Friendly Warning

Drew's thumb and index finger played with Gabrielle's chin, then ran up and down her cheek. "How did you do this?" he asked.

"Do what?" The words were more like a sigh.

"Darken your skin."

She worried her lip, then looked straight into his eyes. "A dye."

"How did you learn about it?"

"An actress taught me."

"What else did she teach you?"

Caution flickered through her eyes, and she turned away from him.

"Not this time, Gabrielle." His hand captured her elbow. "What else did this . . . actress teach you?"

"To beware of men," she replied angrily, twisting to get away. He didn't ease the pressure on her.

"Too bad you didn't pay attention," he said silkily. . . .

The Scotsman Wore Spurs

Patricia Potter

Bantam Books
New York • Toronto • London • Sydney • Auckland

The Scotsman Wore Spurs
A Bantam Book / March 1997

ISBN 0-553-57506-6

Published simultaneously in the United States and Canada

Bantam Books are published by Bantam Books, a division of
Bantam Doubleday Dell Publishing Group, Inc. Its trademark,
consisting of the words "Bantam Books" and the portrayal of
a rooster, is Registered in U.S. Patent and Trademark Office
and in other countries. Marca Registrada. Bantam Books,
1540 Broadway, New York, New York 10036.

PRINTED IN THE UNITED STATES OF AMERICA

RAD   10   9   8   7   6   5   4   3   2   1

The Scotsman Wore Spurs

Prologue

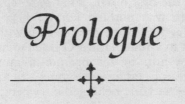

Near San Antonio, Texas
March 1870

Someone else's troubles were none of his own.

Especially an ambush.

Andrew Cameron, the earl of Kinloch, kept telling himself that, even as he spurred his horse into a faster gait in the direction three men had taken earlier. Three men who planned to kill another.

He'd heard them talking last night in a raucous saloon in a no-name Texas cowtown. He bloody hell hadn't wanted to listen, but their voices, rising in proportion to the amount of liquor consumed, had continued to climb.

"We agree then," one of the men had said. "Kingsley will be coming this way tomorrow to hire new drovers for the spring roundup. Won't be no one with him since he's so damned shorthanded."

"Bastard," one man agreed. "No one will cry over his turning to dust."

"Serve him right firing us like that."

"Damn good luck running into that little guy," the

third man said. "Strange coot but the five thousand dollars looked all right."

Drew now swore. As a landless, near-penniless Scottish peer, he had systematically destroyed all dignity and respect his title once held. He was thirty-five, a wastrel of the first order, good only with cards and horses. There was nothing left for him in his own country, so he had come to America, with a letter of introduction to a man named O'Brien in his pocket. It was given to him by his brother-in-law when he'd raised the idea of perhaps becoming a rancher.

But had never truly belonged anywhere, and wasn't sure he wanted to now. He had made a career of tilling his own rows, crooked as they were, and in the process, he'd deliberately avoided caring about anything and anyone. Caring was much too painful.

He'd even found a measure of satisfaction—if not contentment—in his isolation, but last year he'd tumbled from his role as indifferent observer when a four-year-old girl wrapped herself around his heart. He'd vowed never to repeat that uncharacteristic experience. One slip was sufficient for a lifetime.

But he hadn't been able to block out the overheard conversation or the name Kingsley. Unfortunately, there was no law in town to take a hand in the affair—no constable, no military, no anything but liquored-up cowhands itching for a fight.

He'd told himself it was none of his business. And he'd gone to bed still trying to persuade himself of that.

Yet here he was, riding hard in a country he didn't know, chasing men he didn't know, in defense of still another man he didn't know.

Bloody idiot, he called himself as he checked his horse. The men he'd been following had veered off the trail toward a massive granite outcropping. The rocks, rising starkly out of the ground, were a perfect place for an ambush.

Drew considered his options. The first was the

wisest: Mind his own business, turn around and go back the way he'd come. The second held a modicum of danger: Circle wide around the rocks, warn anyone approaching, and look like an interfering fool.

The sound of gunfire from the far side of the rocks immediately reduced his options. He just couldn't ride away. Ambushes offended him; he'd suffered through one himself not long ago.

He spurred his horse toward the outcropping, leaped from the saddle and started to climb. He hoped he wasn't too late. He heard the sound of return gunfire and realized the surprise attack had failed.

When he reached the peak, he looked down. Three men, scattered among huge boulders below him, were firing at a man crouched behind a fallen horse. The animal's stillness told Drew it was dead. *Now* the ambush became personal. He had an abiding affection and respect for horses if not for men.

He found a protected position, aimed the rifle he'd bought in Denver, and fired. He hit two of the ambushers before anyone even knew what was happening. As the third man swung around, Drew ducked behind cover, but not quite fast enough.

He felt a bullet slam into his shoulder, then another tear into him. As consciousness slowly faded, his mouth twisted in bitter self-mockery.

Someone else's troubles were most definitely none of his business.

Chapter One

-------✟-------

Blinking back tears, Maris Gabrielle Parker ruthlessly hacked off sections of her hair just as she was attempting to hack off the terrible memories of the past week.

Don't think about them.

As if she could think about anything else.

Images replayed themselves in her head. The gunshots outside the theater where she'd finished performing. Her father's body jerking from a shot, then plunging toward her to take a second shot obviously meant for her.

Squeezing her eyes shut, she saw the tall lean gunman, face hidden by a hat whose silver band caught light from the hotel front, darting away as doors opened and people started pouring onto the street. She *did* want to keep seeing him, remembering him. She had plans for him. And for a man named Kingsley.

Her father's final words echoed in her mind. A

warning? A deathbed confession? And the unexpected, stunning legacy he left behind. Perhaps that was the most tormenting of all.

She stared back into the cracked mirror on the wall of a mirror in a cheap room in Pickens, Texas, a small town forty miles southeast of San Antonio where her world had collapsed in one violent night.

A haunted face stared back at her. She saw little of the singer who had brought down the house at the San Antonio Palace a week earlier, who'd attracted swarms of unwanted admirers. Instead, her blue eyes looked lifeless, her cheeks thin and white, her lips incapable of a smile.

She was alone now. After spending an entire life with her actress mother and singer father, she was all alone.

And someone wanted her life as well as her father's. They may well try to rectify that unfortunate failure unless she acted first.

The killer, or killers, would be looking for a singer with waist long dark hair and flashy clothes. They would be looking for a readily recognizable woman.

They would not be looking for a grubby orphan lad.

She looked at the hair on the floor and then up at what was left of the long dark hair that had always been her best feature, and she caught a sob in her throat. That hair had disguised a number of imperfections, taking attention away from the too wide mouth and turned-up nose.

"Ah, you have the angel's own hair, just like your mother's," her father had told her repeatedly. And she remembered her mother brushing it, telling her that a woman's hair was her glory.

Gabrielle bit her lip. Her father's voice was stilled, as were the fine hands that had danced so lightly over strings and keys. Tightening her fingers around the scissors, she started cutting again, tears falling silently and mixing with the strands of hair catching in her clothes or falling in desolate-looking piles at her feet.

She cut closer and closer to her scalp. Released of its weight, soft tendrils curled around her face, giving her a decidedly boyish look. Still, she would have to use a small amount of oil to keep it plastered to her head.

Remember the role, she told herself. Play the role. Nothing else matters.

To give herself courage, she hummed an old French lullaby. The sound was lonely, hollow, in the otherwise silent, stark hotel room. It needed harmony, but there was no one to hum along with her. She felt so alone, more alone than she'd ever been in her life.

When the last lock lay in the heap on the bare floor, she removed all her clothing. Opening a newspaper flat on the narrow bed, she laid her dress on it, along with the corset she'd been wearing under it, and her fine button-up shoes and silk stockings. She tied them together with a piece of string, planning to leave the bundle in a church pew. Perhaps the minister could make good use of them.

Then, sitting naked before the mirror, she opened her stage makeup box and began applying judicious amounts of dye. Enough to darken and roughen her fair complexion. Beginning at her hairline, she covered any patch of skin she thought might show, including the back of her neck, then went back and added a few strategic smudges of genuine dirt, which she'd collected for that purpose. The dye, she knew, would last for weeks without washing. She would take enough for another application. By that time she would have accomplished her task. One way or another.

Finally satisfied with the results, she picked up her petticoat and ripped into it strips, then used the strips to bind her breasts. Not that they were all that large, anyway. Her body was naturally slender, and its few curves would easily be hidden by the layers of clothes she planned to wear. Still, she was taking no chances on being discovered.

Her costume, purchased at the only mercantile in the small town where she'd left the stage, looked altogether too new. She would have to do something about that, she thought, as she put on the stiff clothing. Her hat, though, was perfect. She'd taken it from her father's trunk; it dated back to a melodrama in which she and her parents had performed. Her father had bought it off a drunken cowboy for two bits, and it was as disreputable as they came.

Pulling the hat down over her forehead, she grimaced at the smell still emanating from the sweatband. Then she gathered her courage about her like a cloak and turned once more to face the mirror.

Enter Gabe Lewis.

Gone was Gabrielle Parker, beloved and protected daughter of James and Marian Parker. Daughter of a criminal, if she believed what her father had said in his last communication to her. And how could she not believe her father's own words?

The hurt returned. The deep anguish that her frantic activities had tried to bandage over. The anger. The thirst for justice and retribution.

Her hand reached out and clasped the letter that was never far from her, the letter and the newspaper article her father had left in his trunk for her. She'd been sent to that trunk by his last, dying words: "In the trunk . . . letter . . . explains it all . . ." Mustering the last of his strength, he'd clutched her arm, whispering, "The article. Kingsley. It's him. Davis. Danger for . . ." The words faded, then he made one more mammoth effort to speak. "Leave . . . Texas. Promise."

She hadn't had a chance to make that promise, and she had no intentions of leaving Texas, especially after finding the letter her father had written and left alongside a newspaper article. It was, as much as anything, a confession as well as a warning. Undoubtedly the accompanying article had prompted him to write it. Sensing danger, perhaps even fearing for his life, he'd wanted her to know the truth. The letter was dated the day before he'd been shot, and he'd marked the envelope "to be opened upon my death." She'd hadn't believed the contents at first, though she couldn't deny the handwriting was his.

He'd always been larger than life to her, his laughter hearty and his eyes twinkling. He'd been a loving husband, a wonderful father, and a man who would give his last dime to someone in need. It was impossible to reconcile her image of her father with the man his letter described. Impossible to believe he had been friends with the likes of the men he said he once rode with.

And yet, by her father's own admission, he'd committed acts that had forced him to leave Texas and that had kept him away for twenty-five years. Throughout that time, he'd harbored a terrible secret.

It was obvious to her, now, that James Parker had paid for the sins of his youth all his adult life. Finally, he'd paid for them with his death. Now, in her grief and anger—and her guilt that it had been she who had brought him back to Texas when he'd obviously not wanted to come—Gabrielle believed it was up to her to make sure her father's killer paid for his sins as well. Why, dear God, had she begged him to make this trip when the offer was made? Why?

But she had, and now he was dead, and the law could care less. She'd directly accused the man named by her father—a man named Kingsley—but the sheriff had laughed it off. Kirby Kingsley, he'd said, was a man of substance and power; he would not even approach the man about the charge, not on the word of an entertainer.

Gabrielle fingered the newspaper article and read the headline once more. Her hands shaking as she held the paper, she stared almost blindly at the headline, though she knew it by heart. KINGSLEY TO TAKE HERD NORTH.

The article, which included an artist's sketch of a man named Kirby Kingsley, was nearly a column long.

Her eyes scanned the words without really reading them, but they were already burned into her mind. Given what she now knew, she had no doubt that the article had been the cause of her father's uncharacteristic, anxious state in the days before his death. For her, it was the cause of overwhelming guilt. She understood, now, why her father hadn't wanted to come west, and she wished, with utter futility, that he had rejected her pleas. If he had, he would still be alive. It was her fault that he was dead, and she was learning all too quickly that grief compounded by guilt was nearly unbearable.

She was left with one choice: if her father's murderer was to be brought to justice—and it was inconceivable to her that he would not be—she would have to deliver him herself. She had no idea how, but she knew she had to do *something*.

The article, after so many readings, had provided her with the means. Kirby Kingsley was planning a cattle drive. Composed of cattle from many ranches in the central Texas area, it was reported to be one of the largest drives ever attempted. Kingsley would trail boss the herd from a point south of San Antonio to the railhead in Abilene. Drovers were being hired.

She would become one of those drovers.

She could do it. She knew she could. She had played enough male roles to know the swagger, to know exactly how to lower her voice and imitate the language of a cowhand. And although Gabe Lewis didn't look like much, she'd seen enough cowboys to know they came in all sizes, and many were as young as fourteen or fifteen. Children grew up fast in the west.

Her one *real* disadvantage, she knew, were her riding skills. She could ride—barely. She had precious little experience, having traveled mostly by train and coach, but her father had insisted that she learn, at least, the basics. He'd also insisted that she learn to use a pistol for self-protection. One never knew, he said, when one might need to know how to sit a horse or use a firearm to protect one's self.

Her lips thinned to a grim line, and her resolve hardened. She *would* get hired. And she *would* carry out her plan. She would discover the truth, even if she had to use her gun to force it. The powerful Kirby Kingsley would pay for her father's death. So would his hired gun. Though she hadn't seen the killer's face, she felt she'd seen enough to identify him: an uncommonly tall man with cat-like grace and a band of silver on his hat. She would find both of them and force a confession if necessary, perhaps even take justice into her own hands.

She did not care about the price she might have to pay. With grief and guilt still raging inside, the future seemed an enormous black void. Her dreams—her father's dreams—of singing in a great music hall were shattered and she couldn't seem to piece them back again.

Taking a deep breath, Gabe Lewis gave the brim of his awful hat a final downward yank. He stuffed the little money he had into his pockets, tucked the bundle of discarded clothing under his arm and left the room. He needed one final prop before the play could begin.

He needed a horse.

Drew Cameron stretched out in the comfortable chair, nursing an excellent brandy and pondering his future.

For a while, he hadn't thought he had one. He'd almost died from loss of blood, then from an infection. But Kirby Kingsley had simply refused to allow him to die. Having made sure he had the best medical help available, Kirby himself had stayed by his bed day and night. Kirby said it was the least he could do for the man who'd saved his life.

Perhaps, Drew thought, it was saving each other's life that accounted for the odd kindship that had developed between them. Odd because they were so different. Drew, a ne'er-do-well who had been raised with the trappings of wealth among the Scottish aristocracy. Kirby, a hardworking dour rancher who had known only grinding poverty as a boy and young man. Drew cared about little, was attached to no one. Kirby cared deeply about his ranch, his cattle, his brother, his nephews; he felt extremely proprietary about all of them.

Still, the similarities between them seemed to override their differences. Both had been basically discarded as youngsters. And both had rebelled in ways that had injured themselves. The mutual recognition of kindred souls was there, and in the two months that Drew had been at the Kingsley ranch, the Circle K, he'd found the kind of friend, perhaps even the father, he'd never thought he'd have.

During late-night talks over drinks, Drew often sensed a sadness and loneliness in Kingsley. But tonight Kirby was positively morose.

"Still thinking about the ambush?" Drew asked.

"It's unsettling to know someone wants you dead," Kirby said, frowning.

"You think whoever it was might try again? It's been two months."

"I'd know a lot better if those three hadn't got away."

"Two of them are probably still in no shape to try again," Drew said.

"I wish that made me feel better," Kingsley said. "But if they were hired guns, whoever paid them to kill me could just as easily hire others."

Drew was silent. He wished he'd heard more: a name, a town, something.

"And I worry about the ranch. If anything happened to me . . ."

Drew tried to reassure him. "Nothing's happened for two months, and your brother, Jon, seems capable."

"He knows animals. He doesn't know business, or men, and he never will. And my nephews? Hell, Damien has potential, but he's too hotheaded . . . and greedy. And Terry, he's like Jon. Good-natured but easily led. I've worked too damn hard to have everything destroyed."

Drew couldn't disagree with Kirby. As a gambler, Drew studied men: their strengths and weaknesses. Kirby was pure steel; his brother clay.

"Go with us," Kirby said suddenly. "You want to learn cow. There's no better way."

Stunned at the invitation, Drew thought Kirby couldn't be serious. He tried to give his friend a graceful way out of the impulsive suggestion. "Kane O'Brien's expecting me."

Kirby shrugged off the excuse. "If you want to learn the cattle business, you won't find a better classroom than a cattle drive."

And O'Brien would probably be relieved, Drew thought. His brother-in-law had called in a debt in asking O'Brien to take him on. The last thing O'Brien was likely to want—or need—was a tenderfoot in the way.

"Think of it this way," Kirby said, reading Drew's thoughts. "I really want you."

" 'Tis the why of it, I'm wondering," Drew said, his brogue deepening. "I'm no drover."

Kirby was silent for a moment. "I trust you," he finally said.

The simple declaration touched and pleased Drew. Few people in his life had trusted him. Nor had he trusted many people.

With the first tiny spark of excitement flickering inside him, he rapidly considered the consequences of his disappearing on the trail for the next several months. Kirby had already written on his behalf to Kane O'Brien, saying he'd been wounded and was recovering nicely at the Circle K. It would be easy enough to cancel his visit. Other than that, he had no commitments, no obligations.

Yet he felt compelled to argue. "I don't think your nephews would be pleased." Damien was to be second in command, and Damien didn't like him. Drew had seen the signs of growing resentment as Kirby spent so much time with his wounded guest.

"That's their problem," Kirby said. "The fact is I would like you at my back. You're a fair hand with a rifle."

"Ah, that. Every Scotsman is familiar with a sporting weapon. I had a bit of luck, no more. And you noticed I'm sure, I'm not much good at ducking."

"No," Kirby said dryly. "We'll have to work on that."

"I've never done much but toss a pair of dice. You know I don't know anything about driving cattle."

Kirby eyed him with amusement. "You said you used to race in steeplechases, and I've watched you ride the last several days. I don't think there's a damn beast you can't ride, though you'll have to get accustomed to the moves of our cutting horses. You can learn the rest. And the sound of your voice alone is worth the pay," Kirby added.

Drew was confused.

"I heard you sing one day. Nothing soothes restless cattle like a mellow voice."

"I can provide ye with a few Scottish battle songs," Drew said wryly, "and little else."

Kirby chuckled. "Hell, I would be the only trail boss ever to have a Scottish lord as a cowhand. And I'd wager the Circle K that underneath that noble skin lies a true Westerner."

Drew forced a smile. "My title is the least thing I possess to commend me."

His bitterness must have been plain. Kingsley was silent for a moment, then said, "I know you have guts, that you risked your life for a stranger's. That says a hell of a lot to me. And I know you're thinking about raising cattle," Kingsley continued. "You can cut out fifty as your share when we reach Kansas City. Keep them as seed for your own herd or sell them."

"That's above the going rate," Drew observed.

"The going rate usually doesn't include my life."

"I need no reward for that."

"You think my life is worth so little?"

Drew felt his resistance weaken further. He wanted to go on the drive. He wanted it more than he'd ever wanted anything. He'd heard the horror stories—dust, storms, flood, Indians, outlaws. He harbored a curiosity about this exacting land that permitted few mistakes. It was his chance to prove, not only to Kirby but also to himself, that he was more than a clever gambler. Yet he was apprehensive. He had disappointed nearly everyone. He didn't want to disappoint this man.

"And Damien and Terry?" he asked. "What will you tell them?"

Kirby's lips thinned. "I hire. They don't."

The last thread of resistance broke. "Then I accept," Drew said.

He'd played the rake the past fifteen years, consciously trying to destroy his family name, the title, and everything to do with Kinloch. It had been his revenge on the man who'd made his mother's life—and his own—a living hell. But there had always been an emptiness, a vast lonely place where his heart should be. Revenge hadn't filled it. Neither had gaming or drinking or whoring.

Perhaps he'd find something in this new land that would.

A pleased look on his face, Kingsley poured them both another drink. "To a successful drive," he said.

"To a successful drive," Drew echoed as he swallowed the fine, golden liquid.

Chapter Two

— ✛ —

Drew ignored the hoots of laughter from the cowboys watching him as he gingerly—very gingerly—picked himself up off the ground. The fall was ignominious. He couldn't ever remember falling from a horse before.

Kirby had warned him that cutting horses were unlike any other animal, their movements quick and sometimes unexpected when they saw a cow wandering off. The pinto Drew was riding had proven Kirby right, moving sharply when Drew had just relaxed after a very long day in the saddle.

Drew eyed the horse with more than a little asperity, and the bloody beast actually bared its teeth in what Drew was certain was a grin. He winced at the picture they must make.

"Uncle Kirby said you could ride," Damien Kingsley said nastily. "What other tall tales did you hand him?"

Drew forced a wry smile. He had been the target of

unending razing since he'd first gone on the Circle K payroll a week earlier. His Scottish accent and unfamiliarity with the Texas longhorns hadn't improved the image of tenderfoot.

"What do they have for horses in Scotland?" another man scoffed.

Damien, sitting a small roan, snickered. "You ain't going to be any use at all."

Drew tested his limbs. They seemed whole, but every bone in his body ached. As accustomed as he was to riding, a week of sitting in a saddle for eighteen hours a day had strained even his experienced muscles. The thought of three months of days like this shriveled his soul.

Learn cow. That's what Kirby called learning the cattle business. In some peculiar, ungrammatical way, the expression fit. But Drew was beginning to think he'd just as soon jump off the edge of the earth. His enthusiasm for being a cattle baron had dimmed to the faint flicker of a dying candle.

But, dammit to bloody hell, he'd never been a quitter, and he wasn't going to start now. Neither did he want to see the triumph spreading across Damien's face. Even less did he want to disappoint Kirby.

Drew brushed off his hands on the seat of his pants and started for the pinto. He was saved from another attempt to make peace with the bloody animal when Shorty, one of the drovers, interrupted the proceedings with a loud bark of laughter. "Well, lookit that, will ya!" he exclaimed.

Drew shot a glance over his shoulder to see the cowhand pointing northward, past the ranch house and barn, and he turned to look, as did every other man present.

Coming into view around the corner of the barn was the most moth-eaten, woebegone, and decrepit beast he'd ever had the misfortune to behold. And perched precariously on its bony back was a small figure whose hat looked as decrepit as the horse.

"Mebbe Scotty could ride that," one of the men said, laughing uproariously at his own joke.

Drew would have loved to cram that laughter down his throat, along with the nickname they'd given him, but that would just make trouble for Kirby. He wondered how long he could curb a temper that had never been known for its temperance.

They all watched the slow approach of the scraggly duo, and, listening to the men's nonstop taunts, Drew already felt a measure of sympathy for the stranger.

The rider and horse halted just a few yards from the gathered crowd. The lad—and he was a lad, Drew noted—was enveloped by a coat much too big for him. Only a portion of his face was visible. Under the dirty slouch hat, a pair of dark blue eyes seemed to study him before they lowered, then moved on to the other riders.

"I'm looking for the foreman," he mumbled in a voice that seemed to be changing.

"What for?" one of the men said, using his elbow to nudge a companion. "Want to sell that fine horse of yours? That fellow there, with the pinto, may be interested."

Guffaws broke out again, and the boy's eyes came back to Drew, resting there for a moment.

"Lookin' for a job," he said, ignoring the jibe. "Heard they might be hirin' here."

"Pint-size cowboys?" Damien said. "You heard wrong. We're full hired. More than full hired," he added, tossing a disagreeable look at Drew.

"Read about the drive in the newspaper," the boy said. "It said they be needing help. I want to see the foreman."

Drew admired the boy's persistence. But the drive *was* full hired, even at the miserly wage of fifty dollars and keep. A number of much more promising cowboys had been turned down. It seemed every cowboy in the West wanted to ride with Kirby Kingsley on what was being called a historic drive.

"I'll take you," Drew said. "Follow me." Without waiting to hear what the other hands would make of his conspicuous disregard of Damien's words, he headed for the corral.

Leading the pinto by the reins, Drew limped toward the fenced enclosure where Kirby was making a final selection for the remuda, which would total one hundred and eighty horses at ten per man, plus sixteen mules for the two wagons.

"Mr. Kingsley?" He had stopped calling Kingsley by his first name around the other men, having no wish to further aggravate their resentment toward him. He was an employee of the Circle K, nothing more.

Kirby turned around, saw him, noted his limp— and grimaced in the way Drew had come to recognize as a smile.

"Told you about those cutting horses," Kingsley said.

"So you did," Drew replied wryly. "I won't make the mistake of underestimating them again."

"Good. Nothing broken, I take it."

"Only my pride."

Kirby's lips twitched slightly, then his gaze went over to the young rider beside Drew. "That a horse, boy?"

The lad's chin raised defiantly. "It ain't his fault no one ever took care of him. He has heart."

"What's your name?"

"Gabe. Gabe Lewis."

"And your business?"

"I heard you was hiring."

"Men," Kirby said. "Not boys."

"I'm old enough."

"What? Fourteen? Fifteen?"

"Sixteen," the boy said, "and I've been making my own way these past three years."

"You ever been on a drive?"

Gabe Lewis hesitated, and Drew could almost see the wheels turning inside his unkempt head. He wanted to lie. He *would* have lied if he hadn't thought he might be caught in it.

"No, but I'm a real fast learner," he answered. thrusting upward another notch.

"We don't need any more hands," Kirby said, turning away.

The quick dismissal brought a flush to the boy's face. "Mister Kingsley?"

Kingsley swung back around.

The boy's voice had lost its belligerence when the lad spoke. "I'll do anything, Mr. Kingsley. Maybe I'm not so big, but I'm a real hard worker."

Kirby shook his head.

"I need the job real bad," the boy said in one last desperate plea.

Drew watched as Kirby studied the boy. It shocked him that Kirby was actually considering hiring the lad.

"By the looks of that horse, I'd agree," Drew said helpfully, figuring Kirby needed only the slightest push.

Gabe Lewis scowled at him for a second. Baffled, Drew wondered why his help wasn't welcome.

Kirby finally spoke. "Pepper, our cook, was complaining yesterday about his rheumatism. Maybe we could use someone to help him out. You up to being a louse, boy?"

"A louse?" the boy repeated.

"A cook's helper," Kirby explained. "A swamper. Cleans up dishes, hunts cow chips, grinds coffee. You ever done any cooking?"

"Of course," the boy said airily. Drew sensed bravado, and another lie, but Kirby didn't seem to notice. From the moment the boy had mentioned he was desperate, the rancher had softened perceptibly. It surprised Drew. There was nothing soft about Kirby Kingsley.

But it was obvious that Kirby had made up his mind to hire Gabe Lewis—for reasons Drew didn't even begin to understand. The lad could barely sit a horse, admitted he'd never been on a cattle drive, and clearly had lied about his culinary ability. He probably lied about his age, as well; his face showed not even the faintest sign of stubble. Moreover, he didn't look strong enough to control a team of four mules.

Drew considered Gabe Lewis's assortment of clothing. Odds and ends—and far too many of them—hung on a small frame, all dirty, much too large, and thoroughly impractical for the sweltering Texas spring. Was the lad trying to conceal a too-thin body, or did he fear someone would take what little he had if he didn't keep it all close to his person?

"My cook has to agree," Kirby told the boy. "If he does, I'll pay you twenty dollars and found."

The boy nodded.

"You can't cut it, you're gone," Kirby added.

Lewis nodded again.

"You don't have much to say, do you?" Kirby asked.

"Didn't know that was important." It was an impertinent reply, one Drew might have made himself in his younger days.

Kirby turned to Drew. "Get the kid some food. I'll talk to Pepper."

"I need to take care of my horse," the boy said. "Give him some oats if you got any."

Kirby shook his head. "Don't bother. He'll be mixed in with ours. Not that he looks like he'll last long."

"No," the boy said flatly.

Kirby, who had begun to walk away, stopped. "What did you say?"

"I'll take care of my own horse," the boy said stubbornly. "He's mine."

"If Pepper agrees to take you on, you'll ride on the hoodlum wagon," Kirby said. "You don't need a horse. Besides, all the hands put their horses in the remuda for common use. This one, though"—Kirby shook his head—"he won't be any good to us. Might as well put him down."

The lad's eyes widened in alarm. "No. I'll take care of him. He goes with me."

"Then you can look for another job."

Drew couldn't help but admire the boy's pluck. His need for the job was obvious, yet he wasn't going to give up the sorriest beast Drew had seen in a long time.

"Maybe the horse has some potential," Drew said softly.

Kirby didn't hide his disbelief. "That nag?"

"He's been mistreated, starved," the boy said. "It ain't his fault."

"How long you had him?" Kirby asked.

"Just a week, Mr. Kingsley, but he's got grit. We rode all the way from Pickens."

Kirby looked from the horse to Gabe Lewis . . . and back to the horse. Finally, he shrugged his shoulders in surrender. "What the hell. But you're responsible for him. If he can't keep up, I'll leave you both."

"He will. He's already getting stronger." The lad paused. "What's the hoodlum wagon?"

"Damn, don't you know anything?" Kirby's irritation was plain. "It's the wagon that carries bedrolls, extra saddles, tools. A chuck wagon for a drive this size needs every inch for food and supplies."

The lad looked fascinated but said nothing.

Kingsley swore, frowned at Drew, and turned his attention back to the corral.

Drew smiled at the boy, who didn't smile back. He did, however, slide down from the horse—somewhat painfully.

"I'm Drew Cameron," he said.

The boy looked at him suspiciously. "You talk funny."

"I'm from Scotland," Drew explained. "The other hands call me Scotty."

The boy didn't look satisfied but didn't ask any

more questions, either. Silent, he followed as Drew led him to the barn.

Drew stopped beside an empty stall, and watched as the lad led his horse in and began to unbuckle the saddle. Drew poured oats into a feed bucket. The horse looked at him with soft, grateful eyes, and he understood the boy's attachment. Hell, he'd had a horse he'd . . . loved. Too much. Bile filled his throat as he remembered. . . .

"I can take care of him alone," the boy said rudely.

"You got a name for this animal?"

"Billy, if it's any of your business."

"That's a bloody odd name for a horse."

"It ain't your horse."

"No," Drew conceded.

The boy removed the bit from Billy's mouth and took off the halter. Then he returned to the unbuckled saddle and slid it off the horse's back. He struggled with it, and Drew saw immediately that Gabe Lewis was not adept at handling tack. There was no deftness that comes with practice.

Drew's gaze went to the boy's hands. Gloves covered them. New gloves. Upon closer inspection, it seemed that the rest of his clothes were fairly new, too, though effort had been extended to hide that fact. The dirt, while plentiful, was too uniform for it to have been accumulated naturally, and the denim trousers were still stiff, not pliant.

"Don't you know it ain't polite to stare?"

The lad's angry question brought Drew's gaze up quickly. "Sorry," he said, making an effort to be less obvious—though he continued his inspection.

Something else didn't ring true. The lad's speech was odd. The way he said "ain't," as if it were an unfamiliar word. Drew had an ear for sounds. It was a natural talent that had been invaluable in gaming; he could always detect nuances in an opponent's voice: desperation, bluffing, fear. He thought he detected all those things in Gabe Lewis's youthful intonations.

Putting aside desperation and bluffing, both of which could be explained by poverty and need, why would the lad be afraid? Did he have something to hide? Could he be a runaway, or worse?

Drew hadn't forgotten the ambush nor the possibility that someone might try again. And he remembered the ambusher's words. *That little guy.* He very much doubted this slip of a lad could be involved in anything as savage as the ambush, but he had seen danger and dynamite come in much smaller packages.

He immediately dismissed the idea as absurd. Doubtless, the last few months in Scotland, during which he'd worried constantly that he would lose the sister he had just found, had made him overly cautious and far too suspicious. A man he'd never suspected—a trainer of horses—had proved to be a murderer and kidnapper. The experience had been a bitter reminder that people and things were often not what they seemed.

Draping an arm over the top of the stall, he asked, "Where are you from?"

Lewis continued brushing his horse. "Places."

An answer Drew himself had given frequently. He nodded. The boy's business was his own until proved otherwise.

"The bunkhouse is the next building. Take any cot that doesn't look occupied," Drew said, knowing there were several empty ones.

"When do we leave?"

Drew heard an anxious note in the boy's voice. "In two days."

"What do you do?" Lewis put down the brush and turned to look at him, meeting his gaze fully for once. His eyes were almost too blue to be real and they were filled now with cold anger.

Drew shrugged. "Just a cowhand. And if I want to stay that way, I'd better get back to work."

Drew turned and walked away. He could feel those blue eyes boring holes into his back. His spine tingled with the enmity he'd felt and wondered what he'd said, or done, to cause it.

What the bloody hell, anyway. The lad was none of his business.

Gabrielle watched Drew Cameron leave the barn. She had almost swallowed her tongue when she'd first seen him. He was uncommonly tall and lean. He had the same build as the shadowy figure who had killed her father and shot at her. Granted, Cameron's hat bore no band of silver. And he limped. The killer had moved like an alley cat, silent and sleek, as he'd disappeared into the shadow from which he'd appeared. But perhaps Cameron's limp had developed only recently. And he might own more than one hat.

In truth, what made Gabe most suspicious about the Scotsman had more to do with his manner. He'd said he was "just a cowhand," in that distinctive Scottish brogue.

Just a cowhand. She didn't believe it for a second. He was a lot more than a cowhand if she was any judge of people. In her experience, which admittedly was limited, cowhands were uneducated and easygoing. Drew Cameron was obviously well educated and, despite an easy smile, radiated a certain intensity.

Kirby Kingsley didn't treat him like another cowhand either. She couldn't put her finger on it, but something in the way Kingsley and Cameron communicated with each other spoke of a bond that went deeper than that of boss and hired hand.

And dear God, but Cameron was handsome. His hair was a tawny, light brown that shimmered in the sun, and his eyes were golden, with flecks of brown and green and gray. Some would call them hazel, but that didn't begin to describe their unique color. Like his hair, his eyes appeared to shimmer with gold, to flash, even dance—as if he were amused at something only he understood.

No, Drew Cameron might be acting the part of cowhand at the moment, but he was a lot more than that.

And Kingsley? A shiver raced up Gabe's spine, and she reached, almost unconsciously, to pat Billy's neck, seeking the only source of warmth and comfort available to her.

Kingsley wasn't at all what she had expected. She had thought he would be brash and loud and mean as a snake—a wild, reckless sort of man: an image conjured from the descriptions in her father's letter. But then, her father hadn't been wild and reckless, not apparently since his youthful days. And, she realized, that she hadn't taken into account the passage of time. Twenty-five years obviously had changed her father, and it must have changed Kingsley as well.

Kingsley was rich, now, and influential. Power and wealth probably went a long way toward disguising wild and reckless tendencies. But underneath the confident veneer, she was convinced, his heart was still wicked. His eyes were cold, almost completely without emotion, as was his voice. She could still hear him saying that her horse ought to be put down; he'd said it as unfeelingly as he might have ordered a worn-out fence ripped out and burned for fuel.

She had no idea why he had agreed to hire her. It had been clear at the beginning that he hadn't wanted to do it, and she'd sat there on Billy's back, certain her plans of getting Kingsley away from his ranch before seeking justice were hopeless. She'd been on the verge of pulling the Colt out of the coat pocket and confronting him then and there. The temptation had been almost overwhelming. Simply looking at him, being in his presence, had made her head spin and the entire world seem sort of hazy and unreal.

Then, before she'd lost her last shred of self-preservation, Drew Cameron had intervened. As much as she hated to think she owed her success to a man who might have killed her father, she was

certain it had been Cameron's softly spoken words
that had changed Kingsley's mind. Another reason to
wonder about the relationship between the two men.

Gabrielle buried her face against her horse's neck
and released a ragged sigh. He *was* a bag of bones,
which is why she called him Billy, for Billy Bones—a
fact she hadn't been inclined to admit to the tall Scottish drover. She would have given up her new job—
and her chance to get Kingsley—if he'd insisted she
leave Billy behind to be slaughtered. The horse was all
she had. She ran her hand down the horse's neck and
he trembled. When she'd gone looking for a horse to
buy, she hadn't expected to become so thoroughly and
instantly attached to one. But then she'd seen Billy,
with his sad, hopeless eyes.

The liveryman had gone straight past him, but
she'd hesitated.

"You don't want that one. He's done for. Cowpoke
just left him here. Be best just to put him down."

"How much?" she'd asked.

"Hell, you can have him," the man said. "Five dollars for a saddle. But he won't last a day."

But Billy had lasted. She had purchased some oats
and had ridden him slow and easy and the horse had
looked at her with a kind of gratitude that made her
heart break open a little further. He was hers, and she
was going to make him well. Kirby Kingsley be
damned.

Giving Billy a final pat, Gabe made sure he had
water. She added more oats to his feed, then headed
for the bunkhouse.

"Don't need no help." Pepper was adamant. "And I
don't want no kid getting in my way."

Kirby held his tongue and thought about the best
way to pursue this topic. Fact was Pepper was the
best trail cook in Texas, and he would do anything to
keep him. A good cook could make or break a drive.

Drovers often worked fourteen to eighteen hours a day in heat, pouring rain, and every other plague known to man; they demanded good food and good doctoring, and the cook was responsible for both.

"You were complaining yesterday about too much to do," Kirby reminded him gently.

"That was jest complainin', and you know it," Pepper said, his whiskers quivering with indignation. "You think I'm too old, you jest say so and hire someone else."

"I don't want anybody else. You know I went looking all over Texas to find you." He hesitated. "Truth is the kid needs a job."

Pepper narrowed his eyes. "You going soft, Kingsley?" He was the only man in the Kingsley employ that called the owner—and trail boss—by his last name with no courtesy preceding it.

"No, I'm not going soft," Kirby said, hoping to God it was true. "It just seemed a good idea since your rheumatism has been flaring up." It was more than that, he knew. He wanted to help Gabe Lewis because he knew what it was like to be desperate for money, for work of any kind—and unable to find it. Twenty-five years ago, no one would give him a job. He had been taking care of his younger brother, and they both were so damned hungry they would do anything for a meal. *Anything.*

"Won't share my wagon with him," Pepper growled.

Kirby breathed in relief. It seemed the argument was won. "He can travel in the hoodlum wagon and sleep with the rest of the hands," he said. "If it doesn't work out, I'll put him wrangling. Doesn't seem too good at horses, but maybe in a few weeks . . ."

"Probably no good at cooking either."

Kirby thought Pepper was probably right. But the kid could learn. "You'll be doing me a favor," he replied.

Pepper scowled. "I ain't no nursemaid."

Kirby chuckled. There would be no misunderstanding about that. Pepper was as irascible as a coyote in a locoweed patch, and he would give the boy a hell of a time. But if the boy survived that, Kirby reckoned he could survive anything. It would be interesting to see whether Gabe Lewis had as much grit as his mouth had bravado.

Chapter Three

—✛—

Gabrielle's worst fears were realized as dusk came. She'd gotten through supper fairly well. Large containers of stew had come from the kitchen and the hands had gathered outside to eat. She'd stood in line for her share, enduring the curious looks and teasing from the drovers; then she'd taken her plate to a spot under a solitary cottonwood, where the others left her alone to eat in peace.

As night fell, though, the cowboys straggled into the bunkhouse and, not wanting to stand out, she reluctantly followed. Yet, standing in the doorway of the long, narrow, wooden building, she bit her lip nervously and thought about the night ahead.

She hadn't really considered it before. Hadn't realized all the ramifications of being one of Kingsley's hired hands. For days, she'd been existing by clinging to a single purpose. Now she was faced with the reality of her plans, of sleeping in a room with several dozen nearly naked men.

She steeled herself. A role, she told herself. This was simply another role. *You can do it.*

The room was dirty and overcrowded, probably because of all the extra hands being hired for the drive. And, dear heaven, it smelled. Her nose twitched at the undeniably gamy odor.

She'd already picked her space earlier when no one was there. She had hoped to find an empty place, a corner, in which she could make herself as small and as invisible as possible. But the only two beds she'd seen without belongings on them were two upper bunks in the middle of the room.

Now she headed straight for the one she'd chosen and where she'd left her bedroll, trying her best to ignore the disrobing men. But there was no escape from the cowboys who'd thrust off their shirts as soon as they gained the door. Some wore union suits under their shirts. Some did not.

"Sonofabitch, but it's hot for the first of May," she heard one of the hands say.

Gabrielle agreed. She, however, couldn't strip down to nearly nothing as most of them had. Futilely, she tried to keep her eyes on the bare boards of the floor and, at the same time, watch where she was going.

"Hey, there's that kid," one cowboy said. "Old Kirby couldn't have hired him."

Another chimed in. "I heard Pepper grumbling that some brat had been stuffed down his throat."

Gabrielle heard it all, knew she'd been meant to hear. She said nothing, just kept walking, her heart pounding. Suddenly, though, someone was in her path, and she had to stop.

"What's your name, kid?" the man said as several others gathered around, looking at her curiously.

Beneath her hat brim, she threw him the look of bravado she'd perfected during hours in front of the mirror. *Play the role,* she ordered herself. *That's all you have to do.*

"Name's Gabe Lewis," she said off-handedly.

"How old are you?"

"How old are *you*?" she retorted.

"He's telling you it's none of yer business, Jake," another cowboy said with amusement, "just in case you didn't figure it out."

"You really goin' with us?" another man, lolling on a bunk, asked. "In that getup? You'll roast to death 'fore we leave Texas."

"Hell, he won't make the second day."

"If the sun don't get him, Pepper will," chuckled another man.

"Leave him alone," came a voice from the doorway, and though she couldn't see him over the heads of the cowboys, Gabrielle immediately identified it. No one would mistake the burr in his words. Her stomach tightened. She didn't want a protector, or need one. Especially this man.

"They don't bother me," she said.

"None of your business, anyway, Scotty," one of the hands said angrily.

"I'm making it my business," the Scot said, moving toward her until he stood just feet away.

"You got a whole lot to learn, Scotty," said another man, "even if you are the boss's pet."

Gabrielle watched Drew Cameron's face pale, the hazel eyes turn deadly cold. "Go to bloody hell, Jake," he said.

"You gonna make me?"

The bunkhouse suddenly simmered with tension. Faces were filled with expectation and avid curiosity. She watched the Scotsman's hands ball into fists, then relax. "I don't want to fight you, Jake."

"You just good at ambushing men?" the man called Jake taunted, and Gabrielle felt herself go rigid. "I heard you saved Kingsley's hide by shooting some fellows from the back."

She waited for Cameron to answer, to deny the accusation, but he didn't. He simply turned around, nothing in his face signifying he'd even heard the damning words. It was as if everyone stopped existing for him.

Using the moment to reach her bunk, she climbed up and sat cross-legged in the center. She watched as the Scotsman walked a couple of yards, stopped beside the bunk next to hers, and sat down on the lower bunk, obviously oblivious now to others in the room.

Ambush. The word echoed in her head. Again, Gabrielle wondered if it had been he who had killed her father and tried to kill her. And it occurred to her suddenly that if Drew Cameron were her father's killer, he might recognize her despite her disguise. The killer had been standing in the shadows, and she'd caught only a glimpse of him, but she and her father had been well-illuminated by a street lamp. If Cameron were the killer and did recognize her, he might believe she could eventually recognize him. And, if that were so, then it could explain why he'd helped her secure the job with Kingsley. Having found her, he'd want to keep her close by—so he could finish her off in his own good time.

She shivered in the heat. Implausible, yes. She wouldn't recognize herself. Yet . . . why else would he be kind to an itinerant boy?

Her eyes went back to him. Just her luck she would choose the bunk next to his. He was taking off his shirt, and she knew her eyes widened. Unlike most of the other cowboys, he wore no union suit under his shirt and his chest was bare—and stunning. Afraid she'd be caught staring, she couldn't avoid casting furtive glances at the Scotsman. She couldn't help it. Couldn't help noticing the sinewy muscles that rippled when he moved, the light brown hair that caught gold even in the dim light, then blended into a sun-bronzed body. She felt her cheeks flush and her stomach flutter in disturbing ways as she watched him bend down and pull off his boots with careless disregard for his companions.

She finally forced her gaze away, but even as her eyes focused on a piece of flooring, the image of Drew Cameron remained in her mind. She tried again to picture him as the obscure figure that she'd seen standing in the shadow with a gun in his hand, but the image wouldn't come into focus. She simply didn't know what to think. It seemed, lately, that her intuition was failing her.

She sighed, feeling every bit as uncomfortable inside herself as well as outside. Which brought her thoughts around to another problem. Her clothes. She longed to thrust them off. She longed most of all for a bath.

The other occupants of the bunkhouse had already relieved themselves of most of their clothes, some down to their longjohns. Despite her fear of being the center of attention, she noticed the drovers were all otherwise engaged, either lounging on their bunks, talking to the man in the next cot, or starting a poker game at one end of the room. Everyone seemed to have lost interest in her. Drew Cameron, wittingly or not, had diverted their attention.

Gabrielle took stock of her situation. Her well-considered plans had not included a roomful of half-naked men. She felt her skin prickle, and she was only too aware of her strangeness, that she was the only person in the bunkhouse still wearing a hat and jacket. But she was not about to part with either. They were her armor, her shield.

They were also hot as Hades.

Air. She had to get some air. She slipped from the bunk and moved toward the door, passing close by the men playing poker. She pulled her hat low on her forehead, keeping her eyes straight, aimed at the door and avoiding all the near-naked bodies.

"Where you goin', kid?" asked one man at the poker game taking place on the floor between two bunks. "You wanna join us?"

Her pace slowed, and she glanced down at the

cards on the floor. She was tempted. She really was. The glint in their eyes said they were ready to take on a tenderfoot. And she could give them a good run for their money. Stagehands had often entertained her with games of chance when she was very young, waiting for her parents to finish their performances. She had later perfected the skill as she waited for her turns onstage. But she wasn't supposed to have any money, nor any marketable skill. She was, she reminded herself, a penniless, desperate orphan.

"Don't have any money," she said shortly.

"We'll take your marker."

"Like hell we will," said another player.

Drew Cameron suddenly appeared next to her, apparently continuing his role of self-appointed protector. But he said nothing, his eyes studying her with the gleam of amusement she'd seen before. She still hadn't figured whether his apparent kindness earlier had been some kind of secret joke or something more sinister. Perhaps he just enjoyed playing with people, like cats played with mice before finishing them off.

That must be why her skin tingled whenever she saw him, why her blood seemed thicker, hotter. A simple matter of awareness. Not awareness of a man but of danger. She hoped to heaven it wasn't anything more.

"I gotta go see 'bout my horse," she said and turned away, valiantly trying to keep from falling over one of the sitting men.

"That nag," someone chuckled. "Looks like the hindquarters of bad luck. Ain't good for nothin' but Injun food."

In the brief time she'd been in the West, Gabrielle had learned many things. Among those things was that calling a man's horse Injun food was one of the worst ways to insult him. She felt her temper rising. "Empty wagons," she said, looking pointedly at the speaker, "rattle the most."

"Gotcha there," a man she didn't recognize said. "He means you, Hank."

The Scotsman chuckled.

Hank swung angrily on him. "I wouldn't smile if I were you. You're 'bout as handy as a hog playing a fiddle."

Gabrielle started to inch away toward the door, but the cowboy called Hank stopped her. "I'll bet that horse don't last a week."

"He'll last as long as you," she retorted angrily. "But I ain't got nothin' to bet with."

The cowboy shrugged. "That hat."

She hesitated. She needed the hat. It, more than anything else she wore, gave her a sense of protection. But in the few days she'd owned Billy Bones, she'd grown very protective of him. And she believed she'd been rewarded for the love she'd given him. Billy hadn't minded her inexperience. He'd tolerated, without complaint, the unhappy fact that his back went up when her backside came down. *Her* Billy had both courage and heart.

"What's *your* wager?" she asked.

The cowboy grinned. "*My* hat."

The man next to him shoved an arm in the cowboy's side. "Those are the two worst damn hats I ever did see."

Gabrielle couldn't disagree, and she couldn't understand why on earth anyone would want her hat. Still, she pondered the wager. She was going to have to live with these men, day and night, for as long as it took to accomplish her task, and she needed to make friends with them.

But not, she decided finally, at the risk of exposure. She needed the hat. It contributed, more than anything else she wore, to her disguise. If they learned she was a woman, she would never be allowed on the drive. She'd read enough dime novels to know that.

"I like my own hat," she finally said in the gruff

voice that was becoming second nature. "Mebbe next time."

The man next to Hank, the bettor, grinned. "Can't see how either one of you could win that one, anyway. I'm Sandy. This ornery cuss is Hank Flanigan. He's so contrary that if you throw him in a river, he'll float upstream."

Gabrielle smiled for the first time in weeks. Sandy was likable and friendly. She glanced at the Scotsman. His eyes were studying her intently and she had the sudden, frightening sense that he saw right through her layers of clothes, through the eccentric disguise she'd tried so hard to build.

She moved her gaze back to the friendly Sandy, then to the others in the bunkhouse. They were an odd assortment: black, white, Mexican, even one part Indian. The drovers ranged in age from nearly as young as she pretended to be to a man who looked forty or more. Most, however, seemed to be in their early twenties.

She nodded, having already given her name.

"Glad to have you with us," Sandy said.

"Hummmph," said the contrary Hank. "He ain't no bigger than two bits."

"Two bits is a lot of money," another said. "He can't be worth that."

"Still, I think I'll call him Two-Bits," Hank persisted.

"Two-Bits it is," said another.

Gabrielle stood there a moment, letting what was now good-natured laughter crash around her, forcing a smile to her own lips. She had already realized in the past few hours that everyone had a moniker. She supposed hers could be worse.

Her gaze went, again, to Drew Cameron. He was studying her closely, as if measuring her in his mind. His penetrating scrutiny made her stiffen, and she thought, even standing with the other cowboys, he stood out in the crowd. He wasn't any more a part of them than she was.

But who, or what, was he?

"Come on, Scotty," one of the men said. "Join the game."

"So I will," the Scotsman said, amusement returning to his eyes. But it wasn't the kind of amusement one shared with friends. It was another kind, the kind that belonged to a man laughing at himself, or, perhaps, at life in general.

All at once, Gabrielle thought she understood. His casual, lighthearted demeanor was a sham. A face he presented to the world. He used it to lull people into thinking he was no threat to them. Despite Jake's taunting words, it was obvious the other cowboys didn't take him seriously.

But they were making a mistake. A big one.

She wasn't sure what Drew Cameron was, but casual and lighthearted weren't in the running. A shiver ran down her spine. Was he simply an out-of-place Scotsman? Or was he something far more complex and murderous? She was sure of complexity. She wasn't sure about the latter. Her feet turned, and she hurried out the door, the ring of loud masculine laughter following her.

The lad did not come back that night. For some inexplicable reason, Drew found himself worrying about him. Perhaps he'd decided this group too rough for him, after all. Perhaps he'd taken that poor excuse for a horse and left.

The youngster—Gabe—had been bloody uncomfortable in the bunkhouse; that had been obvious. The place wasn't Drew's idea of paradise either, but he'd received enough snide remarks about his stay in Kingsley's house. If he was going to make this work, he knew he had to get along with the other hands. It was too long—and dangerous—a drive to have enemies at your back.

Besides, life in a succession of boarding schools had

taught him he could sleep anywhere and get along with almost anyone. Since his father hadn't been able to stand the sight of him, he hadn't gone home, even during summers and Christmas holidays. Instead, he'd charmed both teachers and fellow students into inviting him home with them; the result had been that he'd rarely spent a holiday alone, and he'd learned how to adapt to an amazing variety of people and places. In short, he'd become a chameleon.

It was a talent he expected to serve him well in winning over the Kingsley cowhands. Already, he'd made inroads. He would continue to take their gibes and joshing in good humor. He'd work hard to gain their respect, and sooner or later they would accept him.

Meanwhile, he was learning a bloody lot—and the price of a few aches and pains didn't seem too high. Indeed, he was taking satisfaction in the physical labor, in stretching himself to the limit. Yesterday's fall had been humiliating—he still felt the bruises—but he had enough confidence in his horsemanship to know he eventually would live it down.

It was still dark, but Drew lost any hope of getting more sleep. The snoring had become ungodly. As had the odor of stale sweat. Hell, he might as well get up and check on Gabe. He needed some fresh air anyway.

Quietly, he rose from his bunk and searched for a clean shirt. He had three with him, and he religiously washed them daily. He doubted such small pleasures as clean clothes would be possible once the drive began, but he would take them now, even at the price of being called a dandy and tenderfoot and a few less charitable names. If the cowhands were aware he had a title, Drew knew he would never hear the end of it.

Walking quietly down the center aisle, Drew took a closer look at Gabe Lewis's bunk. The lad's bedroll and saddlebags lay on top of the unwrinkled blanket, which made it likely he was still somewhere about.

Outside, dawn was beginning to lighten the sky, the first hint of lavender relieving the inky blackness on the eastern horizon. Only a slight breeze stirred, but it was a vast improvement over the stuffy bunkhouse.

Drew took a deep breath of fresh air, then started across the yard, heading for the barn. With his eyes well-adjusted to the darkness, he looked around but didn't see another living soul. He swore to himself. Kirby hadn't seen the need for a guard, even after the ambush weeks ago. Drew had tried to persuade him to post one, but the cattle baron felt safe here, on his own land. Drew, on the other hand, wondered whether his friend was safe anywhere until the man who paid his attackers was found.

The door to the barn was closed but not barred from the outside, and Drew stepped in. A horse whinnied, announcing his presence and others started moving restlessly in the stalls. He passed them, treading quietly, and went directly to the stall where Gabe Lewis's horse had been stabled yesterday afternoon.

The horse was still there, and, when Drew peered inside the stall, it stepped carefully aside. He looked down to see what appeared to be a pile of rags in the corner. When the rags sighed and shifted a little in the straw, Drew smiled. So the lad hadn't given up. Somehow, Drew hadn't believed he would. Probably, before the drive was over, Gabe Lewis would win Flanigan's hat as well.

Thoughtfully, Drew eyed the broken-down horse. He knew horses, and he tended to agree with this one's owner that Billy was stronger than he looked and, indeed, had heart. Well, his owner had heart, too.

Leaving the barn as silently as he'd come, Drew walked over to lean on the top rail of the corral. There he watched the sky grow lighter, daybreak painting the vast canvas with an array of pink and golden hues. Dawn in Scotland, though beautiful in its own quiet way, had never been like this. Nothing here, in this wide-open land, was done on a small scale, and Drew didn't think he'd ever tire of its lonely splendor.

With the day about to begin, he saw smoke

spiralling from Kingsley's house. Marguerite, the cook, was preparing breakfast. Pepper wouldn't take over feeding the men until the drive started. Drew remained where he was, watching the sunrise, until someone rang the great bell outside the ranch house. In minutes, men were pouring out of the bunkhouse, stopping only long enough to rinse their faces at the pump.

Drew went back inside the barn to wake the lad, only to find him standing outside of Billy's stall, stretching his arms above his head, hat in one hand. Drew's gaze stopped at the mop of dark curls plastered to the boy's head, curls that looked as if they belonged to a girl, not a boy.

Sensing his presence, the lad's head jerked toward him, and in the next instant, he stuffed the hat back on his head. Dark blue eyes grew wary. Then hostility, so strong it almost reached out and touched him, filled them before the lad looked away.

"What are you looking at?" he asked.

Drew ignored the hostility and went into the stall, walking over to the horse, running his fingers down its side. It trembled at his touch.

"Get away from him," the boy said. "He doesn't like . . ." The boy stopped suddenly.

"What doesn't he like?" Drew asked curiously.

But the boy's face went utterly still, and Drew was stunned. Control. Complete control. Something one didn't see in a face that young.

"He don't like foreigners," Gabe said after a moment, startling him into remembering his own question.

"And how would he be knowing I'm a . . . foreigner?" Drew asked with amusement.

"Yer accent, of course," the answer came airily and with just a dash of superiority at besting an adversary.

"And Billy can distinguish among accents?" Drew said.

"He's a very smart horse." The slightest twinkle of

mischief shone in those blue eyes before coming under control again.

It was amazing. Despite the boy's grammar and rough demeanor, Gabe Lewis was bright—very bright—and also a little bit of an actor. Perhaps a great deal an actor.

But Drew's amusement quickly faded. Someone was after Kingsley. And there seemed more to this lad than what lay on the dusty surface. Gabe Lewis had claimed to be sixteen and, Drew figured, might be as young as fourteen. But Drew had seen boys even younger than that on Glasgow docks who were thieves and killers. Some had the faces of angels. Some wouldn't have thought twice before staving in a head if a few pence were offered.

Drew decided then and there he would keep an eye on young Master Lewis.

"You might want to discard some of those clothes," he suggested. "It's going to be a bloody hot day."

The boy merely huddled his slight body more into the offensive garments and turned back to his horse. His posture made it clear he wasn't going to take anyone's advice. Well, he'd learn. Drew would bet his saddle that the boy would discard at least some of those layers before late afternoon.

Leaving Gabe to his own devices, Drew went to find the pinto he had ridden yesterday. He was damned if a horse was going to get the best of him.

Sitting behind his huge walnut desk, Kirby reviewed his preparations for the drive. He had cash—wrapped in oilcloth and locked in a strongbox that would go in the chuck wagon—along with powers of attorney from neighboring ranchers participating in the drive. He was leaving his own power of attorney for his brother Jon in case anything happened to him.

When he was finished, he leaned back in his chair,

his fingers toying idly with the pen he held. Through the open windows of his office, he could hear the cowboys in the yard, laughing loudly about some wager one of them had lost. Their energy and excitement were high. Tomorrow was the big day. They would saddle up and ride out with an unprecedented ten thousand head of cattle. Hell, he was excited, too.

Staring out the window, Kirby frowned. He would have liked to go into town to say goodbye to Laura Sellers, but he had no right.

Laura. Even her name was pretty. So was the sound of her voice. He pictured her in his mind. Lovely taffy-colored blond hair, intelligent dark brown eyes, a curvaceous body that made him ache. He had known the widowed dressmaker for five years; her husband Bill had been a lawyer and Kirby's friend until he died a year ago, leaving barely enough for her to live on. She might have returned east, where apparently she had relatives. She'd stayed, though, and started a successful dressmaking business. He recalled the several occasions that he'd paid her a visit. He could do that under the guise of friendship without it causing talk. He'd never asked her out, though, despite knowing she would have accepted his invitation. He hadn't gotten so old or out of touch that he couldn't tell when a woman would welcome his attentions.

His fingers clenched around the pen. When he thought of Laura, the vow he'd made never to marry was strained to the limit. But he still feared that the ugly secret he harbored might destroy him someday, and he wanted to make very sure that no one he loved was also destroyed.

For that reason, he lived a solitary and lonely life except for his brother and nephews, and even then he'd tried to make them independent of him. It was difficult. Since he was fourteen, Kirby had taken care of Jon, who at the time of their parents' death was eight. He had been father as well as brother, and Jon had never completely learned to stand on his own two feet. Nor had his sons.

The pen broke in his hand. The events of twenty-five years ago were as alive in his mind as if they had happened yesterday. He had tried to put them away in a mental box and close it off, but they kept coming back. Lately, they'd been coming back more and more often. He couldn't help but wonder if the ambush several months ago was in some way connected to that long-ago disaster.

Who had hired the gunmen?

Three men came to Kirby's mind, three men who had something to gain by his death, or more likely, something to lose if he remained alive. Yet . . . what could have stirred the pot after so many years?

Probably nothing. Probably his conscience was working overtime. After all, there had been no further attempts, just that one freak ambush that, fortunately, had been waylaid by Cameron's quixotic rescue. Truth to tell, although he was damned happy to be alive, he wasn't sorry the ambush had happened. If it hadn't, he wouldn't have met Drew Cameron.

He smiled at the thought of the Scotsman. Kirby had made few friends in the last twenty-five years—maybe because he'd once used such damned poor judgment in choosing companions, maybe because he was afraid of losing those he might choose. Regardless of the cause, he'd held himself aloof from other men. But something about Drew Cameron made him discard his ordinary caution.

Guts, for example. Plain, old-fashioned guts. The man had taken on three gunmen for a stranger's sake. But there was much more to the Scotsman. He was intelligent, well-read, articulate, and charming. Usually Kirby was suspicious of charm; he'd seen it used to his disadvantage—and almost ruin—once before, but he could find no evil in the Scotsman, only a barrenness that matched Kirby's own.

Drew hid his loneliness well under a smile, a wink,

and a joke. But Kirby often wondered what turned a Scottish lord into a wanderer, a man who would accept a pittance for backbreaking labor.

Kirby sighed. His friendship with Cameron scared his nephews. They had always expected to take over his spread and now they sensed a challenge to that natural assumption. That Drew Cameron wanted no part of it would never occur to them.

What *did* occur to Kirby was that the competition might be good for his nephews. He didn't want to think that he was using a man who had saved his life.

So he thought of Laura instead. Pretty Laura whom he could never have.

Chapter Four

"Head 'em up and move 'em out!"

The call started at the front of the sprawling, brown mass of horned cattle and moved in two directions around the perimeter of the herd, until it reached the back.

Riding drag, the worst possible position on the drive, Drew received the call last, and by the time it reached him, the very earth rumbled with movement and the plain itself appeared to be moving. Great clouds of dust swirled from thousands of hooves, and all of it seemed aimed directly at his face. He pulled up his bandanna for protection, but he couldn't cover his eyes. He knew his clothes would be brown with new dirt within an hour.

He didn't know how his horse stood the unremitting assault, but the pinto seemed to take it in stride. They had been on the trail five days now, and he and the pinto, his horse of choice, had finally reached an understanding. At least, Drew thought they had.

His mind had been wandering a bit when a cow, straggling at the back of the herd, suddenly broke away and veered to the left. The pinto veered after it and Drew was nearly unseated. He gave his head a shake to clear it. No more daydreaming about the green fields and grouse-filled woods of Scotland. He had to pay attention every moment.

The horse turned sharply again, and this time Drew anticipated the move and flowed with it. Within seconds, the wayward cow had been driven back to the main herd, and the pinto settled back into an easy walk. Drew settled in for another long and grinding day.

By midmorning, he was shifting restlessly in the saddle, wishing to bloody hell he could dismount and walk awhile. Walking was a sacrilege to most cowboys, but his body had yet to resign itself entirely to sitting in a saddle eighteen hours a day. The eager anticipation that had rippled through him that first morning, when the drive commenced, had since drained away. His sense of adventure had dimmed as dust, dirt, and heat enveloped him like a malevolent cloud.

Heat. He felt it to the marrow of his bones. The Texas sun was nothing he'd ever experienced—big and bold and burning—and he wondered how anyone ever got used to it. Scotland had three temperatures: cool, cold, and freezing. Based on the past five days, he decided that the Texas counterpart was hot, hotter, and roasting. But today felt especially miserable; the heat was accompanied by a suffocating humidity that hadn't been there yesterday.

His own discomfort made him wonder how Two-Bits was faring. Despite the temperature, the lad still clung to his preposterous garb. The other hands, who were all down to the minimum necessary to protect their bodies from occasional branches and brush, were taking bets on how many days it would be before the cook's louse shed his layers of clothing.

Drew couldn't help but feel sympathetic, as well as

grateful, toward Gabe Lewis. The lad had saved him from being the cowhands' favorite target, taking all the joshing and pranks upon himself. And, God knows, he gave the hands enough to tease him about. His own initial suspicion of Two-Bits had faded to almost nothing; no villain, no matter how young, could possibly be as inept. He'd have been in jail, or dead, with his first unlawful act.

Stories already abounded about the louse's incompetence, and Two-Bits had been banished to the sole duty of collecting cow chips. No one was betting that he wouldn't find a way to fail at that, too. The lad would have been fired on the first day if it weren't for the fact that he tried so hard; even Pepper had to admit that he did.

The day wore on, seemingly endless, and sometime late in the afternoon, Drew noticed the temperature start to drop. The air became heavy, and the humidity went from oppressive to unbearable. It seemed to collect on Drew's skin, and the reins, even through his gloves, felt like wet leather, limp and slippery. And yet he was aware of a peculiar energy in the still, moisture-laden air. A short time later, a sharp wind started to blow. The sky, clear that morning, began to grow thick with dark, ominous layers of clouds; they piled up like a chain of mountains, filling the sky.

The cattle became perceptibly restless. The wind and the wicked-looking sky made Drew nervous, too. For the last hour of the day, he and the other two cowhands riding drag—Ace, a black man, and Juan, a Mexican—were constantly moving, trying to keep the back of the herd together.

By the time the call came to stop for the day, about an hour before dusk, he was flat-out exhausted, and hunger gnawed at his stomach. Since breakfast at dawn, he'd had only jerky during the day, along with warm water from his canteen. He'd changed horses three times during the day and was now riding a black.

When he'd completed his share of work, getting the herd settled for the night, he rode with Juan and Ace to the temporary corral that had been set up for the remuda. There, he dismounted and unsaddled his horse, leaving it in the hands of the wrangler.

Grateful to be on his own feet, he walked toward the chuck wagon, which he knew would have arrived with the hoodlum wagon hours ago to set up camp. The wagons always moved out before the rest of the drive, camping early in order to fill the barrels with water before the cattle soiled it.

As he approached camp, Drew looked for Two-Bits but didn't see him. The coffee was ready, though, and the stew smelled as good as an eight-course meal in a fine Edinburgh restaurant. He poured himself a cup of coffee and took a couple of swallows, using it to rinse the dust out of his mouth and throat.

"Don't get too comfortable," Kirby told him as he sipped his own cup of coffee. "You have the first watch."

Drew nodded, sighing inwardly. He'd told Kirby he didn't want favors. It was obvious he wasn't going to get any. Being the newest man, he was usually assigned to the meanest jobs, and that included first night watch as well as drag.

Pouring more coffee into his tin cup, he helped himself to a bowl of stew and a chunk of fresh bread, then ate as he paced slowly around the campsite. After so many hours in the saddle, sitting held little appeal. Most of the other hands had finished their meals and were drinking their coffee and talking. A couple were unrolling blankets preparing to sleep. Several were playing cards. As he watched, a couple of men wandered off, away from the campsite, to tend to private matters.

Drew's stroll took him past the chuck wagon, where he stopped to talk to Pepper, who was working on a batch of biscuit dough. "Where's the lad?" he asked Pepper.

"Gone after more wood for the fire," Pepper said.

Drew took another drink of coffee. "He get rid of any of those clothes?"

"Hell no." Pepper shook his head in disgust. "Damn fool kid. Almost like he's afraid somebody's gonna steal 'em." The cook looked up at the sky. "On the other hand, could be he's smarter than any of us. He might need them things he's got on real soon."

Drew's gaze turned upward. Although it wasn't yet dusk, the sky was even darker than it had been minutes earlier. Dark clouds churned ominously. And the wind had turned cold. All around the campsite, cowhands were putting on coats.

Seeing Kirby walking toward him, he looked to the trail boss for an explanation. "Is this sort of weather normal?"

Kirby shook his head. "Ain't no such thing as 'normal' in this part of Texas. Weather can turn real strange out here. I've seen blizzards in May." Looking at the sky, he shook his head again. "I don't like this. I don't like it one damn bit." And with that, he walked away, striding across the campsite toward Damien.

Drew gulped down the rest of his food, drank his coffee, rinsed his plate and cup, and left them in the barrel where they were stored. In the few minutes he'd been in camp, the temperature had fallen sharply. He shivered inside his light cotton shirt as he walked to the hoodlum wagon, where he kept his bedroll and extra clothes. He hesitated a moment, then pulled on a wool shirt and his slicker. He might well need it before his watch had finished.

As he started toward the remuda and a fresh horse, Kirby stopped him.

"Be real careful tonight," the trail boss said. "Cattle are always a little spooked the first few nights, and this sky . . ." His gaze traveled heavenward again. "There's a storm brewing. A bad one." Offering Drew a twisted smile, Kirby added, "You might try one of those soothing Scottish melodies."

Before Drew could reply, Damien interrupted. "Hell, that will spook them straight to Mexico," he said nastily.

Kirby gave his nephew a long, warning glance, and Damien glared at Drew.

"I wouldn't trust him with those cattle," Damien said to his uncle.

"I would," Kirby said quietly. "And you'll take the second shift, Damien, so you'd better get some sleep."

Drew felt the enmity practically ooze from Damien before the younger man turned and walked over to flop down on his bedroll. Kirby gave him a nod, then headed over to talk to Pepper, and Drew was left to wonder—not for the first time—how seriously he ought to take Damien's blatant anger toward him. Would Kirby's nephew actually do him harm? He didn't know, and that being the case, he reminded himself to watch his own back.

He saddled a fresh horse from the remuda and mounted. As he rode off toward the herd, he caught a glimpse of a small, semibent silhouette—Two-Bits, hunched over an armful of cow chips, heading toward the chuck wagon.

Relieved, Drew smiled. He hadn't even been aware that he was worrying about the lad. Didn't know why he cared enough to worry. Yet he couldn't seem to keep Gabe Lewis out of his thoughts for long, and he found it comforting in a way he didn't begin to understand that the lad was still with the drive.

He didn't understand his concern for Gabe Lewis any better than he understood why he had let himself get involved with Kirby Kingsley. He usually went out of his way *not* to get involved. Yet here he was, dead tired and filthy and longing for a good snifter of brandy, riding off into what promised to be one hell of a bloody storm. And for what purpose? To tend a bunch of cattle.

Stupid beasts, cows. Didn't possess a grain of sense, nor any redeeming qualities he could name. So, why

was he killing himself on this damn drive in exchange
for fifty of the cursed beasts? One game of chance in
town, and he'd have enough money for a clean room,
a good meal, and a lusty woman.

Pride, he thought. It had to be. There simply was no
other explanation. He'd accepted Kirby's offer out of
curiosity and adventure and now was stuck with a
decision too readily made. He'd never been a quitter,
no matter what else he'd been—or hadn't been.

As he began his first long circle of the sleeping herd,
Drew started to sing softly—a Scottish lullaby that
one of his nurses had sung to him long, long ago, in
another lifetime.

Gabrielle was on her way back to camp with her
latest load of cow chips when she saw Drew Cameron
ride back toward the herd. She wondered whether
he'd heard about her latest debacle. Embarrassment
ripped through her as she remembered each humiliating moment.

Stew had been a last-minute replacement for supper
tonight. The planned menu had been beans, which
she'd put on the fire as soon as they'd stopped at
midafternoon, far ahead of the herd. Pepper had been
busy making bread and had told her to put beans into
a pot with water.

She'd done exactly that, pleased that he had trusted
her with that small chore. But then Terry Kingsley had
arrived, telling them that the herd was an hour
behind, and he'd taken a taste of the beans, immediately spitting them out. The younger Kingsley had
sworn first at Pepper, who'd then turned on her.

"What's the matter now?" Pepper asked sharply,
and when Terry held up his tooth for the cook's
inspection, Pepper let out a single explicit oath.

Gabrielle still hadn't been quite sure what she'd
done wrong. Pepper had told her to put five pounds of

beans in a pot and she'd followed his instructions precisely.

But Pepper had fixed her with his blue pale eyes. "Sonofabitch," he said. "What did I do so bad in my life that a vengeful god saddled me with you?"

Gabrielle had stared at him, uncomprehendingly.

"Any fool could see gravel was mixed with the beans," he said. "Anyone with a lick of sense."

She still must have looked puzzled because the cook went into another spasm of creative oaths, then explained disgustedly. "Sellers mix gravel in with beans to add to their weight. You always have to sort it."

"I didn't know," she said.

"Any jackass knows that," Pepper muttered balefully. "I ain't gonna let you anywhere near this wagon again."

Gabrielle had wanted to sink into the ground. Nothing she did was right. Nothing. She'd tried to swallow, but a huge lump of embarrassment had clogged her throat. She *had* seen some grit toward the bottom, but hadn't seen any in the scoopfuls she'd measured. Minutes later, she'd been banished back to collecting cow chips. At least she was out of sight of Pepper, and hopefully out of mind. She winced as she remembered the outraged barrage of insults.

At least this hadn't been quite as bad as the coffee calamity. Having lived with her parents in rooming houses and hotels, she had never made coffee in her life. So when Pepper had told her to make it "strong enough to float a horseshoe," she had taken him seriously. After searching the compartments and finding coffee beans, she'd hesitantly asked him how much to use. After he'd hollered for a while about how any simpleton knew how to make coffee, his growled instructions had been to "take a pound of coffee, wet it good with water, boil it over a fire for thirty minutes, pitch in a horseshoe and if it sinks, put in more coffee."

It hadn't sounded right to her, but she was hesitant to ask any more questions. They always drew spiked contempt and exasperation. He obviously thought *anyone* should know how to make coffee. So she'd followed the directions—except for putting in the horseshoe—and she still didn't consider it her fault that nobody had told her that she had to grind the coffee beans.

Unfortunately, Kingsley had been the first person to pour himself a cup of the stuff she'd made. He'd taken a sip without looking at it. The reaction was immediate. He spat it out instantly, and his face had gone beet red. She'd been extremely thankful that the words he'd muttered under his breath were incomprehensible.

Pepper's comments, however, had been very plain. Gabrielle had heard inventive swearing in the theater, but everything she'd ever heard paled in the face of the old cook's creative use of the language. And his comments over the coffee were nothing compared to the pinnacle he'd reached when he discovered she'd thrown out his sourdough starter. It had looked—and smelled—like something spoiled to her. How was she supposed to know what it was?

For the following three nights she had been exiled from the chuck wagon, and only today had she been given another chance.

So much for second—and third—chances. She'd lost them. And she only wished she could figure out why she even cared. She wasn't here to learn how to cook or make anyone like her. She was here to find some kind of justice.

She bit her lip, torn between amusement at the beleaguered Pepper and chagrin at her own incompetence and the likely result. If only there had been a cookbook. Or if Pepper had explained something. But neither had happened, and she'd placed far too much faith in her own reasoning ability. Cooking, apparently, was not one of her God-given talents.

She sat down on a dead log, and she couldn't help herself. She started laughing. That coffee *had* been rather strange, and the look on Pepper's face when he'd discovered his treasured starter missing would forever be in her memory. Pure disbelief. Absolute horror. If she hadn't wanted to stay so badly, to complete her mission one way or another, she would have smiled then and there.

The reminder of her goal sobered her. Nothing had changed her conviction that Kingsley had hired a gun to kill her father. And she was still suspicious that Drew Cameron might be that hired gun. But she wasn't sure, and she hadn't figured out how to confirm her suspicion.

She saw so little of the Scotsman. And when she did see him, he confused her so badly she couldn't think. When he was around the campsite, he watched her constantly, watched her with those intense, piercing golden eyes. And when he wasn't watching her, he was doing or saying something *kind*—at least on the surface his words and deeds appeared kind—which only made her more confused.

She didn't want Drew Cameron's kindness. She didn't want to talk to him, didn't want to like him. And she most definitely did not want to feel the butterflies that fluttered inside her every time she looked at him. She didn't understand how she could feel any pleasant sensation over a man she believed might be a murderer—*her father's* murderer.

In fact, she decided, it was her suspicions about the Scotsman that were keeping her from acting on the overwhelming impulse she felt every time she saw Kirby Kingsley—that and the fact she was never alone with Kingsley. She wanted to use the pistol she kept in the saddlebags, force him to tell the truth, even . . . kill him if necessary. It wasn't rational, that impulse. In some dark corner of her mind, she knew that. But when she saw Kingsley, or thought about him, all rational thought fled. Rage and grief overpowered all else. She wanted to hurt him, to do damage to him as he had done to her and those she loved.

It didn't matter what happened next. She couldn't think past that moment. In slightly more rational moments, she knew that if she shot Kingsley, the likely outcome would be that she, too, would die. But at the moment, she simply didn't care. She had no one. Nothing. Except . . . if she were killed, she would miss her chance at finding the man who'd actually pulled the trigger.

So, no, she couldn't confront Kingsley. Not yet. And so she was biding her time. Every morning, she woke up with the sensation that she was living under a cloud as big and dark and all-encompassing as those filling the sky above her at that moment. And every night, she fell onto her bedroll vowing that tomorrow . . . tomorrow would be the day. She would get the answers she needed about Drew Cameron, then seek the justice her soul craved so badly. And in between morning and night, all she could think about was how hot and tired she was, and about her father being dead, about being alone in the world. So alone. So apart from everything and everyone around her.

Enough wool-gathering, she scolded herself. She was competent enough to fetch cow chips and wood, and that might be the only thing that saved her job.

As she finished her search for cow chips, she noticed that the wind had picked up since she'd left camp. It felt good, and she even risked opening her coat and unbuttoning the top few buttons of her shirt to let it cool her overheated skin. She'd been hot and miserable all day under the layers of clothes. How she would make it through weeks, maybe even months, in all these clothes, she didn't know.

By the time she started back to camp, it was nearly dark. As she passed between the herd and the wagon, she slowed, then stopped, at the sound of a man's voice. It was a voice she instantly recognized, and he was singing. She didn't know the song but it was soft and low. A lullaby. She couldn't identify the song, but she was instantly enchanted, both by the melody and the rich, smooth tenor that was singing it. She listened, storing the melody in her mind, until gradually he moved away and she couldn't hear him anymore.

In the silence, she was left feeling more confused than ever. The cursed man had done it to her again. His smile, his kind words. His voice, singing a lullaby. Nothing about him fit the image of an assassin. Yet nothing about him seemed to fit the image of a cowhand either. A part of her—the part of her that was grief-stricken and enraged at an unjust world—wanted to believe the worst of him, wanted to find ulterior motives in everything he did. Wanted to hate him.

But another part of her whispered that he couldn't possibly be a murderer. That he was as lonely and apart from the rest of the world as she was. As lonely as his voice had sounded, singing his beautiful lullaby to a herd of cattle.

Suddenly, as she stood in the dark in the middle of that vast, wide-open plain, all of her own feelings of loneliness, of being isolated from the rest of the world, intensified. Damn Drew Cameron. Damn his smile, and his lullaby. Damn everything about him that made her feel things she didn't want to feel.

Angry at herself, feeling like a fool, Gabrielle buttoned her shirt and coat and started back for the chuck wagon. As she walked, though, she became aware that the sky had lost its last trace of light, and the cool air that had been pleasant only minutes before had turned cold. It bit through her layers of clothing. An instant later, thunder rumbled in the distance.

She quickened her steps and, as she approached camp, she saw cowboys leave the cooking fire and head for their horses. Thunder meant nervous cattle. She'd learned that much.

Pepper barely acknowledged her return. He was packing supplies in the chuck wagon. The fire had been cleared of everything but the coffeepot. "Put that wood in the hoodlum wagon," he said.

When she had dumped her load, she returned. "What can I do?"

He glanced at her. "Storm's coming. Damn bad one. I can feel it. You keep out of the way."

Gabrielle looked at the sky, then at the bedrolls scattered around, abandoned by the cowboys. She started rolling them up and putting them under cover in the hoodlum wagon. Pepper looked up at her once, nodded in approval of her actions, then went back to closing the various shelves and buttoning up the canvas.

By the time she had completed her task, rain had started falling. She saw that Pepper had rigged a canvas flap over the fire, but the wind was fanning it too close to the wagon for safety. With obvious reluctance, he lowered the canvas, and in minutes the fire went out. The night was as black as any Gabe ever had seen. What was more, the temperature had taken another sudden drop.

"Get in yer wagon," Pepper ordered gruffly. "It's gonna hail. I've seen them stones big enough to kill a horse."

As he spoke, she heard the cattle moving restlessly, the plaintive bellowing growing stronger. And the horses, closer yet to the campsite, were whinnying nervously. Among them, the voices of at least two cowhands could be heard, shouting to each other.

When she saw Pepper hurrying toward the horses, Gabrielle ignored his order and followed him closely, using the shape of his shadow for guidance. She arrived at the remuda to find Jake, the wrangler, and Shorty moving the horses from their makeshift corral. They were tying the horses individually onto several picket lines that had been strung tight between a half dozen cottonwoods. Squinting in the darkness, she and Pepper silently joined them.

One by one, they moved the remaining horses, and the task was made infinitely more difficult when, all at once, the rain turned into large pieces of ice, pelting the earth, pelting the shying horses, pelting Gabrielle with amazing force. Some were as large as quail eggs, and she wanted to do as Pepper had ordered, but both the wrangler and Pepper were staying in the open, trying to secure and soothe the horses. She couldn't do less. She moved among the animals, her actions becoming automatic as she carefully tied the nervous animals.

Though she began actually to fear for her life, the nearly panicked horses seemed even more afraid. Steeling herself against the pounding of hail, she stuck with the task at hand, and finally, after what seemed hours, the four of them—Jake, Shorty, Pepper and her—had over a hundred fifty horses and mules tied securely.

Giving a sigh of relief, she longed for the relative comfort and safety of the wagon, but the men were remaining, moving up and down the lines of tied horses, trying to soothe them. She joined them, calming them with a touch, a whisper. All the while, the hailstones came faster, harder, and larger. Her hat and clothing protected most of her, but she felt the blows and knew she would have even more bruises the next day.

One horse, apparently hit hard in the face, tried to rear and became frantic when he couldn't. She moved over to the animal, whispering, even began humming the Scotsman's lullaby that was still running through her mind. Slowly, the horse relaxed.

Lightning streaked through the heavens, providing brief illumination before the sky went black again. Gabrielle stood still, then became aware of a deep rumbling, a trembling of earth underneath her.

"Stampede," Pepper yelled. "Get behind a tree."

The rumbling grew stronger, and the earth shook. Cattle were suddenly everywhere, running blindly, veering as they saw the trees. Terrified horses reared and fought the ropes. Another bolt of lightning shot across the heavens, and balls of ice rattled through the trees, beating out a metallic rhythm. It was a symphony of violence, and Gabrielle had never been more frightened in her life.

She clung to the slender trunk of a tree, terror clawing through her as the huge herd of panicked cattle parted, like a river, around rocks, to either side of the island of trees where she and the men and the spooked horses huddled. She prayed, as she had not prayed since her father had died. She prayed for herself. She prayed for Drew Cameron. She prayed for every man out there in the storm.

"Please, God, make it stop . . . please make it stop. Don't let any of them get hurt. Please . . ." she prayed. And if her prayers for safe passage were focused more on one man in particular, one with a quick smile and a seductive voice, she refused to acknowledge it even to herself.

She hugged a tree, straining to see in the dark, hearing sudden splashing, which meant the cattle were heading across the creek. Loud male voices, shouting above the storm, punctuated the sound of hooves as they moved away. Yet even after the splashing stopped and she knew the cattle were all on the other side of the water, the earth still vibrated under her feet.

For several long minutes, Gabrielle continued to hug the tree. Her insides were quivering, her body shaking from head to toe.

"Two-Bits?"

Pepper's voice had the slightest quake to it.

"I—I'm all right," she said. Peeling her arms from the tree trunk, she took one shaky step, then another, away from the cottonwood. The horses continued to stomp nervously, neighing and pulling at their ropes. She heard Jake's voice, crooning to them.

Still, hail continued to fall, thicker than ever, and she shivered in her misery. But her thoughts were out on the plain, traveling with the cowboys attempting to stop the stampede. She understood the dangers.

"Please God, let them be safe," she whispered again.

"We'd better see to the wagon," Pepper said. "You can bet there'll be somebody hurt."

"Are you sure?" Gabrielle asked, straining to see the cook through the cloak of hail-filled darkness.

"Hell," he swore, "we'll be lucky if a third of 'em ain't hurt or worse after this!"

Gabrielle's stomach lurched. Pepper was not a man to scare easily. She followed his shadow, a dark blob in a freezing black nightmare.

The chuck wagon had been turned over, knocked that way by frantic cattle. Pepper called for Shorty, leaving Jake with the horses, and the three of them tried to right it. But it was no use. The packed wagon was simply too heavy.

"We'll have to wait for help," Pepper said with disgust. He found a lantern, rigged a covering to keep the rain from dousing the flame, and placed it like a beacon in front of the wagon. Then the three of them—Pepper, Shorty and her—huddled against its bottom, seeking shelter from the hail, listening for hoofbeats and a yell to announce an arrival.

The trembling of earth eased. Gabrielle heard something like distant thunder but she didn't know whether it was cattle or actual thunder.

She shivered. She couldn't remember when she'd been so cold, and she realized it wasn't strictly because of the temperature or the icy winds. In the days she'd been on the drive, she'd come to know all the hands by name. Some she liked, some she didn't. But she didn't want any of them to die. Not like this.

A century passed. No one spoke. Eventually, the

hail lessened, then ended, but rain continued, falling in heavy sheets until she felt like a saturated sponge.

"Pepper? Pepper, damn it, where are you?"

The voice reached out from the darkness, disembodied but urgent. Gabrielle's heart leaped to her throat. It was Kingsley. She was sure of it.

"Yo," Pepper yelled.

A dark figure appeared on horseback from the other side of the overturned wagon.

"Everything all right here?" Gabrielle recognized Kingsley's voice.

"Wagon turned," Pepper said, "but no one was hurt. The herd?"

"We stopped them about three miles across the river." Kingsley's voice was businesslike. "I have one man dead, two others hurt."

Dead. The word resounded in Gabrielle's mind, and before the echoes faded, a half-formed, spontaneous plea took its place. *Please . . . please, don't let it be him. Please . . .*

Pepper, who was sitting beside her, rose stiffly from the ground to stand. "They coming in?"

"The injured are. The rest will stay out there with the cattle. I don't want to move them now."

"How bad are they?" Pepper asked.

Kingsley was silent for a moment before he replied. "One's pretty bad."

"I need help getting this wagon upright," Pepper said, his voice matter-of-fact.

"The kid all right?" Kirby asked.

"He's here. Did fine," Pepper said gruffly. "Didn't go losin' his head."

Stunned at the praise, Gabrielle's pride warred with anxiety as she shifted from the ground to her feet. Who was hurt? *Who?* How badly? She wanted to ask but couldn't force the words out.

Shouting for Jake to come help them, Kingsley dismounted, then tied one end of his lariat to two bows of the wagon. The other end he tied to his saddle horn. Gabrielle jumped in shock when he thrust the reins of his horse into her hands.

"You lead the horse away from the wagon while we push it upright,' he ordered. "And for God's sake, stop when I tell you."

Nodding—a useless gesture in the dark, she realized—she coaxed the horse, feeling him strain against the load. They'd gone a couple of yards when the lines slackened just as she heard Kingsley's shout. "Hold there!"

A few seconds later, he appeared in front of her to take back the reins. "Good job," he said.

Then Pepper called to her. "Two-Bits! Come help me get out my doctorin' things. Can't see my own hand in front of my face."

As she ran through the rain to help, the litany continued to run through her mind: *Please, God, please . . . don't let him be dead. Please.*

Drew held his arm stiffly as his exhausted horse walked slowly toward the chuck wagon. Failure, strong and bitter, rode with him.

Two other men guided their mounts alongside his, one man carrying a limp body, the other barely holding on to the saddle horn. The body was Juan's; he'd been caught under the hooves of the cattle when they'd made a sudden turn and run straight into his horse. The horse was dead, too.

Ace had almost died, as well. Drew shuddered, his insides still sick from the events of the past hour. Ace had also lost his horse, but Drew had reached him before the main herd had trampled him, swooping down and hanging half out of his own saddle to lift the black man across his horse's shoulders. The man's leg was crushed, but with any luck he would live.

Still, Drew felt as if he'd failed. If he'd been more experienced, if he'd anticipated the direction the herd would take, perhaps he could have swung the cattle back, away from Juan.

Bloody hell, he'd never wanted responsibility for the lives of others. He had, in fact, tried to avoid such obligations all his life. What a fool he'd been, a naïve fool, ever to think of a cattle drive as a lark. A great adventure.

Well, so now he'd learned—the hard way, as usual—that it was impossible. Over the past few days he'd seen that a trail drive depended on teamwork. And tonight, he'd seen very clearly the full extent of that burden: Everyone on the drive was responsible for every other man. Quite simply, they had each other's lives in their hands.

And he wasn't at all sure he was up to the task. He remembered his father's mocking laughter when he suggested the possibility of purchasing a commission. *I wouldn't trust you with a dog. You're weak. Worthless. Get out of my sight.* How many times had he been told that?

Until he'd believed it.

Shifting in the saddle, Drew tried to hold the reins and his arm at the same time. He'd done something to the arm when he'd picked up Ace, and he hoped it was a bad sprain and not a break.

A light flickered in the darkness ahead, and he narrowed his eyes, trying to determine how far away it was. At least they were moving in the right direction. The heavens were so bloody dark, only the sound of the herd behind him had given him a reference point. The lightning was gone too, but the cold, freezing rain continued to pummel the earth and everything upon it. His horse reached the creek, and he realized instantly it was higher than it had been just an hour ago. As he crossed, he felt the pull of it against the horse's legs.

By the time they reached the chuck wagon, Ace, who had been suspiciously silent through the ride, was swearing. Kirby was standing at the back of the wagon. A small slight figure stood silently with him.

"You'd better get the wagon and horses across," Drew said. "That creek's rising fast."

"As soon as we get you two patched up," Kingsley said. "Jake and Shorty are already moving the horses."

"We gonna talk all night?" The cook's voice materialized out of nowhere.

"Ace's leg is pretty well smashed," Drew said.

The slight figure next to Kirby, whom Drew identified as Gabe, seemed to stiffen but remained silent.

Pepper's voice broke in. "What about you, Scotty?"

"It's not serious. Take Ace first."

Pepper and Kirby helped Ace down from the horse, then lowered him on an oilcloth that had already been spread.

"Bring the lantern here, Two-Bits," Pepper commanded, and Drew watched the lad move quickly forward and shine the light down on the injured man.

"Dangnabit," Pepper exclaimed as he cut away the trouser leg and saw the mangled leg. "I can't do much. Needs a doctor. I can give him some whiskey for pain, bandage it, but he needs more help than I can give him . . ." The cook's voice trailed off just as Ace moaned.

"I can't afford the time or the men," Kingsley said in an emotionless voice. "Can't you stitch him up until we reach the next town?"

"Oh, I could stitch him up all right, but all the jiggling and jostling would kill him for sure."

Kingsley swore.

"I can take him on a travois," Drew said. "I won't be good for a week or more anyway. San Antonio isn't that far. I can catch up with you later."

Pepper shook his head. "There's a cattle town—Willow Springs—no more than fifteen miles east of here. Should have a doc."

"Now, wait a minute," Kirby said. "Before anyone goes anywhere, Pepper, take a look at Drew's arm."

Drew reluctantly shed his slicker and shirt, shivering in the icy rain as the cook tested and probed.

"Sprain," Pepper pronounced. "He's right. He won't be able to herd for a week at least."

"He can't go alone, not with a wounded man and that arm," Kingsley said, then his eyes lit on Two Bits. "You can do without the kid, can't you, Pepper?"

Drew heard a small protest escape the boy's lips but apparently neither Kingsley nor Pepper heard it—or they chose to ignore it.

"Never wanted him in the first place," Pepper said.

"You can take one of the horses from the remuda," Kingsley told the boy.

"I'd rather take Billy."

Kingsley shrugged and turned back to Drew. "That all right with you?"

Drew wasn't sure whether the boy would be more hindrance than help, but he understood Kirby's reasons for not thinking he could manage alone—and that Ace's life might depend upon his having someone along with him. He also understood that his agreement to take Two-Bits would determine whether he was allowed to go at all.

He nodded.

"It's settled then," Kingsley said. "Pepper, you fix Ace as best as you can, then get a sling on Cameron. The kid and I will make a travois. Come on, kid, let's get started."

Drew watched as Kirby strode away, toward the hoodlum wagon. Two-Bits hesitated, giving him a wary look. Drew could feel the reluctance radiating from the lad's eyes, eyes that, in the dim light, were almost black. He wanted to say something reassuring, but he was just too tired and discouraged to make an effort.

Then, Kirby's shout came slicing through the strained silence. "Two-Bits! Get over here."

The lad tore his gaze away and obeyed Kirby.

Drew sighed, thinking it was going to be a long ride to Willow Springs. An instant later, though, he forgot Gabe Lewis when Ace moaned. He leaned down and lifted the whiskey bottle to the man's lips while Pepper cut away pieces of his trouser leg and pulled them from the wounds. The cook hesitated, then poured alcohol over the torn and bleeding flesh. Ace screamed, then lost consciousness.

"You take a sip of that yourself," Pepper advised. "You'll need it to keep going tonight. Town's a good day's ride. Faster you get him to a doctor, better his chances."

Drew nodded and went to get his bedroll and a warm shirt. He was wet to the skin and freezing. His arm ached like bloody hell. He hadn't slept in eighteen hours. And he was facing a long grueling ride with a half-dead man and a green kid, who undoubtedly would cause him nothing but trouble.

Adventure, he thought, was for fools.

Chapter Five

———— ✛ ————

Willow Springs, Texas

"I don't want to leave Ace," Two-Bits protested. "I want to stay here with him."

Drew bit back an angry rejoinder and took a deep breath. He was tired beyond exhaustion and his arm hurt like hell. He wanted to talk to the doctor—privately—then find a bed. Any kind of bed. A floor would do.

Standing in the tiny waiting room of the doctor's office, he tamped down his impatience with Two-Bits's stubbornness. "The doctor says he'll live and the leg can probably be saved," Drew said, wishing he shared the doctor's guarded optimism. He took several heavy coins from a pocket and handed them to his companion. "You get us a room, two of them. I'll be there as soon as I can."

Two-Bits stared at him sullenly, hands in pocket. He made no move to take the money. Drew's eyes narrowed, and finally, with an exasperated sigh, the lad gave in. Nodding curtly, he took the money and left the room.

Drew watched him leave, shoulders sagging, thinking that in truth the boy had a right to stay with Ace. He'd been a surprising blessing on the agonizing day-long trip to Willow Creek, not only keeping pace without complaint but nursing Ace with unfailing kindness.

He didn't know what he had expected, but certainly not the tireless, practical companion who changed bandages with a smile and deftness that seemed to ease some of Ace's pain.

That smile, however, had not extended to him, and while Two-Bits would sit and talk to Ace each time they rested, the boy had little or nothing to say to him. Only a mumbled word now and then.

With a sigh, Drew returned to the inner room where Dr. Sanders was treating Ace. The doctor, too thin and haggard, looked in need of his own services.

"Don't be too long," Sanders said. "He needs to sleep."

Drew murmured his agreement as Sanders passed him on the way out the door, leaving him alone with Ace.

Ace's face was lined with pain. "Doc says I'll walk again, but maybe not as good."

Drew sat on a chair next to the bed. "You're on a horse all the time anyway," he said.

"That's a fact," Ace said, some of the anxiety leaving his face. "Used to pick cotton in Texas before the war. Never wanted to stay close to the ground again."

Drew pulled out a small package of bills. "Mr. Kingsley wanted you to have this."

Astonishment spread over Ace's face as his fingers shuffled through a number of bills. His mouth worked for a moment, his eyes misting. Then he looked at the bills again. "How . . . much is here?" he said.

Drew suddenly realized Ace probably couldn't

cipher. Or read. "Two hundred dollars," he said gently. "Should see you through four months or more." He watched as the man fondled the bills.

Ace shook his head against the pillow. "Never had so much. Never heard of anyone doing this."

"The boss is full of surprises," Drew said with a wry smile.

"Tell him I'm mighty grateful," Ace said.

"I will," Drew said. "You be careful with that."

"I'll pin it to my clothes, right next to my skin," Ace said with a smile, then added hesitantly. "Scotty. . . ?"

Drew lifted an eyebrow in question. He and Ace and Juan—the foreigner, the one black, and the Mexican—had shared the worst parts of a cattle drive, and a bond of sorts had grown between them. When Ace held out his hand, Drew sensed how tentative a gesture it was, how fearful he was that the offer would be rejected.

Drew grinned and grasped the injured man's hand tightly. "You'll be back in the saddle in no time."

Ace looked skeptical but his handshake was firm. "I'll never forget what you did," he said. "Coming back for me like that."

"Anyone would have done the same, anyone on that drive." Drew dismissed the sentiment, but he gave the other man's hand a squeeze before letting go.

Ace shook his head. "No, not everyone woulda done it. And I'll always be beholden to you an' Mr. Kingsley."

Inwardly, Drew squirmed with discomfort. He disliked gratitude.

Ace sighed. "You and me, we never did get to play poker together. That's how I got the name, you know. I drew a straight the first night I came to Mr. Kingsley's ranch. Ace high. First time ever."

Drew had heard the story several times. But, smiling, he let Ace continue. The injured man obviously wanted to prolong the conversation.

Drew just nodded. "You'll do it again. Get some rest now. Take care of yourself. And when the drive is over, I'll look for you. Leave word with the doctor where you'll be. If I ever get a ranch, I'll need a bloody good hand."

Ace's eyes misted slightly. He nodded. "I'll do that," he said.

"Take care of yourself," Drew said.

"You too, Scotty."

Morosely, Drew headed toward the town's one hotel, his thoughts occupied by Ace and his uncomplaining acceptance of a life marred by injustice and tragedy. The other drovers *had* ignored Ace, isolating him as they had isolated Drew in the beginning. But they had never accepted Ace as they were gradually accepting Drew. Bloody hell, but he was weary of class and race distinctions. That was one reason he left Scotland. One of the reasons he loathed his title.

As he reached the hotel, he tried to force all thoughts except sleep from his mind. He'd sell his soul for a hot bath and clean bed. What with a storm, a stampede, and two days in the saddle without sleep, he was as exhausted as he'd ever been. And more confused. For a man who had always considered self-survival and opportunism much-desired virtues, he was finding himself involved in more and more lives.

Feeling oddly unsettled about the perverse direction his character was apparently taking, he entered the hotel, only to find a disheveled Two-Bits sprawled asleep in a chair. The hat was gone, fallen to the floor, but the grime remained. Still, Two-Bits looked impossibly young—and innocent—with long eyelashes covering those indigo blue eyes that always regarded him so warily. Dirt and dust, though, layered the face, distorting and disguising the lad's features.

Damn, but he felt protective of the little imp. And the harder Gabe Lewis tried to reject his protection, the more compelled he felt to offer it. He didn't understand himself, not at all. He'd decided years ago that caring was for fools; it was usually for naught and bloody well painful to boot.

The desk clerk was gone, and it appeared as if the small hotel was full. Looking at the bare hooks where keys would normally hang, Drew noted that they were all empty. He leaned down and shook Two-Bits, who stirred a little, then curled back up. Drew shook him a little harder and the lad's eyes opened slowly. Their blue was glazed by sleep, but an instant later, when he succeeded in focusing and saw Drew standing over him, his eyes flew wide open.

"Did you get the rooms?"

Two-Bits dug around in the chair, then held out a key. "Only had one room," he said with his usual brevity. "Clerk said he was goin' to bed, so I waited for ya." He sat up. "I'll sleep in the livery stable. Already gave the man a quarter."

"We'll share the room," Drew said.

The lad's eyes widened with something like alarm. "Rather be on my own," he sniffed.

Drew hesitated. Two-Bits must be as exhausted as he was. "No baths here, I suppose," he said, studying the boy's grimy face. His must be just as bad, or worse. He hadn't shaved in two days.

Two-Bits looked even more alarmed at that thought, then shrugged indifferently. "Don't need a bath. Everyone knows too many baths make you sick."

Drew lifted an eyebrow. "Pray tell, how many would *too many* be?"

For a moment, he thought he saw a sliver of amusement in the lad's eyes, but it disappeared quickly into a frown, so quickly Drew wondered whether he had imagined it. Two-Bits held out the key, waiting until Drew reluctantly took it.

"Rather sleep with Billy Bones than a foreigner," the boy muttered balefully.

Drew sighed. The lad babied that horse like a mother with her first bairn. Just as Drew had Sir Arthur thirty years ago. His stomach tightened again.

There were few stronger bonds than that between a boy and his horse, especially a boy who had nothing or no one else. Yet the result could easily be pain so deep and excruciating it never went away.

So he let the boy go. Nothing he said, no warning, would make a farthing's worth of difference.

Gabrielle slept in an empty stall next to Billy Bones. Truth told, she could have slept anyplace. She'd never been so weary in her life. When her head hit the straw, she didn't even think about Kirby Kingsley or the Scotsman. She simply passed out.

She didn't have that advantage the next morning, though, when she woke to see streaks of sunlight creeping through the various cracks in the building. She lay there in the hay, remembering how callous Kingsley had sounded as he'd said he didn't want to lose time while a man lay injured, moaning in pain from an injury received trying to save Kingsley's property.

What would Ace do now? Surely, it would be a long time before he could work again. If he ever did. What would a man do out here, being crippled and no longer able to perform the hard physical labor that was his only means of earning a living?

Chewing her lower lip, Gabrielle considered the situation. Most of the money that she and her father had saved, which wasn't much, was in a bank back East. She had brought little with her. But it was sure to be more than Ace had, and she decided to go over to the doctor's office and leave what she could with him.

She rose from her makeshift bed, greeted Billy, and gave him some oats. As she headed for the stable door, she shook the hay out of her clothes and hair. Sweet heaven, she would love a bath. But she didn't dare take one. No one looked too closely at the scruffy Gabe. A clean Gabe would be another matter.

She nodded to the livery owner as she left the

stable, then crossed the town's only street and walked halfway down the block to a whitewashed house with a shingle hanging above the door. Doctor Charles Sanders. Finding the door unlocked, she entered.

"How's Ace?" she asked the long, thin man who was sitting at a desk.

The doctor glared at her. " 'Bout as well as could be expected after being trampled." She shifted from one leg to another, knowing how she must look. She took several bills from her pocket and handed them to the doctor. "Take out your fee and give the rest to him."

The doctor's lips twitched slightly. "I've already been paid, but I'll hand this over to him. I don't usually get offered my fee twice." He offered Gabrielle a smile. "Now I believe in miracles."

She felt her cheeks flush. Must have been the Scotsman. Maybe she had misjudged him. A little, anyway. Ace hadn't been his responsibility. Yet he had been unfailingly compassionate toward the wounded man on the long ride to Willow Springs. And now apparently he'd paid his doctor bill.

"Can I see Ace?"

"He's sleeping."

She nodded. "I'll be off then. Tell him . . . I . . ."

"Asked after him? I will."

She hesitated. "I'd 'preciate it if you don't tell anyone who left the money. Not even Ace. Just tell 'im it was left."

"If he asks. . . ?"

She shook her head.

The doctor shrugged. "All right. I'll see he gets it."

"Thank you," she said gratefully, for a moment unconsciously dropping her role and realizing immediately she'd made a mistake.

As Dr. Sanders gave her a puzzled glance. "Aren't you young for a cattle drive?"

"Not so young" she said.

Something flashed in his eyes, and she would have

sworn he saw beyond her disguise. But he only said mildly, "It's your business," then added opaquely, "Be careful."

She wasn't sure what he was warning her about, but she knew she needed to leave before this too-astute man ruined everything. She nodded and escaped out the door.

The Scotsman was waiting for her at the stable. Both horses had been saddled, and he was talking amicably with the dour stable hand. He turned as she entered and, seeing her, flashed her a quick smile.

That smile, she thought, must have melted hearts in Scotland. Even her heart, as suspicious as it was of him, jerked a little as he turned on the full force of his charm. He had washed, shaved, and put on a clean shirt. Seeing how handsome he looked, she was only too aware of how grimy she must appear to him.

"If I hadn't found Billy here, chomping oats," he said, "I might have thought you'd found easier pickings than those on a trail drive."

"I'm not a quitter," she said, averting her eyes from his piercing gaze.

"No," he said. "I don't guess you are."

It *hurt* to look at him, to see the gold in his eyes sparkle with mischief, the wry grin on his face. Darn it, why did he have to be so appealing?

She felt him studying her, knew he was taking in the hay that was still stuck to her clothes here and there. Her suspicion was confirmed by his question.

"Would you like to take a bath before we leave? There's a bathhouse at the end of the street."

"Told you I don't believe in baths," she said. "Ain't healthy."

He frowned, then started to speak, hesitated, then thought better of it and shrugged. "Suit yourself. Let's go, then."

He swung up on his horse with graceful ease and sat there as if born to it. Gabrielle winced at how awkward she must appear to him, climbing her way onto Billy's back.

"Relax," he said as they started down the street. "Don't fight Billy or the saddle. Use your legs to communicate with the horse. He's smarter than you think."

"I think he's very smart," she shot back.

He shook his head, clearly tired of her rebellious retorts. She didn't blame him. She was tired of them, too.

As they passed the edge of town and turned northwest, Cameron tried again. "How long have you been riding?"

"How long have *you* been riding?"

"Since I was three," he said. "Maybe younger."

Gabrielle blushed, embarrassed at even having tried to challenge him in an arena in which he was clearly a master. At the same time, she stored the tidbit of information he'd offered her. She wanted to know more about him, *needed* to know. But now that she finally had the chance, she was afraid of divulging her interest. Not that she was all that clear anymore about exactly what her reasons were. What *was* clear, she realized, was the more she talked, the more she risked revealing her true identity—in any event, her sex.

Still, she couldn't pass up the opportunity the ride ahead afforded her. Their concern for Ace during yesterday's ride had stifled any conversation.

"If you've been ridin' that long," she began, "how come the first time I saw ya, ya'd just fallen off a horse?"

The Scotsman grinned. "Did you have to remind me of that particular embarrassment?"

Gabrielle stared at him, her gaze riveted to his face. Her resistance to him melted under that grin, and strange things were occurring in her body. Her blood ran warmer, her heart fluttered, and an odd, mysterious ache formed somewhere in the core of her.

At her continued silence, he went on wryly, "If you

must know, I underestimated a cutting horse. He wanted to go right, when I told him to go left. He went right, anyway, and, well . . . I went left. Without him." Amusement deepened the Scottish brogue, making his voice whiskey smooth and sensual. Appealing. Very appealing.

Tearing her gaze away from him, Gabrielle sank further into her coat. "Does he still go right when ya tell him to go left?" she asked.

"Nay," Cameron replied. "Now I go where he wants to go, at least where cattle are concerned. He obviously knows more than I do."

Still, he had been quick enough, and skilled enough a horseman, to save Ace. And saving a man at the risk of his own life didn't fit her idea of an assassin.

Drat the man. Why did he confuse her so?

"How come you work for Kingsley? You ain't like the others."

He cut his eyes toward her. "Why do you say that?"

She had many reasons. Breeding and education topped the list. He obviously had both while most of the hands couldn't read or write. Also, a kind of natural leadership exuded from him, despite his attempts to disguise the fact.

"You just ain't," she said. When he remained silent, she decided to persist. "You like the boss?"

His glance toward her was sharper this time, and she told herself to be careful. She suspected the doctor had seen through her disguise. The Scotsman was no fool, but he'd had no reason to look beyond the obvious. She couldn't give him one. She looked ahead, rubbed Billy Bones's neck in a gesture of supreme indifference about whether the man answered or not.

The Scotsman looked straight ahead as he answered. "Kingsley's a good cattleman."

What kind of answer was that? None at all, she thought. And he knew it. His avoidance of her question sent quivers through her, and she reminded herself sharply that she might be dealing with a man who killed other men for a living. She wasn't sure why this last obfuscation bothered her. The man seldom gave straight answers but seemed to take pleasure in playing word games or changing subjects when something personal arose. She recognized the pattern; her father used to do the same thing. She'd never known why he'd avoided some subjects, not until a few weeks ago.

What was the *Scotsman* hiding? Or did he always try to obscure his true feelings?

But she'd probed as far as she dared. She turned her attention to the trail, trying—mostly unsuccessfully— to do as the Scotsman suggested: Relax.

Dusk was chasing them as they reached the creek where the Kingsley riders had camped the night of the stampede. The cattle would be approximately twenty-five miles ahead, a two- or three-day journey for the cattle, one for him and Two-Bits.

Pulling his mount to a halt at the creek's edge, Drew studied the water in the waning light. It had been a mere trickle two nights earlier before the storm. Now, although the rain had stopped yesterday, the yield from upstream had transformed the creek into a fast-moving river.

Drew had heard of flash floods from other drovers. Added to his own vivid memory of the hail and torrential rain and icy wind, his memories of Texas would not be favorable ones. Oh, it had its points— spectacular vistas, magnificent sunsets, and a vastness unequaled by any other he'd seen. But it was no place he wanted to live, and he decided then and there that his ranch—if he ever built one—would be located in a more reasonable climate, where the ground wasn't so hard that water ran across it like an ocean every time it rained. Yes, he'd choose some nice reasonable terrain. And Texas wasn't it.

Two-Bits, who had been trailing behind him for the past five miles, appeared with Billy and stopped beside him. For several minutes, they both sat looking at the water they would have to cross. Drew had intended to go farther tonight. Kirby had already lost two men—Juan and Ace—and Drew knew he couldn't afford the loss of a third for long. But he didn't like the looks of the creek, especially the debris that was moving rapidly along the swollen waters.

He looked at Two-Bits. "We can try to cross it now or wait till tomorrow."

The lad hunkered down in the saddle and frowned. He looked like a little elf, that small build in so many clothes and the ridiculous hat shielding his face as well as his thoughts.

"Could be worse tomorrow," Two-Bits said.

"Can you swim?"

The boy nodded. Drew hesitated, weighing the veracity of the response. If the lad swam like he cooked, they could be in trouble. Then there was the question of whether or not Billy was strong enough to withstand the current, although Drew had to admit, the bedraggled horse looked a hell of a lot better than it had days earlier.

"You certain?" he asked.

Two-Bits answered by moving Billy toward the edge of the water. The horse went willingly enough.

"Wait here," Drew warned, making up his mind. "Let me cross first." He could judge then how dangerous it would be for a weak horse and an inexperienced rider.

His pinto plunged into the water and walked nearly the whole way, swimming only several feet before regaining its footing and making the bank.

When he and the wet horse were on the other bank, Drew turned and nodded to Two-Bits, who started Billy into the river. Drew watched as the horse carefully picked his way halfway across, then started the short swim. Drew was just breathing a sigh of relief when a log came barreling down the creek and hit the horse's withers.

Billy panicked, and Drew saw the animal lose his direction. In the next instant, he started swimming downstream, his big equine body struggling to regain its balance. Trying to decide what to do next—whether to plunge in and help or wait and see if Billy and Two-Bits worked it out together—Drew held his breath. Two-Bits clung to Billy's neck like a leech, and Drew heard and saw the lad trying to coax his panicked horse into swimming in the right direction. But it was a losing battle.

Two-Bits slipped slowly to the right, sliding around Billy's neck and finally fell off as the horse plunged frantically in the water. It was immediately apparent the lad had lied again—he couldn't swim a stroke.

Drew swore, keeping one eye on Two-Bits as he jumped from his horse's back, yanked the sling off his injured right arm, and hit the water. He saw the lad go under, then bob up only to go under again, limbs flailing.

He started swimming, ignoring the pain in his sprained arm. Through the corner of his eyes, he saw Billy scramble up to the bank, but Two-Bits was being tossed quickly downstream by the powerful current. As he swam, he saw the lad's hands attempt to grab a large floating limb—and miss. He quickened his strokes, and he was only a few feet away when he lost sight of the lad's head as he disappeared under the muddy water.

Drew swam underwater but, blinded by the mud and silt, he could only reach out and search with his hands. He felt cloth, then a hand, and he pulled, struggling to get to hard ground. The water was freezing, and the boy's clothing added weight and bulk, making it difficult to move. His weak right arm didn't help matters a bit.

Finally, Drew's feet touched the creek bottom. His arm hurting like hell, he managed to lift the now-limp form, carrying him up to the bank. Falling to his knees, he laid Two-Bits on the ground and pulled off his hat, which hung from a thong around the boy's neck. Gabe was bloody lucky he hadn't strangled. Shivering, muttering oaths under his breath, Drew started peeling off the boy's thick sodden clothes.

He stopped suddenly. With only a couple of layers to go, it was plain, even in the muted glow of twilight, that the body beneath the water-soaked clothing was not as it should be. Not as he expected to find it. Rather, it was soft and curved. Curved quite nicely. It was, in fact, the body of a girl.

Drew's mouth actually fell open, his hands frozen in place on the open edges of Gabe Lewis's shirt—the second layer from the real thing, as best as he could tell. His gaze shot to the skin. It was pale, almost white in the last rays of a setting sun, in contrast to her neck and face that were now streaked with dirt and something else. His fingers touched the skin, and when he took them away and looked at them he saw a brownish cast. Dye!

He swore again, long and inventively, even as he studied the delicate features that should have obviously proclaimed her gender. Would have, if not for the always present grime. No wonder she didn't take baths. Bad for the health, indeed! Bloody hell, he'd always prided himself on being observant, and she'd totally duped him.

But this was no time to ponder the obvious. He turned the slight figure over, onto her stomach, and straddled her, using his hands to force water from her lungs. The pressure on his sprained arm sent pain slicing from his fingers to his shoulders, but he gritted his teeth and kept up a steady rhythm. After a minute or so, he was rewarded. Beneath him, he felt her body convulse, then a rush of water poured out of her. He shifted off of her to sit beside her as she sputtered and gasped.

Relief flooded him. And anger. She could easily

have died. Another minute or so in the water, and he wouldn't have been able to bring her back.

She started shivering as well as gasping and sputtering. They were both wet and freezing. And, he noticed, with the sun nearly gone, the temperature had dropped. They needed a fire.

Then he needed an explanation. A bloody good one.

Cold. She'd never been so cold. And air. She couldn't seem to get enough of it.

Slowly, painfully, Gabrielle returned to consciousness. For a minute or two, she coughed and choked without understanding what had happened. Awareness seeped in gradually, though, and she began to remember sliding off Billy's back, into the water.

For another awful minute, the memory of swirling darkness closing over her head and not being able to breathe overwhelmed her. But, finally, her present freezing state overcame all else.

She rolled to her side, moaning. It was so cold. Her eyes blinked open. She was lying on the bank of the creek. And it was not quite dark. About as dark as it had been when she'd taken Billy into the water.

Billy. Where was he?

Worried thoughts about her horse gave her the strength to struggle to an upright position. She looked around, still sputtering a little, teeth chattering, but she didn't see the horse.

What she did see, quite suddenly and with breathtaking clarity, was that her coat was gone and also her top shirt. The buttons of her flannel shirt were open. And what remained of her clothing—a single, light cotton shirt and the bindings around her breasts—were soaking wet and plastered to her skin.

Sucking in a quick breath, she twisted around and her gaze flew to meet Drew Cameron's. He was sitting, head propped on his knees, staring at her.

She stared back.

He cocked one eyebrow at her.

She gulped.

All the while, her mind worked furiously—as furiously as it could, given that she still felt decidedly muddleheaded—to invent some story she thought he might believe. For it was patently clear that her charade was over, and that any second now, he would demand to know why in bloody hell she'd been dressed up like a boy—yes, she was sure that's how he would put it.

But he didn't demand any such thing. He didn't speak at all. He merely stared at her in silence and he kept it up so long that she wondered if he actually knew that his silence was far more discomforting to her than any question he might pose or accusation he might make.

Desperately, she looked around. He'd started a fire, but it was small and still weak, giving precious little warmth. But her gaze was inevitably drawn back to the dripping man next to her.

Seeking to break the tension, she cleared her throat to speak. "Billy?" she asked, her voice weak and croaky.

"He made it across," Cameron replied, his tone as calm as his appearance.

Except that he wasn't entirely calm, she finally noticed. He was shivering nearly as badly as she was. In fact, she realized it had been he who must have rescued her from the creek.

When she spoke she made no attempt to disguise her normal speech patterns or her voice. "Is it your mission in life to go around saving people's lives?"

"No," he replied in carefully measured tones. "In fact, I try my best not to. I especially try bloody hard not to save fools from themselves."

She knew he meant her, and she knew from his carefully modulated tones that he was furious. Well, he had a right to be, she supposed.

She saw his gaze skim over her, take note of her

quaking shoulders and chattering teeth. Then he stood and glared down at her. "Your saddlebags and bedroll are soaked, and so are all your clothes," he said. "I have some dry ones. Get what you need from my bedroll while I look for more firewood."

Gabrielle watched him disappear behind some trees. Orders came easily to him, just, apparently, as saving lives did.

Who was he? The question posed itself in her mind for at least the hundredth time as she struggled to her feet. Hugging herself against the cold, she made her way unsteadily to his horse and unbuckled his bedroll. He was right; his things had survived the creek without getting soaked, probably because he'd wisely wrapped them in oilcloth. She found two shirts, including the one he'd worn yesterday, which she took out to put on. It smelled of soap, and she realized he must have taken time last night to wash it.

Darting a quick look, she stripped off the clothes from her upper body and pulled on the Scotsman's shirt. It swallowed her nearly whole, going below her knees. The cotton felt fine against her skin, and she knew it was good—and expensive—material.

Who *was* he? The question reverberated in her mind again and again. Where did a fifty-dollar-a-month cowboy get the money for a shirt like this? Or for those fine-tooled boots he wore? Or for the expensive saddle he used?

He could be a gambler, she guessed. He did play cards, and he had the cool, deceptively casual demeanor for it, as well as the almost frightening perception. But why on earth would a gambler want to work his hands to the bone on a cattle drive?

No reason she could think of.

So perhaps, he was a hired gunman. That made better sense. Not that she'd ever met one, but it seemed to her that the profession would require the same calm demeanor and piercing insight required of a successful gambler—in addition to an expertise with a gun. And he *did* wear a gunbelt. But then so did all the other hands.

Could he be a gunman? Hired, perhaps, by Kingsley to protect him? And, maybe, even kill for him?

But she didn't *want* Drew Cameron to be a hired gun. She didn't *want* to think of him as a murderer. She wanted to think of him as the man who had risked his own life to save Ace—and to save her.

Could there be two men in that one body? A cold-blooded killer and the Scotsman who thought nothing of jumping in icy water to save a ragged, homeless boy?

With her thoughts in turmoil and shivers racking her body, she pulled off her wet trousers, realizing only too well how naked she was. There was only Cameron's shirt between her and the world. Taking the pair of trousers she found in his bedroll, she pulled them on. They enveloped her like a bass swallowing a minnow. She couldn't walk, she couldn't move. She could only stand there, holding the danged trousers up with two hands.

"A wee bit large, I would say," came an amused voice, the Scottish accent lilting and appealing, yet very, very masculine.

Without turning to look at him, she tried to take a step, but her foot caught in the trouser leg. She started to fall, but her downward journey was stopped when his arm shot around her waist, catching her. Her hands flew automatically to his chest, bracing herself, which meant that she had to let go of the trousers. They fell instantly in a puddle around her feet, shackling her and leaving her naked, but for his cotton shirt.

"Let me go!" she demanded, panic edging her voice.

But when he started to, she promptly lost her balance again, and his arm tightened around her once more.

"Steady, there," he murmured.

The amusement in his voice was infuriating. With

her face flaming, Gabrielle looked down to see a pile of kindling alongside her feet; clearly, he'd dropped it to catch her. She also saw that if she tried to pull up the trousers it would only result in more complications. Instead, she tried to step out of them.

Cameron caught her arm and stopped her. Then his hand came up under her chin and tipped her face upward until she had no choice but to look directly at him.

His eyes had lost all hint of laughter. They were golden, tawny, like his hair, the gold dominating the gray and brown and green, like those of the jungle cat she'd seen in captivity in St. Louis. They were looking at her with the same hunter's gleam, too, as if he'd caught his prey and was trying to decide whether to play with it or go directly for the kill. She had no doubt, then, that Drew Cameron, the Scotsman, could be a very dangerous man.

She tried to back away, but he held her still, studying her face closely. Then, slowly and deliberately, he let his gaze travel up and down her body, making her feel as if he were ridding her of the one garment she wore. When he'd finished his inspection, his eyes came back to lock with hers.

"Well, Gabe Lewis," he said. "Just who and what are you?"

Chapter Six

⁜

Drew waited for a reply. When none came immediately, he nudged a little. "Let's start with a name."

"It *is* Gabe . . . Gabrielle," the woman said slowly.

And she *was* a woman. Not a girl, which he'd believed at first. She met his gaze square on—for the first time, if he recalled correctly. Perhaps she'd realized that if she gave him a chance to look at her for long, he might see beyond the grime.

And she was right. He was seeing a great deal.

While he wouldn't call her beautiful, not in the sense of the fashionable ladies he'd known, she had a charm and appeal that went straight to his heart. The water had washed off much of the dirt, and her skin appeared nearly flawless. Her short dark hair clung around her face in wet curly tendrils, framing the large dark blue eyes. And those eyes were lovely. Dark blue, they fairly sparkled, like the twilight sky above them twinkling with the first stars of the evening.

Gabrielle. The name fit her a bloody sight better than Gabe.

It occurred to him that people saw what they expected to see. Otherwise, he could never have been so blind as not to see what had been before his eyes. He had accepted her as a boy because there had been no reason to look beyond the scruffy hat and clothes and grime, no reason to question the short hair and boyish attire.

Still, he'd always considered himself more observant than most. The fact that a slip of a girl had outsmarted him stung, even while it amused him.

But why the masquerade?

She shivered, and he realized that his questions would have to wait.

"I'll get more firewood," he said. "Can you keep that fire going?"

She nodded.

He hesitated. "Like you cook and swim?"

She grinned suddenly, and he was enchanted. He'd not seen her smile before, and it transformed her. Her entire face took part: her nose wrinkled, the corners of her eyes creased, and her cheeks dimpled.

"I did take care of fires for Pepper without burning the chuck wagon down," she defended herself.

But there was a wry note, and Drew suspected the chore had not gone altogether smoothly. He still hesitated.

"Truly I can," she said. "You need to change clothes before you get pneumonia." She paused briefly, her enormous eyes focused on him. "Thank you for coming in after me."

"Did you think I wouldn't?" he asked gruffly. "But why in the bloody hell did you tell me you could swim?"

She lifted one slender shoulder in a shrug. "I knew you wanted to get back. I didn't want to delay you."

"Don't ever do that again," he warned her. "Don't ever lie to me when I ask a question." Her appeal, as she stood there in naught but his shirt, only slightly mellowed his anger. He hated lies. His entire childhood—such as it was—had been a lie, and it had nearly destroyed him. "I should have thought you learned that lesson with Pepper."

Her eyes darkened and she had the grace to flush.

Deciding to leave her with that thought for a few moments, he went to his bedroll, rummaging through for the extra shirt. The only dry trousers were the ones she'd tried to wear. He looked to see that they were lying on the ground, where she'd stepped out of them.

Seeing the direction of his gaze, she leaned down, picked them up, and threw them to him. "You can have them," she said, a tentative smile curving her lips. "They don't suit."

He was barely aware of her words, however. His head was reeling from what he'd seen of her when she'd leaned over. Her legs were lovely, her body slender and firm. The soft cloth of the shirt clung to curves he never would have dreamed were there.

He had known some true beauties, had bedded more than a few, but none had the appeal of this halfdrowned pixie. Was it merely abstinence? He'd not been with a woman since he'd left Scotland. But he was afraid it wasn't merely lust that suddenly gnawed at him.

Sighing, Drew took the shirt and trousers to the privacy offered by a cottonwood tree. He quickly changed into the warm, dry clothing, wondering as he did so if the cold, wet ones wouldn't serve him better. His blood could stand some chilling.

He searched for additional firewood for several minutes, needing the time to quiet his desire, to control a burning ache that had started smoldering inside him. He wanted some answers, and he'd need all his wits about him to extract them from this devious imp. She was a good little actress . . . and liar, he reminded himself. And his instincts had already failed him miserably where she was concerned.

He continued to remind himself of what a liar she was as he approached the still struggling fire she tended. She was huddled next to it, apparently trying to catch what little warmth she could.

After adding the wood to the fire, he sat down next to her. She looked up at him with a charming smugness, her breasts moving beneath the cloth of his shirt. Bathed in starlight, shadowed by darting flames, she was bewitching, a beautiful sprite whose magnificent eyes could inspire Celtic legend. He should have known they couldn't belong to a lad; they were altogether too beautiful.

More than that, something about them, something he perceived in their depths, made him feel alive, every sense tingling with anticipation. "Gabrielle," he said softly. "An unusual name."

He watched her tense, the shoulders bunch together. She said nothing.

"*Very* unusual for a cook's helper," he continued thoughtfully.

"Appearances can be deceiving," she said. "Take you, for example. I don't think you're exactly what you seem, either."

She was perceptive as the devil, too.

"But I don't think I left any doubt as to what sex I am," he countered.

A frown flickered across her brow, and she hugged herself protectively. He could almost see her mind work frantically, forming explanations he might accept. Somehow, he felt they wouldn't be the truth.

She looked into the fire, away from his eyes, and he *knew* he was right. "I'm running from someone," she finally said.

"Why?"

She hesitated. "He . . . wants me," she finally stuttered. "He followed me everywhere. I thought I could lose him on this trail drive."

"Who is he?"

She hesitated. "I can't tell you."

"You're going to have to do better than that, Gabrielle," he said in a deceptively gentle tone. "You tell me, or you tell Mr. Kingsley."

Her face went white, and she actually shrank away from him, as if fending off some kind of an attack. "He wouldn't let me stay," she said desperately.

"Probably not," Drew agreed.

She looked up at him with her eyes pleading. "Please don't tell him."

"Why?

"I won't have any place to go."

Drew heard a crumb of truth in what she said. But only a crumb.

"Who is after you?" he asked again.

Her eyes clouded and for a moment he didn't think she was going to answer. Shivering slightly, she reached for a piece of wood and put it in the fire. Then, as if she'd reached a decision, she replied, "A man. He and my . . . father arranged a marriage."

Her lips were trembling slightly. So were her hands. Desperation edged her voice. But arranged marriages had gone the way of slavery; a woman could always say no.

He must have looked skeptical because she continued slowly, almost jerkily, the way a person sometimes did in revealing an awkward truth—or a lie.

"I . . . refused," she murmured. "He was much older than me . . . and ruthless. He swore if he couldn't have me, no one would." Tears misted her eyes. "Someone tried to help me leave St. Louis . . . but he was attacked, almost killed. Everyone who's tried to help me . . ." She faltered.

Warning bells rang inside Drew's head. A part of him—that new, protective instinct he seemed to have unwillingly acquired—wanted to take her and hold her, assure her that no one would harm her, not as long as he was around. His arms itched to do just that, his fingers tingled with the need to touch her face. But a louder, more persistent part of him, the part that had guided him through many a cutthroat game of poker, the part that had become adept at measuring people as a means of self-preservation, kept him from following through on the impulse. Something about her explanation didn't ring true. Oh, he believed that she was desperate, and it was clear that she was afraid of *something*. But the rest of her story? Bloody unlikely.

"He hired detectives," she continued haltingly. "I thought I could lose him on this trail drive. They would never think to look for a boy." Shadowed by the flames, her face looked earnest, hopeful. "Don't tell Mr. Kingsley."

"Why not?" he said. "I think he would help a damsel in distress."

"I've read about cattle drives," she said, her hands now clenched together. "No women allowed."

She had the right of that, anyway. It was undoubtedly true that Kirby would send her packing to the nearest town the instant he found out who—and what—she was. And if she really was in trouble, she would be easy to spot. Those vivid blue eyes were a certain giveaway. He'd never seen any like them.

"I don't like liars," he said coldly, trying to put some distance between them. Every time he looked at her, his body reacted in extraordinarily rebellious ways.

She bit her lip, but he gave her credit. Her eyes met his directly. "I had no choice," she said simply.

"Who is this man?"

"A banker from St. Louis," she said. "My father was very successful, but then his business failed. He owes . . . a great deal of money."

Drew raised a skeptical brow. "And he was willing to sell his daughter?" Something flickered in her eyes. Anger? Denial? But this time she did look away and said nothing.

Drew sighed. What kind of desperation would drive a young woman to cut her hair, don some of the most uncomfortable—not to mention downright ugly—garments he'd ever seen, and bear the hardships of a cattle drive? He might consider the particulars of her story to be pure fiction, but he didn't doubt for an instant the reality of her fear.

And parts of the story *would* explain her incompetence at cooking, something most women had at least a passing familiarity with. Most Scottish peeresses knew little more than how to order meals. He imagined the same might be true of well-to-do American families.

"You *won't* tell Mr. Kingsley?" she said, her voice genuinely shaking.

"I'm not sure," he said. "He has a right to know. If anything happens to you . . ." He cut himself short and ended with a shrug.

She drew herself up, the set of her chin determined. "I may not be able to cook very well, but I can take care of myself."

"Oh, yes, I see that you can," he drawled. "Just as you took care of yourself crossing that creek."

She looked at him in reproach at being reminded, and he had to grin at her gall. Her frown deepened, but at the same time, her lips twitched a little, then a little more, until a beguiling smile of utter mischief spread across her face. He felt his blood warm again, realized his breath had suddenly become ragged.

"I really can take care of myself—most of the time," she said earnestly. "And I'm learning. I just need a chance."

Her words struck a chord inside. If the story about her father using her to pay his debts *were* true . . . well, he himself had experienced the pain of a father's betrayal, as well.

There were other kinds of betrayals, though. Such as the betrayal of a friend. His friend, Kirby Kingsley, had wanted him along on the cattle drive because someone had tried to kill him and whoever it had been was still out there. The possibility that Gabrielle was connected in any way to the three brigands who'd ambushed Kirby was preposterous. Still, her presence *was* odd and, if nothing else, would certainly be an unneeded diversion.

She was sitting there, large blue eyes regarding him hopefully, as if he were her last chance.

"Why Kingsley's drive?" he asked suddenly, watching her face carefully.

He saw her swallow before she replied. "I read about it in the paper. The article said Kingsley needed hands, and I thought . . . well, it seemed like the perfect place to hide."

Her fingers were twisting nervously in her lap. Drew noticed the blisters on her hands, hands that he was sure had been smooth until a week ago. Yet he'd never heard her complain, not on the long ride to Willow Springs nor on the exhausting return. Most women he'd known wouldn't have lasted half a day.

Bloody hell. He'd never been one for rules. He'd never followed any and had, in fact, taken pleasure in breaking them. So why should he respect some rule about women not being allowed on trail drives? It went against his grain to deny a fellow renegade the help she needed.

Besides that, he respected gumption. Grit, they called it here. And she had more than her share of that.

"I won't say anything . . . for now," he said, vowing silently to keep a close eye on her.

Her eyes closed briefly, and relief flooded her features. When she opened her eyes, she met his gaze directly. "Thank you," she said softly.

He uttered a short laugh "Don't thank me yet. I admire a strong instinct for self-survival and I admire your, shall we say, *inventiveness*. But"—he lifted a eyebrow in warning—"although I might concede you your tale, or at least part of it, I don't like lies. They offend me. And you're very handy with them."

She started to say something, but he cut her off.

"Neither do I like disloyalty, and you're placing me precariously close to that," he added grimly, all amusement gone. "If I feel, at any time, that it's important for Kirby to know about you, I *will* tell him."

Her fingers were locking and unlocking again. He wished he knew what was going on inside that devious mind of hers, but she was very good at hiding her emotions. Too good, he thought again. Something was not right. He knew it.

Yet the bare truth was that she interested him in a way no woman had before. He wondered how she would look in a fine dress, her hair washed and coiffed. Probably not any more appealing than she did in his much-too-large shirt, short curls drying around her face, a tentative smile on her lips.

He lifted a hand to touch her face, his fingers caressing the skin. She stiffened, her eyes widening a little in alarm. Yet he saw something else in them, too, and when he felt her shiver, he sensed that it wasn't all cold or fear.

"It's a crime to hide your body under those clothes," he said.

Her lips parted, and she started to speak, but before she could, he leaned over and touched his mouth to hers lightly, lightly enough that she could move away if she wished. Her breath caught, her lips trembled slightly under his, hesitating. Then, with a quiet whimper, he felt her yield, her lips turning soft and pliant beneath his.

What had been meant as exploratory suddenly became something else. Need burned straight through him with stunning force. And suddenly he was lost in something far more, far greater, than anything lust could explain.

The moment the Scotsman's lips touched hers, Gabrielle knew her world had changed forever. Oh, she had been kissed before, more than once. but she'd never felt this . . . magic. It was as if she'd been asleep all her life and only now was being awakened.

His arms went around her, and she felt a warmth spreading through her like rays from the sun on a clear summer day. And with that warmth came something else, something new and mysterious and irresistible. His lips teased hers, rocking back and forth, twisting first one way, then the other, and she found herself responding with wanton abandon. Swirling eddies of desire rippled through her. She felt his body tense and his hands tremble as they touched her hair, her shoulders, moved up and down her back, and she knew he felt it too, this barely restrained passion.

Her arms crept around his shoulders, her hands instinctively stroking the back of his neck. He made a low, growling sound deep in his chest, and his mouth opened over hers, coaxing hers to do the same. The sensation of his tongue teasing the corners of her mouth was wildly exciting, but exciting didn't begin to describe the way she felt when she let her lips part beneath his and his tongue enter her mouth.

Shocking. Exhilarating. Electrifying. It was all those things. And it was also a little frightening. His arms tightened around her, and his mouth grew hard and demanding. And suddenly fear overwhelmed her, fear and confusion over the bewildering ache that was building in the deepest part of her—a longing for something she didn't understand. She needed something. And the strength and power of that need terrified her.

With a small cry, she jerked back, fighting for breath and for control. He released her immediately, though he kept one hand on her shoulder, his fingers playing with a short lock of hair.

"Gabrielle, are you a virgin?" he asked.

She was glad it was too dark for him to notice the heat creeping into her cheeks. She felt hot all over, on fire with passion—and with shame. How could she have been so intemperate? So *wanton*.

Apparently taking her silence for assent, he swore softly, oaths she'd never heard before. When he was through, he sighed, then said in a much resigned voice, "Ah lass, has no one ever told you not to play with fire?"

She wished she had a sharp retort, but she didn't have it in her to think of one. She longed only to reach out and touch him again. Gratitude, she told herself. What she felt was gratitude. After all, he had saved her life today.

At least, her shame wasn't compounded by the thought she might be kissing her father's murderer. For Drew Cameron could not be the man who had done it. If he had, he would have seen her picture on the playbills posted all around San Antonio, and he would have recognized her by now—he wouldn't be sitting here kissing her, much less rescuing her from drowning. So, no, he was not a murderer.

But he *was* Kirby Kingsley's friend.

She shivered, remembering the Scotsman's comment about loyalty. And she wondered again about his relationship to the cattleman.

"Gabrielle?"

She looked toward him. She didn't want to. She didn't want to see the disdain she was sure would be plain on his features. She *had* been wanton. But she'd never lacked for courage and she never made excuses.

His mouth was set in a rigid line, his golden eyes glowing like a jungle cat's. Then he surprised her again. "That was inexcusable of me," he said. "I'm sorry."

Then to her amazement, he rose and walked away from the fire, seeming to fade into the shadows.

Utterly bewildered, Gabe pulled her knees up and hugged them with her arms as she stared at the fire, her body still hot and needy . . . and lonely

• • •

Drew walked for what seemed like hours. They needed more wood, he told himself. The night was cool again, and they had only his two dry blankets between them; hers were soaked through. But when he picked up the first piece of wood, he stared at it in the darkness, then tossed it away. Gabrielle could use both blankets. He could use a bit of a chill to tame his internal heat.

He groaned. He heartily disliked being honorable. But despite his frequenting of disreputable taverns, his reckless gambling, his open flouting of convention with actresses, he'd never knowingly taken advantage of a woman. He'd never seen the attraction of bedding a woman who didn't return his enthusiasm for the act of lovemaking. Nor had he ever bedded a virgin. He'd left that vice to his father, who'd made his life hell for being a bastard but who had created a village full of them at Kinloch. The late earl of Kinloch had made no distinction between willing and unwilling, but he went to any lengths to keep his noble friends from knowing about them, dispensing money to keep mouths shut. Dispensing money, Drew thought bitterly, that should have been his inheritance.

The familiar hatred for a man long dead, for the hypocrisy and lies that were his heritage, welled inside him. He had tried to conquer that particularly destructive emotion after wasting his youth in harboring it. Still, it came back to nip him now and then.

That was one reason he'd left Scotland. To get away from hating. He didn't want to hate anymore.

He was thirty-three, and he'd spent most of his life gambling, whoring, and drinking. All the while, he'd lived with an emptiness the size of a crater, but he had only discovered why he felt so empty after meeting Ben Masters and his half-sister Lisbeth. He'd never seen love until then, refused even to admit it existed. Now, he knew it not only could exist, it could flourish, given the right people to share it.

Observing Ben's and Lisbeth's love for each other

had given him a small taste of love—and an enormous appetite for more. Still, he wondered whether it was too late, whether he could ever accept—or believe— the fact that anyone could love him.

He had followed Ben and Lisbeth to America, a place where the land was new and unexplored and the future more important than the past. He had hoped that here he might lose his demons.

When Drew returned to the fire, Gabrielle was asleep, wrapped in his blanket. Only a few scattered embers remained of the fire. He sat down and stared at them as they smoldered into ashes.

Chapter Seven

———— ✛ ————

Drew woke to the sound of crying. A soft heartbroken sound. He fought his way out of grogginess and focused on his surroundings.

Night still dominated the sky, though to the east a hint of dawn edged the horizon and the stars were already fading.

Turning his head to the side, he saw Gabrielle's form, tossing about as if she were fighting off an attacker. Mixed in with her whimpers, he heard bits and pieces of mumbled words.

"No, father. No. Mistake." Then a long, agonizing, "Noooooooooo."

The despair and anguish in her words tore at his heart. Rolling to his side, he moved quickly over to her. The blanket had come off during her thrashing, and the shirt she wore was tangled about her waist, leaving her mostly naked. He caught a glimpse of sleek perfection before he covered her. Then, taking her by the shoulders, he shook her gently.

"Gabrielle," he said softly. "Wake up."

She started, her body jerking, then her eyes flew open. She sucked in a sharp breath and stared at him without recognition.

"Gabrielle," he said again, and her eyes lost some of their confusion and started to focus on him. He noticed the trail of tears on her face, the sheen of wetness in her eyes. "It's all right," he said awkwardly, unused to comforting. "You're safe."

Her eyes blinked rapidly several times, and, finally, the pent-up breath rushed out of her lungs on a soft moan. Struggling to sit, she looked at him, then down at her body, as if suddenly aware of what she was wearing and how little she was covered. Several of the top buttons of the shirt had come undone, exposing a fair amount of skin, which, in the shadowed darkness before dawn, appeared white in contrast to the dark fabric framing it.

She fumbled with the buttons before looking at him. "I must have had a nightmare."

"Aye," he said. "I think you did. You mentioned your father."

He couldn't see the expression on her face, but her tone was wary as she spoke. "Did I say anything else?"

He shrugged. "Something about a mistake. That's all."

She was silent for a moment, then said, "I'm sorry I woke you."

He wished his gaze wouldn't keep falling to the gentle rise of her breasts, nor his memory returning to her near naked form. The thought made him turn away so she wouldn't see what shouldn't have been in his eyes, his mind.

"It's all right," he murmured.

He saw as well as heard her breath catch—her chest rising sharply. His heart pounded and he knew he should look away. But he couldn't. He felt as out of control as a schoolboy.

He took her hand, swallowing it in his own. "Gabrielle?" he whispered.

And then she was in his arms again, though he was uncertain about which of them had made the move.

Devil be damned, but he wanted her. *And you might well be damned if you continue.* But his body ignored the mind's message as her body clung to his. He tried to tell himself it was clinging for all the wrong reasons; she'd had a nightmare, she was frightened, she needed comforting—not passion. Yet it felt so right, her body against his.

But just as he was adjusting himself to the rightness of the situation, and in the slowly growing light of dawn, she looked at him steadily, searching his features.

"Who *are* you?"

Caught off guard, he chose not to understand. "You know."

"I don't mean your name," she said, reproach coloring her tone. "And don't tell me you're an ordinary cowhand. Because you're not."

"There's no such thing as an ordinary cowboy," he said.

"But you're more *extra*ordinary than any of them," she persisted.

It bloody well took every bit of his self-control not to kiss her again. "Am I?" he said, rather pleased at the observation.

She glowered at him. "What did you do before you came on this drive?"

"I was a gambler. I *am* a gambler," he corrected himself.

Her scowl turned to interest. "A good one?"

"Very good," he replied immodestly.

"Then why. . . ?"

He didn't answer immediately. He wasn't going to help her one bloody bit. Besides, he liked watching the way her mind worked. She just bored in like a coyote going for a rabbit. "Why what?"

The glower returned. "Why are you on this cattle drive?"

"You asked me that before," he observed.

"And you didn't answer."

"Didn't I?"

If glances, even from very pretty eyes, could kill, he'd be under six feet of dirt.

"You know damn well you didn't," she said, then immediately looked chagrined at the words that had popped out of her mouth.

He'd been right, Drew realized—she had been raised as a lady and wasn't used to swearing.

He threw out a small bone. "I was bored," he said, and it was at least part truth. He had no intention of sharing his deeper reasons. He wasn't used to sharing any part of himself, and now didn't seem a particularly good time to start, not with the creative and cunning Miss Lewis.

She eyed him speculatively, the soft illumination of dawn revealing a bright intelligence in those lovely eyes. He'd always liked intelligent women. But he also liked honest ones.

"Boredom doesn't seem like a very good reason to . . ." She trailed off, as if suddenly uncertain.

"To what, Gabrielle?" He prompted.

She stared at the ground. "To do something so dangerous."

He laughed. "You're scarcely one to talk about danger. At least I wouldn't have joined a cattle drive as a cook's helper without being able to sit a horse or make a cup of coffee."

"Yes, you would have," she shot back.

The rejoinder rocked him. She was right. He might have done just that.

"*I* usually recognize my limitations," he countered. He just didn't pay much attention to them.

But she was smiling in triumph as if she'd read his every thought. It was most disconcerting.

"What are they?"

"What are what?" he replied, deliberately misunderstanding.

"Your limitations. I didn't think you had any."

Bloody hell, but she was good. She could feint with the best of them. Everything about her stimulated him—with the possible exception of her clothes. The mystery, the sharp wit, the self-confidence of a woman who could sit there with only a shirt and a dirty face and short tousled hair and challenge him on an intellectual level.

"Limitations?" she prompted after a long silence.

"I would much rather hear about yours," he said smoothly.

"You know mine," she said. "I can't swim." After a moment, she added, "or cook."

"Isn't that a little odd?"

"I don't know? Is it?"

He chuckled. He couldn't help it. He liked her more every moment, even as part of his brain warned him. Danger, though, had always been appealing to him. Danger in a pretty package was even more fascinating. Their eyes met, and awareness rippled between them. The air was hissing, crackling, sparking a thousand tiny charges up and down his spine.

"I thought every woman knew something about cooking."

"I thought every trail hand knew how to stay on a horse."

She touched a nerve. He'd always taken pride in his horsemanship and had ridden horses to championships in races in Scotland. "At least I'd been on a horse before joining a cattle drive."

She blushed. She was good at shielding some emotions, but she couldn't seem to control the color that pinkened her cheeks.

"You're right," she finally said. "It was rather . . . optimistic of me. It looked easy enough."

He turned his head so she wouldn't see his smile.

"You did well after the stampede and with Ace."

"I like him," she replied quietly.

He liked the way she said it—with directness and honesty.

"He's a good man," Drew said, "and what happened was bad luck."

Her gaze fell to her hands in her lap. "It could have been worse if you hadn't been there."

Drew felt uncomfortable again. He'd been in the right place at the right time, nothing more. "It's the job," he replied.

"You could do anything you wanted," she said, returning to her previous point.

"I'm suited for very little," he said. "My skills, such as they are, are mostly in the field of gaming. If I don't wish to do that, I have few options."

She shook her head. "You could get any kind of a job with your education."

He raised a questioning eyebrow. "And what do you know about my education?"

"It's a good one," she said evenly. "I would guess a university."

"I drank my way through one, yes," he said, amusement mixing with a little resentment at the deadly accuracy of her observations.

"And you obviously have breeding."

He chuckled. "Everyone has breeding, lass, or they wouldn't be here."

Her lips pursed with concentration. "That's not what I meant."

"And what did you mean?"

"Your manners. The way you walk and talk. It radiates . . . confidence and wealth."

"And wealth equals breeding?"

Her jaw set and those blue eyes became turbulent . . . and angry. He was mocking her, just as he had mocked himself for the last twenty years.

"Obviously not," she said, her tone acerbic. "But you still haven't answered my question."

"Which one?"

"Why you're on this drive."

"I thought I had."

"No answer that I believe."

"Then that makes us equal," he said sharply.

She looked as if he'd struck her. Her eyes clouded, and her body stiffened. He'd known she lied to him, but he still felt like a bully kicking a hapless kitten. He reminded himself that kittens had claws.

"An adventure," he said, trying to dispel the sudden tension between them. "An adventure as well as a job. An opportunity to see the West in ways few do." It was another part of the truth, but he wasn't able to keep the biting sarcasm out of his tone. "Don't you know, lass, the Scots have an abiding fascination with all things American?"

She frowned, clearly puzzled. "Why?"

"Because we're old and you're new. We've lost our opportunity, and you have yours ahead. The English have basically taken our land, and they consider independence a fault. You consider it a virtue."

It was a rather pompous speech and he'd rather enjoyed the telling of it, again deflecting personal questions he had no desire to answer.

He darted a quick glance at the sky. The black sky had turned a soft gray. The sun would be tipping the horizon before long.

He looked down at his hand. It was still locked in Gabrielle's. With a courtly gesture he'd learned as a child, he brought her hand to his mouth and kissed it, lingering over it longer than he should have. He wanted to do more. Cursing himself for his rather rare gentlemanly behavior, he snapped, "We might as well get an early start." And with that, he stood.

She hesitated, looking at him with those damnably delectable eyes, her long sooty black lashes adding to her look of vulnerability. He reluctantly released her hand, which he'd been holding with his right hand. His arm was still sore and couldn't bear much weight. But he offered her his left hand and pulled her up, effortlessly lifting her to her feet. Gabrielle Lewis weighed little more than a feather.

She looked so damn bloody vulnerable. He suddenly thought of his brother-in-law and his sister. If she really were in trouble, Ben could help. "I have a friend," he said slowly, "who is a lawyer in Denver. He used to be a U.S. marshal. He'll help you. You can trust him completely."

"A marshal?" she repeated softly.

"You can catch a stage in the next town," he added. "I have enough money . . ."

"No," she said flatly. Then as if she realized how her rejection of his offer sounded, she continued, "Thank you, but . . . I just don't . . . can't trust anyone. You don't know . . . this man."

Drew felt his suspicions rise again as something furtive appeared in her eyes. She seemed to shrug into herself, then let her gaze fall from his. At that moment, he knew absolutely that she'd lied, that at least some part of her story was false. Yet, what could be so important, or so dangerous, that a pretty woman would hide behind those bloody oversized clothes and cut her hair? What could be so bad that she would suffer the dangers and hardships of a trail drive?

"You will still keep your promise?" she asked tentatively.

He shouldn't. He knew he shouldn't. Yet he couldn't bring himself to believe she had lied for some nefarious purpose. He would hold his tongue for the moment but keep a wary eye on her. Hell, he would keep an eye on her anyway, now that he knew what lay underneath the grime.

"As I said last night," he replied, "I won't say anything for now. I won't promise more than that."

She chewed on her lip for a moment, then started to say something, but he put his finger to her lips to stop her. "And if I find out you're lying . . . about something important," he added softly, "you'll find I'm no gentleman."

She didn't flinch, he would give her that. Still, as he turned away, he wondered whether the con artist had been conned.

He walked over to test the clothes spread out over bushes and limbs. They were not quite dry, but he was not in the mood to be any more gentlemanly than he already had been.

"I want to leave in a few minutes" he said coolly. "Can you be ready?"

"Yes." Her voice was quiet but sure. Most women would take hours, but then he'd never met one quite like Gabrielle before.

No, Gabe. Gabe Lewis. He had to get used to the name again.

The day wore on awkwardly for Gabrielle. There was little time for conversation and even if there had been, the Scotsman made it clear he wanted none of it.

Oddly enough, Gabrielle felt she had lost a friend. By turning down what appeared to be a completely unselfish offer—money and a reference to his ex-marshal friend in Denver—she had sparked his suspicion. Or had it simply been a test on his part? One she'd failed.

Aches and bruises from the long ride made every mile a physical misery as well, but she could live with that. She found it more difficult to live with her lies than with Drew Cameron's withdrawal.

She tried to persuade herself again that she was playing a part, just as she had on stage so often. But each time she saw the Scotsman's cool golden eyes and sardonic smile, she cringed inside. Cringed even more as she recalled the times he had, more or less, called her a liar.

She wanted to blurt out her suspicions about Kirby Kingsley, to say that she had lied for good reason, but there was still too much she didn't know. She didn't know how closely the Scotsman was involved with the man she suspected of killing her father. And, although she was now certain that Cameron couldn't have been the shooter, she wasn't certain whether or not he knew the shooting had taken place.

Could a man who saved one life condone the taking of another?

She didn't think so. And she most fervently didn't want to believe it of him. But then, he was adept at playing roles, too. Didn't that indicate he had something to hide?

And what about Kirby Kingsley? She knew with complete certainty that he had something to hide— had been hiding it for twenty-five years. As she pondered the reasons for the journey on which she'd embarked, she recalled her father's dying words and the words in his letter.

She'd been so *clear*, so *sure*, that in leaving her the letter, directing her to it and to the article about Kingsley, that he'd been telling her that Kingsley was responsible for killing him. She was still sure. But not as sure as she had been.

Somehow, in the past three days, something had happened to create tiny, niggling doubts. Perhaps it had been the storm or the dunk in the creek, in both of which cases she'd been terrified and certain that death was imminent.

More likely, she thought, the hot flood of sensation created by Drew Cameron's kiss last night had finally caused her to wake up from the dream state in which she'd existed since her father's death. For she realized now that she'd felt frozen, suspended in time at the moment she'd seen her father clutch at his chest and start to fall. Inside, all she'd been able to feel were grief and fear and rage. She'd been driven—and perhaps blinded—by them ever since.

But no more. The Scotsman's passion, if it had accomplished nothing else, had shocked her back into living. Into *feeling*. Oh, the grief and anger—and loneliness—were still with her. But she no longer felt controlled by them.

And with her new clarity of thought, she realized that she couldn't simply walk up and shoot Kirby Kingsley. She might have done it a week ago—if she'd had the opportunity, if he'd done something at that moment to stimulate her rage into action. And she thanked God that the occasion hadn't arisen. For she was no murderer.

But if she weren't going to kill Kingsley, she still felt compelled to bring him to justice. Somehow, she had to find a way to prove that he had ordered her father's murder. *Somehow* . . .

Gabrielle spent a good part of her time thinking about ways she might gather evidence against Kingsley. It seemed an impossible task, given that it was unlikely he'd brought a signed confession along with him on a cattle drive. Finally, she realized she was merely driving herself crazy, and she forced herself to stop thinking about her father's murder and about Kingsley, and instead to think about the good times. . . .

She thought of her parents. Her mother had been very beautiful, much more beautiful than she was. She had inherited her father's wide mouth and willful chin, but her mother had shown her how to make the best of herself. Marian Parker would turn over in her grave if she could see her daughter now in such hideous, dirty clothes and cropped hair.

Then again, perhaps she might have winked. And she certainly would have been gently amused by her off-spring's mishaps as a louse. Gabrielle smiled, remembering her mother's warmth and open-mindedness.

She remembered, too, seeing her parents together. The way her father had looked at her mother, as if she were the only woman on earth. When her mother had died two years ago of pneumonia, part of her father had died, too, and the gleam in his eyes and laughter in his voice had never returned.

Gabrielle had always hoped for a love like her

parents had found. She'd always wondered if she ever would find a marriage as fine and whole as theirs had been. The dark side, though, was always the ending, and she wondered now whether the joy was worth the grief.

She had no one to ask.

Emotion clogged her throat and blurred her vision. She stared at Drew Cameron's straight back as he rode ahead of her. Would he betray her to Kingsley, she wondered. Or would he keep her secret, as he'd promised. The question pounded at her throughout the last hours of the long day.

She knew when they got close to the herd, because the cow chips were fresher. At last she saw the cattle in the distance and heard their soft lowing as they grazed. She followed the Scotsman around the cattle, both of them riding slowly so as not to spook the herd. They headed directly for the chuck wagon, where they found Kingsley sipping a cup of coffee and Pepper stirring a pot of beans.

Both men looked up as they approached. Kingsley's typically severe expression didn't change, nor did Pepper's.

"Thought you might be staying in town," the cook grumbled, looking directly at her, making it clear that he was unhappy she hadn't.

"We wouldn't want to be disappointing you," the Scotsman said, his accent pronounced.

The corners of Kingsley's lips twitched slightly, but his eyes remained hard, even cold. "Took you long enough," he finally said, turning to Drew. "You know we're damned shorthanded. Take a fresh horse. You're on night herd."

Drew smiled slightly. "Aye, sir," he said with mock subservience, but he headed toward the remuda without another word.

Gabe was furious on his behalf. They'd eaten only two short meals of hardtack and jerky that day.

They'd had no coffee. And Cameron had been in the saddle for nearly twelve hours already.

The fact that Kingsley hadn't even asked about Ace infuriated her even further. It also strengthened her belief that he was a man who could kill another man without remorse or conscience.

"Pepper can use some help," he said to her, then started to turn.

"Don't you want to know about Ace?"

Kingsley stopped and turned back to her. "Why? There's nothing more I can do."

Gabe slid down from her horse to face him. She knew she shouldn't say another word, but she was tired, and hurting, and she wanted to lash out at the man who used people so easily.

"He might be crippled for life," she said.

Kirby's reply was curt. "That's the risk of a trail drive," he said. "Every man knows it. And now you know it, too. You can quit anytime." He turned and walked toward the remuda, where she saw him saddle and mount a horse, then ride out from the camp area.

"Damn young fool. Shoulda stayed in town," Pepper muttered as he stalked back to the chuck wagon.

The words were meant to be heard, and Gabrielle set her chin stubbornly. They weren't going to get rid of her that easily.

"What do you want me to do?" she asked, following him.

"Really want to know?"

She stared at the old cook blindly, tears of anger and frustration clouding her eyes. What *was* she accomplishing here?

Pepper's scowl faded. "It ain't that bad, boy. You did awright the other night. Mebbe you ain't a complete loss."

"The other night?"

"Durin' the storm. When you helped out with the horses and the wagon and didn't go losing your head.

Mebbe you have some promise. You watch me and mebbe you'll learn something." With another dubious "mebbe," he turned away.

Dubious or not, the faint praise lifted the weariness from her shoulders, and she knew a kind of pride deeper than any she'd felt after a successful performance. Pepper, she realized, was a much more critical house than any she'd played to.

"You wanna try cookin' them beans again," he asked. "We'll be needin' a new batch for the night riders."

She did. She nodded. Drew Cameron would be one of those. She'd show him how competent she could be.

"But I ain't letting you near my starter," Pepper added ominously.

She couldn't stop a small smile. He glared at her. But she suspected she saw a twinkle in his eyes.

Kirby Kingsley rode the perimeter of his cattle, telling himself he was out here to check the night herders. The truth was, he wanted to remove himself from the accusing eyes of the boy. Those eyes had bored right through him, as if searching his soul and finding it wanting.

Hell, the kid hit the mark, only he didn't know how closely. Gabe Lewis obviously believed him hard-hearted because he hadn't asked about Ace, but he had crimes on his conscience that were a hell of a lot worse.

He hadn't told the kid he did hurt for Ace and had provided the best he could for him, but that he couldn't have stood knowing that Ace had lost a leg, or even his life. This was his fifth trail drive, and he'd lost more hands than he wanted to remember: He'd lost them to rivers, to rustlers, to Indians, to stampedes. He'd learned to do what he could, then try to forget them. It never quite worked, but he damned well tried. Otherwise, he would never boss another drive.

But God, that kid's blue eyes haunted him.

He spurred his horse into a gentle trot, seeking out Drew Cameron. It probably hadn't been fair to send Drew out, but he wanted to talk to the man alone, and he sure as hell couldn't do it around the chuck wagon.

Kirby found him at the back of the herd. Most of the cattle had finished grazing and were down for the night. They seemed well content at the moment. Drew was sitting toward the back of his saddle, humming a tune as all the cowhands did at night.

As he approached the Scotsman, he spoke, "Drew?"

Drew nodded wearily. "He'll be all right," he said. "The doctor even thought he might be able to save the leg. He'll be crippled, though."

Kirby nodded.

"I told him he could work for me if I ever get a ranch going."

Kirby smiled stiffly. "You will. I've never seen anyone learn so fast."

"I'm not sure the others agree."

"They do," Kirby said. "I've heard them talk."

He was glad Drew had the tact not to mention his nephews. He'd been making excuses for them to himself, but in truth, he couldn't excuse their jealousy. They hadn't stopped sniping at the Scotsman even while the others had accepted him. His acceptance had become complete when he saved Ace; there wasn't a man now that wouldn't partner with the Scot, except Damien and Terry Kingsley.

"I half-expected the kid to stay in town," Kirby said.

He could have sworn he saw Drew's body stiffen slightly, but his answer sounded casual enough.

"So did I, but he's no quitter."

"Was he any trouble?"

"Outside of nearly drowning, no," Drew said. "He

told me he could swim. He can't. Something to remember."

Kirby chuckled. "He does seem to exaggerate his abilities."

"I'm surprised you let him stay."

Kirby shrugged. "I was hungry once. Real hungry. I lied and stole and cheated for food for my brother and me. I know what desperation will do." He hesitated, then asked. "Did he tell you anything about himself?"

"Not much," Drew replied.

"Sometimes ... I have the feeling that he ... knows me."

When Drew remained silent, Kirby sighed, still wondering why the boy—and those angry eyes—preyed on his mind.

"Want a relief?" he said.

Drew shook his head. "I like it out here alone."

Kirby understood. God knows, he'd felt that splendid isolation enough times. The clouds had gone and the sky was clear. The only sound was the soft, contented lowing of the cattle and an occasional bit of a song from another hand who'd drifted by.

"I'll be scouting ahead. It's good to have you back."

He didn't wait for an answer but spurred his horse away from camp, riding alone under the bright moonlit sky. He didn't want to admit even to himself that it was a boy's eyes that kept him from heading toward camp—and sleep.

Chapter Eight

———— ✜ ————

Beans, beans, beans. Sitting on the ground next to the chuck wagon, Gabrielle separated the gravel from the beans and hoped that after this cattle drive, she'd never see another bean as long as she lived.

Three weeks out, they had stopped in midafternoon on the bank of the Red River, where Kingsley announced that they would remain for the night, giving both men and cattle a chance to rest before making the treacherous crossing. On the other side was Indian Territory, a term that produced any number of harrowing tales from hands who'd been there and lived to tell about it.

"Dang it," Gabrielle muttered when a handful of unsorted beans and gravel fell out of her hand and into the pot. Muttering under her breath, she began picking out the offending matter, vowing again that, when this hellish journey was over, she'd never eat beans again. Lord, they *lived* on beans. Beans and salt pork. And pepper. An unholy amount of pepper. The old cook had certainly acquired his moniker honestly.

In fact, she'd come to see that Pepper was much more than a cook, or even a doctor, for the drive. He acted as stake holder for bets, banker, barber, confessor, and mediator. Pepper handled all with a crankiness that bothered no one. It was, apparently, not only accepted but expected. A supplicant was disappointed if he didn't receive a growl and a "Hell damn I ain't no twenty people."

On this drive, he was also acting as a teacher. Under Pepper's contrary tutelage, she had learned to prepare a decent pot of coffee—and a pan of beans. He still wouldn't let her near his precious starter, however, nor the Dutch oven where he baked his sourdough biscuits. And she still collected cow chips—or wood, when it was available—and cleaned the pots and pans. Pans had to be washed mostly with sand because the rivers were always muddy, being stirred either by their own cattle or by the herds ahead of them. Busy from dawn until well after dark, she had lost track of the days. One day had merged into another in the endless drudgery of the drive.

The hands kept up their spirits by making bets. They made bets on anything and everything: whose beard would be the longest when they arrived at the railhead, how long it would be before Scotty gave up trying to shave every day, how long it would take to cross a particular river, when—not if—they would encounter Indians. She'd even discovered they'd made bets on how many days she would last the drive and how long it would be before she took off her hat and coat. She could have told them those were two bets they were all bound to lose.

While the cowhands were making bets, she was working alongside Pepper to keep them fed, and there was simply no end to the work involved in feeding eighteen hungry, tired drovers. Efforts to do so were made far more difficult by the lack of clean water and the dust; the farther north they went, into the endless plains of north Texas, the worst the dust became.

Gabrielle sighed and gave her hot forehead a swipe with the back of her hand. As she did so, she let her gaze wander around the camp—heaven help her, hoping for a glimpse of the Scotsman.

She'd seen little of him during the past two weeks. Kingsley had taken to scouting ahead a lot of the time, often staying overnight, leaving Damien in charge when he was gone; the younger Kingsley, who didn't try to hide his animosity toward the Scotsman, made sure that Cameron was kept busy. Cameron still rode drag—the dirtiest job on the drive—and caught the first night shift, the time when the cattle were still restless. The result, as far as Gabrielle was concerned, was that she saw him only when he galloped up to the chuck wagon to grab a quick meal before falling down onto his bedroll for a couple of hours' sleep. He was always asleep in seconds.

She knew he was, because she watched him. She couldn't help it. Couldn't help remembering the touch of his lips on hers, and the tender fierceness of his hands on her body. She wondered if he remembered, too. If he did, he gave no acknowledgment of it. His golden eyes seldom rested on her for more than a moment.

Still, she consoled herself, he'd kept his promise. He hadn't told Kingsley that she was a woman—for if he had, she wouldn't still be here—and she supposed that counted for something.

As for her purpose in being here, Gabe wondered more and more often if this journey were nothing more than a fool's errand. Even if she could have found the time, she hadn't yet found the nerve to go through Kingsley's belongings, stowed in the chuck wagon. Not that she had any real hope that such a search would produce anything conclusive, but it was the only means she had available to learn anything about him. With him gone so much, it was impossible for her to make any sort of personal assessment of the man. She only knew the drovers respected him, though they didn't seem particularly fond of him.

When he was in camp, the only person to whom Kingsley spoke more than a few words at a time was Drew Cameron—which, as she came to think about it, made it even more peculiar that the Scotsman was always assigned the worst jobs. If he truly was Kingsley's friend, then the trail boss was going to extraordinary lengths not to let anyone think he played favorites.

As her mind wandered back to its favorite topic— the Scotsman—she marveled that he continued to perform all the odious duties assigned to him without resentment or protest. He did everything with unfailing good nature and a cocky grin, as if to say to the world he could handle anything dished out. What she couldn't understand was why he even would *want* to.

In some ways, he was more of a mystery to her than Kingsley.

She sighed as she finished sorting the beans, dumping them into a pot and adding water. Pepper insisted on seasoning them, just as he did his famous sonofabitch stew. She had no idea what went in the latter, and she didn't want to know.

"Need some wood." Pepper growled. "Take that horse of your'n and go fetch some. Ain't none any-place close."

Nor was there. Numerous trail drives crossed here, stripping the land. There wasn't a twig or branch to be found anywhere.

Gabrielle welcomed the thought of riding her horse. She was tired of riding on the hard bench of the hoodlum wagon, though she was pleased with her progress in handling the team. She'd earned the cal-luses that now covered her palms.

Giving Pepper a cocky grin—she considered it the ultimate challenge to get him to smile back—she dusted off the seat of her pants and headed for the remuda. When she spotted Billy, she felt a surge of pride. He had gained weight, his coat was glossy, and he was swiftly becoming a perfectly respectable-looking horse. Although the horses were considered common property, no one ever rode him except her. They knew he was her horse.

"Before long," she whispered, "I'll have to change your name to Sir William. What do you think of that?"

He nuzzled her hand in search of the treat she always gave him, munching the proffered oats quickly. "Greedy boy," she scolded, then saddled him, occasionally stroking him as she did, telling him what a fine fellow he was. He always seemed to understand, arching his neck a little and picking up his tail.

After saddling him, she rode to the hoodlum wagon and found the sling she'd made for gathering wood and cow chips. Even Pepper had been impressed with her inventiveness. He'd also been impressed—though he hadn't actually said so—that she could sew. Since then, she'd been pressed into mending shirts and buttons and trousers for the trail hands, a chore that he usually—and reluctantly—would have performed.

Swinging wide of the herd, the memory of the stampede still alive in her mind, she headed upriver. The afternoon was lazy. A slight breeze, coming over the river, took the edge off the heat, and the sky was as blue as blue could get. She felt a measure of freedom on these wood-searching trips, a relief from the tension of always acting a role, always being onstage.

She rode a couple of miles before finding a small stand of trees that had not yet been picked clean. Tying Billy to a bush, she went to work. Wincing slightly, she cut down a small tree, begging its forgiveness. One of the cowhands had told her Indians did that, and she'd fancied the idea. When she deemed that she'd collected enough, she packed the wood in the sling and tied it to the saddle, then mounted and started back slowly toward camp.

As she approached the herd, the loud, plaintive bawling of an angry cow caught her attention. She looked to see that one man on horseback—she identified him by his hat as Damien Kingsley—was separating a small calf from his mother and leading it away by a rope. The mother tried to follow, but another drover had lassoed it and was pulling it in another direction.

The frantic cries of mother and calf stirred her anger. She applied her heels to Billy's sides and cantered over to Damien.

"What are you doing?" she asked.

He looked at her with disgust and spoke curtly. "He's too small to travel or cross that river," he said curtly.

She understood immediately what he was planning to do, and her stomach knotted. She looked at the calf tugging to get away, and at the mother bawling plaintively.

"He can go in the hoodlum wagon," she said.

Damien closed his eyes for a moment with an expression of pure disgust. "Hell, just what we need. A fryin'-sized pilgrim trying to tell us how to run a trail drive. Go back to the chuck wagon."

"No," she said.

Damien's neck turned red. He was a good-looking man and would have been even more so if his countenance weren't so marred by dissatisfaction. It had been her observation that he blustered his way through things, rather than think them out, and she often wondered why Kingsley left him in charge when he was gone.

Family. Damien was part of Kingsley's family. It was the only explanation. The hurting came back. Kirby Kingsley had family. She didn't.

Sliding off Billy's back, Gabrielle went over to the calf and stroked its sleek head. Damien started to yell at her to get away and do as he'd said, but he was interrupted.

"What's wrong?"

The sound of Drew Cameron's voice brought Gabrielle's head up fast, and she marveled that she hadn't heard him approach.

"I have to put the calf down. You explain it to him," Damien said. "Damn fool kid." Without waiting for a response, he began again to drag the calf away.

"No," she yelled, throwing her arms around the calf's neck as it looked at her with great brown eyes.

Damien swore.

"Gabe, he'd never be able to keep up," the Scotsman explained, jumping down from his horse to walk over to her. "He'll kill himself trying. Putting him down is the kindest thing to do. And Damien has to take it away from the others . . . the smell of blood makes them crazy."

She wanted to say that it would make her crazy, too, but with the sound of the cow and calf bellowing at each other ringing in her ears, all she could do was stare at the Scotsman, pleading with him not to let this happen. In some remote corner of her mind, she knew she was being irrational. She didn't care. Other calves might die, but this one . . . she simply couldn't let it happen. Not with the mother crying right in front of her.

Half-choking on the words, she managed to say, "I'll take care of it," she said. "The wagon . . ."

Cameron looked at her for a moment, their gazes locking, then, with a sigh, he rolled his eyes heavenward.

Speaking to Damien, he said, "I'm off now. I'll be going back to the chuck wagon. Look, your uncle would be happy if we saved one of his cows. You know that mother's going to go looking for her calf and might wander off. Gabe can take the calf in the wagon and tie the mother behind."

"Sonofabitch," Damien swore. "You gonna do that for every calf born on the drive?"

Drew shrugged. "There's no harm in trying it on this one, is there? And it will save you some time. You'll have to take that calf off a long way if you don't want to spook the whole herd."

Damien snorted in derision. "My uncle will think you're crazy."

"Probably," Drew said easily.

With her breath lodged in her lungs, Gabe waited for Damien's decision. She could almost see his mind working. If the calf disrupted the camp, he could blame it on the Scotsman. And not having to take the calf off *would* save time.

"Go ahead," he said finally. "Take him."

Gabrielle breathed again. Quickly she slipped the rope from around the calf's neck. It ran to its mother, who immediately started nuzzling it.

Cameron took the rope off his saddle, walked over to the cow. She watched as he slipped off the other drover's rope, and put his own on. He grinned at her with that devil-go-to-hell smile that made her legs unsteady and her breath short and ragged.

"Know anything about calves?" he asked.

She shook her head.

"I think you're going to learn cow real fast."

Gabrielle's adoption of a calf—and the Scotsman's part in it—made them both the butt of jokes the rest of the evening.

"Got a bull that needs a ride," one drover quipped. "Been complainin' 'bout walking too far."

"Scotty's got a soft streak," said another. "Hey Scotty, what about a game of cards?"

"Hey Two-Bits, that calf would make one hell of a sonofabitch stew."

Gabrielle suffered through the taunts and Pepper's scowl. The cook's response made all the other heckling seem like congratulations.

"Weren't your place to buck Kingsley," he said.

"Nobody likes puttin' down a calf, but ain't nothin' else to do with 'em. Kingsley will tell you that. You jus' wait."

But Kingsley didn't tell her any such thing. To her utter amazement, when he had heard the story, he had merely looked at the Scotsman as if he were insane, then back as her as if he expected no better.

"That damn calf causes any problems I'll shoot him myself," he said. "You'll want to do it yourself after a day." And with that, his lips thinned, and he walked away.

Stunned, Gabrielle looked at the Scotsman, who was leaning against the back of the chuck wagon. He winked at her, and her heart skipped a beat, all thoughts of Kingsley wiped instantly from her mind. Even covered with dust, Drew Cameron was an extraordinarily striking man, his tawny hair and golden eyes and wide sensuous mouth making it almost hurt to look at him.

Who *was* he? The question was never far from her mind. She'd never known a more complex man. A Scot in the American West who claimed he was bored and wanted an adventure. An educated man who possessed all the polish and charm of the upper class of British society, who nevertheless said he was a gambler by profession—and a good one. A man who saved other men's—and one particular woman's— lives at the risk of his own, without hesitation.

A man willing to endure the ridicule of his fellow cowhands and his trail boss to help her save one out of a thousand calves bound for slaughter.

Again, the question begged asking: Who *was* Drew Cameron?

Her eyes held his across a mere three feet, and the connection between them was so strong, so bone deep, that she actually felt her legs turn to water. She swayed on her feet, her heart beating so loudly that she was certain he must be able to hear it.

Slowly, as their gazes held, the smile faded from his

face, and his gold-flecked eyes seemed to soften in a way she hadn't seen before. She saw him suck in a quick, sharp breath, and she knew that he felt it, too, this explosive attraction radiating between them.

But Pepper and Kingsley were on the other side of the campfire talking. And soon the cowhands would be coming in for supper. Through a haze of longing, she knew she couldn't simply go on standing there, staring at him. Still, she couldn't tear her gaze away.

It was the Scotsman who broke the tension. Pushing away from the chuck wagon, he took a step toward her and raised a hand to the side of her face. She felt an instant of panic, thinking he had forgotten her role, forgotten she was supposed to be a boy, and was about to do something that would make the sky come crashing down upon her, certainly, and perhaps upon him, as well.

But the moment passed quickly when a half smile appeared on his face and a gleam returned to his eyes. His hand merely brushed past her cheek, then retreated, turning palm-up between them. She looked down to see a coin, lying on his palm, as if it had been plucked from behind her ear.

"Magic," he said in that lilting brogue, which seemed especially strong. "A slight of hand. The art of illusion. Remember, few things—or people—are ever what they seem."

He took her hand and put the coin in it and her fingers closed around it. His eyes bore into hers for a moment with an intensity that seared through her soul. The he sauntered over to the fire, poured himself a cup of coffee, and wandered over to greet several other drovers who were arriving—leaving her more mystified than ever.

The Red River crossing was a nightmare Drew never wanted to repeat.

They lost no men or animals. But they came close.

Too bloody close. A number of cattle became mired in quicksand, and the drovers had to dismount, duck into the water and tie the animal's legs together, then pull them out. It was long, dangerous work.

Yet when it was over and both men and cattle were resting, Drew admitted to himself that he felt a sense of accomplishment such as he had never known. He was wet, muddy, and nearly dead from exhaustion as he collapsed near the chuck wagon with the other drovers. Still, he felt exhilarated. Even Kirby was smiling—a spare smile, but a smile nonetheless.

There was much to be said for physical labor, Drew thought, lying flat on his back, not moving a muscle. It could hurt like hell, but the rewards of knowing he'd stretched himself to the limit—and won—soothed the physical pain. Yes, pride was a fine thing.

Letting his head roll to the side, he looked around the camp. Most of the drovers not on duty lay spread out on the ground, too tired to jaw, as they so picturesquely called conversation. Two-Bits—he continually had to remind himself to think of Gabrielle that way—was busy at the cook fire, relieving Pepper, who was tending minor injuries.

Drew watched her, trying not to think of what lay underneath the layers of clothes she still wore. He wondered why no one else saw through them to the slender curves, why no one had noticed the delicate bone structure of her face.

He wished *he* could stop noticing. And remembering. He wished his body would stop reacting to the memory. Illusions. He had made that little speech about magic as much for himself as for her, to remind himself that she had secrets and that he detested secrets.

But as he watched her hunch over the fire, he felt an admiration he'd never felt for a woman before. Nothing daunted her, not stampedes or wounds or Pepper. She'd endured unmerciful teasing over the calf with her head held high. And she'd held on to that calf in the hoodlum wagon on the crossing despite the animal's frantic thrashing to return to its mother.

Indeed, he liked her spirit as much as the body that contained it. And, oh, he did like her body. . . .

Drew was still enjoying the view—or rather his memory of it, swaddled in shapeless rags—when he saw Kirby approach. Tearing his gaze from Gabrielle, he lifted a questioning eyebrow at the trail boss— which was about as much as he was capable of moving.

Kirby stooped down to talk, balancing on the balls of his feet. "You're becoming a real cowman. I was watching you out there."

Drew started to offer his usual sort of reply—"I didn't do anything the other hands weren't doing"— but then stopped himself. He *had* done a good job. And it pleased him considerably that Kirby, whom he respected, had noticed.

"Thanks," he said simply, swallowing his discomfort of accepting any kind of praise.

"You want to move on up?" Kirby asked. "Take point?"

The pleasure spread. The point man rode near the front of the herd. No more eating dust.

"I think I could tolerate it," he replied.

Kirby gave him a rare smile. "We'll stay here tomorrow, let the cattle rest and calm down a bit. Some of them had a rough time. I'll be riding out in the morning. I'll probably be out scouting most of the time, now that we're entering Indian Territory." He hesitated, then continued. "Damien will be in charge."

Drew grinned. "I appreciate the warning, though it isn't really necessary. Damien's all right. Just has a burr under his saddle, and I think I'm it."

Kirby's lips twitched. "You're catching onto our lingo real fast, even if I've never heard burr said with that many r's." He unwound and stood. "I hope to hell you're right." He hesitated a moment, then continued, "That kid's doing real well, better than I ever thought. Keep an eye on him for me, will you?"

Drew nodded.

Kirby let out a deep sigh. "Every time I look at him, I can't help seeing myself at that age. With a younger brother to look after and not so much as a pot to piss in, things were pretty tough." His eyes grew bleak. "You get mighty reckless when you're hungry."

Drew understood about hunger, not for food but for a sense of belonging. His hunger had made him reckless, too.

Following the direction of Kirby's gaze, he looked over at Gabrielle. What was she hungry for, he wondered. Hungry enough to make the desperate, reckless choice to come on this cattle drive.

Sighing, he turned back to Kirby. "You turned out pretty good," he said.

Kirby's eyes went dark, almost blank. "You do what you have to do to hold on to your own," he said. Then he spun around to leave, glancing over his shoulder long enough to say, "Just look after him for me." Then he strode away.

The night was deep before Gabrielle was finally able to close her eyes. She had bruises where the calf had fought her as she held on to it during the crossing. She knew now what Kingsley meant in saying she'd want to shoot the animal herself after a day. Still, every time she looked into those huge brown eyes, she was more determined than ever to save the poor thing.

The object of her crusade—Sammy, short for Samson—was currently lying contentedly with its mother behind the wagon.

But it wasn't Sammy that kept her awake; it was the vision of the Scotsman and Kirby huddling together near the fire, talking.

Damien Kingsley had been watching, too. It had been obvious to her for some time that he felt displaced

in his uncle's eyes by Drew Cameron. Watching
Damien, she could see the barely suppressed anger, the
envy, even the chagrin, stamped on his features. It
would take a blind fool, she thought, not to realize that
feelings as powerful as those Damien was harboring
were dangerous to have around on a cattle drive—and
she was neither blind nor a fool.

She hoped that Kingsley and the Scotsman weren't
oblivious of the potential danger either. She hoped
Damien would control his temper and not, finally, do
something terrible. Shuddering, she refused to allow
herself to consider exactly what "something terrible"
might entail.

Worried, frustrated that she could do nothing to
prevent Damien Kingsley from doing exactly as he
pleased, Gabrielle scooted over onto her other side,
facing away from the fire and the men. As she tried
once more to fall asleep, it occurred to her to wonder
if she looked at Kingsley the same way Damien looked
at Drew Cameron: with pure malice.

Odd, but since yesterday, when he'd let her keep
the calf, she didn't feel quite the same about the trail
boss. Not that he'd been kind. But she was quite
aware that he would have been well within his rights
to order her to give up the calf. And she even acknowledged that it would have been the sensible thing to do.
She couldn't have stopped him. Yet he hadn't, and the
paradox of humanity existing in a ruthless murderer
had her baffled.

At the moment, she was too tired to think about it.
Tomorrow, she decided, burrowing into her bedroll,
she would go for a ride on Billy. Pepper had said she
could, that they would be resting for the day and that
he wouldn't need her until the afternoon. That's what
she needed: some distance.

Tomorrow, she would let Billy take her far away
from beans and Pepper and Kirby Kingsley. Far
away from Drew Cameron. Far away from the
lowing cattle and the clatter of pans.

· · ·

Kirby rode hard, deep into Indian Territory. He led a second horse that he would ride when the first one gave out. He planned to cover enough ground to scout out campsites for the next three—possibly four—days. He wanted to make it through Indian Territory as quickly as possible, knowing that Kiowas and Comanches, along with renegades from other tribes, still hunted this area—and not only for game.

As he rode, he considered the decisions he had to make. Decisions about Damien and Terry, and about his own future. The ambush several months ago had reminded him of his mortality—and his sins. He could do damn little about either, but he didn't want his brother's and nephews' lives ruined, too.

Gold brushed the sky as the sun tipped the horizon. Wisps of cloud wandered aimlessly overhead. The prairie stretched out for miles, looking benign and peaceful. But Kirby knew differently. He'd passed this way before. Jagged outcroppings of rock and deep gullies made it perfect for ambushes. And he thought a lot about ambushes these days.

He hadn't gone far, was probably no more than several hours from camp, when his spine started tingling. For a moment, he thought it only nerves. When the shot rang out, shattering the quiet of morning, he called himself a fool.

His horse whinnied in pain, reared. Kirby held on, looking around sharply, reaching for his rifle. He saw a flash as the sun glanced off metal. An instant later, pain struck him from behind, fierce and burning.

He felt himself falling—then he felt nothing at all.

Chapter Nine

———— ✠ ————

Riding point was one hell of a lot better than riding drag. Simply breathing clean air was a novelty. The pinto obviously enjoyed it, too, Drew noticed. The horse's steps were quicker, his head higher, his spirit almost exuberant.

Damien Kingsley, however, was not a happy man. He was in his usual position, at center front of the herd, with his brother Terry riding right point and Drew riding left. To say Damien was unhappy about the new arrangement was an understatement. But he hadn't tried to change his uncle's orders, for which Drew was relieved. He didn't want to be the cause of a quarrel in the Kingsley family, and he wasn't sure how he felt about Kirby using him to test Damien's limits—for he knew that was what his friend was doing.

When the drive left the Red River that morning, Kirby had been gone a day and a half. But no one was really surprised. The trail boss had said he would be gone several days. Now that they had left Texas, everyone was aware of increased danger and the need for moving quickly and having campsites planned well ahead.

Drew cast a glance upward, at the huge blue sky. Not a cloud in sight. Only a huge red ball of the sun beating mercilessly down upon the parched land. It was going to be another hot one.

He felt a moment's sympathy for Gabrielle, still enveloped in all those clothes. Then he reminded himself he'd offered her an alternative, an introduction to Ben Masters and the money to reach Denver and she'd rejected it. Hadn't even considered it briefly.

Had she refused because he'd said Ben was an ex-marshal and she was running from the law? The question plagued him, along with the even more troublesome one: Should he have told Kirby that his scruffy, troublesome louse was a woman? He felt guilty that he hadn't. But he would have felt even more guilty if he'd broken his promise not to tell and Gabrielle had been injured as a result.

He didn't want to see her hurt in any way. He wanted to protect her, as unfamiliar and uncomfortable as the feeling was. When he'd looked for her that morning at breakfast and found her gone, his stomach had clenched and his heart had started to pound. It had pounded harder when Pepper told him she'd gone riding on Billy.

Bloody hell, why couldn't he keep his mind away from her? Why did it constantly jerk back to her, and the mystery surrounding her?

His horse snorted, then whinnied. He snapped back to the present, wondering what had alerted the pinto. Expecting to see an escaping steer, he saw, instead, something moving toward them from the north-west, too far away to identify. As it approached, the form resolved into two forms, then into two riderless horses.

At the same time that Drew made the identification, he noticed Damien angle to the left and increase his speed; the foreman had seen the horses, too. Following Damien's lead, Drew spurred the pinto into a gallop, heading toward the oncoming animals. As he drew nearer he recognized the animals as Kirby's favorite bay and roan geldings.

Drew reached the horses a few seconds after Damien, in time to see the younger man catch the tired beasts, then reach over and touch, first the saddle, then the rump of the bay. Damien looked at his hand, then held it out to show Drew.

"Dry blood," he said shortly. "The bay's been grazed on the hindquarters, but the blood on the saddle came from someplace else."

Or from someone else. Drew stared at Damien's hand. "Another ambush?"

"Looks like it," Damien said curtly.

Drew hesitated, giving Damien time to consider his next move, then pushed, even though he expected an explosion in doing so.

"I'll go look for him."

Damien didn't explode. Instead, he asked. "You ever done any tracking?"

"Not much," he answered honestly.

Damien hesitated. "Uncle Kirby said you can use that gun." It was a question more than a statement.

"I can," he replied simply.

Damien took a map from his pocket and studied it before looking up at him. "I'll stop the herd at the stream about a mile ahead," Damien said. "Take Terry and two others. Shorty and Legs are probably the best trackers. When we bed the herd down, I'll send two more after you."

Drew nodded, surprised that Damien was allowing him to go, equally as startled by the deep pain in the man's eyes.

Drew spurred his pinto back to the herd, and to Terry.

"Kirby's horses," he said briefly. "Looks like

trouble. Damien wants you and me, Shorty, and Legs to go look for him."

Terry didn't ask any questions but gave the reins of his horse a pull to the right, turning to head back down the line to find Shorty, who was tall, and Legs, who was short.

Drew took that time to ride to the remuda and get a fresh horse, then joined the other two as they rode up. "The horses came from the northwest," he said, joining them, pacing his horse with theirs. No more words were spoken as they raced in front of the herd toward the open prairie.

The drive stopped early, and Gabrielle wondered why as she pulled up the team hitched to the hoodlum wagon. She no longer needed someone with her under ordinary circumstances. She jumped down and began to unhitch the team of mules even as she pondered the possible reasons for an early end to the work day.

She'd seen Damien Kingsley race past her on his way to Pepper's chuck wagon. He'd ridden alongside the wagon for a moment or so, obviously imparting some news, then turned and raced back to the herd, again passing her on the way.

She untied Sammy from inside the wagon and helped him reunite with his mother, which he did by greedily groping for milk. Then she rushed over to Pepper.

He had already lowered the chuck box and boot containing supplies and pots and pans. In minutes a fire would be blazing, and coffee boiling.

"Why are we stopping so early?"

He glared at her, his pale blue eyes looking even more watery than usual. His hands kept moving, as did his mouth, though it didn't say anything.

"Pepper?"

"The boss . . ." He hesitated, then said reluctantly, "His horses came back."

She looked at him, not understanding.

"Without him," Pepper said. "Terry and Scotty and some others have gone out looking fer him.'

Gabrielle frowned, still puzzled.

The old cook gave an exasperated sigh. "They found blood on his saddle."

Gabrielle swallowed hard.

"Damien wants to know everyone who's been out of camp for the last two days."

Gabrielle felt her face go red. She didn't know how much showed under the makeup, but cold waves suddenly washed through her body.

"He doesn't think someone . . . here . . . ?"

Stiff-legged and wobbly, she jerkily went to the hoodlum wagon to fetch the necessary wood and cow chips. She automatically started a fire, her thoughts racing around like ants on a hot surface. What could have happened to Kirby Kingsley?

Once the herd was settled, several more men rode out to look for Kingsley. Speculation among them was rife. Some supposed Indians, other outlaws. Even a wild animal. Kingsley could have been injured, tried to mount and failed, leaving a trail of blood. They all dismissed any possibility of an assailant from their ranks, though Damien had asked pointed questions.

When he got around to asking her, her stomach knotted, but she answered honestly. Yes, she'd been riding the day before. No, she hadn't seen anybody. She hadn't really been that far from the herd, just far enough to be by herself. Damien didn't seem to think it odd that she'd wanted to be alone and seemed to accept her answers at face value. Still, her stomach continued to knot and twist as she wondered what he could have done if he'd known she had a motive for wanting to do his uncle harm.

She also grew sick thinking about Drew out there. What if there were Apaches, Kiowas, or Comanches?

She felt the level of tension rising as the day wore on. The drovers were silent, no longer joshing each other and telling tall tales about fantastic exploits. They came in, ate, and rode back to their posts, filling in for those on the search party.

Evening came and the knot in her stomach grew larger. Tempers were frayed. Pepper cursed several times as he leaned over to get something, once groaning as he straightened. She'd offered to help, and he'd turned on her, a string of oaths flowing from his mouth.

She finally left, went over to Billy Bones, and curried him, needing something to do to keep her from going crazy. She'd sought justice, but now she wanted it by the law. She found herself hoping they would find Kingsley.

And she prayed nothing would happen to the Scotsman.

Legs was a bloody fine tracker. Drew took note of his fellow drover's talent, watching as the man moved swiftly and surely, pausing only occasionally to lean down from his horse and study tracks.

Drew had heard that Legs was half-Indian, but his light blue eyes seemed to put the lie to that rumor, and no one had seemed wont to push the point. Legs had a ferocious temper and a reputation with a knife. But he was also superb with horses, and he could read trail signs like other men read books.

They hadn't been out much more than three hours when Drew sighted buzzards circling around. He yelled, then spurred the pinto into a gallop, hearing the others race behind him.

The buzzards were still circling, and that gave Drew hope. He'd learned enough by now to know that they waited until their prey was dead. He dug his spurs deeper, feeling a spurt of speed as he approached a form lying on earth packed firm by thousands of cattle hooves.

He dismounted before the horse fully stopped, and

ran the last few yards to drop to his knees before the still figure of Kirby Kingsley. His friend had two bullet wounds in him: one had struck his side, entering in front and exiting in back. The other had grazed his head.

Drew put his fingers to the pulse in Kirby's neck and breathed a little easier when he felt a fluttering response. It was thready and weak, but Kirby was still alive. Just.

He swore. There had been no attempts on Kirby's life since the ambush nearly three months ago. Terry had dismounted and joined him, along with one other man. Legs was riding on past, looking closely at the ground leading to an outcropping.

"He's still alive," Drew said. "Barely. Whoever shot at him must have thought he was dead."

"Must be Indians," Terry said.

"Not unless they've been shoeing their horses," Shorty said, staring at the ground. "There's three different sets of horse-shoes here."

"Sonofabitch," Terry swore. "Uncle Kirby had two horses. That means there was only one gunman. And Injun horses don't wear shoes."

"And outlaws or Indians would've taken Kingsley's horses," Shorty said.

Drew was silent—all of them were—as the implications became clear. Shooting Kirby had been a deliberate act, probably committed by one gunman, who hadn't been after the horses.

"How is he, Scotty?" Shorty asked.

Drew shook his head. "He has a head injury that's been bleeding some. Also has a bullet that went through him, and he's lost a hell of a lot of blood. We'd better get him back to Pepper."

Terry Kingsley stood up. "I'll take him on my horse."

Drew nodded. "Let me try some water first. He's been out here awhile."

Shorty passed him a canteen and Drew held it to

Kingsley's mouth, allowing a few drops to moisten his lips. The trail boss didn't respond.

He handed the canteen back, then he and Shorty lifted Kirby up onto Terry's horse. They were about ten miles from camp. It would be a long way back.

Gabrielle watched three men ride up, her heart pounding with a mixture of relief and dread. Drew was alive and clearly unharmed, riding as tall as ever in the saddle of his horse. But Terry Kingsley was carrying a fourth man, slumped in front of him, and she saw as he approached the camp at a loping canter that the man was Kirby Kingsley.

The search party rode directly into camp and up to the chuck wagon.

Shorty jumped down and threw his reins to her. "Hey, Two-Bits, take care of my horse for me."

Pepper was there instantly, as two men lifted Kingsley down. She crept closer, leading Shorty's horse behind her. But she was stopped cold when she glanced at the Scotsman. His gaze speared her, glittering with suspicion and angry questions. Gabrielle felt herself shiver inside.

Then Damien Kingsley came racing into camp, and the Scotsman's attention went to him.

Damien jumped off his horse to drop down beside Pepper. Others came to join the circle that had formed around the trail boss. No one spoke, though, as Pepper's hands ran over the injured man's wounds. Pepper was as close to a doctor as they were going to get. The nearest real doctor was over a hundred miles away.

Finally, Pepper looked up at her. "Get some water and my box."

His box was a precious commodity, filled with medicines and home remedies and a bottle of whiskey. Handing the reins of Shorty's horse to another drover, she ran to do as she was told. All the while, she was aware of Scotty's gaze.

He was still looking at her when she returned to set the box next to Pepper. The cook was cursing and shaking Kirby, trying to rouse him. When that failed, he dribbled some water down his throat, then a thimbleful of whiskey. Kirby's throat worked convulsively and Pepper's face relaxed slightly.

"What happened?" Pepper asked, looking up at Scotty despite the fact that Terry Kingsley stood nearby.

"Bushwacked," the Scotsman said softly. "Legs is still out there trying to pick up a trail."

"Indians?" one hand asked.

The Scotsman shook his head. "They were after Kingsley. Didn't even bother with his horses."

"But why?" the drover asked.

Damien Kingsley looked at the Scotsman. "Yeah, why?"

Gabrielle wanted to know why, too. She wanted to know whether it had anything to do with her father's death. Coincidence? How many times were people ambushed in Texas?

She looked down at the unconscious man, a hurricane of emotions buffeting her. She believed he was the man responsible for her father's death. Her father had as much as said so. But if that were so, then who had shot *him*?

She should hate him; but looking at the pale, still form of a strong man she felt only a peculiar sadness. She looked away, wanting to escape.

"Boil some water," Pepper said as she tried to inch away.

Fighting the tightness in her throat, she poured water into a pot and set it on the spit already in place, then stood watching Pepper as he washed away the dirt from the wounds. Every touch of the cloth on the jagged flash made her wince.

Kingsley. She heard her father whispering the name

as he died. Why would Kingsley's name—not hers or her mother's—be the last word on his lips if he hadn't been trying to tell her something vitally important? His tone had been accusing . . . hadn't it?

She looked at the man on the ground. The man who always scowled at her, who at the best of times appeared harsh and cold. The man who'd dumped a badly injured drover in a one-horse town with no money and without so much as a backward glance. She despised that man.

She looked away even as she heard one of the drovers ask how Kingsley was, and heard Pepper's mutter, "Up to someone else."

Gabrielle turned away. Up to God? Was that what Pepper meant?

Would she ever know what happened—and why— if Kingsley died? Would she would ever be safe again?

She backed away, almost forgotten, as Pepper swabbed at the trail boss's wounds. She looked back, saw the Scotsman's eyes on her. He wore no hat, he seldom did unless he was riding drag. His face was bronze now, and tawny hair fell over his forehead. The muscles around his jaw were clenched and his golden eyes appeared to see right through her. There was no humor in them now, no amusement. Her heart beat hard under his intense scrutiny, and she felt like a butterfly pinned to a board.

Finally, he let his gaze fall from hers, turning his attention to the preparations that were underway to move Kingsley to a bed made up close to the fire.

Gabrielle stood there feeling lost and bereft as she watched him stoop next to Kingsley. Concern and white hot anger were obvious in the way he looked at Kirby Kingsley.

Given that fact, he would never believe her, nor would he believe Kingsley was responsible for her father's death. Not anymore than the law had. Not unless she could get proof.

She couldn't get that unless Kingsley lived.

She started to pray for the man she believed her father's murderer, or the one who had paid him.

Kirby Kingsley wasn't going to like the delay. Each drover knew that, including Drew. The schedule was crucial; the first herds reaching Abilene would fetch the best prices. Nearly twenty ranchers had contributed to the herd, and their success—or failure—depended on Kingsley.

Yet Kirby remained unconscious, and Pepper argued they shouldn't move him. They couldn't leave him with one or two men—all they could spare—with Indians and ambushers in the vicinity. They could make up a day later, Pepper said, and Damien agreed.

As late afternoon faded into night, and night into morning, the campfire kept burning, and all the drovers kept vigil around it, leaving only to take their turns at watch.

Drew prepared to get a couple of hours sleep before he had to go on watch, but he delayed his rest when Legs returned. The drover-tracker had little to report. He'd found only one set of horse tracks, and he'd followed them into a creek and lost them. Whoever had shot Kingsley was still out there.

Or here. The thought nagged at Drew. Would someone follow a cattle drive three weeks just to find an opportunity to get Kingsley alone? Or could the shooter be someone on the drive?

The idea that the shooter was living among them nagged at him as he lay down on his bedroll and tried to catch some sleep. So did the memory of the expression on Gabrielle's face when she'd seen Terry riding in with Kirby. A myriad of emotions crossed her features as she'd stood watching Pepper work over the trail boss—and relief and shock hadn't been among them.

Drew recalled that she had gone riding yesterday. He had never seen her with a gun, but that didn't mean she didn't own one—or couldn't have taken one from some drover's holster, stored in the hoodlum wagon, while the man slept.

Drew didn't like the direction of his thoughts, but he couldn't help them. His heart told him that Gabrielle couldn't be responsible. But his common sense, as well as his suspicious nature, forced him to admit that it wasn't impossible. Why had she lied to him? Could she be working with someone else? Why was it so important to her to be on this trail drive, and finally, had he made a possibly fatal mistake in not telling Kirby about her deception?

The questions followed him into a brief, restless sleep—along with the determination that he was going to have another talk with Gabrielle. And this time, he was going to get some straight answers.

Gabrielle drew the cool, wet cloth across Kingsley's face, then dunked it back into the water bowl. She'd finally persuaded Pepper to get some rest, promising to call him the moment Kingsley showed any sign of waking. If he ever did.

She studied the trail boss's feverish face, listening to his ragged breathing, thinking how odd it was that she was sitting here, nursing him. Even stranger to think she genuinely wanted the man she thought had killed her father to live. She told herself it was only because she wanted the chance to hear any words he might utter, that she wanted him to admit his part in her father's death.

But it was more than that, and she knew it.

A weakness of character? Her father had as much as identified him as his murderer.

The night was quiet. A few of the drovers remained around the fire, sleeping or simply lying on the bedrolls. Once in a while, one would come over and ask her how the boss was doing. Kingsley, she was learning, had won a singular respect and loyalty from his hands.

Still, as her gaze moved over the men in camp and as she thought about the others, out on their watches, she had to wonder if one of them wanted to kill their boss. She'd heard Damien's questions, known the possibility was being considered.

It was hard for her to imagine. She was coming to know the drovers well. They were loyal to each other and to Kingsley. They seemed to aspire to little more than a paycheck and a good meal, and their dreams appeared limited to the next town, where they hoped to find a glass of whiskey and a loose woman.

Only the Scotsman didn't fit. And Kingsley's nephews, who probably had much to gain with Kirby's death. They stood to inherit a vast ranch and the wealth and power that went with it. But Terry Kingsley struck her as too mild-mannered and ineffectual to plan anything more complicated than a poker game. Damien, though . . . well, that was another story. Damien was bright enough. And he certainly appeared angry. Still, his concern for Kingsley a few hours earlier had seemed quite genuine; he'd looked worried sick. And, in the end, Gabrielle couldn't persuade herself that Damien was capable of murder.

She added several pieces of valuable wood to the fire and watched the shadows dance across Kingsley's face. It was a harsh countenance, and he seldom if ever smiled. A hard boss, the hands all agreed, but fair. They didn't ask for more than that.

Sighing, Gabrielle wriggled inside her hot, dusty clothes as the Scotsman rode in from his watch. He wore no hat, and his tawny hair fell over his forehead, partially covering his handsome, sun-bronzed face. As he dismounted and walked toward her, she noted the sheer elegance of his movements—the way he rode, the way he walked, everything about him spoke of grace and confidence and strength.

"How is he?" Drew asked as he stooped beside her.

Gabrielle cast a quick glance at him. "No change."

He looked pure exhausted. She ached to smooth away the lines of fatigue crinkling his eyes. She longed to stand in front of him as Maris Gabrielle Parker and see in his eyes the admiration she'd seen in others, not the doubt and questions and suspicions.

The chasm between them widened at his next question. "Pepper left you alone with him?"

Whether they were meant as an accusation or not, the words struck her like a blow to the stomach. His eyes, which sometimes appeared so golden, were hard now, the gold in them eclipsed by a glittering agate.

"He was tired," she said. "I—don't think he's feeling well."

His eyes cut to hers. "That makes things easier for you, doesn't it?"

"Why should it?" She challenged him.

His eyes didn't leave hers. "If Pepper is ill, he won't look too deeply into the peculiarities of his . . . what is that expressive word? . . . louse." His voice was unemotional, cool, with an underlying hint of ruthlessness.

The good-natured, usually subtly amused Scotsman was displaying another side. The geniality was gone, and now she wondered whether it had ever really been a part of him or merely a skin that covered what he really was.

And what was that?

"No," she simply.

"No what?"

"It doesn't make things easier," she said.

"I saw your face when we brought . . . Mr. Kingsley in," he persisted.

"And . . ." she prompted slowly, wondering what indeed had been in her face. She'd been so swamped by conflicting emotions that even she didn't know exactly how she'd felt.

"You weren't exactly . . . surprised."

"Wasn't I?"

"And you were gone from camp the morning he was shot."

She nodded noncommittally.

"Where did you go?"

"For a ride."

"North?"

"Yes."

"You didn't see anything?"

"No."

His eyes seemed to peel layers from her. Layers of pretense, layers of lies, layers of feelings even she didn't understand.

I want him to live, too, she wanted to scream at him. *I want him to tell me what happened twenty-five years ago. I want to know if he had my father killed—and if so, why. And if it was Kingsley, I want him to pay for it. But if he dies now, I'll never know the truth. And I'll never feel safe. So he can't die. Not like this.*

But the words went unspoken. Drew Cameron was Kingsley's friend. He would never believe her, any more than the sheriff in San Antonio believed her.

For several long minutes, Gabrielle remained frozen, held prisoner by Drew Cameron's unrelenting gaze. Then, suddenly, the tension between them was broken by a quiet moan, coming from the man lying on the bedroll between them.

As she grabbed the wet cloth, wrung it out, and wiped Kingsley's forehead again, she cast a quick glance at the Scotsman and saw he was watching her as if he expected her to plunge a knife into his friend. She applied her attention to her patient.

Kingsley moved again, and he spoke a few unintelligible words. Leaning down, she put her ear close to his mouth. Most of the words were broken, but she heard several quite clearly.

"Sorry ... so sorry." Then another one, "Murderer."

Chapter Ten

Kirby Kingsley's mumblings turned more coherent as the night wore on, and Drew convinced Gabrielle to get some rest. But despite Drew's patient prodding Kirby could tell him nothing about his attackers. He'd seen only the glint of sun on a rifle.

The pain that lined his face couldn't conceal the bleakness in his eyes as he came to the same conclusions Drew had reached earlier: The ambush three months ago was not an isolated, freak occurrence, as Kirby had wanted to believe.

Kirby had refused to go to the law then, saying he'd have to go all the way to San Antonio and the attacker would be long gone in any event. Drew had accepted that explanation at the time; now he wondered whether Kirby hadn't had another reason.

As Drew sat at his friend's side, he felt a deep and burning rage. Kirby was weak from loss of blood, his jaw was clenched and his forehead creased in an expression of severe pain, and his skin was gray. Only two days before he'd been a strong, healthy man still in the peak years of his life.

"Who?" Drew asked him. "Who would go this far to see you dead?"

Kirby looked up at him, his gaze desolate. "I have no idea."

"You murmured some words as you woke up," Drew said.

Alarm spread over his friend's face, and Drew's gut tightened.

"What?" Kirby asked.

"Don't you remember?"

Kirby shook his head, wincing a little at the pain that ensued from his head wound.

Drew frowned, remembering Kirby's words. "You said something about a murderer. About being sorry."

Kirby closed his eyes, heaving a tired sigh.

"You *do* know something." Drew spoke in urgent tones. "Tell me—what did you mean?"

Kirby hesitated, opening his eyes to look around.

"No one's listening," Drew said. "The only hands here are all asleep—and snoring."

Seeming reassured, Kirby sighed again. "Those things I said—they happened twenty-five years ago."

"Someone with a long memory?"

Kirby's brow furrowed. "It doesn't make sense. There's no reason . . ."

"No reason a woman should be involved?"

Drew saw surprise flash through Kirby's eyes at his question.

"No," Kirby said. "No reason at all. Why would you ask?"

Drew hesitated. He should tell Kirby about Gabrielle. Now. But if Gabrielle didn't have anything to do with this—and he couldn't believe she did—he would be betraying her.

"No reason," he said. "Just satisfying myself on a point. Look—you need to rest. We can talk more tomorrow."

Kirby didn't argue. His eyes drifted closed on another long sigh.

Drew fetched his bedroll and stretched out near Kirby. He was going to make bloody sure Kirby wasn't alone, especially not with Gabrielle or his nephews. Pepper would watch over him during the day in the chuck wagon, for despite Pepper's age and stiff limbs, he was good with a gun and he was loyal to Kirby.

Earlier Pepper had pronounced his boss on the mend, claiming his poultice had warded off infection. Drew remained a bit skeptical but was inclined to agree with Pepper's conclusion that Kirby would live.

This time. He wouldn't give odds on the older man surviving a third attack.

Drew swore silently. He'd cared for few people in his life, wasn't at all experienced at it, and now he wondered if he ever wanted to be. There was a lot to be said for being concerned only for oneself. Not that he'd done such a bloody good job of that either. Yet here he was, feeling responsible for two people: Gabrielle and Kirby. And for some reason, he couldn't rid himself of the notion that those two people's interests clashed in some way.

Frustrated, Drew closed his eyes and rolled to put his back to the fire. He needed some sleep. Kirby would insist on starting the herd tomorrow.

But sleep was a long time coming. And even when it came, visions of a blue-eyed, short-haired temptress plagued his dreams.

Loud swearing and pans crashing woke Gabrielle from a sound sleep under the hoodlum wagon. Alarmed at the disturbance, she pushed herself up onto an elbow, and rubbed her eyes.

"Two-Bits!"

Hearing her name being called—and none too pleasantly—she slipped on her shapeless coat and hat, though her eyes were barely open. They were open far enough, though, to see that it was still nighttime. As she rolled out from under the wagon, she squinted in the darkness and made out several forms moving about. But Pepper hadn't yet started the fire.

"Gabe!"

Scrambling to her feet, she hurried the thirty or so yards between the two wagons, the distance marking the space where the drovers slept when they weren't on watch. Some were up, others were slowly rising from bedrolls. Several were cursing—loudly.

Ten feet from the chuck wagon, Gabrielle was brought to a halt as she recognized another shadowed form, milling around in the darkness.

Sammy.

She'd left him with his mother, who was tied to the back of the hoodlum wagon, and she'd expected him to stay put. Obviously he'd had other ideas.

The calf had made his way to the chuck wagon, where he was stumbling over cowhands' sleeping bodies, bumping into the chuck box, sending pans crashing to the ground—and generally wreaking havoc. Confused by all the human noise, as well as the noise he himself was creating, the calf started running first in one direction, then another, stepping on drovers as he went.

As Gabrielle watched the rampaging calf, trying to decide how to catch him, Pepper appeared from inside the chuck wagon. She couldn't see his expression in the dim, predawn light, but she felt his burning glare. She would hear about this all day. Sleep was important to the hands, who usually got little of it. And they were lucky that the sound of clattering pots hadn't yet spooked the cattle.

She said a small prayer. Sammy would be lucky not to be invited to supper tonight—as a main course. Cowpunchers, she'd learned, became very protective of their charges and were loath to kill their own cows. They might buy a cow from another herd to butcher, but even that was rare. Sammy, though, was stretching the sensibilities of this bunch of cowhands to the limits.

"Sonofabitch!" Legs's familiar complaint came the loudest.

"Get that damned calf out of here!" Damien exclaimed.

Starting to feel a bit panicked herself, Gabrielle looked around. She had no rope, and when she tried to grab Sammy as he went past her, he butted her aside. Off balance and still only half-awake, she went tumbling to the hard ground. The calf continued stalking the camp. No one else even tried to stop him. They were all watching her.

Determined, she regained her feet and studied Sammy, who was running every which way, trampling on everything in his path, human or otherwise.

"Sammy," she said coaxingly as she stood.

Sammy didn't respond.

"Sammy!" She tried to force a note of authority in her voice.

Sammy backed away. She looked around, and she thought her eyes must be playing tricks on her in the dark. But she had good night vision, and it did seem as if every drover present—about eight of them—was grinning. Including Drew Cameron. Even Kingsley, who was semipropped against a wagon wheel, appeared to have a small smile on his lips.

Knowing she'd be listening for days to the story of Two-Bits and Sammy, the calf that destroyed Kingsley's camp, she tried not to smile herself. Smiling did not fit her part—the gruff boy of few words. Instead, she concentrated on the calf, only too aware that she was the center of attention—and amusement.

Discarding the idea of getting a rope—Sammy seemed in no mood to stay still long enough for her to get it around his neck—she tried to think of a way to get the calf to come to her. The mother was tied to the chuck wagon, and she supposed it would work if she used the cow to lure her own calf. But then they'd have two bovines trampling the cooking area, and that would send Pepper into fits.

She thought rapidly, recalled the sound of the cow's mournful cry to her calf. How did it sound? She could mimic almost anything, having inherited her father's ear for sound and ability to reproduce it.

Without expectation of success, she made an effort to approximate a cow lowing and was astonished when the calf slowed and, finally, came to a stop. She made the sound again. The calf turned to look at her, his panic seeming to fade. She took a couple of steps toward the hoodlum wagon, and tried the plaintive lowing again. The calf followed. Slowly, she back-stepped her way across the camp, trying not to trip on the men or bedrolls in her path. Finally, she reached the hoodlum wagon, and the calf came up to join her, heading directly for its mother.

Gabrielle watched in relief as the mother welcomed her calf and it huddled next to her. Behind her, the camp was quiet; not a single drover uttered a sound. Then, a minute later, the clatter of pans signaled that Pepper had decided to start breakfast. Dawn couldn't be far behind.

With her back still turned to the rest of the camp, Gabrielle became aware of someone standing behind her. She knew who it was without looking. Her body reacted to the Scotsman whenever he came near her, almost as if she were a magnet to his steel.

"How did a banker's daughter learn to do that?"

She heard his whispered words as his breath tickled her ear. Her body stiffened, as much a reaction to his closeness as to his words.

She turned toward him. He was so tall, she had to look almost straight up to see his face. He had washed and changed shirts, and the smell of soap mixed with leather spiced the early morning air.

"That was a fine trick," he added, his voice soft, even seductive, not harsh as it had been the last time he'd spoken to her.

"I've always been good at imitating voices," she said.

"I've noticed. You never slip, do you?" he observed softly. "You've got your voice completely trained."

"It's not trained," she replied—being truthful, for once. "It's just a natural . . . talent."

She returned his gaze steadily for a moment or two longer, then had to look away. He saw too much, asked so much. And she always wanted to answer.

"I see Mr. Kingsley is better," she said.

The Scotsman was silent for a moment, clearly not ready to leave the subject of her voice control—and other unacknowledged talents. Finally, though, he let out a sigh and answered her question.

"Aye, he's better. We'll be starting back on the trail today."

She glanced upward at him, surprised. "He's that much improved?"

"No," Cameron replied, leaning against the wagon. "But he insists. He'll ride with Pepper. He can always use Pepper's bunk."

"Does he know . . . ?"

"Who shot him? No. He only saw the reflection of the sun off a rifle sight."

She hesitated, then asked, "And does he know *why*?"

The Scotsman's features tensed. "He says not."

Another moment of silence passed, then he said, "You don't carry a rifle."

It wasn't a question, but she shook her head.

"Can you shoot?" His tone was casual, but his expression was not; his gaze, as he studied her face, was piercing.

Her fears told her to lie, to say, "No, I've never held a gun in my life." But common sense warned her that she'd never get away with it. He'd know instantly that she was lying.

Thinking quickly, Gabrielle replied, "A little."

"What does 'a little' mean?"

"It means . . ." She lifted one shoulder in a quick shrug. "A little. I thought it would look odd for me not to have a gun if I was going to join a cattle drive, so . . ." She shrugged again. "I bought a gun. I tried it a few times."

She risked a quick look at him. He was still staring at her—hard. But he didn't have that half-enraged, half-cynical expression she'd come to recognize as a sign that he thought she was lying to him.

" 'A few times,' " he repeated slowly. "And did you hit anything you aimed at?"

"Well . . . maybe once or twice." She hoped her furtive glances at him would be interpreted as embarrassment, for she couldn't seem to prevent them.

"Well, then," he began, "I'd say a few lessons might be in order."

Her gaze flashed up to meet his.

"I'll teach you," he said, throwing her completely off balance.

She didn't *want* him to teach her. She was already afraid of him, of how he made her feel, and every time he came near her, her fear grew.

Feeling more than a little desperate, she protested, "But I don't like guns."

"But Gabe Lewis would," he said, his lips twisting into an amused smile.

He had her there. And he knew it. Gabe Lewis *would* jump at the chance to learn to shoot.

"But . . . why? I mean, what difference does it make if I know how—"

"I think it's fairly obvious what difference it makes," he cut in, his voice as smooth as glass. "The past two days have proven beyond a doubt that, out here, one needs to know how to protect oneself. And if you own a gun, you should understand how it works and how to use it."

She could think of no argument that sounded even remotely sensible. She already knew she was beaten as she asked, "How do I know you're any good?"

One fair eyebrow shot upward. "I'm a Scot," he said simply. "We learn to shoot almost before we can walk. Every gentleman knows how to hunt."

His tone as he said the word *gentleman* caught her attention; for an instant, his cool and casual voice had hinted at contempt.

Carefully, she said, "You were a *gentleman*?"

"That's very debatable," he replied, his smile disappearing.

Through the layers of charm, she saw a deep bitterness that even he, who was so good at masking his thoughts and feelings, couldn't hide.

"I don't think so," she said softly. "I think you must have been a very fine gentleman."

He seemed taken aback. "Now, what makes you think that?"

"The way you cared about Ace," she said. "Not many of the others did."

He shrugged as if that meant little.

"You believe in loyalty."

"Doesn't everyone?"

She shook her head. "No, I don't think so."

"And I thought *I* was cynical," he said, the side of his mouth twitching again.

"And you keep promises."

The half-smile evaporated instantly. "Is that a reminder?"

"No," she said. "A thank you."

"Don't thank me yet," he warned. "I came bloody close to telling Kirby today, and I still might."

"You think I'm a danger to him?"

"I don't know what you are," he replied. "And I don't like puzzles."

"Are you sure?" she asked, looking up at him through her lashes, a tiny smile curving her lips.

She hadn't been trying to seem seductive, only teasing. But for an instant, his eyes glittered brightly, his gaze holding hers in a look that made tendrils of heat curl through her. Then, however, his gaze skimmed over her, taking in the hat and clothes. And he grinned. She could have slapped him.

"I'm bloody sure," he said. But his eyes still held a hint of amber fire, and she knew he was seeing past the clothes that would have shamed a beggar to her real self. And he had seen quite a lot of her.

Blushing, she looked away. Damn the man! Why did he have to confuse her so?

"When we stop tonight," he said, "I'll take you for a shooting lesson."

Lord, were they back to *that* again?

"But I don't *want*—" She stopped short, having looked up to find she was talking to the air. He had walked away, his long legs carrying him quickly beyond hearing range—unless she shouted. Which she wasn't about to do.

"Sonofabitch," she said, trying out the word for the first time. She'd heard it often enough lately. The cowhands used it rather like glue, to stick every other word together. They also used it to describe any and all troubles. In fact, she heard it so frequently that she didn't even think of it anymore as an obscenity. It was a perfectly acceptable expression. Descriptive, too.

"Sonofabitch," she repeated. But, although it helped to vent her frustration, she discovered that swearing did nothing to alleviate it.

Drew grinned as he walked back to the place he'd called his bed last night and gathered up his bedroll. Bloody hell, he enjoyed sparring with her.

He felt better than he had all night, his suspicions about Gabrielle having been laid to rest—or nearly so. He didn't think she had lied about her lack of shooting experience. And the distaste in her voice, when she said she didn't like guns, definitely had been real.

Later today, he would know for sure if she had told the truth. Oh, he knew she would try her damnedest to squirm out of their lesson, but he wouldn't let her, if only because he'd meant it when he told her she should know how to protect herself. Kirby would agree with him on that, would even force it on the lad he knew as Gabe.

As Drew tossed his bedroll into the back of the hoodlum wagon and got on with his duties for the day, he considered his ulterior motives in teaching Gabrielle the finer points of marksmanship. Of course, he would have to take her far enough away from camp that the cattle wouldn't be spooked by the sound of gunfire. Far enough that the two of them would be alone.

Far enough that he could kiss her again.

The farther the cattle drive had moved across the plains, the fewer gullies and streams there were—and Gabe was finding it more and more difficult to maintain her privacy. Unfortunately certain functions still had to be performed.

That morning, she relied upon her usual excuse—the search for wood—to disappear for a few minutes. But she had to walk quite a distance before she found a couple of stunted, mostly dead trees, and it occurred to her as she returned to camp that the lack of convenient shields might become an even bigger problem before the trip was over.

But it wasn't her lack of privacy that most concerned her at the moment. So far, she'd managed to wash her underclothes and her short hair in the hoodlum wagon with a pail of water, when everyone was asleep. If she had to, she'd come up with a way to take care of other personal matters.

But the Scotsman . . . he was a far greater problem.

He was like a dog with a bone. And she was the bone, much to her discomfort.

What made it so completely intolerable was her reaction to him. She didn't understand it. She had been courted in more cities than she could remember. Admirers had flocked backstage after performances, and invitations to dinner had been legion. Wealthy men. Handsome men. Influential men. But she'd never felt the kind of attraction for a single one of them that she felt for Drew Cameron—this fevered anticipation, with heart pounding, pulse throbbing, and blood quickening. All the clichés from books and plays had come alive inside her.

As she helped Pepper get breakfast ready, she found herself both dreading and eagerly anticipating the end of the day, knowing she would see the Scotsman again. And that they would be alone. Her state of anxiety made her somewhat absentminded and earned her a scowl from Pepper, and she tried harder to shove her own troubles aside and focus on the task at hand.

Pepper, she noticed, seemed to be complaining more than usual about his rheumatism, and he left more than usual for her to do. But then, she reasoned, he was also doctoring Kingsley, changing bandages and worrying over him like a mother bear over a cub, mumbling to himself as he did so.

"People go gettin' shot. Ain't no civility no more," he muttered as he puttered slowly about. "Ambush," he added disgustedly.

Kingsley, still on his bedroll by the chuck wagon, tried to move a little but pain added more creases to his lined face.

"Shouldn't be moving," Pepper mumbled.

"Got to go on," Kingsley said and tried again.

Sympathy warred with anger inside Gabrielle, as she watched him. She shouldn't care about his pain, but she did. He'd lost a lot of blood, and the gash alongside his head was ugly. His head must hurt like the furies, and she was sure that even his smallest movement made it worse. Still he persisted, struggling to his feet, until he was upright, hanging on to a wagon wheel.

His eyes were as hard as stones, his face harsh, and

she wondered again what engendered the loyalty she'd encountered among his hands. Perhaps, she thought, because he *was* a hard man, a man who would do anything to hold on to what was his.

The question was, What did *anything* include?

After the hands had eaten, she hitched up the mules to the hoodlum wagon as one of the wranglers hitched mules to the chuck wagon, and both started out. The broad beam of the disreputable hat stayed low on her forehead, protecting her face from the sun. Looking at her gloved hands on the reins, she wondered whether they would ever be as they had been, smooth and without calluses.

How could the Scotsman have any interest in her? Other than to have his questions answered, that is. And did she really want him to be interested in her as a woman? The questions bedeviled her throughout the long, hot, dry day.

Sammy was in the back of the wagon, bawling his protest against the indignity. But he still couldn't keep up with a ten-mile trek. Not yet. Even if he could wreak havoc in camp.

Sammy. Think about Sammy. Think about the theater. Think about music. Don't think about Kingsley. Don't think about the Scotsman.

Don't think about how the devil she was going to persuade Drew Cameron that she didn't know how to shoot a gun.

Billy Bones was actually playful. Frisky. Spirited.

Drew wondered about the changes Gabrielle had wrought upon the horse. It appeared to him that patience, food, and affection had produced nothing short of a miracle. He had been too occupied with his own duties, as well as thoughts of Gabrielle, to notice before, but as he watched the woman and the horse riding beside him, he catalogued the differences. Billy held his head high, his steps were quick and sure, not dragging as they had been when the two appeared at the Kingsley ranch nearly a month ago. His coat was sleek, and his eyes clear.

And Gabrielle? Well, she still had a ways to go, but her seat had improved; she no longer appeared as if she was in danger of falling off at any second. And although she still looked like the ragamuffin he'd first glimpsed, he now noticed the straight back, the willful chin, and the fierce passion in her startling blue eyes.

He longed to get his arms around her.

They rode for a half hour before stopping, far enough away that noise wouldn't stampede the cattle. Drew dismounted, then went over to Billy Bones and offered Gabrielle his hand.

She hesitated, then gave it to him, slipping down into his arms. He enjoyed the feel of her against him, and his hands imprisoned her for a brief moment. She fitted there.

Too well. He didn't want to let go.

She seemed to slide even closer to him, her disreputable hat hitting his chin. While one hand kept her imprisoned, the other released the tie under her chin and took the hat from her head, letting it glide to the ground.

He could see her eyes now, the beautiful blue eyes that could make a man weak. Hell, they *did* make him weak. Her dark hair swirled in tendrils around her face, and he knew why she always kept the damn hat on. She looked utterly female to him now, and the confusion in her eyes made him feel protective. And lustful.

It had to be magic, he thought, sorcery of some kind, that she practiced upon him, for he simply had never felt this way with any other woman. Tender and protective and, at the same time, nearly overwhelmed with desire. His hand brushed a curl from her face, and he knew she'd washed it recently. The texture was silk against his fingers, the softness of her skin irresistible.

He leaned down, letting his lips brush hers, and her response stifled any scruples or reservations he had. Her lips were warmly inquisitive, and her hands circled his neck tentatively, her fingers creating rivers of fire that raged through him.

His kiss deepened and her body pressed instinctively into his until the ache in his loins became agony. He wanted this woman, and he'd ceased to care if it was right or wrong, or if it made one whit of sense.

The kiss became frantic, his tongue entering her mouth and searching, seducing until, suddenly, she jerked away.

Staring up at him, panic filling her gaze, she took a quick, ragged breath. "Scotty . . ."

"Drew," he said. "My name is Drew."

She simply continued to stare at him, her eyes bright with a mixture of passion and fear.

"Say it," he said.

"Drew," she obeyed.

He liked the sound of it. The husky quality of her voice was sensual, enticing.

His thumb and index finger played with her chin, then ran up and down her cheek. "How did you do this?" he asked.

"Do what?" The words were more like a sigh.

"Darken your skin."

She worried her lip before answering. "A dye."

"How did you learn about it?"

"An actress taught me."

"What else did she teach you?"

Caution flickered in her eyes, and she lowered her gaze and tried to turn away.

"Not this time, Gabrielle," he said, his hand capturing her elbow and turning her back toward him. "What else did this actress teach you?"

"To beware of men," she said angrily, twisting to get away.

He didn't let go.

"Too bad you didn't pay attention," he said silkily. "A trail drive is hardly a place to avoid them."

"I thought you were going to teach me to shoot," she said, tugging her arm from his grasp.

"I thought you didn't want to learn."

"I changed my mind."

"So did I. I would much rather do something else."

With her arms wrapped around her waist, she gazed up at him, and he saw in her eyes a thousand different things: fear and passion, defiance and longing. Mostly, though, he saw her confusion.

His heartbeat quickened. She was smart and funny and full of grit, and he liked her. He liked her quite a lot, despite knowing that it was a bloody fool thing to do.

He knew nothing about commitment, about caring deeply for someone. Most of all, though, he feared her secrets. He didn't think he could survive the ruin inevitably caused by secrets and lies. Not again.

Drew sighed. He wanted to touch her, to kiss her, to bed her. He ached to do it. And he could. He knew it as surely as he knew his own name. Yet, he hesitated. And finally he backed away, thinking as he did so that it was a bloody poor time to develop a conscience.

"All right," he said, drawing the pistol from his holster and holding it out to her.

Gabrielle stared at it as if it were a rattlesnake, and he knew instantly that she'd been telling the truth. She really didn't like guns.

"I've got my own," she said, and she turned, opening the flap of her saddlebag and pulling out her weapon.

Drew's eyebrows shot upward in surprise. He didn't know what he'd expected—probably a derringer, a lady's gun, or some falling apart ancient pistol. But she turned back to him holding a Colt. Putting his own gun back into its holster, he took it from her and examined it to find that it wasn't new but was perfectly serviceable and in excellent repair. It was also loaded.

He emptied the bullets from the chambers and offered it back to her. Before she took it, she bent down, picked up her hat, and plopped it back onto her head. Then, with some hesitation, she took the gun from his hand, seemingly uncomfortable even holding it.

"Just feel it," he said. "Get comfortable with it."

"How can you ever be comfortable with a gun?"

The question startled him. He'd never *not* been comfortable with a gun. Guns of various kinds always had been a part of his life. Hunting was often a social event. He'd never enjoyed it, but his father had made sure he acquitted himself well as a boy. As a man, he'd disdained hunting as he'd disdained so many things his father worshiped.

"In this country," he said, "it appears a necessity."

"And in Scotland?"

"A gentlemanly skill," he said with self-mocking amusement.

"The two seem at odds."

"Aye, they should be," he said, his smile fading. "But that's not the way of the world—not this world, in any event."

"Is America really so different from Scotland?"

"Today it is," he said. "Where I come from, shooting people is frowned upon."

"I think I would like Scotland," she said.

"Ah, but it has a bloody past."

"And we have a bloody present," she said in a low voice.

"Aye, but civilization will come. It always does," he replied, watching her face.

Grief. It darkened her eyes and tugged the corners of her mouth downward. It was real, and it was recent. He watched her struggle to regain control.

"You sound disappointed," she finally said.

"Opportunity often disappears with the coming of civilization," he replied. "With order comes rules."

"And you don't like rules?"

"Not much."

"And you're looking for opportunity?"

"Isn't every man," he said, then added, "and woman?"

The air was sizzling between them. He was barely aware of the words being spoken. He couldn't take his eyes from her.

"And how far would they go . . . for opportunity?"

"Ah, now that is a good question," he said. His hand touched her chin. "How far would *you* go?"

She moistened her lips, her eyes locked with his. Then, abruptly, she stepped back, as if burned, and turned her attention to the gun in her hand.

"Are you going to show me how to use it?"

She always changed the subject when he asked anything personal, and he was determined to get beyond that gate. "You haven't answered my question. How far would you go, Gabrielle?"

She looked at the gun. "I think you must have been a snake-oil salesman."

"Ouch," he said. "You wound me. I do have a few standards, and wasting alcohol in such a fashion wouldn't meet them. I'm an adventurer, yes. A gambler admittedly, even a rogue at times, but never a charlatan."

Her eyes lit with interest. "A rogue?"

"Of the first order," he admitted cheerfully.

"What does a rogue do?"

He raised one eyebrow. "Ah . . . a well-bred young lady would know better than to ask."

She looked down at her clothes. "Do I look like a well-bred young lady?"

He chuckled. "You look delectable. And I suspect you *are* a lady."

She studied her fingers, playing nervously with the gun.

He put a hand on hers. "Be very careful with that. I like my body parts."

She looked startled. Alarmed. She really *didn't* like the gun.

"Hold it firm, lass," he said. "Try the trigger." He watched her for a moment, then pulled the dilapidated hat from her head.

"That's an improvement," he said, grinning.

She started to grab for it, but he threw it several feet away and grabbed her when she started to go after it.

"I can't put my arms around you with that bloody hat in my face," he said lazily.

Her shocked gaze flashed to his, but before she could protest, he stepped behind her and put his arms around her, lifting her hand holding the gun. "To teach you the intricacies of the weapon, lass," he said in a voice meant to be reassuring. Or was it? He enjoyed teasing her, enjoyed knowing he had her as off balance as she had him.

"It seems simple enough," she retorted. "You pull the trigger."

He chuckled. "Try it. Aim at something."

She looked around, her eyes lighting as they reached him.

"I dinna mean me," he said. "And there are no bullets."

"I can wish, can't I?" she retorted.

"Ah, lass, that's an unkind thing to say." He looked around, spied the hat.

His large hand fit around hers, showing her how to grip the gun. "Pull the trigger easy," he said. "Never rush a shot."

When he was satisfied that she understood the basic principle, he loaded the gun and handed it back to her.

"Now aim at the hat and pull the trigger. Slowly. The pistol will jerk, so be prepared."

She gave him an indignant glare. "My hat?"

He shrugged. "A bullet can hardly do it any more harm."

"Hmph."

She half-turned away from him and took aim at the hat. He had to stifle a laugh as he watched her chew her bottom lip and squint in concentration. A full minute passed, he could swear, before she finally pulled the trigger, and when she did, her whole body jerked as the revolver kicked in her hands. The bullet stirred a pile of dust two feet to the left of her hat.

But he wasn't concerned with her lack of accuracy. Her hands were shaking, and he suddenly realized what courage it had taken for her to pull the trigger. Her distaste for guns went beyond a simple fear of the unfamiliar, or even a healthy respect for a lethal weapon. It was something primal, something born of experience. And it was connected to the raw grief he'd seen in her eyes only a short while ago.

Feeling as if he were finally getting close to unlocking a great mystery, he moved to put his arms around her again. "Gabrielle," he began, once more taking hold of her gun and lifting it. "It won't hurt you. Hold it like . . ."

He trailed off, suddenly aware of her body trembling in his arms. But was it fear? Perhaps. Some of it. Or could she be as aware as he was of the electrifying heat surging between them? Could she feel the waves of tenderness and yearning that poured out of him, having her here, like this, surrounded in his embrace?

He tried to ignore his hunger, tried to keep his voice even, but he heard the hoarse quality of it as he spoke. "Squeeze slowly," he said, "and hold it in both hands."

She leaned back, into him, as she fired again, guided by his hands. The bullet hit the hat, sending it scooting across the ground a foot or so before it came to rest on its side. She made no sound of triumph, uttered no cry of satisfaction. Instead, she seemed to sink into him.

Hell, he'd known holding her was a mistake. Yet, he'd done it anyway. Even through her layers of clothing, he felt her curves, the curves he'd first seen in the moonlight, when she was clad only in his shirt.

He let go of her hands, and her arms fell to her sides, and he heard a slight thud as the gun slipped from her fingers. When he turned her around to face him, it rocked him to see tears glistening in her eyes.

His hand came up to touch her face, to wipe away the moisture. "Gabrielle?" he whispered her name, his heart pounding.

She looked at him with an intensity that burned through him and a longing that matched his own.

The warning bells were going off inside his head, loud and clear. *You care too much,* a voice told him. *She'll hurt you, betray you, lie to you.* But he didn't care. For once in his life, he was going to ignore the voice and follow his heart, devil be damned.

Throwing caution to the wind, Drew pulled Gabrielle into his arms and brought his mouth down to cover hers.

Chapter Eleven

Gabrielle's response was pure desperation, a shelter from the intense pain surging through her. Her lips sought Drew's with frantic urgency.

Holding her father's gun, feeling it, remembering the lessons he'd given her with it . . . remembering another gun and the shot fired that had taken her father from her . . . all of it had come flooding back to engulf her with grief. It hadn't taken any effort at all to pretend she didn't like guns. She'd wanted to throw the Colt away, to run from the memories that swamped her.

Instead, she buried herself in Drew's embrace, lost herself in his kiss. He felt so warm, so strong, so *alive*. He made *her* feel alive. She knew in her heart that there was something strong and pure and splendid between them. There had been from the night at the river when he'd saved her life. And she wanted it. She wanted him.

She felt the pain of grief fade, replaced by

something stronger, more urgent. His mouth caressed hers, giving without demanding. Asking. Waiting.

Her hand went to his face in an impulsive, exploring gesture. She knew so little about him, had suspected so much. And yet, she knew she was losing her heart to him.

The tenderness of his lips, the fierce longing in his kiss, the protectiveness of his arms around her, made her feel safe. And complete as she'd never felt before.

The warmth of his touch as his hands circled her waist drifted inward, spawning tremors that ran to every part of her body. His lips were smooth and strong, gentle beyond comprehension. She hadn't known it was possible for there to be such sweetness between man and woman. Her lips melted under his, her body sliding against his until they were almost one. Electric, hot tension flowed through her, right down to her toes.

The kiss turned searing, full of need, full of promise. She felt his body changing, his manhood suddenly pulsing against her, and she knew a corresponding quivering in the innermost part of her. She whimpered with need, with the voracious ache growing deep in her body. Her body strained toward his, arching into him, as his arms tightened around her.

Her whimper drowned in his groan.

His mouth opened, and his tongue began a sensual courtship, magnifying the throbbing yearning within her, the exquisitely painful and delicious need. Her tongue met his with wanton abandon. When she thought she could bear it no more, his mouth left hers, his lips kissing a path to her neck where he ignited a ring of fire with his tongue. She clung to him, feeling the heated tension of his body.

"Gabrielle," he whispered, his very breath sending quakes through her body.

She thought she would explode with the growing need inside her. She looked up at him, at the hazel eyes lit with gold. She swallowed, unable to speak.

"Who are you?" he asked softly. "A sorceress?"

She could only shake her head.

"Ah, Gabrielle. The bloody hell of it is I don't care."

His arms pulled her closer. Heat seared her everywhere as their bodies touched and his lips came down on hers again. And she responded with passion rising from deep within her. Her mouth caressed his, asking, wanting, demanding in some primitive way that she didn't understand..

"Scotty . . ."

"Drew," he corrected, whispering in her ear. "Andrew."

She barely caught his words. She felt dizzy, full of trembling, pulsating sensations.

"Bonny lass," he said. "My gallant, bonny lass," he murmured before his mouth joined hers once more and his hands began to make their way through her layers of clothing.

Her heart was beating rapidly, yet the flow of her blood seemed to have slowed to a heated crawl, as she waited, breathless. His hand touched her breast with several layers still separating them. Yet she felt her breast tighten, harden, his sensitive fingers creating rivers of feeling flowing through her.

He groaned, then started peeling away her clothes: the jacket, then the outer shirt, a second shirt, until he reached the boy's undershirt. Freed from layers of cloth, her breasts strained against the last fabric binding them. And they were sensitive. Her breasts were suddenly so sensitive.

He unbuttoned the undershirt, then untied the binding around her breasts. Slowly, gently, his hands caressed parts of her that no man had ever touched. When he stopped suddenly, she felt a terrible loss. But he took her hand and led her to a dry nest of pine needles, where he guided her down until she was on her knees. He knelt beside her, kissed one hard nipple, then the other. Her back instinctively arched, and she moaned.

Looking down at his tawny hair, she saw the sun's rays had sprinkled it with gold, and thick tendrils had been swept in different directions by the breeze. She touched it, ran her fingers through the thick strands, her hand pressing him to her breast.

And then he lifted his head, and his eyes—golden and fiercely tender—searched her features. "Gabrielle?"

She merely nodded, and her hands went to his shirt. She tried to unbutton it, but her fingers were suddenly awkward. They became entangled in the holes, and she looked to him for help.

He gave her a smile filled with tenderness as his hands caught hers and, together, they finished unbuttoning his shirt. She watched with fascination as it fell open, revealing a hard chest sprinkled with golden hair. Her fingers played with his chest, tracing the outlined muscles, stopping at his nipples, then following the path of hair downward toward his trousers.

She lifted her eyes to his. "You don't have the body of a gambler."

His brows knitted together. "And how would ye be knowin' that?"

"I've seen some," she said airily, trying to regain some of her reason. Her hand, though, was still exploring. And her mind was none too clear. "Gamblers are usually quite . . . like jelly. Because they sit so much," she explained hastily as if afraid he might take offense.

He chuckled, his hand catching hers and bringing it to his mouth, nibbling on her fingers as he watched her, amusement and passion mingling together. "Jelly-like?" he repeated. "I suppose that does rather describe some gamblers I've known."

"Of course, I've never seen any . . . like I'm seeing you," she continued, rather shocked at her own words and their implication.

"I should hope not," he said, "But I'm flattered you don't think I'm . . . jellylike."

Her hand pressed against the rock-hard stomach as if testing it, then wandered up to his shoulder. Her gaze met his, and she felt as if she'd been struck by lightning. Mesmerized, she fought for breath, fought for reason.

"I used to race horses occasionally in Scotland," he said. "Racing steeplechases keeps you fit."

"Steeplechases?" she echoed in astonishment. There seemed no end to his talents.

"Aye. Have you heard of them?"

"Of course," she said, wishing she weren't so dazed, wishing she were alert enough to fit this new puzzle piece into the picture of him she had created in her mind. "I've read about them in books and newspapers. And I went to one once. In New York." She didn't add that, at the time, her family had been playing a local theater.

"But you're larger than most jockeys," she said.

He grinned. "Which is why I had no real future," he said.

She digested that for a moment, then filed it in her mind as she did everything about him. But still, why were they talking about steeplechases?

Her eyes met his, and she knew suddenly that he was deliberately trying to cool the air, to reduce the electricity, the overwhelming sexuality that reverberated between them. His eyes lit, and she knew that he knew exactly what she was thinking.

"You wretch," she said, wanting him closer, wanting so much more than the careless insouciance behind which he always hid. She wanted his strength and generosity and tenderness. She wanted his passion. She ran her fingers seductively up and down his chest, silently exulting when his body shuddered in response.

"I'm not in the habit of taking virgins," he said, his voice hoarse.

Her hand stilled. If he stopped now, she couldn't bear it. The thought of never reaching the pot of gold that lay at the end of the rainbow he'd created inside her was simply unthinkable.

"I'm not a virgin," she said.

I don't like liars. His warning sounded in her mind as the words left her mouth. But she couldn't stop. Not now.

His gaze held hers, searching wanting, she suspected, to believe. She made herself hold steady. She hadn't been wrong. He was honorable. Kind. Gallant. He had saved her life. He had kept his word. And he made her heart sing.

She leaned over, her lips touching his, and then his were crushing down, hungry and demanding, upon hers. He took her down, his body moving on top of hers, only their trousers separating them. Her sensitive breasts touched the bare skin of his chest, feeling the tickle of the springy golden hair. She lost her breath for a moment in the deliciously erotic sensation. But then another, stronger sensation took its place.

He pressed against her, his manhood swelling and pulsating even through cloth, creating a need inside her so strong, so carnal, she gasped.

He moved quickly, stripping away his trousers, then hers, then he sat back on his heels to gaze down at her. And she let her gaze wander over him, his form all grace and power. Reaching out, his hands explored her body, slowly, seductively until she arched uncontrollably. His hand touched the most intimate part of her, caressing until she felt on fire. Then, he positioned himself above her, his manhood barely touching the curve between her legs, then slowly lowered himself until his naked body covered hers, his manhood resting against her.

His lips rained kisses everywhere, her eyes, her cheeks, her neck, and then back to her mouth. With his knee, he nudged her thighs apart, and suddenly she felt him pressing against the most sensitive part of her. His lips slid down her neck, and he whispered her name. She felt his manhood probe deeper. She bit her lips as the pressure inside her increased. But she couldn't prevent the sound that escaped her when pressure suddenly turned to pain, sharp and unexpected.

"Oh!"

"Bloody hell."

He stopped, his face buried against her neck, his breathing ragged, every muscle in his body tense. She could feel his manhood throbbing inside her. And slowly, as the pain receded, her body instinctively arched up toward him, aching for whatever lay waiting.

Still, he hesitated, and, nearly frantic, she wondered if he actually might leave her, even now. Instinctively, her arms tightened around him, at the same time that the passage inside her seemed to wrap about his manhood, embracing it.

Groaning, murmuring incoherent words against her skin, he started moving again, slowly at first, then with an accelerating rhythm, until she didn't think she could bear more, that she would disintegrate from the white hot heat.

Waves of pleasure increased a hundredfold before erupting into a glorious fireball of sensation. Convulsive spasms rocked her at the same time she felt him tense, then suddenly, plunge into her deeply, with total abandon a final few times. And they held tight to each other, riding the aftershocks of pure pleasure.

As he collapsed onto her, she continued to feel his fullness, felt herself wrap around him and hold him close. She had never felt so drained, yet so utterly content.

Drew fought to suppress the anger inside him as he basked in fulfillment. But in the end, he lost the battle. She had lied to him again. He couldn't deny the pleasure her lie had afforded him, but pleasure was a fleeting thing. Betrayal lasted a lifetime.

Sighing, he rolled away from her, stretching out on his back next to her to stare at the late-afternoon sky. The sun was sinking toward the horizon and, overhead, bright blue was dappled with pink and golden tones.

Her hand was intertwined in his, and she was silent, but her fingers moved against his. She had given him the greatest gift a woman could give a man, and he felt humbled by it. She must have had many chances before this, for she was lovely and completely desirable. He wanted to say tender things to her. He *should* say tender things.

But he simply couldn't catapult the lie.

"Why?" he asked. "Why did you lie to me?"

He felt, more than saw, her flinch.

A moment of silence passed, then in a low, clear voice, she said, "Do you really have to ask?"

He turned his head and looked into her eyes. God, but they were blue. Such an intense blue. And all that intensity was focused on him. Tenderness, something that might even be close to love, surged through him.

But he didn't want love, didn't trust it. He had no idea how to give it, or take it.

"I told you never to lie to me again." His voice wasn't even his own. It sounded scratchy, harsh.

"I'm not sorry," she said softly. "I could never be sorry for what just happened. Please don't you be."

He wasn't. Deep in his heart he wasn't. That's what scared him.

Scared? Bloody hell, he was *terrified*.

His hand went to her face, tracing its contours, hesitating at the corner of her mouth. "How many other lies?" he asked softly.

She hesitated, and he knew there were others. A heavy lump settled in his heart. He didn't know if he could survive many more untruths.

"How many?" he said again.

Her fingers pressed tightly against his. "There are . . . some things I can't tell you," she said.

"There's no one after you," he said, probing as he watched her eyes.

She nodded her head. "That *is* true."

His anger transferred to that other person, that unknown assailant who would dare to harm her. "Why?" he asked. "Why can't you tell me the all of it?"

"Because I don't know the all of it," she said. "I only know that a person I loved very much was killed. And someone shot at me."

"A person you loved?" Jealousy stirred within, completely unfamiliar, distinctly uncomfortable. "Who was it?" he asked.

"A relative," she said.

"I thought you *did* know all of it," he said. "Your father the banker, selling you in marriage to a creditor. A friend being hurt trying to help you." He suddenly realized his anger ran so deep because he cared so much about her. Each of her lies was a dagger in his heart.

He rolled away from her and buttoned his shirt, then found his pants and pulled them on. He threw her clothing over to her, ignoring the pain in her eyes.

"Drew?"

"Get dressed," he said coldly and turned away, going over to the horses. He closed his eyes, an avalanche of regret rolling through his body. He had to get her out of his system. But how could he when she'd claimed a deeper place than anyone ever had? How could he love a woman he didn't trust?

His father's voice, speaking words he hadn't wanted to hear, echoed through his mind. *Your mother was a whore. You're not my son. Is that what you wanted to know?* He hadn't wanted to know, but he'd *needed* to know. And the words had explained so much. But they'd come too late, when he was grown, and the damage had been done to a bewildered little boy who had never understood why he was hated so. By the time he'd learned why, he'd already lost any ability he might have had to trust. And he'd already been convinced he wasn't worthy of someone else's love.

He felt as if he'd been given a glimpse of heaven only to be jerked back, mere moments later, into hell.

He turned. Gabrielle had pulled on her trousers and a shirt. Her short hair was tousled from his hands, from their lovemaking, and her lips were swollen. Her eyes, as she straightened to look at him, were beseeching, but her back was ramrod straight.

"I'll never be sorry," she said defiantly.

A gnawing ache filled his belly. He wanted to take her in his arms and whisper sweet words to her. He wanted to slide back into her and know the ecstasy of their mating. He wanted to do all that, and more— and he could; she would welcome him.

But he didn't trust her.

"*I* am," he said bitterly. "Let's go."

Mounting his horse, he rode away, leaving her to don the remainder of her clothes, mount alone, and ride in his dust.

Gabrielle knew she'd made a mistake. She had known it from the beginning, but she hadn't realized how truly dreadful a mistake it had been. Not until she'd seen the emptiness, the pain, the utter desolation in Drew's eyes. Eyes that had completely dismissed her.

She wanted to tell him the truth. All of it.

But how could she? She'd seen for herself Drew's affection and concern for Kingsley. How could she tell him that she thought his friend was a murderer? How could she make him choose?

And what if he chose Kingsley?

She would die.

But could that pain be worse than what she was experiencing at this very moment? Would it really be any worse to have him choose his friend over her than to have him ride away without a backward glance only minutes after he'd made love to her?

She could still feel the fullness of him inside her, the touch of his hands on her body, the tenderness of his kisses on her lips.

She also felt the tears trickling down her cheeks.

What had she done?

Chapter Twelve

---✦---

The following morning, Gabrielle bounced along on the seat of the hoodlum wagon, her eyes peeled for Indians. She thought the terrain appeared incapable of sustaining any form of life. The plains were an endless sea of parched dirt, broken only by piles of stones and scrub. The desolation surrounding her was a match for her mood.

She'd spent a restless night, wondering if she should tell Drew everything. Should she trust his instincts and basic integrity with her life? The answer was always the same: She wanted to tell him. But what if he didn't believe her? What if she were forced to leave the drive, never to know the truth about Kingsley? Worse, what if, by telling Drew, she put him in danger, too?

The wagon banged over a rock she hadn't noticed, and she nearly fell off the seat. Trying to stay alert, she gripped the reins of the mules and sighed.

She'd learned a few new facts about Kingsley that morning over the breakfast cook fire. A couple of the drovers had been talking, and she'd overheard one say that the trail boss had started the Circle K twenty-five years ago with a small stake.

Twenty-five years ago. At that same time, her father had left Texas for the East, with a stake of his own and a secret that would eventually kill him. Impossible that it could be coincidence.

But what could she do with the information? It proved nothing. It merely helped to confirm her suspicions.

The day wore on slowly. She spent many hours watching the wagon ahead of her, thinking about the injured cattleman riding inside of it. Thinking, too, about Pepper, for whom she'd come to feel a grudging respect, even affection.

He hadn't felt well again this morning. His arthritis, he'd said, was acting up. He'd left many of his chores to her, including the bread baking, which told her exactly how ill he must feel. Bread and pies were his pride. He'd never allowed her to touch either. She had watched and learned, though. Her bread hadn't been as light as his, but it had been acceptable.

She should feel proud, she guessed. Satisfied with her accomplishment. But all she felt was heartbroken. And no matter what she tried to think about, her mind wandered back to the look on Drew's face as she'd seen him over the cook fire—cool, impersonal, indifferent, his eyes devoid of emotion.

The look haunted her throughout the long, hot day.

Every movement of the wagon hurt like hell, but Kirby was more concerned about Pepper than himself. As he lay on the hard bench inside the chuck wagon, trying not to fall off as they bumped over the rock-hard ground, he pondered the old man's behavior. He wasn't convinced that arthritis was the only thing causing Pepper difficulty. Watching him now, through the wagon's open front, Kirby noted Pepper sitting stiffly on the seat, driving the mules automatically without his usual picturesque curses. The simple fact he wasn't grousing was a sure sign that something was wrong.

Dammit, *everything* had gone wrong on this drive. The stampede, Juan's death and Ace's injuries. The ambush. The delays. This morning, he'd noticed that even Cameron had grown tight-lipped and silent, and Kirby had to wonder if the devil was riding his trail.

Shifting on the bench in a futile effort to get comfortable, he heaved a sigh. He wished Damien would return from scouting. He'd been gone since yesterday before dusk and should have been back by now. Maybe, he thought, it hadn't been wise to send his nephew out as scout, but he'd had little choice. Somebody had to do it, and no one else knew the territory or had the experience.

With another deep sigh, Kirby peered through the front of the wagon and spoke to his cook. "Pepper?"

"Huh?"

"You all right?"

"Gettin' old, that's all."

"That kid . . . ?"

Pepper grunted. "He's doin' okay. Better'n I 'spected."

Kirby was silent, weighing the response. It was high praise, coming from Pepper, but had the kid really earned it—or was Pepper saying it because he knew he was failing?

Thinking about the trail ahead, Kirby remembered a trading post thirty miles north where there was a doctor. He'd see to it that Pepper got a good looking over when they got there.

He eyed the old man's back. "We've seen a lot of drives together, haven't we, Pepper?"

"Yep."

"Are they getting harder or are we getting older?"

"Mebbe you outta leave 'em to yer nephews."

"You think they're ready?"

Pepper's reply was silence.

"I don't either," Kirby sighed.

Pepper grunted.

"What do you think of Cameron?"

"Scotty?"

"Yeah."

"Don' know what he's doin' here. He ain't no drover."

"He's learning 'cow.' "

Pepper shook his gray head. "He's a wanderer, that one. Never does stay still. Ridin' off every chance he gets."

"You saying you don't trust him?"

"Ain't sayin' nuthin' of the kind," Pepper growled. "He saved Ace. That's a fact. Jus' sayin' he's a wanderer."

"Like you."

"Like I *used* to be." Pepper was silent for a moment or two, then grumbled, "I didn' tell ya b'fore 'cause I wanted t' come along, but I've got me a bad ticker. It's been slowin' me down some, more 'n I reckoned on."

Kirby stiffened. He'd known Pepper for twenty years or more. The old man had been cook for the outfit, on and off, throughout that time. He would disappear for a year or two then come back. "Just got itchy feet," he'd report. He'd obviously recognized a kindred spirit in the Scotsman.

"I want the doc at Haley's Trading Post to check you out," Kirby said.

When Pepper didn't protest, he felt his heart sink, and as he lay back on the bench and closed his eyes, worry pressed down on him. Worry about Pepper, about where Damien could be, about getting the herd to Abilene without further mishaps. Most of all, he worried about who was out there, waiting for him, waiting to kill him.

He counted three possibilities. Three men's names. And he thought about those men, and the man he'd been when he'd known them, as he endured the long, hot, pain-filled day.

Drew worked the pinto to get a wayward cow back into the herd. Really, the pinto sprinted ahead of the steer and drove it back where it belonged without much effort on his part. Still, he enjoyed the action and almost would have welcomed another sudden spurt of independence from one of his charges.

Hell, he'd have welcomed *any* diversion from thoughts of Gabrielle.

Because of the danger from Indians, the wagons were staying close now, not moving several miles in front of the herd. He could see the back of the hoodlum wagon, jostling along in the ruts other wagons had made as they passed this way. Riding left point he couldn't even get her out of his sight, much less his mind.

Don't think about her. Think about something else. Think about owning a ranch. Think about Ben and Lisbeth. Think about anything but Gabrielle....

He thought about Indians. Not that he knew enough about them to occupy his thoughts for long. He had seen a few in towns, usually on foot, and he'd listened to tales about their horsemanship, their fierceness, their atrocities. He'd heard enough to make him want to know more about the wild men of the plains. The part of him that was Scot sympathized with their desire to remain free, to fight off their would-be conquerors, as his people had fought the English for several hundred years. His people, too, had been slaughtered.

As he was dwelling on these gloomy thoughts—which, anyway, were an improvement on even gloomier thoughts of the woman driving the wagon ahead of him—he saw Damien riding toward the herd.

He spurred his horse forward, wondering what had

kept him so long. He knew Kirby had worried like hell.

"Small detachment of cavalry ahead," Damien said, pulling in to ride beside him. "The lieutenant says a bunch of renegade Kiowas took off from the reservation with some of their families. They've been sighted north of here. Some Utes, too. Those two tribes are blood enemies. And both are probably needing food."

Frowning, Drew muttered, "All we need now is to get caught in the middle of an Indian war."

Damien hesitated, then said, "Uncle Kirby says you're good with that rifle. Go on up and ride with the wagons." Without waiting for a reply, Damien rode back to warn the other drovers.

Drew spurred his horse, heading for the chuck wagon. When he reached it, he paced alongside the bench. Pepper grunted at his arrival. Kirby, his head still wrapped in bandages and his face sheet-white, was sitting on the bench beside the cook. He was holding a rifle.

He nodded to Drew. "Damien told you?"

Drew nodded.

"We can't lose this wagon," Kirby said. "There's no place in Indian Territory to replace it."

"We won't," Drew said.

"If we see any Indians, we'll try to bargain with them for a few head of cattle. Don't shoot first."

"I understand."

Kirby glanced at him. "You ever shoot from horseback?"

Drew shook his head. "Just that night of the stampede, and then I wasn't aiming at anything."

"It's hard as hell to hit anything," Kirby said. "Wait till your target's close."

Drew shifted in his saddle. "How close?"

"Within touching distance," Kirby said with a wry smile.

Drew looked at him askance, thinking he couldn't be serious.

Kirby raised an eyebrow. "Still thinking about the cattle business?"

"Aye," Drew said. "Never a dull moment."

Kirby nodded. "I'm glad you're with us. Now, you'd better go back to the hoodlum wagon and tell the kid what's happening. You teach him anything about shooting?"

"One lesson," Drew muttered.

"Better give him another one tonight."

Not bloody likely, Drew thought. But he nodded, then started to turn his horse around. He stopped, though, when he caught a glimpse of Pepper's face under the brim of his hat. While Kirby's was pale, Pepper's face was a dull red. And his hands were decidedly unsteady on the reins.

Drew's gaze went back to Kirby. Kirby met his gaze, and Drew saw instantly that he wasn't the only one who was worried about the old cook.

"My horse needs some rest," he said. "After I talk to Two-Bits, why don't I drive your team for a while." It was a lame excuse. Ridiculous, really. The remuda was just to the right of the herd, and he could have replaced his mount any time he wanted. But Kirby nodded, and Pepper didn't argue. Something was wrong, Drew realized, something more than worry over renegade Indians.

He turned the pinto and rode back to the hoodlum wagon, pacing his horse next to Gabrielle.

She looked at him warily from under the hat that now sported a bullet hole. Her expression was curious—and guarded.

"Army says there's Kiowas and Utes north of here," he said. "Keep your eyes open. I'm going to ride in the chuck wagon with Pepper and Mr. Kingsley."

She gave him a short nod in reply.

"Pepper doesn't look well," he continued, wondering whether she'd noticed anything.

"He says it's his arthritis acting up."

So she had noticed something, although Drew couldn't help but think it might be more serious that arthritis.

He continued to ride next to her, reluctant to leave her side, yet having no real excuse to stay. "Remember what I taught you," he said finally.

She turned her head and met his gaze directly, and he saw in her eyes all the pain and confusion he'd caused.

"I remember *everything you taught me*," she said.

His jaw tightened, his lips thinning to a grim line. He had not even bid her goodbye yesterday when they'd returned to camp. Bloody hell, he'd felt deceived all over again, bewildered by the slip of a girl who had turned him inside out, then twisted his guts with lies.

"About the gun, lass," he said.

"I remember."

"Stay right behind the other wagon."

She nodded.

He hesitated, then rode ahead again to the chuck wagon. Slipping his rifle from the scabbard, he handed it to Kirby, then took the lariat from his saddle horn and tied one end to his reins. Moving to the back of the wagon, he leaned over and tied the other end of the rope to the back bow. Then he slipped down and took several rapid strides to swing up onto the bench. The other two men made way from him.

He took the reins from Pepper and watched as the older man made his way inside to lie down on his bench.

Kirby spoke quietly. "He just told me he has a bad ticker. I may have to leave him at Haley's."

"Haley's?" Drew said.

"Trading post where we'll get supplies. It's two days away, maybe three if we run into trouble. And that seems to be all we're doing." He paused for a moment, then asked, "How's the kid doing?"

Drew shrugged. "Indians don't seem to worry—" He stopped short, realizing he'd almost said "her."

Perhaps, he should. Perhaps Kirby should know. Bloody hell, Kirby definitely should know. Yet Drew couldn't quite bring himself to give up Gabrielle's secret.

"Has there ever been a woman on a cattle drive?" he asked, hoping to hell he sounded more casual than he felt.

Kirby gave him a knowing look. "Getting lonesome? There's usually some, uh, soiled doves at Haley's. Competition's pretty stiff when a trail drive hits."

"Just curious," Drew said.

"I know of one or two men who take their wives along on drives," Kirby said. "But there's damned little privacy on the trail, and I wouldn't want one along. What in the hell would you do with a woman on a drive, anyway?" He gestured ahead with the barrel of his rifle. "Next water hole we come on, most of the men will take a bath."

Drew had his answer, and it only served to make him feel even more torn in his loyalties. Should he honor his bond of friendship with Kirby? Or should he honor the bond he'd created last night with the woman who had given him her virginity? The woman whom, despite lies and everything else, he was coming to love. God help him.

The day wore on. Undulating expanses of prairie stretched as far as Drew could see, and there was no sign of galloping, painted braves. Kirby rested inside the wagon with Pepper, and Drew drove the team, with three rifles lying at his feet.

They stopped early in the afternoon beside the Washita River. Drew unhitched the team. Pepper got down and opened the wagon boot, where all the pans and the staples were housed. But as Drew helped him take out the Dutch oven, the cook fell, his hand going to his chest. Drew caught him. The cook's precious oven clattered to the ground.

As Drew eased Pepper down to lie on the hard-packed earth, Gabrielle, who had unhitched her own team, sprinted toward them, her face full of distress.

Pepper struggled to sit, leaning against a wagon wheel. Seeing Gabrielle, he frowned and waved her away. "Don' jus' stand there. Get supper started."

Drew watched her face. There was nothing blank about it now, nothing concealed. Anguish filled her eyes.

"Pepper?" she whispered.

"You deef?" the cook said. His face was no longer red but a pasty color, and his breathing was labored. His hand clutched at his chest, but his gaze was steely.

She shook her head. "I'll start the fire."

The old man seemed to relax. "You can do it now. You can do it all. Smart lad." He closed his eyes, and his body slumped against the wheel.

Kirby, who had climbed out of the wagon as quickly as his injuries allowed, kneeled next to Pepper, taking his hand. "Don't do this to me. Damn it, Pepper, don't do it."

Drew leaned over, felt for a pulse in the man's neck, unsurprised to discover that there was none. He stood, heaving a sigh as he leaned against a wheel. Then he glanced at Gabrielle.

She was standing absolutely still, tears glistening in her eyes. She turned away, stumbled. Then, with a shuddering sigh, she straightened, turned, and walked briskly toward the hoodlum wagon.

He went after her.

They reached the hoodlum wagon at the same time, and he watched as she reached blindly inside for wood, spilling several pieces as she lifted out others.

He put his hands on her shoulders, and she jerked away, huddling against the wagon. Her shoulders heaved.

"Gabrielle," he said softly.

She turned around, used the back of her hand to wipe away a tear. "I'm all right," she said.

"I don't think you are."

"Why do you even care?" she said, her voice filled with bitterness.

"God help me, I do," he said.

"I don't need you," she said. "I don't want you."

"Ah, lass . . ."

She spun on him. "I'm not your lass." Reaching down, she picked up the wood she'd spilled. "Pepper," she said with dignity, "would want me to get supper."

And with that, she walked swiftly away, leaving him standing there, in awe of her courage—and aching to hold her and take away her pain.

They buried Pepper as the last glow of the retreating sun bronzed the horizon. Every man not on duty stood at graveside while Kirby, a Bible in his hand, read a passage from Psalms.

Gabrielle stood beside the grave with the others, twisting her hat in her hands. She barely noticed the curious stares the drovers cast at her short curls. All of them were holding their hats, too, and it would have been stranger still for her to have kept hers on. At the moment, she didn't care what anyone thought. She was simply miserable and couldn't imagine things getting any worse.

Kingsley's voice was awkward, broken as he spoke. She had come to realize that the two men—the rancher and the cook—had been friends for a long time. Kingsley's pain as he read the Twenty-third Psalm was obvious. She didn't want to sympathize with him, but she did.

When he finished, each person turned a shovelful of dirt into the grave. She took the shovel from Drew, her hands unsteady as their fingers touched for a split second. She scooped up her share of dirt and tossed it in, then passed the shovel on to Damien. Drew started a song, a hymn she recognized, and the others joined him. She mouthed the words, knowing that her contralto voice would give her away, if her curls already hadn't. And then the men moved slowly away, leaving Kirby and Drew to raise a rough wooden cross that Drew had fashioned.

She had cooked some salt pork and beans, along with fresh bread. The bread still didn't have the lightness of Pepper's, nor the beans the spice, but she heard no complaints. The drovers always muttered as they ate Pepper's beans—right before they came back for second helpings. She figured she had not yet earned their muttering. It was a sign of affection and respect.

She would make them mutter, she thought, if it was the last thing she did. For Pepper, she would make them mutter.

Haley's Trading Post had been raided and burned. Only a dog remained, lying beside one of eight mounds of earth, its head tucked between its front paws. The animal barely managed to raise its head to acknowledge the newcomers as Drew rode in with Kirby and Damien beside him.

Drew looked at the ground as they cautiously approached, applying the tracking skills he'd learned over the past month. Unshod hoof tracks were overlaid with shod ones, which probably meant that soldiers had reached the trading post too late but, given that all tracks led off in the same direction, had gone after the culprits.

The tracks headed northwest. The drive was headed straight north. Perhaps, he thought, they could avoid trouble. Although, all things considered, that was probably too much to ask.

Neither Kirby nor Damien spoke as they dismounted and walked slowly around to inspect the devastation. Viewing the scene, Drew thought their silence was appropriate. He dismounted, too, and looked over the burned-out timbers, guessing there had been at least four buildings and a corral. The smell of smoke and fire still lingered, but when he touched a charred piece of fencing, it was cold. Two days, he thought, perhaps three.

Looking at Kirby, who was standing at the line of graves with his hat in his hand, Drew saw his friend's shoulders slump. He looked tired. Hell, he had to be hurting, both physically from his wounds and internally from Pepper's death.

Five days after being wounded, the trail boss had insisted on riding again and on assuming the duties of scout. Drew had argued against it, and for once, Damien had been on his side as they'd both tried to persuade Kirby to let someone else do it. But their arguments had fallen on deaf ears. Drew knew they'd been lucky to convince Kirby, at least, to take someone else with him.

Drew didn't understand Kirby's reluctance. It was evident to everyone on the drive that someone had tried to kill him. Was he *trying* to get himself killed? It almost seemed that way. When he left the herd to go riding across the open prairie, grim resignation etched into his face, it was as if he were riding out to meet his death. As if it were his destiny.

Shuddering, Drew tried to shake off the morbid thoughts. Told himself he was letting the burned ruins around him and the days of endless, empty prairie get to him.

Besides, with no gunmen in sight, they had more immediate problems. Kirby had stopped the herd five miles back at a water hole, and they were here, at the trading post, to order supplies. Supplies that wouldn't be here, waiting, when the wagons arrived.

Walking over to stand next to Kirby, he looked at the graves. "Friends?" he asked.

"Not particularly," Kirby said. "Haley wasn't the friendliest man on earth. He overcharged drovers and sold guns and liquor to the Indians. But he was the only damned supplier in a hundred miles."

Gesturing toward the remaining seven mounds, Drew asked, "And the others?"

Kirby sighed. "Last time I was here, Haley's had five men and three women working for him. One kept the store, two were half-breeds who handled the stock. There was a blacksmith, and then there was Benedict."

"Benedict?"

"A doctor of sorts." Kirby uttered a harsh laugh. "He could drink more than any man I've ever seen and still remain standing. His fee was usually a bottle of Haley's rotgut. But when he was sober, he could heal man or beast better than any sawbones I've ever known. Stayed here because he had an Indian wife. Whites ostracized her and him, too. Haley left them alone."

Kirby shook his head. "She's one of the reasons Haley had no trouble with Indians. She was a chief's daughter or something. Then, too, Haley wasn't particular about what he traded."

Drew looked around. It would have been a hell of a lonely existence out here in the middle of nowhere. A lonelier death.

Damien walked up to them. "We're running short of supplies, Uncle Kirby. What do we do now?"

"I'm worried more about those damned Indians," Kirby said, waving the hand that held his hat to include the ruins. "It looks like a passel of them."

Damien grunted something affirmative. "Yeah, and it looks like the army's on their tail."

"Humph," Kirby grunted.

Drew knew Kirby shared his fellow Texans' disdain for the U.S. Army, a dislike that ran back to the American 'Civil War.' Tensions still openly simmered from the bloody conflict.

At that moment, their attention was drawn to the lone survivor of the massacre: the dog. They all looked at the end grave when the animal lying next to it let out a brief, plaintive whine.

Drew glanced at the well and saw that the top had been burned. Walking over to his horse, he got his canteen, then walked back to where the dog lay. He poured some water into his hat and offered it to the animal. The dog whined again and tried to stand but couldn't. The animal was holding one of its legs awkwardly, and Drew noticed a deep wound. He pushed the hat under the dog's nose and watched it drink, slowly at first, then frantically.

When the animal was through, it lay down next to the grave again, its head resting on the mound.

Damien drew his six-shooter from its holster.

"No," Drew said sharply.

"It's best for the animal," Damien said. "What in the hell do you want to do with it? Leave it here to die of thirst?"

Drew looked back at the motionless dog, keeping vigil over its master's grave. He couldn't bear to see the beast's loyalty and devotion rewarded with a bullet.

"Two-Bits," he said, "can take of him."

"Ha!" Damien snorted. "Like that damned calf that's always running all over the camp? Besides, we'll be getting a new cook, and who'll take care of the damned animal then?"

Drew shot a look at Kirby.

"He's right, Scotty," the trail boss said. "You know it."

Drew shook his head. "None of us thought Billy was any good, and look at him now. Another month and he'll out-race any horse you have. Two-Bits has a way with animals, you know that."

All three of them turned their gazes back to the dog, who suddenly looked up at Drew as if sensing an ally. Liquid brown eyes regarded him sorrowfully. Of medium size, with thick black and white fur, a long nose, and an intelligent look in his eyes, the animal looked to be a mongrel.

Kirby sighed in resignation. "If you can get him away from that grave, you can bring him along."

Drew flashed him a grateful smile, going down on one knee to run his hand along the dog's fur. It trembled but didn't move, nor did it make a sound. He took the injured paw and flexed it. The leg wasn't broken, but the wound looked infected.

"Come on, boy," he said, urging to dog to its feet. But the animal only looked at him. Drew fished in his pocket and found a piece of jerky, offering that. The dog sniffed it, then put his head back down between his paws.

Damien walked away, snorting in disgust.

Drew swore. Then he thought about Gabrielle, and in his mind he saw her smile. He hadn't seen that dimpled smile recently, not, in fact, since their abbreviated shooting lesson.

He rubbed the dog's head. " 'Tis time for the living, my wee friend," he said in a low voice meant only for the dog's ears. "And I'm knowing a body who needs ye as much as ye need her."

The dog ignored him. Clearly, he didn't understand Highland speech.

Drew sighed, reached down and started to pick up the beast—and promptly got bitten on the wrist.

"Bloody hell!"

"So much for good intentions," Kirby said. "We don't have all day for this."

Drew scowled at the dog. Then, tearing off a piece of his shirt, he tied the dog's mouth shut, ignoring the growling protest. "I canna' leave ye here," he said. He looked up at Kirby. "You don't know who his owner might have been?"

Kirby shrugged. "There's always a lot of dogs around. Might have been Benedict's. I don't think Haley ever cared for a living thing."

Sometimes that didn't matter. Drew knew that as

surely as he knew his own name. He'd tried his bloody damnedest to be loved, only to be kicked and beaten. He'd always come back for more. Too many times.

He picked up the dog and mounted his horse, his left arm holding the squirming furry bundle, trying to ignore its frantic attempts to return to the grave.

"He'll try to come back," Kirby warned him.

"Maybe," Drew said, knowing that Gabrielle would tame the beast. He was sure of it. He didn't trust *her*. But he trusted her gentleness and her compassion.

Dammit, she would love this bloody dog.

Chapter Thirteen

———— ✦ ————

Gabrielle loved the dog from the first moment she saw him. She loved him even more after hearing of his vigil at the grave. But what she loved most was that Drew had brought the animal to her.

With his eyes conveying both tenderness and amusement, he dumped the dog into her arms. "I've brought you some more trouble," he said, his brogue thick and lilting. "And I'm thinking this wagon will soon be resembling a bloody ark."

Joy rushed through her. He *hadn't* entirely given up on her. Yet the knowledge frightened her, too, because she was afraid to hope, afraid to care too much.

Really though it was too late. She already cared too much. Her heart wanted to burst whenever she looked at him, and when their gazes met, she felt tremors of warmth in that place he'd awakened inside her.

She gathered up the ragged piece of fur and hugged him close. Unable to express her gratitude to Drew in words, she let her eyes thank him.

"You'll have to be after naming the beast," he said. "No one knows how he was called."

"Honor," she said suddenly, thinking of the dog's steadfastness by his master's grave. "I think I'll call him Honor."

And Honor was no trouble at all. He was just sad, and Gabrielle spent more time that day with him than she should have, talking to him, telling him that his master had gone to a wonderful place and that he, Honor, had a new home.

Well, maybe he was a little trouble. Because she gave the dog so much attention, supper was late, the beans gravelly, and the bread overcooked. Damien scowled, which he did very well, and Kirby muttered something about how he must be going daft, letting her keep the "damned beast." But he didn't make her give the dog up.

The following morning, as they crossed the river and pushed north, Honor sat next to her on the bench of the hoodlum wagon. She flicked the reins, urging the mules onward, trying to keep pace with the chuck wagon being driven by one of the wranglers. Because of the increased threat of Indian raids, the wagons were still staying closer to the herd than usual. Nerves were stretched to a fine point. Arguments and fights had broken out last night after Kingsley reported his findings at Haley's. Supplies were dwindling, including coffee and sugar.

Gabrielle reached over and stroked the dog, who tolerated her affection without enthusiasm. He'd stopped whining though, and he seemed more relaxed than when Drew had handed him to her. She was still afraid to untie him, afraid he might go back to the ruined trading post.

The plains seemed endless as she looked out across them, her eyes watchful. She was the sole cook now, until Kingsley replaced her. Before he did, she planned to use the access that her new position afforded her to sneak a look at the trail boss's belongings. Not that she had any expectation that such a search would produce hard evidence that Kingsley had murdered her father. It was simply the only thing she could think of to do that might, at least, give her a clue about the man she'd found so difficult to know.

She stroked Honor again as guilt welled up in her. She didn't want to use Pepper's death for her own advantage. She had grown to care about the man and his gruff ways.

Nor had she been raised to think it was acceptable to invade someone else's privacy. She couldn't help feeling she was betraying her parents and herself by spying on Kingsley. While her father's last words still echoed constantly in her mind, she nonetheless had formed a grudging respect for the powerful cattleman.

He had hired a young, desperate boy, and for that insolent youth he'd allowed a broken-down horse to come on a long, hard trail drive. He'd stayed the execution of a newborn calf who'd had to be carried in a wagon. He'd given a reprieve to a dog who was sure to have died and who would need to be fed from their dwindling supplies. And he'd been close to tears, speaking over the grave of a man he'd called friend for twenty years—she was sure of it.

Gabrielle was desperate to reconcile Kingsley's behavior with the image she had painted of him in her mind as a cold-blooded killer, and for that reason alone, she would put aside her scruples and her self-respect to search his belongings. She had, at best, ten days on the trail before they reached the next town, where Kingsley would try to find a new cook. Ten days to learn the truth.

And ten days of being totally responsible for the care and feeding of sixteen drovers—with only limited supplies to accomplish the task.

Hoofbeats interrupted her thoughts, and she peered around the edge of the wagon to see Kingsley himself galloping toward her.

"Canadian River ahead, about one mile," he

shouted. "We stay on this side overnight, then cross at dawn."

She nodded, watching as he galloped off to tell the others. Since nearly drowning, she'd come to hate river crossings, although some were worse than others. She hoped the Canadian River was shallow and skinny.

It wasn't. It was wide and fast-moving, and although the drovers declared that it wasn't very deep, it seemed plenty deep enough to drown in. Gabrielle prepared supper for the drovers, all the while casting unhappy glances at the obstacle she would have to cross, come dawn.

The hands were especially quiet and tired. The constant danger of Indian raids meant they were all doing extra duty, the number of guards on every shift doubling. Throughout the evening, Gabrielle watched weary-eyed men come in for coffee and food and a couple of hours of sleep, then go out again.

Kingsley came in just before sunset from scouting ahead on the other side of the river. Pouring himself a cup of coffee, he tasted it gingerly, then gave her a nod.

"Coffee's right good," he said.

Gabrielle shifted her gaze away from him, confused and at the same time pleased by his praise.

He took a plate of beans and fresh bread and squatted near the fire, where Jake and Legs were already eating.

"You handling everything all right?" he asked her.

She nodded.

"A lot to ask of a kid."

She looked away.

"You think you can hang on another week or so?"

Again, she nodded.

"Dammit, kid, you got a voice?"

She shot him a quick glance. "Didn't know you wanted a voice. Thought you wanted a cook."

Jake and Legs guffawed.

Kingsley smiled too, a crooked smile that was unexpectedly appealing. "Prickly, aren't you?"

She shrugged.

"We got another month to go," he said. "Maybe more. This is too big a job for a stripling."

"And it wasn't too big for an old man?" she retorted without thinking.

Kingsley went rigid, his face paling, and Gabrielle knew she'd gone too far. He'd been fond of Pepper. She'd as much as said he'd killed the old cook by bringing him along, and that hadn't been her intention at all.

Kingsley held his silence, merely finished his meal and coffee, found himself another mount, and rode out to check the herd.

Jake rose and stretched. "I'm going to catch some shut-eye. Have the midnight watch."

Legs stood up, too, and they both walked over to flop down onto their bedrolls.

Gabrielle was alone, the only one near the chuck wagon. Her heart pounded, and she tried to find a reason why it wasn't a good time to carry out her plan. But she knew it might be the only time she would have.

She found an excuse—molasses for the coffee—in case anyone came back into camp and saw her inside the chuck wagon. Then she took a deep breath, looked around to see that no one was in sight but sleeping cowhands, and scrambled into the back end of the wagon.

There was a large box tucked against the back of the bench. She'd seen it several times when fetching something for Pepper. She leaned over to examine it in the dwindling light. The box, one foot long and about six inches wide, was locked. She didn't know what she expected to find in it, but the fact that it was locked caught her attention. It probably contained money, but maybe Kingsley also kept letters in it, or a diary.

Frustrated, she played with the lock for a moment, not wanting to break it or make it look as if it had been forced. After several minutes of futile efforts, she gave up, deciding that she would have to wait. Sooner or later, they would be near a town or a trading post, and Kingsley would buy supplies. Which meant he'd need money. She'd make sure she was around the next time he opened his strongbox, so she could get a glimpse of the contents, and maybe see where he kept the key.

She was still staring at the box when she heard the Scotsman's voice.

"Thinking about taking up banditry?"

Gabrielle pivoted on the balls of her feet. He was standing at the back of wagon, leaning to look inside, an elbow resting where he'd untied a flap.

"I was looking for molasses," she replied indignantly.

"Are you now?" he said softly. "I thought I saw some outside."

"I thought we would need more. It'll be a long night."

"Aye," he said, "and it'll be the devil's own work trying to keep the cattle out of that river tonight. They're as jumpy as the drovers."

Grateful for the change of subject, Gabe moved away from the box, over to a small barrel of molasses, then realized she had nothing to put it in. She felt her face grow hot and knew she had to brazen it through.

She sat down in the middle of the wagon, surrounded by barrels and boxes and Pepper's bed, which she'd declined to adopt, and said, "I forgot to bring in the jar to refill it." She took off her hat and looked up at Drew with eyes that had seldom failed to get her what she wanted.

He wasn't buying it. A muscle in his cheek jumped, and his eyes were cool as he spoke. "Just what are you looking for?"

She decided to go on the attack. "What are you doing here? I thought you were on watch."

"Did Kirby tell you that?" he said. "Is that why you thought it safe to rummage through his things? Is it money you're after? If it is, I can give you some."

Gabrielle felt as low as a worm under a rock. He had thought her a liar, and now a thief. She could hardly deny the first, but the second charge struck straight through to her heart. She couldn't bear to look in his face and see the disappointment. Disappointment in her.

Suddenly, Gabrielle knew that Drew Cameron was more important to her than anything else. More important than Kirby Kingsley, more important than finding justice.

"I don't need money," she said as she stood, bowing her head so she wouldn't hit the top of the wagon. She made her way to where he stood at the opened flap and reached out, asking for his hand.

He gave it to her, wrapping her hand in his, and she felt his strength and his warmth. It would be so easy to slide into his arms, she thought. But the anger in his eyes kept her from acting on the impulse. Instead, she scrambled down without his help to stand beside him.

When she was on her own two feet, weak as they were, she pushed the hat back on her head, pulling it down over her forehead. Then, peering up at him from under it, she searched his features.

She knew that she already had strained his patience to the breaking point. Finding her trying to break into Kingsley's strongbox was undoubtedly the final straw. She'd given him more reason than he ever would need to tell Kingsley what he knew about her.

Unless she gave him a better reason *not* to tell.

Gabrielle turned to survey the camp. Coffee was plentiful, so were the beans, staying hot over coals. A few drovers were asleep under trees. The next watch wouldn't be over for another hour.

Turning back to Drew, she said, "I'm taking Honor for a walk. Would you go with us?"

His eyes narrowed suspiciously. "Aye," he said.

She was aware of his watching her as she went over to the hoodlum wagon to fetch Honor. The dog regarded her approach with little enthusiasm, his head between his paws.

"Ah, Honor," she said, with a lump in her throat. "How can I make you feel better?"

"Time," the Scotsman said behind her. "Time and patience."

She turned around and looked at him. "Do you have time and patience?"

"It's running out, lass," he replied. "Your hourglass is nigh onto empty."

His warning was unmistakable. So was the cool glint in his eyes. She saw no hint of the tenderness he had shown her before, and she doubted that telling him the truth would bring it back. But it was all she had to offer.

Silently, she untied the dog's rope, attached to the wagon wheel. Honor got to his feet readily enough, though his tail still hung glumly between his legs. She gave a slight tug on the rope and he came along, leaving Sammy to bawl in dismay at being left behind.

As she walked, with Drew behind her, Gabrielle felt as tightly wound as wire between telegraph poles.

She reluctantly left the safety of the hoodlum wagon and headed for the patch of scraggly trees upstream that she had scouted earlier. Other trail herders had destroyed almost every patch of green, cut most of the trees, and polluted the water.

They walked in silence for a quarter of a mile, away from any listening ears, over a small rise, where they found some privacy by a giant cottonwood. The tree was too large to be turned into firewood easily and so had managed to survive the cattle drives it had seen pass by. Honor sniffed the ground, his tail raising a trifle as curiosity won over mourning. Gabrielle tied him to the cottonwood, then sat on one of the roots that jutted up from the earth.

The Scotsman leaned against the tree, obviously waiting for explanations she was still loath to give. Her heart's cadence became erratic as she looked up at him. A day's growth of beard roughened the stark planes of his face, and his eyes had the predatory gleam of a mountain cat. His hard, lean body was all power, all strength, and she blushed, remembering the feel of it, bare and warm and vital, on hers.

"Gabrielle?"

She swallowed hard, still uncertain whether this was a good idea. But she would lose him, for sure, if she said nothing. She might lose him anyway, but at least by telling him she had some chance.

Her gaze met his. "I don't know where to start," she said slowly.

"The beginning is usually a good place," he said. "Is Gabrielle your real name?"

"My middle name. My whole name is Maris Gabrielle Parker." She held her breath a moment, wondering if he would recognize it. But his eyes reflected only interest, not familiarity.

"And why is Maris Gabrielle Parker masquerading as a boy on a cattle drive?"

"I didn't lie about someone being after me," she said softly.

"But you did lie about the reason," he finished.

She lowered her head. "Yes."

"So, what *is* the reason you're being followed?"

She couldn't keep staring up at him. She held out her hand. He hesitated for a moment, then took it and sat next to her.

The silence stretched between them for several moments.

"Gabrielle?" he persisted.

"I don't know whether I can trust you," she said desperately.

An instant of silence passed, then he spoke in ironic

tones. "*You're* worried about trusting *me*? And what in bloody hell have I done that makes you think you can't?"

She hesitated, then said slowly, "You're friends with . . . with Mr. Kingsley."

She felt his body stiffen beside her, felt his fingers go rigid as they were wrapped around hers, but he didn't speak.

"Swear you won't tell him," she said desperately. "Swear it."

"I canna' do that," he said. "Not till I know what I'd be swearing to."

She looked at him, pleading. "I think that Kirby Kingsley had my father murdered."

Drew's mouth actually dropped open. "Kirby?"

"Yes," she said miserably.

He stared at her for a moment, then uttered a harsh laugh. "You're daft," he said, letting go of her hand.

She wrapped her arms around her waist, hugging herself as she shook her head. "I'm not daft. My father . . . James Parker . . . was killed three months ago in San Antonio. In the street. I was with him. The gunman shot at me, too, but Papa threw himself on top of me before the man could get a clear shot. I didn't get a good look at the gunman, only a quick glimpse. He was at the end of the boardwalk, a long way off, and it was dark. Papa died in my arms, but . . . but before he died, he said, 'Kingsley. It's him. Danger.' "

Drew went on staring at her for what seemed a long time as if she'd lost her mind. Finally, he gave his head a shake, saying, "This is insane. Maybe we'd better back up. Tell me what were you doing in San Antonio."

Gabrielle bit her lip. Many considered actresses and singers, who entertained in saloons as well as music halls, to be only one rung up on the ladder from the oldest profession in the world.

"Gabrielle?" Drew's voice had sharpened, and a

quick glance at him told her he would accept nothing but a full confession. Well, that was what she planned to give, whether he liked it or not.

"I was performing at the San Antonio Palace," she said. "I'm a singer, and my father played for me."

"A singer?"

"And an actress," she said, almost defiantly.

She held her breath as she watched her reply register. Comprehension slowly spread across his features, and the gleam in his eyes grew brighter.

"So that's how you did it," he said. "I wondered how a well-brought-up miss managed to walk like an urchin off the Glasgow docks."

"I've played boys on the stage," she explained, her tone as dull and hopeless as her mood.

His next words startled her.

"Why Kirby?"

She blinked at him. "I told you what my father said as he died."

Drew shook his head. "But *why* would Kirby want to kill your father—or take a shot at you?"

Gabrielle hesitated.

"Gabrielle, for God's sake—"

"My father and Mr. Kingsley and two other men committed a crime together twenty-five years ago."

Drew pulled back, frowning. "Explain."

Gabrielle swallowed. "When Papa was dying, he also said some other words. 'In the trunk. Letter. Explains it all.' I—I found the letter in his trunk, and it was with a newspaper article about Kirby Kingsley and this cattle drive. Papa had seen the article and written me the letter in case"—she drew a small, ragged breath—"in case anything happened to him, so I would know the truth."

She paused, casting a glance at Drew, trying to gauge his reaction. His face was inscrutable.

"Go on," he said.

"Papa wrote that he and Kingsley and these other two men robbed a bank. A clerk was killed during the robbery. Afterward, the men, including my father, agreed to separate, take different names, and never meet again." She looked at Drew, begging him to understand. "They could still hang, you see. All of them."

Drew frowned. "But if they changed their names, how did your father know that Kirby was—"

"There was a sketch of Kingsley with the article about the drive. Papa recognized his face."

Drew held her gaze for a moment, then looked away, sighing as he stared at the river flowing at their feet.

Gabrielle stared at the muddy water, too, its surface glittering under the last rays of the sun. She felt very much like Honor, lying on the riverbank several yards away. Heartbroken. As if life might as well end here, for the future loomed empty and lonely before her. Empty and lonely without Drew Cameron. He simply *had* to believe her.

Finally, Drew spoke. "Gabrielle," he said softly. "Did you talk to the law?"

"Of course," she replied, her voice barely a whisper. "They didn't believe me any more than you do. Kingsley was too important to be accused or even questioned."

Drew sighed. "What did the sheriff say about your father's letter?"

"I didn't show it to him," she said, a hint of defiance creeping into her voice. "I knew he didn't believe me, and I didn't want to ruin my father's name, not without proof."

The silence was deafening. Gabrielle could almost hear the unasked questions, the doubt, and futility filled her.

"You don't believe me," she said.

Drew ignored the question. Instead, he spoke in an odd, curious tone. "You said this happened in May?"

She nodded.

"Kirby was attacked in March," he said slowly. "He was ambushed."

Her head jerked around, and she looked him in the eye. "Mr. Kingsley?"

"Aye," Drew nodded. "Some coincidence, wouldn't you say?"

"Ambushed?" she repeated. "Are you *sure*?"

Again, he nodded. "I was there. I overheard three men in a saloon, plotting the ambush. Someone had offered them five thousand dollars to kill Kingsley. The next morning, I followed them and . . . well, let's leave it that their plans went awry."

Gabrielle was stunned. She didn't doubt Drew's story for an instant—and she was certain he'd foiled the bushwhackers' plans. But if someone had attacked her father *and* Kingsley, then who . . . ?

A shiver raced up her spine, and Drew's next comment only gave voice to her sudden fear.

"Four men," he said. "And you think you know who two of them are. Who are the others?"

"I don't know," she breathed. "My father didn't give me their names in the letter, and I supposed they'd be different from the names he knew, anyway."

"So it would seem," Drew murmured. "But suppose you tell me what you thought you would discover on the drive? Did you believe Kirby would confess to you?"

Gabrielle let her gaze fall to her lap, her fingers toying with the ratty edge of her coat. "I didn't know. Perhaps I thought I could *make* him confess. I even . . . thought I might kill him myself."

In the silence that followed her announcement, Gabrielle drew a long, steadying breath. Without looking at Drew, she continued. "When I left San Antonio, I was . . . I didn't know what I should do. I kept seeing my father, lying on the street in a pool of blood. I didn't have anyplace to go. No other family. All I could think about was getting some kind of justice for my father, no matter what it cost." She waved a hand in a helpless gesture. "Then, somewhere along the trail . . . I think it might have been the night of the stampede, or maybe the night we"—she shot him a quick glance—"the night we spent by the creek, after Willow Springs. Anyway, something happened, and I realized that I couldn't shoot Kingsley. I couldn't shoot anyone!" Her hands closed into fists in her lap. "But I still wanted justice. So I thought I would try to find some kind of evidence that would prove he'd had my father killed. That's what I was doing in the chuck wagon. Looking for something—anything—that would tell me once and for all that he did it. Or at least explain why it happened."

When Gabrielle stopped speaking, she was breathless, her heart pounding in her chest. Frightened of what she'd see, she turned to look at Drew and found him looking at her as if he'd never seen her before.

"You planned to shoot Kirby," he said slowly. "Then you planned to gather evidence against him. You thought he had murdered your father—and also tried to murder you. And all this time, you've given no thought at all about what he might do if he discovers who you are." He shook his head in wonder. "You scare the bloody hell out of me, lass."

"I don't think anything scares you," she countered.

"*You* do," he said. "Anyone who risks a stampede, drowning, and an Indian attack, all for revenge—"

"It's *not* revenge," she interrupted.

"Then what is it?"

"Justice."

His mouth curled up at one side in cynicism. "Another word for revenge."

"Drew, I have to *know* what happened. Can't you understand that?"

"Of course, I can," he said, his expression softening. "I can even understand how you might have wanted to kill the man you thought killed your father. But I don't understand what you hoped to accomplish by sneaking and skulking about camp—except perhaps to get yourself killed."

Scalded to the quick, she defended herself. "I'm not sneaking and skulking."

"What do you call it then?" he asked.

"Trying to find the truth, with or without your help."

"It'll be without."

"But he killed my father! And he tried to kill me!"

Drew shook his head. "I don't think Kirby Kingsley killed anyone. I think it's far more likely that whoever ambushed Kirby—*both* times—is the one who had your father murdered."

Gabrielle clenched her teeth. She knew Drew made sense. The possibility Drew raised made sense to her, too. But her father had said it was Kingsley. She knew she wasn't mistaken about that. And she'd been clinging to that belief for too long to let it go so easily.

"Because you're Kirby's friend," she accused him. "You *wouldn't* think him a murderer."

"That's right," Drew agreed.

"And if you're wrong?"

He paused.

"If he's innocent," she continued, "I can't hurt him by just watching him."

"If he's not, you can get killed."

"So you admit it's possible?"

"No," he said slowly. "No, I don't. I just want you to consider the risks and consequences of your own actions."

"Do you?" she shot back.

A look of chagrin passed over his face. "Not usually. Perhaps that's why I don't leave here now and go straight to Kirby. But then I've never been an example to emulate."

Her hand found its way back into his. "I know what I'm doing, and I'm not going to get myself killed." She hesitated, biting her lip for a moment before continuing. "And I should probably tell you that I don't need any shooting lessons. My father taught me to shoot years ago, so I could protect myself. I hate guns, particularly after seeing my father killed . . . but I do know how to use one. And I'm not a child."

She could see him trying to be angry at her for lying about her lack of skill with a gun, but, with a sigh, he lost the battle. Instead, for the first time during their conversation, she saw amusement dance in his eyes.

"No, you're not a child," he said. "We certainly agree on that. Exactly how old are you?"

"Twenty-three."

He reached up and took off her hat. She shook her head, delighted to be free of the thing, then she caught him staring at her. Staring in a completely different way. Not as if she were an addlebrain but with admiration, even awe.

"Bloody fool thing to do," he muttered, but his eyes said something else altogether.

"Will you tell him?" she ventured.

They both knew she meant Kingsley.

"Do you know what you're asking of me, Gabrielle?" he said. "Kirby is my friend, and I don't have that many friends that I can simply toss them aside. You're asking me to betray him."

"Not if he's innocent," she said. "And would you want to be a murderer's friend?"

He sucked in a quick breath, holding it as his face underwent a change. The amusement faded from his eyes, and the admiration.

Carefully, he said, "And that's what you've thought of me all this time, isn't it? That I was knowingly a friend to a murderer."

She stared at him, realizing too late the trap she'd sprung on herself. But she wasn't going to lie anymore, not to him. "I thought . . . maybe. I mean, the two of you were obviously close. He—He talks to you, more than he talks to anyone."

Drew's eyes narrowed. "Keep going. What else did you think, Gabrielle?"

Her gaze darted away from his, skimmed over the shadowed landscape, came to rest on Honor, still lying, unmoving, on the riverbank.

"You thought I might have colluded with Kirby to have your father killed?" he asked, his voice harsh.

"At first I thought it was a possibility. But not for very long," she replied.

" 'Not for very long,' " he repeated solemnly, mocking her. "Just *how* long? And while you're at it, tell me how much of your . . . how do I put this delicately . . . your willingness was a reflection of your true feelings—and how much was bait?" Shoving himself to his feet, he looked down at her icily. "What did you want to learn from me, Gabrielle, after *ensuring* that I didn't tell Kirby about you?"

"It wasn't like that," she stumbled, stunned by his fury, by the hard set of his face, his coldness. Instead of dispelling his mistrust of her, she realized now that she'd only succeeded in deepening it. "It wasn't," she pleaded again. "Drew, wait! Please! Drew!"

But her words met his back. She watched, her heart splintered, as he strode away.

Chapter Fourteen

───────── ✦ ─────────

"Drew, wait! Please! Drew!"

Drew heard Gabrielle's frantic words as he turned away, unable to listen to any more explanations, any more lies.

He lengthened his stride, wanting to outrun the sound of the husky voice that had very nearly stolen his heart.

Andrew Cameron, earl of Kinloch. Such a noble title, he thought bitterly, for a man made the target of so many schemes and lies. After learning of the greatest lie of all, he'd thought he would never be hurt by one again. Expect nothing, and a man could never be hurt.

But now he felt mortally wounded. For without being able to say when or how it had happened, he realized that he had begun to trust Gabrielle. She'd made him start believing in people again, believing that there was honor and loyalty and love, and that he might, at long last, have a piece of them.

Maris Gabrielle Parker had just smashed that assumption into the ground. His brother-in-law Ben and his sister must be an anomaly, the exception that always proved the rule.

It hadn't been the lies, though he couldn't quite understand the logic of using lies in search of the truth. No, it wasn't the lies themselves. What had hurt was the fact she'd believed him capable of murder, that she'd used her body to ensure his betrayal of a friend.

At the remuda, he saddled Beelzebub, so named because he was difficult to control. Damien liked the black horse, but the other drovers avoided him. Drew mounted the sidestepping beast and headed at a full gallop across the river. Once on the other side, he raced over the prairie, determined to outrun the demons pursuing him—the betrayals he'd thought he left behind him in Scotland.

The earl of Kinloch. The *fool* of Kinloch. He heard his own laughter grabbed by the wind and carried off.

He also heard Gabrielle's voice: *Do you really want to be friend to a murderer?*

Damn her.

He spurred the horse, aware of faltering light, of the night encroaching on the open prairie. He didn't stop until he saw the foam on the horse's mouth. Dismounting, he began walking the horse to cool him down. He had no idea how far he had ventured from the campsite, nor did he notice his surroundings. He did notice that Beelzebub's sides were heaving, and as he walked he began looking for water for the overheated horse. In all his life, he had never mistreated a horse, and that he had done so now did not improve his black mood. Damn the devil, he'd ridden the animal nearly to the point of collapse.

He guessed he must be five miles from camp, at least. Beelzebub tried nipping his shoulder, showing his disgust for the night outing, but then the horse neighed, and Drew heard an answering whinny.

He stopped. A horse, or horses, were out there. He drew his rifle from its scabbard on the saddle, and stood still, listening. His eyes scoured the prairie, finding a ravine not twenty feet away, and he walked Beelzebub to the edge. He could slip down into it, if necessary.

A hawk cried from a distance. Or was it a hawk?

At about the time he was envisioning bands of marauding Indians swooping down upon him, he made out the lone figure of an approaching horseman, and an instant later, he recognized the shape of the rider's hat. He waved his hands over his head, and the figure moved into a trot, coming to a stop in front of him.

Kirby Kingsley looked down, his face partially hidden by his hat.

"Jake said you lit out like a scorched rabbit." Only a slightest hint of a question colored the trail boss's tone.

"So you came looking for me?"

"Along with renegade Kiowas," Kirby reminded him, "there's ambushers out here, remember?"

"They're after you, not me."

"Maybe. But I don't think the Kiowas would give a damn who it was."

"I needed some time to think."

"Should I ask about what?"

"No."

Kirby dismounted and turned back in the direction from which he'd come. "You with me?"

"Aye," Drew said.

They walked in silence for a while, but Drew felt none of their usual easy companionship. He was keeping things from Kirby, information the man had the right to know. And for the life of him, he couldn't understand why he didn't simply open his mouth and say it: "Gabe Lewis is a woman. Her name is Gabrielle, and she came here to kill you." But the words were lodged in his chest, and he couldn't make himself say them.

Instead, Gabrielle's own words echoed inside his head: *Kirby Kingsley killed my father! And he tried to kill me!* He didn't believe it was true for a second. But he did believe that her father had been killed and that someone had shot at her. He believed it in the same way that he knew Kirby had been ambushed twice.

The question was, What in bloody hell could he do about it?

"This country makes you feel mighty little," Kirby said, breaking the silence.

"Aye," Drew said, only now taking in the details of the scene around him—the high prairie in the last shadows of twilight. They were surrounded by a sea of sedge grass, broken occasionally by a deep ravine. There wasn't a tree in sight. It was vast and lonely and starkly beautiful.

"The Highlands has the same effect," he said.

Kirby glanced at him. "You miss Scotland?"

"I miss the green hills," Drew said. "I miss the pipes."

Kirby chuckled. "Can't say I agree with you, there. Heard a Scotsman play those pipes once near a herd of cattle. Scared them clean to New York."

Drew smiled. "That's one way of getting them there."

"Nothing but bones, though. Didn't bring a cent."

"I'll try not to indulge, then."

Kirby cocked an eyebrow in his direction. "Can you play those things?"

"A little. I didn't bring them to America, though."

A few seconds passed, then Kirby asked, "You ever think about going back?"

"No," Drew said. "There's nothing for me there."

"The title?"

"Ah, the title." He heaved a deep sigh. "What a grand thing a title is. People bow and scrape even if you don't have a farthing, even if you've accomplished nothing but to be born. 'Tis not something I take pride in, that title," he said. "Maybe that's why I like your country. A poor man can become a king if he works hard enough. Look at you. You told me that young Gabe reminded you of yourself long ago. Now you own a good part of Texas."

Kirby didn't reply for a moment, and when he finally did speak, his voice was rough with more emotion than Drew had yet to hear him express.

"The kid does remind me of myself," Kirby said. "At his age, I was as desperate as he was that day he showed up at the Circle K. My father was killed at San Jacinto, during the Texas fight for independence, and my ma died a year later. Bank took our farm, not that it was much. I was seventeen, my brother eleven. I begged and stole. Did anything to keep my brother alive."

Drew didn't want to hear anymore. He knew Gabrielle couldn't be right, that Kirby was no murderer. Yet a part of him was afraid that he was about to learn he'd been twice a fool. He didn't want to know that he'd saved the life of a man who had done murder.

"You ever do anything you regretted?" Kirby continued. "I mean all your life."

Drew felt sick. "Aye," he said. "I think everyone has, and I more than most."

Kirby gave an impatient snort. "I doubt that. You're a good man, Drew Cameron. I wish I had ten more of you."

Waving a hand in dismissal, Drew said, "It's a game for me, Kirby. An adventure."

"I think you want it to be," Kirby said slowly. "But it's not working out that way, is it?"

Drew looked at him askance. "I'm not sure what you mean by that."

Kirby shrugged. "If you think of life as a game, you don't put your heart into it. And so you don't risk having your heart broken when things go wrong—like when men die in stampedes and drought kills off half the herd." He hesitated, then continued. "But I've been watching you, Drew. You're a natural with horses and cattle. And you're a natural with men. Most of my hands would do anything for you."

"I don't want them to do anything for me," Drew said curtly.

"No," Kirby agreed. "Then you're taking risks."

Drew eyed him speculatively. "And what about you? Aren't you taking those risks?"

"Yeah, and I'm no damn good at it either," Kirby said wryly. "It breaks my heart every time I lose even a single calf. And when it's a man . . . well, I swear each time that I'll never boss another cattle drive. But I can't say that I've minded the rewards of taking those risks. And there are plenty of those, too. Like being out here on the high prairie, on a night like this." Looking up at the sky, now twinkling with stars, Kirby sighed. "But I've been damned lonely, too. I've survived for twenty-five years by limiting all the risks to myself. Making sure I was the only one who was taking them. And looking back, I can't say that I think it was the right thing to do."

He turned his head to meet Drew's gaze. "I hope you don't do the same," he said. "I can see you twenty-five years from now, in the same boat I'm in. No wife. No family of your own. No real friends. And I wouldn't wish it on an enemy, much less a friend."

Before Drew could even begin to form a reply, Kirby announced, "I think the horses are rested enough." And swinging up into the saddle, he pushed his mount into an easy canter.

Drew watched him for a moment, moved by his friend's very personal confession—and confused as the devil about why Kirby thought it had anything to do with him.

· · ·

Honor's tail wagged for the first time as his tongue swiped Gabrielle's face. It was some balm to her shattered heart, but not much. She didn't even care anymore whether Drew went to Kirby Kingsley or not. She'd seen the pain in his eyes, and she knew she had caused it.

When she'd made her way back to camp, she tied Honor to a wheel of the chuck wagon, then looked for something to do to keep from bursting into tears. She poured herself a cup of coffee, tried it, and threw it away. The drovers would like it. A horseshoe could indeed float on it. Testing the beans with a spoon, she decided that they were suitably soft. For lack of anything else to do, she added a few pieces of kindling to the hot coals and sat beside it, watching the sun slide below the horizon.

Booted footsteps approached, and she looked up to see Damien. He squatted next to the fire, taking some coffee and juggling the hot cup in his hands.

"Jake says Kirby took off after Scotty," he said. "You wouldn't know anything about that, would you?"

She shrugged.

"Uncle Kirby shouldn't be out there alone with Scotty."

Her head snapped around. "Why not?"

Damien gave her a sideways look. "It's just that things seem to happen when he's around," he said bitterly.

Gabrielle started to retort that, yes, things like people's lives getting saved happened when Drew was around—but she thought better of it. Damien was the one man she tried to stay away from.

He stood. "I'm gonna get some shut-eye. Call me when they come in."

She nodded, her own anxiety rising at the thought of Drew out there on the dark prairie, alone but for Kingsley—and raiding Kiowas and ambushers. She waited for an hour, hoping for their return, sitting by the fire, listening to the crackling flames and the soft lowing of cattle. Several other drovers came dragging in, took a cup of coffee, then went to the blanket rolls.

But finally, she added a few more pieces of wood to the fire, then went over to her own wagon. She petted Sammy, then crawled under the wagon, luring Honor under with her. She wrapped her arms around him, holding his soft, furry body close, and he tolerated her embrace. Eventually, after a long, unhappy time, she fell asleep.

Drew was dead tired when he awakened at dawn. When he and Kirby had returned to camp, he had taken the midnight watch, knowing he might as well for he wouldn't be able to sleep.

As he tossed his bedroll into the hoodlum wagon, he spared only a second's glance at the small bundle of blankets and fur lying scrunched against the wagon's back right wheel. He had work to do. He couldn't waste any more time being furious or feeling wounded.

When everyone was awake and fed, and the camp was packed and ready, Drew mounted the pinto for the morning's river crossing and rode to the bank. There he waited, his job being to control the cattle once they started across. The chuck and hoodlum wagons would go first, with Jake taking them across one at a time. No one trusted Two-Bits with a crossing yet.

The river was not very deep, but the current was fast. Jake got the chuck wagon over easily, then returned for the hoodlum wagon. Drew watched Gabrielle hand Jake the reins of the mule team, then scoot over on the bench to hug her dog, whom she had tucked between her and Jake.

The wagon made it to the middle of the wide river,

then seemed to get stuck. The word *quicksand* flashed through Drew's mind, and his heart skipped a beat. Jake snapped the whip and the mules plunged ahead. But the wagon didn't budge. Jake gave it another try, the mules strained in their harness, and, suddenly, the wagon simply keeled over onto its side. Drew watched in horror as both Gabrielle and the dog slid off the bench, into the river.

He didn't think about how angry he was, or how hurt. He didn't think of anything except that she couldn't swim. He kicked the pinto forward, plunging into the water, at the same time he caught a glimpse of Kirby, on the opposite bank, doing the same.

When he reached the overturned wagon, Drew prayed that she hadn't been pinned beneath it as he dived off his horse and into the muddy water. He came up empty-handed and looked around. He saw the dog climbing out on the far bank, but Gabrielle wasn't with him. Then, downstream, he spotted a dark head, bobbing above the surface.

"Bloody hell!" he swore, throwing his arms above his head and swimming as fast as he could toward her. But just when he thought it was hopeless, that she was moving too fast away from him, he saw her gain a foothold. Stumbling, she made her way to the other bank and struggled out of the water.

Her hat was missing, and so was her coat—or perhaps she'd surrendered it to the current, realizing it was weighing her down. In any case, as she stood on the bank, shaking the water out of her eyes, her cotton shirt plastered itself to her body, revealing for all to see her decidedly feminine figure.

"Bloody hell," he swore again, standing in the river, watching helplessly as the scene unfolded.

Five men on horseback were lined up on the bank in front of her, staring, astonishment plain on their faces. Then Kirby emerged from the water to meet her—and stopped dead, a yard away, his eyes riveted to her dripping form.

Drew didn't know what he hoped to accomplish by sheer virtue of his presence, but he swam like hell for the bank. As he climbed out, he saw Gabrielle register her predicament, then stumble away. He started to go after her, hesitating when he was met with Kirby's accusing gaze. Knowing he'd have to face the trail boss soon or later, he chose later, and strode after Gabrielle.

He caught up with her a hundred feet or so from the riverbank, beneath a small grove of trees.

"Gabrielle, are you all right?" he asked.

She gave him a sketchy nod, half-turning away from him. His gaze skimmed over her. She looked no worse for wear, save that she was coughing a little and wouldn't meet his gaze. Dripping wet, without her coat, she looked exposed and horribly vulnerable, and it didn't help at all when she wrapped her arms around her shoulders in a protective gesture. Drew wished he had something on to give her—a jacket, an extra shirt. He had to settle for simply standing beside her.

They both watched as the drovers righted the hoodlum wagon and got it up the bank. At some point in the process, the dog came looking for Gabrielle, getting as close as possible before shaking himself, thereby spraying muddy river water in all directions. Gabrielle's flock increased when Sammy and his mother arrived, having made the crossing. The calf came right to Gabrielle, gently butting her.

Drew was on the verge of smiling, thinking whimsically that it was as if Gabrielle's animals were all seeking her approval at how well they'd done. But then Kirby arrived, and it was plain that he was not amused.

He spoke directly to Drew. "You knew about this?"

"Aye," Drew said.

"This have anything to do with last night?"

Drew didn't answer.

"Sonofabitch," Kirby muttered. "You, my friend, can plan on riding drag from here to Abilene."

Then he turned his wrath on Gabrielle, who, Drew thought, looked a little like a half-drowned puppy.

"And you, young lady," he growled, "I'll have an explanation from you as soon as we get the cattle across." He started toward his horse, then stopped, turning back to Drew. "You stay with her," he said through clenched teeth. "I want both of you near the wagons until all the cattle cross."

"I'm more valuable with the herd," Drew protested.

"A goddamn woman," Kirby muttered to himself. "Didn't used to be this blind."

"She's a bloody good actress," Drew sympathized wryly.

"Yeah, and what *else* is she?" Kirby growled.

Drew resented Kirby's implication—and the sudden blaze in the rancher's eyes. He guessed he understood it, though. What kind of woman, indeed, would hire onto a trail drive for three months, with eighteen men?

Bloody hell. He still hadn't figured that out for himself.

"Stay with her," Kirby ordered again, then strode off to deal with his herd.

Reluctantly, Drew followed a crestfallen Gabrielle to the hoodlum wagon that had been pulled up beneath a few trees. He felt like part of the Pied Piper's brood as he walked in a path made of river water behind a cow, its calf, and a sodden dog.

Damn the woman. Yet, he reluctantly admitted to himself his anger had been tempered by stark fear for her. His heart had stopped when he'd seen her tumble into the river, and it hadn't started beating again until she'd climbed safely out onto hard ground. He might be angry. He might be wounded to the quick at being used by her. And he certainly didn't trust her as far as he could have thrown her.

But he still cared about her. He didn't want to see

her hurt. If she'd died in the river, a part of him would have died, too.

Feeling as confused as Gabrielle looked, Drew swore creatively as he reached the chuck wagon. She stood there, all five feet three inches of her and probably less than a hundred pounds, with her back stiff and her chin lifted in determination. The woman was all grit.

"I'm sorry," she said to him, most of her bravado gone.

Drew frowned in bewilderment. "You're apologizing to me for nearly drowning?"

She shook her head. "I'm sorry I've placed you in this . . . awkward position with Kingsley."

Drew snorted. "Why be sorry now?"

"He's your friend," she said simply, a tear hovering at the corner of one blue eye.

"That didn't matter before."

The lower lip quivered, and Drew watched her try to bite it into submission.

"It does now," she said.

He wanted to believe her. But wanting didn't make it so. Turning away from her, he watched the drovers herd the cattle into the river.

A small sigh seemed to ruffle the air behind him. He could almost see her shoulders slump. Disappointments of a lifetime kept him from turning to her. Past betrayals stiffened his resolve.

"Drew?" Even her voice trembled. God, it was killing him, not to turn around and sweep her into his arms. He didn't do it. But he did turn back to face her, giving her what he hoped was a look of cool indifference.

"I—I . . . you . . ." she stuttered, more tears forming at the edge of her eyes.

"Yes?" he asked icily, though his heart was thumping hard enough to be heard across the river. He wanted to kiss those trembling lips, wrap his arms around the sodden clothes that continued to drip.

"Yesterday . . ." she began again.

Drew closed his eyes and, again, he felt the heat of her, the desire, the need, the pure want that had exploded into glorious splendor before he was so quickly tumbled back to earth.

Feminine fingers tentatively touched his arm. He wanted to respond, to savor their warmth. She'd made him feel whole for the first time in his life. Whole and wanted and needed.

He opened his eyes and looked at her. Maybe at any other time, he would have believed the earnest, desperate plea he saw in her eyes. Maybe he would have believed that she was truly sorry and honestly cared for his needs and feelings in this mess she'd created. But he had something she wanted now, something she needed.

"I won't give you away," he said curtly. "I'll back your lies just so I can prove you wrong. Is that what you want?" He wheeled around without waiting for an answer, without waiting for a chance to be trapped, to be used again.

He heard her whispered "no," as he strode away, heading down toward the river. He was barely aware that the dog was following him, tail tucked between his legs.

There was a polecat in the woodpile.

Kirby Kingsley fumed inwardly as he went about managing the river crossing. Profound disappointment filled him. He'd trusted Drew Cameron as he'd trusted few other people in his life. He didn't like to think that the man had brought along a woman for his own private amusement, but he couldn't think of another explanation.

Still, it made no sense. Hiding a woman on a cattle drive simply didn't fit what he knew of Drew Cameron's character. The man was as honest as any Kirby had ever met, sometimes painfully so.

That led him to blame the woman. What kind of witch was this "Gabe Lewis"? If she wasn't Cameron's woman, what was she doing here? Or did she have something to do with those two ambushes? He couldn't dismiss the nagging thought that they had something to do with the crime he'd committed so many years ago.

He banished the thoughts from his mind. The only thing that mattered now was getting ten thousand cattle across a river. As he went after a heifer that had started drifting downstream, Kirby thought that the damned drive had been cursed from the get-go—and now he knew why.

Gabrielle spent the day making pies and loaves of bread by the dozen, and beans that were seasoned exactly like Pepper's—or nearly so. She put out the blanket rolls from the hoodlum wagon to dry, then took an inventory of the dried goods in the chuck wagon. And in between tasks, she made sure there was plenty of fresh coffee in the pot available for the drovers, who continued to stop by all day to grab a cup.

She tried, in effect, to make herself indispensable. She didn't want to leave the drive and not entirely because she wanted justice.

She would have given almost anything if she'd thought Drew would just *trust* her again. She had little hope of that, however, and prayed only that she could make him not hate her. If she had to leave the drive, she knew she would never see him again. And he would always believe the worst of her. She couldn't bear the thought of it.

She thought of telling the truth now, immediately, simply facing Kingsley with all of her suspicions. But what if he *were* guilty? Chances were excellent that he and his nephews, who undoubtedly would back him, were good with their guns. They might try to silence Drew as well as her, and Drew wouldn't stand a chance against all three of them.

On the other hand, if she accused Kingsley of being a murderer in front of all the hands and it turned out that he was innocent, Drew would never forgive her.

It seemed hopeless. No matter what she did, she was damned to lose Drew—and possibly her life.

And she most fervently did not want to die. When she'd started out on this trip, she hadn't cared about anything save killing the man who had killed her father. But, as she'd said to Drew, somewhere along the way, things had changed. She didn't feel as if she were alone in the world anymore. Here, on the cattle drive, she'd found a sort of place for herself. She had men to feed and animals who needed her. And, if he only would let her, she had a man who she suspected needed love as badly as she did.

At the moment, that man was standing at the top of the rise overlooking the river, a silent, solitary figure. Keeping an eye on him from a distance, Gabrielle tried to imagine what he was thinking as he watched the activity from which he'd been banned. His last words had held such bitterness: "I'll back your lies just so I can prove you wrong."

She didn't want him to lie for her, didn't want him to compromise his rock-hard integrity for her sake. Didn't want him to feel torn apart by conflicting loyalties.

She understood about loyalty, having felt an intense allegiance to her parents; moving as they had from city to city, from performance to performance, she'd had little opportunity to form other lasting friendships. In a few short weeks, she'd come to feel deeply loyal toward Drew. Whatever she did now, she had to find a way not to betray him. Nothing else—not justice or revenge or anything else—mattered more.

Throughout the day, Gabrielle bore the inquisitive looks of drovers as they came in for coffee or hardtack before returning to the river. Their looks didn't bother her; she was accustomed to worse. And she was enormously glad to be rid of the dirty, hot coat and the tattered hat. Her clothes dried on her body, and as her hair turned into a cap of wispy curls, she brushed it, feeling free and light.

When supper was over and she had enough pies for the next two or three days—and she could find no more duties to perform—Gabrielle dusted the flour off her hands and went to sit on the riverbank to watch the last cattle cross. By the time the crossing was complete and the herd was grazing a half mile from camp, dusk had settled over the prairie. The sky turned blood red, the colors violent and clashing.

Suddenly, Gabrielle became aware of a presence behind her and swung her head around. Kingsley stood above her, his shirt damp with sweat, his cheeks dark with bristle, his eyes cold. He looked every inch a killer.

"I want an explanation," he said. "You're obviously not in need of a job." His gaze went over her assessingly, even insultingly, as she rose. "I suspect you could find one in any saloon."

She could, and she had, but she wasn't ready to tell him that. Besides, it wouldn't matter to him what kind of a job it might be; he obviously preferred to believe the worst. From the corner of her eye, she saw Drew approaching.

Kirby held up a hand, stopping him.

"Was it Scotty who brought you along," he asked her, "to keep his bedroll warm?"

Her eyes opened wide. The thought that she might have planned all this only to be with a man was absurd. And it was just about the last accusation she had expected.

"No!" she exclaimed. "Drew didn't even know until—"

"Until?"

"Until the trip to Willow Spring. I fell in the water

then, too," she said defiantly, her mind working fever-ishly. How much, or how little, could she get away with telling Kingsley?

"Weeks," Kingsley said, visibly angry. "He's known for weeks and kept it from me. He had no right."

Guilt flooded her. *She'd* had no right drawing Drew into her conflict. "I told him someone was after me. That my life was in danger. I begged him not to tell anyone, that you might make me leave the drive."

"You were right about that much," Kingsley said. Then he paused. "Is it true that you're being pursued?"

"Yes," she said flatly. "Someone tried to kill me."

He was silent a moment. "Scotty does have a gal-lant streak," he mused aloud.

"He wanted to tell you. He wanted *me* to tell you, but I made him promise not to."

Kingsley's furious gaze seemed to cut right through her. "A cattle drive's no place for a woman."

"I have no place else to go," she said desperately.

"How about the law?"

She couldn't tell him that she'd already been to the law, had, in fact, accused *him*. "They won't help."

"You sure the law isn't looking for *you*?"

A slight, almost sympathetic note crept into his voice, startling her. In fact, everything about the conversation startled her. She had expected accusations, dire suspicions, threats—things that a man who murdered might say or do. Instead, his angry eyes were actually beginning to twinkle.

She swallowed. She had been preparing herself to tell Kingsley the truth, to confront him with her suspicions if she could minimize the risks. But he wasn't asking the dangerous questions, and everything she had told him thus far was true.

"Can I stay?" she asked.

He hesitated, assessing her, then simply nodded.

"Until I can find a regular cook," he said. "And then we'll see."

His mouth edged into an unexpectedly charming smile. "Poor bedeviled Drew," he murmured, then turned away, leaving Gabrielle feeling more perplexed than ever.

Chapter Fifteen

————— ✦ —————

Despite the inconvenience and indignity of it all, Gabrielle found herself fervently wishing for the good old days of being Two-Bits. Whatever scorn Drew seemed to harbor for her now, it was a feeling obviously not shared by the other drovers.

During the past three days since her gender was revealed, Gabrielle had been courted, fussed over, and cosseted. She had ceased being insignificant Gabe Lewis and was, instead, an object of intense and fascinated male interest.

She had received a sample of what was coming the very evening of the fateful river crossing. While she had been adding wood to the fire, one of the drovers rushed to her side, took it from her, and fed the fire himself, leaving her empty-handed and stunned. Before she could form a protest, ornery Hank Flanigan, who—a lifetime ago—had wagered his hat against hers in the Kingsley bunkhouse, approached her shyly. His face pink under a thatch of hair the color and texture of hay, he had shifted awkwardly from one foot to the other, his shabby hat in hand. Then, he'd shyly thrust it at her.

"You'll be needing a hat, ma'am. Miss. I mean, well, you'll just be needing a hat, that's all."

Another man had shuffled up to her. "Sorry we gave you a rough time, ma'am. We was just joshing."

"You be needing any help," Legs had chimed in, "you just call me."

She couldn't lift a sack of flour or a piece of wood without one of the drovers trying to take it from her. On the other hand, Damien Kingsley hadn't offered anything but a leer. She hated that most of all, because it made her realize that he and the other drovers must be recalling the many times she'd been alone with the Scotsman.

Well, she wasn't alone with him anymore. He wouldn't even come near her.

The oddest thing of all to her, though, was Kirby Kingsley's reaction to her "new" presence in his camp. She certainly hadn't expected him to be so tolerant. He even seemed amused in a cynical sort of way. She'd seen him talking with Drew shortly after his conversation with her on the riverbank. When their discussion was over, Drew had shot her a quick enigmatic glance, then jumped onto his horse and ridden off to night watch. Kingsley had turned and, seeing her standing there watching, he'd actually chuckled before turning to walk away. She didn't understand it at all.

Since then, Kingsley had made few appearances in camp. Despite protests about the safety of his actions, he had insisted upon scouting ahead again. He was gone nearly all day, riding in only at night to give directions about the next day's trek.

All Gabrielle really wanted, though, was the former closeness she'd shared with Drew, and she feared she had made that impossible.

Still, even with all the clumsy masculine offers to help, she stayed busy. Too busy. Three baby calves had appeared at her wagon, shyly dropped by drovers. Sammy was old enough now to stay with his mother, but each night she had to find the other calves' mothers, and she'd rigged a system of using different-color bandanas to make the feat possible. Honor had taken it upon himself to keep the calves safe, herding them back if they tried to wander off. Billy Bones still demanded her attention, too, and so did Sammy, as did a passel of hungry, lonely drovers.

So the days passed, quickly and busily even as her inner loneliness grew deeper, more aching, more piercing. Kingsley had made it clear that he would find a new cook as soon as possible, and time was escaping like sand in an hourglass.

She looked up from the pans she was scouring to see that Kingsley himself was galloping in, which meant he had news of some kind. He was quickly surrounded by the drovers not on watch. She hesitated in the edge of the circle of men.

"Army says they got those Kiowas. Lieutenant claims it was a glorious victory," he added dryly. "Army always says that, even when they get their tail whipped, but they tell me there's no more danger. Not from those renegades, at least."

The drovers cheered.

"Means we can spread out the herd some now," the trail boss said. "And go back to regular watches."

Another cheer.

"But that doesn't mean there aren't other dangers out there. Cheyennes are on the warpath, and some of the other tribes aren't above cow rustling, so don't get careless."

The drovers nodded in acknowledgment.

"I'll ride out and tell the others," Kingsley said, pouring himself a cup of coffee. "Damien out there?"

"Damien, Scotty, Legs, and Hank," Terry Kingsley offered.

At the mention of Scotty, the trail boss glanced at Gabrielle. She tried to keep her face from turning red, but, feeling her failure, she turned away as tears stung her eyes. That happened a lot lately, and it was terribly humiliating. Two-Bits wouldn't have cried.

But even while she tried desperately to control her expression, wondering why she'd never had that problem before, Gabrielle met Kirby's news with relief. She had feared for Drew, for all of the drovers, every time they left the campsite.

The men finally drifted into a poker game.

Now that the imminent danger of an Indian raid seemed to have passed, Gabrielle decided to ride Billy Bones out into the evening. Night came late, so she had perhaps two hours of light left. She needed desperately to escape both prying eyes and adoring looks.

She found her saddle in the hoodlum wagon and saddled Billy, who whinnied in excitement. He looked a different horse these days, his sides filling out, his coat shining from her frequent brushing. He obviously felt very much the fine fellow again.

Honor whined to go with her. The calves had all found their mothers, drunk their fill, and sunk to the ground to sleep. Only Sammy stood tall, proclaiming his new strength and independence.

"All right," she told Honor. "But you must stay right beside me."

He wagged his tail slightly in evident agreement, then watched as she mounted Billy with all the grace of a sack of potatoes. She still hadn't mastered that particular skill.

Gabrielle sighed. She'd had precious little time to practice her horsemanship. Her rump still came down when the horse's back came up.

"Miss, ma'am, uh . . ." Legs stepped in front of her horse. "It ain't safe for you to go out there alone."

No one had cared when she was just plain Two-Bits.

"The Kiowas are gone," she said.

"But there's all kinds of varmints out there, Miss Gabrielle."

"I'll have Honor with me," she said, feeling an acute loss of freedom.

"I'll go wi' you," he said hopefully.

Ducking her head shyly, she shook her head and used the one excuse she knew would work. "I, um, need some privacy. I'm sure you understand."

Legs's ruddy half-Indian face froze with embarrassment. "You won't go far?"

"I won't go far," she lied as convincingly as possible.

She refused to wear spurs. No matter how blunt they were, she thought them cruel. Instead, she twitched the reins, and Billy understood. He started off in a long, loping stride, Honor at his heels.

Gabrielle rode and rode, and rode some more. Her duties were done, supper over, a fresh pot of coffee sitting on coals for those coming off watch. She'd even made hardtack for the men to chew during the next day's drive. She tried to keep track of landmarks. She shuddered at the thought of becoming lost, but she had to get away. She had to think, to plan.

Except her planning so far had led to disaster. You could never tell just one lie, she mused. Even a small one told with good intentions seemed to spawn a pit of deceit.

No wonder Drew hated lies so much. Still, she wondered at the passion beneath his censure. Clearly, he'd been lied to and painfully so. But by whom?

A woman? Was that why he kept such a distance even as his eyes lit with fire every time he looked at her?

She tried to concentrate on her riding, on doing what Drew had instructed her to do. Relax. Go with the horse. Don't fight him. But she still held on to the saddle horn for all she was worth, and her rhythm didn't match Billy's at all.

Honor suddenly barked and ran in a wide circle, then stood at attention, listening. He barked again, then started running to the left.

"Honor!"

The dog paused for a second, then dashed away.

Gabrielle cried out again. She couldn't lose him. Drew had placed him in her care. Terrified, she clung to the saddle horn and urged Billy into a gallop across the rough prairie after the dog, whose black and white tail fluttered like a flag in the tall grass. She prayed, incredulous when she realized that she wasn't bouncing as badly as before.

She nearly overran the dog, who was now sniffing something on the ground. She dismounted. A tiny whimper came from the grass. Gabrielle leaned down and saw Honor busily licking what seemed to be a wriggling blanket.

She moved closer, and her foot hit something soft. A cry caught in her throat as she saw a buckskin-clad woman lying still, a red stain darkening her clothing. Gabrielle leaned down and touched her. She was cold.

Gabrielle swallowed hard. The woman's black hair was shoulder length and in braids, her body slim to the point of being skeletal. The blanket beside her squirmed again, and Gabrielle leaned down to examine it. A child, surely not more than several months old, was swaddled in the wrap, a weak mewling escaping its lips.

A quick inspection showed the child to be a boy, and much too thin. But he seemed not to have any wounds.

The soldiers, she thought. The soldiers and their glorious victory. This woman must have escaped with her child, only to die from loss of blood.

Honor whined and tried to lick the child again.

Gabrielle's tender heart nearly broke at the orphan child's plight. An Indian baby. Few would want him even if he did live.

She picked up the child and crooned to it as Honor stood by expectantly, eyes bright and hopeful, awaiting praise for his find.

She gave it. "Good dog," she whispered with

feeling. And for the first time, Honor wagged his tail in feverish excitement.

Why, Gabrielle wondered, had a woman taken a child on a raiding party? Or had she? Both were terribly thin. Perhaps they had been starving on a reservation.

She would never know. But then, she did know that she needed to get back to camp. Sammy's mother could provide nourishment for the hungry baby. And she would need help to give the dead woman a proper burial.

But if Gabrielle had thought it difficult to mount a horse with both hands, she found it nigh on to impossible with one arm holding a baby. She looked up at the sky for inspiration. Fire seemed to consume the heavens as the sun dropped below the horizon. Urgently, she returned to the boy's mother. Sadness tore at her, but she had to be practical. What had the woman used to carry the child all this way?

Reluctantly, she placed the child on the ground and examined his mother. Though her face was gaunt, she was young, her still staring eyes dark, almost black, her face aquiline. Gabrielle wondered whether she was of Spanish descent, from below the border, and adopted into an Indian tribe. She said a brief prayer over the woman and vowed to convince a few drovers to come and bury her. But she found no cradleboard, no sling.

Gabrielle swallowed hard, then reached to close the woman's eyes. Finally, she tore the blanket into strips, then fashioned a sling for the baby. She looped it around the saddle horn until she mounted, then placed it around her own neck so she could hold the child securely with one hand while trying to keep aboard Billy by clutching the reins with the other. Praying that Billy wouldn't choose this particular time to display his friskiness, she pressed her knees against the horse's sides.

As she started back to camp, the sky melted into a soft twilight blue.

"Bury an Injun?"

"Keep an Indian brat?"

"You must be loco."

Gabrielle pressed the child protectively to her breast as Damien and the other drovers battered her with disapproval. It didn't help that several of them had been out searching for her when she hadn't returned.

"Nits make lice," Damien added balefully, echoing a sentiment she'd heard before.

In the East, where most of her life had been spent, people shared a fascination for the "noble savage." But she'd been in Texas long enough to hear accounts of Indian atrocities. From campfire talk she also knew that many of the drovers had lost someone to Indian raids and that Texans—all Texans—seemed to hate Indians with unbridled passion.

But she'd never supposed that hatred would include a helpless infant or his dead mother. Even the adoring Hank had remained silent when she'd asked for someone to go out onto the prairie to bury the woman.

"Where is she?"

The Scotsman's low, melodic voice broke through the silence. Her own heart thumped at the soft sound that nonetheless dominated the clearing. She hadn't even noticed him ride in and join the group at its fringes, so intent had she been on protecting the baby in her arms.

As one man, the drovers surrounding her turned to stare at Drew Cameron.

He took a few steps closer, and Gabrielle felt the force of his personality as the other men stood back.

"Kirby won't like it," Damien said. "He's got no more use for redskins than any of us have."

"Kirby isn't here," Drew pointed out.

"He's checking the watches," Damien said. "But I'm next in command, and I say you stay here. We can't risk losing another man."

Drew ignored him and looked back to Gabrielle. "Where is she?"

Gabrielle thought he could probably hear her heart pound with gratitude that *someone* understood why she couldn't let the mother of this child remain prey to every scavenger on the plains.

"Honor can take you," she said. "He found them."

"Cameron!" Damien's voice was a warning.

Drew raised an insolent eyebrow, almost daring Damien to interfere.

"There could be other redskins who escaped the soldiers," Hank ventured.

He cast a quick look at Gabrielle, then lowered his eyes to the ground.

Legs shrugged. "Hell, I'll go with you."

Gabrielle remembered that he was half-Indian himself. She wondered how he stood all the disparaging remarks about at least part of his heritage. She caught his eye, and he shrugged, a smile tugging at the corner of his mouth.

"We don't want that kid here," Damien said, retreating from one lost position.

"You want to shoot him, Damien?" Drew asked. "All by yourself?"

Gabrielle clung to the bundle.

"I didn't say that," Damien said.

"Then what are you proposing to do with the wee bairn?" Drew asked, and Gabrielle didn't think anyone missed the threat wrapped in his velvet tone.

"She should have left it there, with its mother," Damien blustered, looking to the others, but suddenly the men were looking away. Down at the ground. Up at the sky.

"Damn it," Damien said, staring hard at each one of them.

Gabrielle gave Drew a tremulous smile, moved by that deep streak of decency he kept trying to deny.

A wistful ache settled in her heart. He was so close, yet so far away. His eyes studied her, gentling at the sight of the baby, but he was still withholding that part of him he'd given so briefly one summer afternoon.

Legs snorted. "If'n we're goin', we'd better be on our way," he said. "Due west, you say?" he asked her.

Gabrielle nodded, her eyes still on the tall Scotsman. "Thank you. Thank you both."

Drew shrugged. "Got some shovels?"

"In my wagon," she said breathlessly as she stared at his golden eyes, a huge lump blocking her throat. Only the wriggling child in her arms forced her back to reality.

Drew's eyes followed hers to the bundle. "What are you going to do with him?"

"How did you know it was a him?"

His mouth turned up in that grin she'd missed. "He doesn't chatter."

Indignation mixed with cautious hope at his teasing. "All females don't chatter," she retorted. "*I* certainly don't."

Legs grunted impatiently. "I'll go saddle the horses," he said. "You'd best get the shovels, Scotty. Sometime before dawn," he added dryly before starting toward the remuda.

Drew fell in next to Gabrielle as she headed for the wagon. "What *are* you going to do with the baby?"

"Feed him."

"With what?"

"Sammy's mother," she replied.

"Have you ever milked a half-wild longhorn?"

"No."

"Ever milked *anything*?"

She hesitated, saw the tightening of his jaw, then admitted sheepishly, "No."

"Don't start now," he warned. "Get one of the men to do it. Most of them come from farms."

"But they—"

"Just smile at them," he said. "Hank's your best bet. He has the worst case of puppy love I've ever seen."

"But—"

"And don't worry about the bairn. None of them will hurt the wee one."

"Because of you," she said.

"Nay. They were just talking. Most of them have reason to hate Indians, but none would hurt a bairn."

She loved the way he said *bairn*, the way the sound rolled lazily off his tongue.

They reached the wagon, and she hesitated, then held out the baby for him to hold. Drew took him readily, his arms holding the child with ease, his mouth curving into a smile as he looked down at the tiny bundle without a trace of embarrassment or awkwardness. She watched a moment, transfixed by the image, then climbed into the wagon to find two shovels and the scrap of cloth she had taken from the Indian woman's dress.

When she emerged with them, Drew gave her a sad, world-weary gaze. "He'll have a hard life, no matter what you do."

"He'll not," she said fiercely. "I'll make sure of it."

"And how will you be doing that, lass?"

"I'll raise him," she said, realizing at that moment that she meant it.

" 'Tis not like a calf you can give back to its mother," he warned.

Gabrielle looked into his eyes, but knew there was no use protesting. He was as sure of her fickleness as he was of his own name. She would simply have to prove him wrong. Somehow. Some way.

Legs rode up, leading another saddled horse. He looked at the baby in Drew's arms, then at Gabrielle, then shook his head as if at two crazy folk. "You ready, Scotty?"

"Aye," Drew replied. He looked back to Gabrielle. "You said the dog could lead us?"

Gabrielle reached down and petted Honor, then held out the piece of fabric for him to sniff it. "Go find her, boy," she said.

The dog wagged his tail as if in understanding, then started out in an easy lope toward the west.

Drew smiled as he handed the baby back to Gabrielle. Their hands touched for a moment, but he jerked his away as if scorched. He took the two shovels and handed them to Legs, then mounted the second horse without stirrups, his body seeming to soar into the saddle in one graceful movement.

"Don't try to milk that cow," he warned Gabrielle again. "Swear it."

He knew her too well. She wished she knew him as well.

She nodded.

"Not good enough, lass. I want your word on it," he persisted.

"I will not try to milk the cow," she replied obediently.

His eyes, still filled with doubt, pierced her one last time before he and Legs rode off into the night.

Chapter Sixteen

✣

Drew kept pace with Legs, both of them holding their mounts to an easy canter as they followed the dog, loping ahead of them.

It was a bloody smart dog, Drew mused. Gabrielle had unquestionably been right when she'd surmised that Honor had been a working dog. Drew had seen similar dogs in Scotland, herding sheep and cattle with astounding efficiency.

Drew tried his damnedest to keep his mind on the job ahead and not on the woman he'd left behind. Gabrielle might be a liar, but he couldn't doubt her tender heart—at least, when it came to four-legged creatures and infants. Still, he was suspicious of how long her commitment to the bairn would last. He had witnessed her determination, but taking in a child was far different from giving refuge to a calf or a horse or a dog.

The latter commitment was temporary. The former was for life.

His own mother had proved that. He had vague memories of receiving affection as a very young child. But later his mother had lost herself in wine and laudanum and had fled when her husband vented his wrath on her son. He'd been eighteen before he'd learned why. And while part of him had pitied his mother; the other, the wounded self, had despised her for not leaving the husband who had hated and abused them both.

By then, his childlike trust had been broken forever, and he'd never regained it. He doubted now whether he ever would—or indeed would want to. And his experience with Gabrielle made him think he'd be insane even to try.

Her trickery and deceit had proved to him once again that others were not to be trusted. Oh, he found much about her to admire, but that merely served to make him even more wary of her. His regard for her was a weakness he couldn't afford. She had already ripped open his protective armor, the aura of indifference and superficiality he'd presented to the world. He was frankly afraid of what she could do to him if he let her any closer. He didn't want to experience— wasn't entirely sure that he'd survive—that pain and bewilderment again, the devastation of abandonment by someone he thought loved him.

He glanced over at his companion.

Legs was smirking at him. "Thinking about Miss Gabrielle? Never would have expected such a pretty woman 'neath them filthy clothes."

The dog increased his pace, forcing them to do the same, and eliminating the need for Drew to answer. Legs was right. She was a pretty woman. Too pretty. He hadn't missed all the male glances sent her way, nor the jealousy he felt when she returned a drover's smile.

A bark cleared his thoughts. Evidently the dog had found the object of their search. And Drew had a job to do.

• • •

I promised.

Gabrielle kept telling herself that as she went from one man to another, seeking two willing hands to milk a cow.

Sheepishly, one after another declined. Several refused, she knew, because Damien had warned them off from helping her with the baby. Two others said they'd never milked a cow before. Others simply disappeared when they saw her coming.

She'd glared at Damien for his part in the joint refusal, then returned to the child. The infant desperately needed nourishment. She had tried to crumble a biscuit in some water, but the baby couldn't eat the soggy mixture.

She was pleading with him once again to open his little mouth and try when the flap of her wagon opened and she saw Kirby Kingsley's face. Her body stiffened as she prepared to do battle for the child in her arms.

"Damien told me you found a baby?"

She tightened her arms around the infant and nodded.

"How old is it?"

She lifted one shoulder in a small shrug. "I'm not sure. I think not more than a few months."

Kingsley shook his head. "Scotty's calling this Noah's ark. Just how many more orphans were you planning to adopt?"

Her eyes met his in the flickering light of the oil lamp. She couldn't suppress a small shudder, waiting for some kind of angry ultimatum. Instead, a small twinkle in his eyes jolted her expectations.

"I'm not—I mean . . . they seem to find me," she stammered with a bit of a quaver but a lot of defiance.

"Damien says you're trying to find someone to milk that damn cow."

She nodded.

"For an Indian baby?" he asked. "You know what kind of trouble you're inviting?"

"Everyone keeps wanting to tell me," she replied.

"I've spent half my life fighting Indians," Kingsley said. "So have most of the people in Texas. And other places I could name."

"Not this baby," she declared. "Your nephew Damien said that nits make lice. Is that your belief, too?"

"No, it isn't," he said steadily. "Legs is one of my best hands. Ornery as hell but as loyal as they come." His voice was soft, almost soothing.

It was too much. She didn't want this man's sympathy. She didn't want his understanding. She didn't want to like him. Gabrielle fought the tears welling behind her eyes.

"I'll milk the damn cow," he said. "Isn't as if I've never done it before. Did my share of milking when I was a knee-high to a grasshopper. Be interesting to see if I still have what it takes."

Before she could say anything, Kingsley disappeared, the canvas wagon flap falling back into place behind him.

Stunned, Gabrielle could only stare at the spot where he had stood. Kirby Kingsley would milk a half-wild cow for an Indian baby no one wanted. Would a cold-blooded murderer care about an Indian child—or any child, for that matter?

Her stomach did somersaults. Had she been so very wrong all this time? And Drew Cameron so very right? If she *were* wrong, how could she ever explain to Kingsley what she'd suspected of him.

The baby in her arms whimpered, and she lowered her head to whisper to him. "You'll be all right, little one. I promise. I won't let anything happen to you."

Warmth settled deep inside her as the crying stopped and the baby looked up at her with great, dark, solemn eyes. The warmth curled around her heart and squeezed. The child was so small, and yet he gazed at her with such wonder and unconditional trust.

And soon he would have milk to drink, a safe place to sleep. And love. She'd make sure he had that. Since her parents had died, she'd had a great deal of love inside her, aching to be spent.

She would have liked to spend a great deal of it on Drew Cameron, but she despaired that he ever would allow it. He was so hard, so cynical—yet so incredibly tender and compassionate. Unfortunately, he was also completely unforgiving.

Gabrielle sighed and turned her attention to making a simple bed for the baby in a large box that had held tins of fruit Pepper had brought along for special occasions. She lined it with flour sacks to make a soft mattress, then laid the baby in it, covered him with her folded blanket, and climbed out of the wagon.

Kirby Kingsley was squatting next to Sammy's mother as one drover clutched the mother's head, trying to keep her still, and a second held back the bleating calf. Every time Kingsley pulled a teat, the cow tried to kick him, and he moved quickly to avoid her hooves as several of the men whooped and hollered.

Finally, Hank stepped up. "Come on, boss, let a real farmer do it."

"Real farmer, hell," Kingsley muttered, avoiding another hoof. "I was milking cows before you were born."

"Mebbe so," Hank said, "but 'pears you've lost the touch."

The cow kicked again, this time overturning the pan holding a trickle of milk.

Kingsley rose in evident disgust and invited Hank to try his hand at the task. He winked at Gabrielle, and she recognized his ploy for what it was. He knew very well how to milk a cow.

Hank knelt, and she watched his hands tug and

squeeze until a steady stream of milk started filling the pan. When the level rose to halfway up the pan's side, he stopped. Dodging the cow's hooves, he handed the pan to Gabrielle with a deep bow. "There you go, ma'am."

"Ain't no way to milk a cow," grumbled an onlooker. "You just let me do it tomorrow."

"Ah, you couldn't get milk from an already full pail." another said. "I'll do it tomorrow, Miss Gabrielle."

"We'll wager on it," said another, resorting to the drover's time-tested method of settling disputes.

Gabrielle's eyes found Kingsley's. His eyes were smiling, although his lips were in their usual grim, straight line. And she knew she would have no dearth of milkers from now on.

She nodded. She owed the rancher. Again.

During the following week, the baby no one had wanted became everyone's baby. Perhaps it had been Kingsley's tacit approval, or the child's own sweet, docile personality. Whatever the reason was, the child thrived. Because Gabrielle had been called Two-Bits, Drew had jokingly referred to the babe as Ha'Penny. And the name had stuck, even though Gabrielle had wished for something more dignified.

"How's the Ha'Penny?" Hank would inquire when he rode in.

"C'mon, Ha'Penny, smile," Shorty would tease.

"Ha'Penny been eating awright?" asked Terry. "If that bottle I rigged up for him wears out, just let me know. I've got a second pair of gloves you can use . . . ten nipples."

Even Damien's frown disappeared as he watched the Penny gurgle and smile at Honor, who kept a cautious eye on him.

The drovers, Gabrielle realized, seemed to love children. And they clearly worshiped women. She guessed they all wanted homes and families someday, so they were making do with what they had. Which meant that someone was always playing with Ha'Penny.

Everyone but the Scotsman. Although he had handled the babe with such ease and tenderness that first afternoon, he'd shied away since. To Gabrielle, it seemed as clear as a Texas summer day that he feared any kind of intimacy or attachment. And she wondered for the first time whether it was her lies that kept him away . . . or whether they were only an excuse.

But why would he need an excuse? What—or who—had hurt him so badly that he couldn't even allow himself to get close to a baby?

She vowed to herself to find out. The question was, When? Her responsibilities were multiplying at a dizzying rate. Ha'Penny ate every three or four hours, and she couldn't leave him at any time. She had to look after Sammy and the other calves. Billy was always whinnying for attention. And she had a horde of demanding drovers to feed, doctor, and pacify.

Gabrielle had never dreamed a person could do so much, or that a life could be so full. She had thought hers full when she'd been traveling and performing with her parents, then with her father, but she'd never experienced the deep satisfaction she did now. She'd never felt the kind of joy she did when Ha'Penny smiled at her, or Honor wagged his tail and nuzzled her, or Sammy butted her for attention.

Or when a pan of beans satisfied the drovers. Or when a cup of coffee brought a masculine grunt of approval.

Or when the Scotsman gave her that searching look that, lately, held the faintest hint of . . . of what? Approval? She could only hope.

Bleached buffalo bones. Thousands of them dotted the trail as the drive reached the last crossing of the Cimarron River.

Drew had never seen anything like it. He never wanted to see anything like it again. Such desolation left him with a sickening sense of waste.

Both he and Kirby were silent as they rode ahead of the herd. After numerous arguments with his nephews and Drew, Kirby had reluctantly begun taking one or the other of them with him when he rode ahead to plan campsites.

"Old maids," he had called all of them. But they had pointed out that too many ranchers were depending upon him for him to take foolish chances, and finally he'd conceded that they were right.

Drew never took his eyes from the rolling plains, always looking for a telltale flash of sun glinting off gun metal. His gut told him that the danger Kirby had attracted was still real and immediate.

And gnawing at him were his suspicions about Gabrielle. He worried that by keeping her secret from Kirby he might be betraying a friend, or worse, increasing the danger to both of them.

Kirby stopped at the riverbank. "The Cimarron," he said. "We're not far from Kansas now. And Caldwell. We can get supplies there."

"No more Indians?"

"Probably not," Kirby said. "But we'll face angry farmers instead, and they can be every bit as dangerous."

Drew stared across the shallow riverbed. In three weeks—four, perhaps—they would be in Abilene, and he'd have decisions to make.

Kirby had one now.

"Are you going to try to find a new cook?" he asked.

Kirby gave him a sly half-smile. "Interested in the outcome, are you?"

Drew didn't want to be. He knew he—and probably Kirby—would be better off if Gabrielle took her growing flock and left the drive. But where would she go with an Indian child—never mind the horse and the dog? And what would happen to all the calves she'd rescued along the way? Who else would have the patience to tie colored rags to mother and calf so they could be reunited each night?

Who else would make him feel so alive?

"You haven't answered the question," Kirby persisted.

Drew sighed heavily. "Aye," he admitted wryly. "I guess it does."

"I'm still trying to figure her out," Kirby admitted. "But the drovers seem content enough, and it'll be hard as hell to find a decent cook this late in the drive."

"Aye," Drew responded.

"I've noticed you've been avoiding her," Kirby said.

"I have no intention of . . . being involved with a woman," Drew said after a moment's silence. "Nor do I wish to dally with the marrying sort."

"And you think Gabrielle's the marrying sort?" Kirby asked with amusement.

"Aye, she's a lady, for all those foolish clothes."

"Some very strong emotion must have driven her to wear them," Kirby said thoughtfully. "I should like to see her in a dress. I think she's probably very pretty."

Jealousy, still unfamiliar and uncomfortable, snaked through him, and he knew Kirby noticed, because he chuckled.

"Don't worry, my friend. If I felt free to marry, there's a lady back home."

If I felt free . . . ? Meaning?

Drew knew the question must have been plain in his expression, for Kirby gave him a shrug and a sigh of resignation.

"I did something long ago that could come back to haunt me someday," he said. "It's kept me from marrying, from having children. I've got some old ghosts living with me. And as long as they're still around, I'll inflict them on no one else."

Old ghosts. Drew recalled his discussions with

Gabrielle about what had happened twenty-five years earlier.

Feeling awkward and embarrassed and horribly presumptive, he began, "If you don't mind, I'd like to hear about those ghosts of yours."

Kirby studied him for a moment. "Hell, I've kept it a secret too long. Maybe if I hadn't . . ." He clamped his lips shut, hesitating. But then, he continued slowly. "Twenty-five years ago, I was real hungry like I thought young Gabe Lewis was. And I had a kid brother to look after. There weren't any jobs. Cattle weren't worth anything then—there were too damn many of them and no way to ship them. I took up with three other boys about my age. We ran wild as hell, most of it out of just plain misery. We robbed drunks coming out of saloons, filched goods from the stores. Then one of my cohorts suggested we rob a bank. It would be easy, he said."

Kirby heaved a sigh. "To make a long story short, a clerk was killed. All of us, including my brother Jon, who was holding the horses outside, are equally responsible under the law. Ain't no time limitation on murder," he said. "All of us could still hang."

They could still hang, you see. All of them. Drew's heart thudded in his chest as Gabrielle's words echoed in his brain. Bloody hell, she'd been right. And as other things she'd told him raced through his mind, he went cold all over despite the blistering heat. *My father . . . was killed . . . I was with him. The gunman shot at me, too. . . .*

Bloody, *bloody* hell!

Fighting for control over his voice, Drew asked Kirby, "Do you think that . . . old robbery could be behind the recent attacks on you?"

Kirby shot him a scowling glance. "Someone trying to silence me, you mean? I thought about that. But I don't know where the other three men are. And, dammit, it's been nearly twenty-five years. I probably wouldn't recognize them if I did see them."

But Gabrielle's father had recognized Kingsley's picture in the paper, Drew thought. Perhaps someone else had, too.

He had to find a way to keep both Kirby and Gabrielle safe. And he would try his bloody damnedest to do it without betraying *either* of their confidences. But if he couldn't . . . well, the hell with it. Their lives might depend upon them sharing their information with each other, and if it meant breaking his word to keep their blasted secrets, that was better than standing by and watching them get killed. A lot of good his self-respect and integrity would do him when he was standing over their graves.

But first . . . first he would try to do it their way.

Feeling as if he were picking his way through a briar patch blindfolded, Drew said, "Kirby, I think one of the men who committed that robbery with you is your ambusher."

Kirby's head jerked toward him, the sky blue eyes piercing him like steel. "Why?" the rancher asked.

Drew gave him a negligent shrug. "Just a hunch," he said. "I'm a gambler, remember? I live by my hunches. And they're almost always right. So, tell me—how can we find these three men?"

"We?" Kirby cocked an eyebrow.

"We," Drew reiterated solemnly, holding the other man's gaze. "As soon as we get the cows to the railhead."

Kirby winced. "Cattle," he corrected. "*Cattle.*"

Drew grinned, hoping it didn't look as forced as it felt. His mood was anything but lighthearted. Whoever had ambushed Kirby knew where he was going and had had plenty of time to reach Abilene before the herd. If *he* were the killer, that's what he would do, rather than take the chance of finding the trail boss somewhere on the plains alone. The bastard probably thought he'd killed Kirby and would wait in Abilene to make sure.

That same killer would learn that a woman named

Gabrielle was also on the trip. A woman on a trail drive was news, and Drew had learned how fast gossip spread.

"I want you to think back," he said to Kirby. "Remember everything you can about each of those three men—anything distinguishing about them that wouldn't have changed over time."

Kirby met his gaze, held it.

"You think he'll be waiting in Abilene, don't you?" he said.

"Don't *you*?" Drew replied.

Day had melted into dusk when they approached the spot where the drive at stopped for the night. Muted pastels colored the sky with whimsical patterns, setting the stage for Drew's favorite time of day. A slow, lazy time. A time that was normally quiet, peaceful. Restful.

Instead, chaos greeted them when they rode into camp.

Two wagons were pulled up near their own, two dilapidated, tattered vehicles overflowing with boxes and furniture. A man dressed entirely in black was shouting balefully at Gabrielle as Honor ran barking in circles around a skinny, whey-faced boy who cowered against the wheel of a wagon, plainly wanting to play with the dog and trying to get past the shrieking man to do so.

"Jeremiah!" the man warned in a booming voice. "Stay away from that beast!"

The boy slunk farther against the wagon, and Honor slunk underneath.

"I am *not* giving you this baby," Drew heard Gabrielle shout back at the man as she clutched the child to her.

"You're interfering with the Lord's will," the man said, drawing himself up rigidly. "And you, woman, should be ashamed, dressed like a whore of Babylon."

"Oh, I don't know," Kirby interrupted pleasantly.

"I'd think a whore of Babylon might be wearing fewer clothes."

The man spun around, his face mottled with anger. He struggled to control it as he noted Kirby's air of command. "At last, a man in authority," he said. "I'm sure you'll agree that the little savage should go with us."

"Savage?" Drew said softly. "I think savagery has to be taught, and it's not always the province of your American Indian."

The man whirled to face him and drew himself up straight. "I'm the Reverend Joseph Dander. I understand that the infant is an orphan, and I'm demanding that you give him to us to be raised righteously."

"Demanding?" Kirby said in a tone every hand on the drive would have recognized as dangerous.

"Demanding," the man replied, oblivious. "We've come to bring the Word to the savages. You can't stand in the way of the Lord."

Kirby's eyes cut to the boy cowering near the wagon wheel.

The others sitting in the reverend's party—three women, four other men, two older boys, and a girl— looked on with anxious expressions."

Kirby's eyes narrowed.

Drew looked at Gabrielle. He recognized the determined glitter in her eyes and knew that no one was going to take that baby from her. Not without a fight.

The reverend reached for the child, and Gabrielle backed away. Drew moved forward, placing himself between Gabrielle and the reverend.

"What in the hell are you doing out here?" Kirby growled at the man.

Reverend Dander turned to him. "We've been called to save the savages."

"You got food with you, then?"

"Food?" The man looked blank.

"Food," Kirby repeated. "You want to save them, then supply something they need. Salvation means precious little when you're starving to death."

Drew's gaze remained fixed on Gabrielle, and he noted her surprise at Kirby's unexpected defense. The amazement melded into approval, and a small grin soon made her eyes fairly dance.

"Are you a disbeliever, then?" the reverend challenged, his cheeks flaming with fervor.

"That's none of your business," Kirby said with deceptive laziness. "Be assured the baby will be well cared for." His eyes turned toward the thin boy with the frightened face. "I would suggest you take care of your own flock."

Reverend Dander's body went stiff with indignation. "The Lord will provide."

"I expect you were hoping *we* would help the Lord," Kirby said sarcastically.

The man's face gave him away. That was exactly what Dander had expected, Drew thought.

Kirby looked again at the reverend's forlorn band. "You're going west with just those two wagons?"

The reverend nodded.

"Hell, don't you know there's hostiles out there, along with outlaws who'd kill you for your horses?"

"The Lord will protect us."

Kirby's lips straightened into a thin line. "That might be good enough for you, but what about those children? They look to be starving, and I don't think they're so anxious to meet their maker."

For the first time, the man's stiff back dropped, and his maniacal gaze lost some of its shimmer. "We *are* hungry. We had a broken axle and—"

"And you want another mouth to feed?"

"It's our duty!" the man snapped.

Kirby shook his head, then turned to Gabrielle. "How much food do we have left?"

"We're running low," she replied. "Just one more sack of coffee, a barrel of flour, a bag of beans, and some remnants of bacon. But we can probably spare a little of each."

"I-I was hoping we might get a cow," the reverend said hesitantly.

Kirby spun on him. "We don't slaughter steers— our own or other ranchers', " he said. "Besides, your family could never use all the meat before it spoiled, and I'll not waste an animal. You're welcome to join us tonight for a meal, and you can have what supplies we can spare." He hesitated a moment, then added, "For the children."

"And the Indian baby?" the reverend persisted.

"He stays with us," Kirby said, glancing at Gabrielle.

Reverend Dander visibly struggled between his need for food and his desire to save a heathen. He surrendered to hunger as he sniffed the bacon and fresh bread on the fire. "We would be grateful," he said stiffly.

But Drew suspected that he hadn't given up. Seeing Gabrielle looking helplessly between the chuck wagon and the fire, realizing she didn't trust the good reverend enough to put the infant down, he strolled over to stand beside her.

"I'll take the bairn," he said in a voice meant only for her ears.

She hesitated, obviously reluctant, and when she looked up at him, he held her gaze steadily.

"I won't let Ha'Penny out of my sight," he assured her.

Her eyes searched his in a way that did extraordinary things to his heart, that somehow stormed the barriers he'd erected to protect himself.

He reached for the child, and without further hesitation, Gabrielle handed him over. He felt nine feet high as the bairn snuggled against him, trusting and content.

He saw Kirby's amused eyes on him, felt the reverend's frustration.

He closed out both and did what he had vowed never to do. He lost his heart. Entirely.

Chapter Seventeen

Gabrielle kept an eagle eye on the reverend and his brood.

She'd known precious little about the West before she and her father had started out eight months earlier. But she'd had a university's worth of education thrust upon her since joining the drive.

She could eye the newcomers now with something akin to pity. They knew even less than she had. At least, she'd had the good sense to be frightened, to know she was doing something dangerous. And she had been alone, risking no one's safety but her own. At least she'd thought not. Now she knew that one tenderfoot could cost lives. One mistake could kill.

Her observation of Reverend Dander's band made her search her own conscience. Her preconceived notions had been proven wrong. She'd misjudged the drovers, believing that her "sort"—Easterners—had a monopoly on civilized sentiments. Though the drovers expressed theirs in starkly different ways—mainly with curses and wagers and joshing—their courage, kindness, and steadfastness humbled her.

Kirby Kingsley had also humbled her. She no longer questioned the Scotsman's loyalty to the trail boss. Although loath to show any weakness, the trail boss was a good man, decent to the bone. He was not her father's killer, and she owed it to him to tell the whole truth. Perhaps she would have discerned his character earlier had she not been so grief-stricken and obsessed with the convenient belief in his guilt.

Stubbornness, she knew, was her greatest fault. Once set on a path, she had difficulty leaving it. Her stubbornness was the reason her father had finally consented to come West. It was the reason he had died. Kirby Kingsley was not at fault.

Kingsley's startling defense of the Indian nations had astounded her, as had his ploy to get Ha'Penny milk from the cow. Clearly, he was a man who despised prejudice and injustice. And she had committed both against him out of her fierce but misguided desire to find justice for her father.

Justice? No, in honesty, she couldn't call it that. She had not set out from San Antonio with justice in mind. She'd only been seeking someone to blame for her sudden, unbearable loss.

Worse, still, she had tried to use the Scotsman to accomplish her ends. Not deliberately, perhaps. But could he ever see it otherwise?

As she stirred the pot of beans over the cookfire, she glanced toward Drew. He still held Ha'Penny, and she didn't miss the tender look in his eyes as he whispered comforting words into the babe's ear. She wished she could hear what he was saying. She wished he were whispering in *her* ear. Certainly not until she told Kirby Kingsley the truth, told him everything she knew.

But when? And how? She would have to find a way.

Reverend Dander's gaze followed her throughout

the meal, his mouth pursed disapprovingly at her trousers and cropped hair. In honor of the visitors, she used the last of their canned fruit for dessert. The six children gobbled everything as if they hadn't eaten in a month.

"Where exactly do you plan to go?" Kingsley asked the reverend.

Dander shrugged. "Wherever we're needed."

"You mean you have no destination?"

Dander looked indignant. "The Lord will guide us."

"You know anything about any of these tribes?"

"I know they need the Word of God."

Kingsley's sigh was loud enough to be heard in God's vicinity. Several of the drovers smirked, and one laughed outright. Kingsley silenced them with a look.

"They have their own god," Kingsley said. "They have their own religion, and it's a right fine one. If you don't respect that, you'll never be welcome among them. Now, if you'll excuse me, I have to speak to my wrangler." He rose stiffly and strode off in the direction of the remuda.

Gabrielle watched him, more curious than ever about the man she had been so sure was a murderer. Seen with new eyes, he was far more interesting and complex than she'd realized.

She gathered up the dishes. She would have to wash them and start a new pot of coffee before being through with her chores. At least she had water to wash with and not just sand. She gave Honor the few scraps that remained on the plates, then turned to walk toward the river.

She hesitated when her gaze was caught by Drew's. He was sitting by the fire, Ha'Penny tucked in the crook of one arm and his supper plate balanced on his thigh. His golden hair and eyes both seemed to reflect the firelight. Dear Lord, how she loved him, loved the gentleness in him that he tried so hard to hide.

Hesitating, she approached him. "Will you come with Ha'Penny and me to the river?" she asked.

He cast her an ironic glance. "The good reverend will suspect the worst."

"He does already," she replied.

"In that case . . ." Drew handed her his plate and rose, babe in arms. "Aye, I'll come with you."

Ha'Penny gurgled, letting out a tiny squeal of excitement, and Gabrielle tore her gaze from Drew's to see that the baby had grabbed the end of the red bandana tied around his neck and was tugging on it, clearly delighted with his toy.

"Little Ha'Penny," she said. And raising her gaze to Drew's once more, she smiled.

His gaze burned through her with fierce intensity, but he only looked at her for a moment, before saying, "Let's go."

She nodded.

They walked side by side to the river, with Honor bounding ahead of them. When they reached the bank, Gabrielle set the pans at the water's edge, then turned to see Drew at the top of the bank, making a bed of sedge grass in which to lay Ha'Penny. She joined him, and they both looked at the baby, lying happily in his cozy spot. His eyes were growing droopy, his movements lazy, and she hoped he'd fall asleep.

Still looking at the babe, Drew spoke quietly. "Are you sure you don't want the reverend to take him?"

Her gaze flashed to him. "To be raised like those sad, silent children?" she asked.

"There's something to be said for silence."

She searched his features, looking for a hidden meaning in his words, but clouds, scurrying across the moon, put his face in shadows. "Who would want silent children?"

He rose to stand beside her, and his voice was suddenly tight, as if each word was forced out. "My father used to say that they were the only kind worth having."

"Your father?" she repeated cautiously, wanting him to continue. He'd said so little about himself.

"We were talking about Ha'Penny," he said. "How can you raise a baby alone? Perhaps it's best to give up the child."

She gazed at him sorrowfully. "How can you say that?"

"I know women often grow weary of bairns," he said. " 'Tis sometimes best to let them go before they . . ."

She waited for him to continue, and when he didn't, she said, "You think I'll grow tired of Penny and abandon him?" She couldn't disguise the hurt in her voice.

He shrugged, taking a few steps along the bank to stand with his back to her. "It's been known to happen."

As it happened to you, she added silently, knowing she was right. Though his words had been spoken dispassionately, she recognized the pain behind them.

Walking over to him, she turned to face him. "It will never happen to Ha'Penny," she said quietly. "I have some money, and I can always sing."

"With a child tugging at your skirts?"

Gabrielle supposed she ought to be indignant at his lack of faith in her, but she wasn't. Instead, she felt like crying. She understood now, she thought, the source of his pain, and it made her ache for him.

No one had loved a small boy, least of all the father and mother he spoke of in such toneless phrases. But had the grown man allowed anyone to love him? She doubted it, doubted he'd ever permitted anyone to get close enough to give him what she knew he needed. It explained so much—why he kept his distance from everyone, why he had avoided Ha'Penny. Why he was so angry—so hurt—over what he perceived as her betrayal.

"I will take care of Ha'Penny," she said to him. "I will watch over him and love him."

"Isn't this maternal streak rather sudden?" he said wryly.

"I'm old enough to know my own mind," she said. "And I've always thought I would have children someday."

He hesitated, shoving his hands into his back pockets to look up at the clouds racing across the moonlit sky. "If you wanted children, why haven't you married?"

She spoke past the lump forming in her throat. "I haven't met anyone I wanted to marry." *Until now* . . .

"Ah, bloody hell." He shrugged. "I donna pretend to know a woman's mind."

"You're just suspicious of them?"

His golden eyes bored into hers. "Haven't I reason to be?"

His words and the brief glance he gave her were full of skepticism, and she couldn't deny it was deserved. She had lied to him repeatedly. She had lied to his friend. Though she'd considered her reasons good ones, he obviously did not.

"I'm going to tell him," she said. "I'm going to tell Kingsley everything."

His head jerked toward her, his eyes spearing hers in the darkness. "Everything?"

"Aye," she said, trying a tiny smile.

His mouth twitched at one corner, but he didn't actually return her smile. Quietly, he said, "Kirby might well ask you to leave."

She nodded. "I know."

"You don't have to tell him, Gabrielle," he said. "I won't."

"Don't you think I know how much it's been hurting you to keep my secret?" she said softly.

"It was my choice, lass."

"I *made* you choose, and I'm sorry for that. And I don't want you to have to keep choosing—not any longer."

Drew was silent. She wished she could see his expression, wished she knew what was in his eyes. How she yearned to see again the passion and longing, there in his tawny gaze.

She swallowed hard. Had her decision come too late?

"What made you change your mind?" he asked.

"The man who defended Ha'Penny wouldn't hire someone to kill for him."

"No," Drew agreed. "He wouldn't."

He could have said more. He could have said that he'd tried to tell her that. Instead he simply looked at her, and as the clouds broke overhead, letting the moonlight through, she saw in his eyes a slow thaw beginning.

She would have liked to help the thaw along a little further, but at that moment, Ha'Penny decided he'd had enough of adult conversation and let out a loud protest. Honor, who had been lying beside the babe, guarding him, hopped up and uttered a quiet "Woof," also telling them that it was time they paid attention. Gabrielle walked over to scoop Ha'Penny into her arms, cuddling him, which brought immediate satisfaction to his tiny face. Content once more, he let his eyes drift closed.

Drew looked at the baby, then gestured with a nod toward Honor. "I think Honor has deserted the calves for Ha'Penny," he said, amusement coloring his tone. " 'Tis the greater need in his eyes."

Gabrielle loved the sound of laughter in his voice. "He's probably been waiting all his life to be a nanny," she said.

"Aye," he said. "He's a fine dog."

"Have you ever had a dog?"

"Nay," he said. "My . . . father did not believe in keeping pets, and I was sent away to school when I was verra young."

"Sent away?"

"Aye, 'tis the way of it in Scotland, and Britain, too."

"It must have been lonely."

He shrugged. " 'Tis the way of things," he said again.

His words said almost nothing, but those unvarnished facts told her more than he knew.

"Is your father still alive?"

"Nay," Drew replied. "He met the devil ten years ago," Drew replied.

"And your mother?"

"She died when I was away at school."

"And you had no brothers or sisters?"

He smiled suddenly, a wistful half-smile. "I have a half-sister. She's in Denver."

Gabrielle remembered his offer made weeks ago of someone in Denver who might be able to help her. "You mentioned someone in Denver?"

He nodded. "My sister Lisbeth's husband."

"You're close to them?"

"Not close, really." He hesitated, then spoke in that careless, indifferent tone she'd come to recognize as veneer for his deepest feelings. "You see, Miss Parker, I'm a bastard, in fact if not in law. My so-called father gave me the use of his name because he dinna want the world to know he'd been cuckolded. But it dinna lessen his hatred o' me." Ice edged Drew's words, and his brogue deepened as he continued. "I grew up wi' no real family. 'Twas not till a year ago that I learned of my half-sister. Nor did she know of my existence. So, you see, we've only recently discovered each other."

Tears welled in Gabrielle's eyes, and she reached out to touch his arm. She felt him trembling and had to bite her lips to keep a cry of sadness from escaping, sadness for the stark loneliness of this splendid man's life. It nearly put her own recent grief to shame.

Drew looked at her hand on his arm, then raised his gaze to meet hers. She knew he saw her tears.

"All that I spoke of occurred a long time ago," he said. "Ye ha' far too tender a heart, Gabrielle."

"But a shallow one?" she asked, remembering his comments about her maternal capacity.

"I dinna say that."

"But it's what you think."

"I think a child is one bloody hell of a responsibility, 'tis all," he said.

As if to emphasize that point, Ha'Penny chose that moment to rouse once more, his eyes opening and his face screwing up before he let out a holler. There was nothing wrong with his lungs, Gabrielle thought. Again Honor jumped to his feet, staring at her, reminding her of her duties.

She tested the babe's bottom and found it dry. "Would you be wanting some attention, then?" she crooned softly. "Or is it time to eat?"

He was so soft, so sweet cuddled against her. She bowed her head, letting her cheek touch his. She already loved him with all her soul, with all the yearning of a heart that hungered to love.

The baby quieted again, though he stayed awake, looking at her with his great dark eyes. He was such a solemn little thing.

She looked at Drew through the wetness in her eyes. "I will always love him," she said. "I know you don't believe me, but I will. He'll smile and laugh and learn to play. And to trust." *As I would like you to trust.*

Pausing for a moment, she began thoughtfully, "You said your friend in Denver is a lawyer. Could he help me adopt Ha'Penny?"

Drew regarded her warily. He obviously disapproved. But she knew no lawyers, nor how to go about finding a trustworthy one. She did know that she would trust any man that Drew trusted.

"The bairn may have relatives," he said.

"Living?" she said skeptically. "Not his mother. And his father probably died in battle."

"Probably is not good enough," he said. "Ben will want to make sure."

It was another subtle challenge to her integrity. Did she care enough about the child to try to find surviving kin who might take him?

"I want to be sure, too," she said.

The corner of Drew's mouth turned up in a slight smile, and his eyes warmed considerably.

"I intend to finish the drive though," she added. "If Mr. Kingsley will let me after . . ."

The smile disappeared from Drew's face. "I'm not sure you should," he said. "When whoever shot at Kirby discovers he's not dead, they'll come after him again. I don't want them to find you, too."

She frowned. "So you really think the two incidents are connected."

"I don't believe in coincidences," he said simply.

But Gabrielle sensed that he knew more than he was telling her.

"No outsiders will know Mr. Kingsley survived until we reach Abilene, will they?" she said worriedly.

"We'll be going into a small town tomorrow for supplies," Drew said. "News travels fast out here, especially about a drive as big as this one."

She shivered, thinking about the possibility of another ambush. Of Kirby Kingsley being shot. Of *Drew* being shot, because he would try to protect his friend. Suddenly, she realized that she didn't care nearly as much about finding her father's murderer. Nothing, not even that, was worth another life.

"No one would fault you for leaving," Drew said, obviously misunderstanding her shiver.

"No," she said. "It's too late for Mr. Kingsley to get a new cook. He needs me. And so do the calves and Billy and Honor and all the hands." *And you need me*, she added to herself. *And if I leave now, I'm afraid I'll never see you again.* "I won't go," she announced. "Not unless Mr. Kingsley makes me."

Drew's eyes darkened, he swore under his breath.

Then his hand went to her cheek, touching it lightly. "I don't want anything happening to you, lass," he said.

Too late, she thought. It's already happened. *He* had happened to her. And she would never be the same.

His hand was hard, callused, against her cheek, yet it was the finest texture she had ever felt. "Drew, I don't want to leave you," she whispered. "I *can't* leave you."

Drew groaned, and suddenly his lips were on hers, hard and forceful and demanding. She felt the fierceness of his desire—and the tenderness she'd feared she had lost forever. He joined his mouth with hers in a delicious, erotic mating that made the tension build inside her, that wondrous craving that made her entire body sing. Tremors ran through her as his hands ran up and down her arms, trailing fire.

His arms came around her, and he started to pull her to him, then stopped, foiled in his efforts by the baby she held.

"Bloody hell," he swore softly. Then, with a groan, he pulled away far enough to look down at Ha'Penny. When he lifted his gaze to hers, the pure, undisguised passion in his eyes sent waves of heat wafting through her.

"I want you, lass," he said, his voice ragged.

She gave him a breathless smile. "He'll go to sleep after I feed him." And it was just as well this way, she thought, for she couldn't have made love with the baby awake and there, with them.

The backs of his fingers brushed her cheek, then clasped her chin gently. She felt so small next to him, even fragile.

"I'm not sure this is even wise," he said slowly, but his voice was thick with need.

"I've never been terribly wise," she said.

He smiled at her. "Neither have I."

She shook her head. "Oh, but you are."

He snorted softly. "Ye donna know me."

"I do," she said. "I know your generosity and your integrity and your gentleness. I know all I need to know."

"No, lass," he said softly. "Donna make me into something I am not. I've led a profligate life. I hav'na had any ties, and I donna want any now. I ha' bloody little to offer anyone but trouble."

His words held a warning she had no intention of heeding. From her parents' example, she had learned to believe in love. Now that she was testing it for herself, she felt greedy for more. She would value every minute she spent with Drew Cameron, regardless of the outcome. The awakening feelings, the glorious splendor, the sweet magic—no matter how short-lived—would last a lifetime in her heart.

Gabrielle swallowed at the emotions welling in her throat and put her hand to his face in a gesture of trust, of love.

His eyes softened. "I never expected . . ."

But he didn't finish the sentence. Ha'Penny began crying again.

She gave Drew a rueful look. "He's hungry. I have to feed him soon."

"Aye," he replied. "You go. I'll see to the dishes."

She nodded. "And after Ha'Penny's asleep . . . ?" She let the question trail off.

"I'm not on duty until morning," he replied.

"We could . . . take a walk."

"Aye. We could."

Gabrielle swallowed, the invitation in his eyes leaving no doubt about where their walk would end. But she had one other thing she had to do first.

"I want to talk to Mr. Kingsley," she said, "before we . . . before our walk."

Drew nodded. "I'll stay near the wagon and listen for Ha'Penny for you."

She hesitated. "I don't want to tell him that you've known all this time."

"Then, that won't be telling the truth," he admonished gently. "If you don't, I will."

Again, she hesitated. "Drew, I never meant to make you a part of it."

"I made myself a part of it," he said. "I'll go with you if you wish."

She shook her head. "No. I have to do this alone."

Taking her hand in his, he kissed her palm.

Gabrielle felt the warmth of his lips travel throughout her entire body. An hour. Perhaps a bit more. He would be hers again. For a while.

Drew watched Gabrielle walk back to camp with Honor at her heels, and as he stood staring after her, the sense of belonging that had evaded him all his life flooded him.

Still, foreboding nagged at him. He had bloody little to offer Gabrielle, not even the faith that he knew how to love. And he couldn't, wouldn't, disappoint a child. He'd never offer something he couldn't deliver or make a promise he couldn't fulfill. So wasn't it better not to offer anything at all?

Still, he ached like bloody hell. He tried to smother the flames licking at his groin, but nothing he told himself worked. He wanted Gabrielle as he'd never wanted anything in his life.

With a humorless, self-deprecating laugh, he turned to the dishes Gabrielle had left by the water. As he knelt to scrub them, he thought about how he must look. If only his old gambling companions at the Edinburgh clubs could see him now, washing dishes and dressed as he was. He'd always taken pride in his clothing, choosing fine fabrics and careful tailoring. And here he was, his cotton shirt and denim pants dulled with dust and dried sweat, his hair untrimmed and combed with fingers instead of a brush. He was used to excellent meals; now his menu consisted of beans and jerky and bread. His hands, more accustomed to cards than to cattle, were sun-browned and callused.

Yet he'd never felt better in his life. No more mornings after from heavy drinking the night before. And no more nagging regrets—regrets that he'd won money from people who couldn't afford to lose it, regrets that he was wasting a life simply to get even with a man long dead.

His companions had enjoyed him because he was good with a quip and a joke, but he'd had damned few friends he'd trust at his side in times of trouble. Westerners had an expression: *I'd ride the river with him.* Drew had never had a friend with whom he'd ride the river—not until he'd come West. Now he had several. Kirby. Shorty. Hank. His brother-in-law Ben. Men he could trust. It was a fine feeling.

And then there was Gabrielle. Pretty, independent, stubborn Gabrielle. Gabrielle, who was offering her heart to him.

He had been able to resist her when he felt she was using him. But her confession today had been like a crack in a dam; all his defenses came tumbling down. It had taken courage for her to admit she'd been wrong, and even more to admit it to someone she'd schemed against. He'd admired her before for her grit, for her determination, but never more than he did now.

He wanted to tell her what Kirby had told him earlier, that he had participated in a robbery many years ago. But it was Kirby's business, Kirby's secret, Kirby's past. Still, the rancher would surely grasp the connection when Gabrielle told him about her father.

If she told him.

Drew clenched his jaw, shoving aside the doubt that had leaped into his mind. She would tell him. She had said she would. And he would not doubt her again.

Quickly finishing the dishes, he took a few minutes

to wash up a little himself. Then, gathering the dishes, he headed back to camp.

He had a rendezvous to keep with a lady.

Kirby Kingsley watched Drew approach camp, carrying an armload of dishes. He'd seen Drew and Gabrielle leave camp, he carrying the baby and she the dishes, and the dog running in circles around them.

He hid a smile behind his coffee cup. He envied Drew and Gabrielle a great deal. They were so obviously falling in love. Their glances alone would ignite dynamite, although both, he'd noticed, were trying desperately to conceal their feelings.

He liked Gabrielle, enough to risk keeping her on the drive despite her gender. She had learned fast, had taken over easily from Pepper, and she never complained. She was gutsy, and really quite pretty once she'd washed off the trail dust and lost the coat and hat that had nearly swallowed her.

He did wish he knew more about her, though. Drew Cameron was his friend. Hell, he seemed to be his guardian angel. He would have liked to keep the Scotsman on after this drive, but he doubted that would be possible. Drew was not the kind of man to take orders for long. He was doing it now because he wanted to learn. But once he'd mastered these lessons, he would seek new challenges.

He watched Drew dump the dishes into the chuck wagon, then walk to the back of the hoodlum wagon, where he stood for a moment or two, speaking to Gabrielle. She was visible, sitting inside the wagon, feeding the baby.

Finally, Drew walked over to join him at the fire. Four drovers were playing poker a few feet away, and several others were already asleep. All was quiet from the Dander brood, too, tucked up inside their wagons.

"A bonny night," Drew observed.

Kirby smiled to himself. The Scotsman added a special flavor to the drive, no doubt about it. Some of the other hands were even answering in *ayes* and *nays*.

"Could be some rain coming," he replied.

"Will you be scouting out in the morning?"

Kirby nodded.

"Is Terry going with you?"

"Don't think there's any need. Not till after Caldwell. We haven't met up with anybody who might report that I'm still alive."

Drew paused, then said, "What about that army lieutenant?"

Kirby shrugged. "He's heading straight south."

"Still, I'd feel better if someone rode along with you."

"You want to go?" Kirby thought he knew the answer before it came. Hell, anyone would rather ride scout than eat cattle dust. And while the Scotsman already seemed to have a sixth sense about danger, maybe he could teach him something new, the rudiments of scouting.

"How would Damien feel about it?" Drew queried.

"Damien's needed here to ramrod the cattle while I'm gone."

Drew was silent for a moment. Then he said, "Perhaps I should wait to say yes. By tomorrow, you may not want me around."

Kirby looked at him, baffled. "What the hell is that supposed to mean?"

But Drew didn't have a chance to reply. At that moment, Gabrielle emerged from the hoodlum wagon and came toward them, and Kirby noticed that her steps were missing their usual lightness.

Coming to a stop before him, she said, "May I see you alone, Mr. Kingsley?"

Kirby looked at Drew, whose eyes were enigmatic. Then he stood and guided Gabrielle away from the fire, out of camp, toward the river's edge, where conversation would be private.

"Are you quitting on me?" he asked her.

"No, sir," she replied, "but you might soon be asking me to."

"Scotty just told me the same thing," he grumbled. "I would like to know why."

"I've been lying to you."

"Hell, I knew that."

She turned to face him, looking straight up at him as she said, "I joined your cattle drive to kill you. I thought you'd killed my father."

Kirby was too stunned to speak. It was all he could do to keep his jaw from dropping open. His mind shuffled frantically through the past, seeking some clue for what in hell she could be talking about. He gave up. Surely the man who'd been killed in the robbery couldn't be Gabrielle's father.

"Who . . ." he began.

"My father was once Jim Davis," she said.

Kirby's blood ran cold at the name, and it nearly froze in his veins as she continued.

"All my life, though, I knew him as James Parker. He was shot down in San Antonio nearly four months ago. He . . . mentioned your name as he died."

Kirby could barely think for the memories, the sheer force of emotion. The four of them, his old gang: Sam Wright, Jim Davis, Cal Thornton, and him. And on the fringes, as far away from danger as he could keep him, there was Jon. Standing there, on the bank of the Cimarron, the nightmare became real again.

"What name—" He broke off, cleared his throat and tried again. "What name did your father say? Kingsley or—"

"Kirby Kingsley," Gabrielle replied. "He recognized you from a sketch in the San Antonio paper with an article about the drive. He'd torn it out."

Kirby couldn't catch his breath. That damned picture. Someone had sketched him, and it had been a good likeness. But he'd changed in twenty-five years; he hadn't thought . . .

"Did your pa say anything else?" he asked.

"Yes," she said slowly. "He was losing blood pretty quickly, but . . ." Her voice quivered, trailed off, then began again. "He said, 'The article. Kingsley. It's him. Danger.' And I thought he meant it was you who'd shot him—or that it was you who'd hired the gunman."

She took a ragged breath. "He also told me about a letter he'd left in his trunk. He'd written it to me because he'd seen the article and the sketch, and I think he was worried something would happen to him. He wanted me to know why." She paused, then finished, "The letter told all about a robbery. But you already know about that, don't you?"

Kirby didn't even consider trying to bluff his way through this. She already knew the truth. And he was damned tired of lying, of hiding. Besides, whoever had shot Jim Davis, he realized, had to be the one behind the attempt on his own life. The connection was too direct, too clear, for it to be otherwise.

"Which one were you?"

Her question jolted him from his thoughts. He immediately knew what she meant, but he wasn't quite ready to answer. He was finding it hard to give up the habits of a lifetime.

Sighing, he looked out across the river. "Tell me first—what happened to your father? Where did he go after the robbery?"

She was silent for a moment, then said, "He went East, met my mother, who was an actress, and joined her in touring the country. She died two years ago, and he and I continued touring together. I wanted to come West. He didn't want to come but . . . but I convinced him."

Kirby heard the guilt in her voice. Christ, he knew how guilt could eat away a soul.

He heaved another sigh, remembering Jim Davis, his friend who was always whistling or humming a tune. He'd played a mouth organ, too. And he had been the most reluctant of them all to rob the bank, the one who had suffered the most when the clerk was shot. But Cal Thornton had convinced them all that no one would be hurt, that they were only stealing money from greedy bankers. Kirby hadn't realized until later that they were stealing from ranchers and small farmers and merchants, who lost everything they had in that robbery.

"If you thought I murdered him," he said, "why didn't you go to the law?"

"I did," she admitted. "No one would believe you could be involved in murder. They wouldn't listen to me and finally they wouldn't even talk to me anymore." Her voice dropped to a murmur as she added, "They didn't put any credence in a singer and sometimes-actress accusing one of the most powerful men in Texas of murder."

"So you decided to beard the lion yourself," he concluded, shaking his head. "Young lady, I don't know whether you're the bravest woman I've ever met or the craziest. If you thought I was a murderer, didn't it occur to you that I might have killed you, too?"

She looked at the ground, seeming to study it as she replied, "I didn't care if I died. When I left San Antonio I was . . . well, it didn't seem to matter what happened to me."

God, he could almost have cried for the pain he heard in her voice—a voice far too young to feel such grief.

Uncomfortable with such strong emotion, and with the protective instincts she roused in him—that he was now certain she'd roused in his Scotsman—Kirby sought to divert them to less painful ground. Giving her a brief, sideways glance, he said, "So, you're a singer, like your pa?"

She nodded. "And an actress, like my mother, though Daddy and I both liked singing best and, after Mama died, that's all we did. We had an engagement at the Palace in San Antonio. My name *is* Gabrielle, but my full name is Maris Gabrielle Parker."

Kirby remembered her. He remembered several ranchers talking about the lovely singer at the Palace. The name had meant nothing to him, nor had he any inclination to travel hours to see a performance. Now he wished he had. Perhaps he would have recognized Davis, perhaps he could have somehow prevented . . .

"Mr. Kingsley, my father was a good man," Gabrielle said, her gaze meeting his directly once more. "Everyone liked him. I couldn't believe . . . I mean, he never said anything about Texas. I didn't even know he'd ever been here. I don't understand how . . . how he could have . . ."

Kirby heard the grief in her voice. And the bewilderment.

"You would have had to be there to understand," he said quietly. "You would have had to be there."

Chapter Eighteen

Gabrielle held her breath as Kingsley hesitated.

Anguish deepened the lines in his face as he began to speak. "Both your father's father and mine had small farms along a river near what is now Austin." He gave her a fleeting, half-smile "When they weren't much older than I thought Gabe Lewis was, they both fought against Santa Anna, then settled on adjoining property that fronted on a creek. Your father and I played together when we were small. My brother was much younger, and your father had no brothers or sisters."

He gave a short nod. "We had good land, some of the best, because of the water. Apparently, it was *too* good, because another rancher tried to buy out both Jim's and my father's land. When that didn't work, our fathers were conveniently killed while taking cattle to New Orleans. Apaches, it was claimed. But we never believed it. Especially when the bank called in their loans and the farms were promptly sold to the man who'd been trying to buy us out. My mother was already dead, and Jim's mother died soon after losing the ranch.

"I was seventeen, and my brother Jon just a kid. Your father was sixteen. We were angry, bitter, hot to get even. The rancher wanted us out of the area, made sure we couldn't get work. My brother was hungry. Hell, all three of us were hungry. Then we started running with Cal Thornton and Sam Wright."

Shaking his head slowly, Kingsley hooked his thumbs in the top of his trousers and took a couple of paces along the edge of the riverbank. Stopping, he swung around to face the river again, then continued. "Cal said he came from north Texas, said the same thing had happened to his pa that happened to our fathers. Sam was his shadow. I never did know much about him. One night we all got liquored up—Cal provided the bottle—and we talked big about how it would solve all our problems to rob just one bank. Cal goaded us on. We were fool enough, young enough, and desperate enough, to listen when he explained how easy it would be. He swore to us that no one would be hurt.

"The next morning, neither your father nor I wanted to go through with it. But Cal had the tongue of a serpent—said we owed it to our fathers, taunted me for not taking better care of my brother." Kingsley shook his head. "That was all I needed to hear. I was already feeling guilty as hell about not taking good care of Jon. So we finally agreed."

When Kingsley paused, Gabrielle took a deep breath. Her father had never spoken about his parents, and she'd always wondered why; if she asked, he simply said they'd been dead a long time. Perhaps, she thought, he'd never talked about them because any mention of them would have led to reminders of a past that he wanted to forget.

"I've often wished to God I could take back that

day," Kingsley continued. "And I know damned well Jim felt the same. He said so. Right after we did it."

Gabrielle recalled her father's letter, its every word dripping with remorse. Hesitantly, she asked, "What . . . what happened that day?"

"We rode into town at midday and watched the bank until all the clerks had left but one. Then we went inside. Jon was to wait outside with the horses. Your father stood guard at the door, and Cal held a gun on the clerk while I rifled the cash drawers. When Cal told the clerk to open the safe, the man said he didn't have the combination. Cal hit him until he remembered it. Then, when Cal had taken the money out of the safe, he turned and shot the clerk. For making him wait, he said."

In her mind's eye, Gabrielle could see the horror on her father's face as clearly as she heard it in Kingsley's voice. Two frightened youths—hardly more than boys—who'd lost their homes and families. She ached for her father, and for the man now telling the tale with such visible pain.

"We ran out," Kingsley went on. "Damn, but I was scared—and sick to my soul at the easy way Cal had shot that clerk. It was so damned pointless. But I kept thinking of my brother—and, admittedly, myself— and we rode like hell out of there. When we divided the money we decided it was best to separate. Each of us would change our name and head in a different direction. Jon and I went south to another part of Texas, Jim headed east, Sam was supposed to go west, and Cal north. I never saw any of them again."

Kingsley sighed deeply as he came to the end of the story, and silence settled between them. The night was still except for the distant lowing of cattle.

Then he took a few steps toward her and reached out, placing a large hand on her shoulder. "Gabrielle, Jim Davis was my friend," he said softly. "I'm sorry."

Somehow, his sympathy touched her more deeply

than had anyone's since her father's death. Gabrielle nodded. "Thank you," she said tearfully.

"Now—" He looked at her expectantly as he let his hand fall from her shoulder. "Tell me why you decided not to shoot me dead the first time you saw me."

Lowering her gaze, she turned away from him to face the river, watching the reflection of the half-hidden moon and stars ripple across the black surface as she spoke. "I told myself I wanted to wait until you were away from your ranch," she murmured. "That I was waiting for the chance to get you alone. But, looking back now, I don't think I ever really would have done it. At least, I hope I wouldn't have. Then, the night of the stampede, with Juan's death and Ace getting hurt"—she let out a ragged sigh—"I don't know. Somehow, having so many horrible things happen at once sort of shocked me out of where I'd been, inside myself. And I realized that I couldn't kill you. That I couldn't kill *anybody*."

Kingsley was silent for a moment, then said, "And now? Why, after all this time, did you suddenly decide to risk telling me the truth?"

"Because in the past few weeks, I've seen who you are," she said simply. "I know now that you couldn't possibly be responsible for my father's death. Oh, I wanted you to be, or I would have admitted the truth to myself sooner. I thought . . . I thought I wanted justice. But now I wonder whether I only wanted to blame someone besides myself."

"Hell, girl, you had no way of knowing your papa would be running into danger in Texas. For God's sakes, don't blame yourself!"

She turned her head to look at him. "Then who?"

His head turned toward her and their gazes met, and she saw his face harden in the sliver of moonlight.

"I can make a good guess," he said. "Cal Thornton. Some months back, just about the same time your father was shot, someone tried to ambush me. Drew saved my life."

Gabrielle hesitated, then spoke in a voice that was barely audible. "Someone shot at me, too. The gunman who killed my father. When he'd shot Papa, he took aim again to fire, but Papa threw me down under him as he was falling."

Kingsley's eyes widened. "Dammit . . . Gabrielle. You mean to say you came after a man you thought was gunning for you, too? All by yourself?"

Mortified that she'd so misjudged Kingsley rather than for her own reckless behavior, Gabrielle flapped her hand helplessly. "I was only thinking about Papa, that I couldn't let anyone get away with killing him. Besides"—she waved her hand again—"I knew once I cut my hair and started being Gabe Lewis, no one would recognize me."

"Well, hell, that's the truth," Kingsley muttered, though his tone held a trace of amusement. "You sure had me fooled well enough."

"Until I fell into the river," she said, adding disconsolately, "Twice."

His lips twitched. "Poor Drew," he said. "How much of this does he know?"

Gabrielle wanted to lie for Drew. She wanted to tell Kingsley that Drew knew nothing, had concealed nothing from him. But she knew she couldn't. "He knows everything," she said. "I told him just a few days ago. And I swore him to secrecy," she added hurriedly.

"Dammit, but that man must be a vault of secrets," Kirby murmured. Then, abruptly, he asked, "What made you decide that I couldn't be involved in your father's death?"

"A lot of things. But mostly what you did for Ha'Penny," she admitted.

He grinned suddenly, and the transformation was so unexpected, she was startled. She also thought he should do it more often.

"I was afraid I'd lose my cook—and maybe even my best hand. I've seen the way Drew looks at you when he thinks nobody's watching."

She bit her lip. "You won't blame Drew?"

"No," Kingsley said. "He keeps his word, and God knows it must have pained him. He tries so damn hard to mind his own business." A chuckle escaped him. "And fails so miserably."

Oh, she did like Kirby Kingsley. Her father's friend. A lump rose in her throat as she wondered if he would become her friend, too. At that moment, she knew she would like that very much.

"I think Jim did very well for himself," Kingsley said softly. "I envy him. And I'm sure your mother was a wonderful woman, too."

Gabrielle nodded. "She was. It nearly broke Papa's heart when she died."

Kingsley sighed. "I'm glad that he found someone. I didn't have his courage. I was afraid someday . . ." His voice trailed off.

She saw the loneliness now. No wonder he kept everyone at arm's length.

"Mr. Kingsley, I know it isn't enough," she said, feeling horribly inadequate, "but . . . I'm sorry that I misjudged you so badly for so long. I don't have any excuse to offer that makes up for believing what I did of you."

He gave his head a quick shake. "Forget it. People think and do all sorts of things when they're grieving that they'd never do otherwise. It's best not to dwell on them but to just move on. The thing we've got to do now is figure out how to find Cal Thornton before he finds us." Frowning, he muttered, "I'd stake my life it's him. Now that I know about Jim—and you. One way or another, it seems you're in as much danger as I am."

Gabrielle didn't want to believe him, but it would have been plain stupid not to. "And you're sure it was this Cal Thornton," she said. "What about the other man, Thornton's friend?"

Kingsley shook his head. "Sam didn't have enough sense to put on a hat during a rainstorm. No, it's Cal, all right. The only other question is why. Why, after all these years?"

"He must think he might be recognized," she said. "He must be in a position where you could see and identify him."

"After all this time?" Kingsley shot her a dubious look. "And what about your father? From what you said, he'd just come back to Texas."

She thought hard. What else would her father and Kirby Kingsley have in common? What, after all these years, could have spurred this sudden burst of violence?

Kirby also had a thoughtful look on his face. "At least," he finally said, "Thornton can't have any idea that you're with us now. But maybe it would be best if you left before we reach Abilene—so you'll have no obvious connection with me."

Gabrielle looked at him. She knew he was only thinking of her safety, but . . .

"I want to stay," she said, her heart suddenly pounding. "Besides, I got a glimpse of the man who shot my father."

Kingsley's head jerked toward her.

"I didn't see much," she admitted. "It was dark, and he was at the end of the street, in the shadows. But I know he had a silver band on his hat, and his build was . . . was like Drew's. He was very tall and lean, and he moved . . ."

"Like a cat," Kingsley finished for her. "Smooth, fluid, like it doesn't take any effort."

She nodded. "Yes."

"Hmm." Kirby stared at the ground for a moment or two, then as a sudden thought struck him, he looked at her quickly. "You didn't think that Drew . . ."

Miserably, she nodded. "When I first saw him, I did. But not for long. And not at all after . . . after the trip to Willow Springs." Gabrielle felt heat rising in her cheeks, felt Kingsley staring at her, and was glad the moonlight was obscured by the clouds.

"Sonofabitch," Kingsley swore softly, "I think it's time I turned in my spurs. Things going on under my nose, and I don't see them. Hell, I should—" He broke off, and even in the watery moonlight, Gabrielle could see his face turn a ruddy red. An instant later, he started sputtering an apology. "I keep forgetting you're a lady. I didn't mean that the way it sounded."

Gabrielle couldn't hold back a giggle, blessed relief after so much worry.

"It's hard getting used to Gabrielle after Gabe," Kingsley said in his own defense. "Gabe eventually made a real fine louse." He gave a crooked smile. "Wonder what Pepper would have thought. In fact, I wonder if the old dog knew from the beginning."

Gabrielle somehow liked the thought, even if it didn't say much for her acting abilities. "I miss him," she said.

"We all do. He was a fine man," Kingsley agreed. "Question is, what do we do now? At least, now I know something about why someone's trying to kill me, and I thank you for it, but I want you out of danger. You should go back East."

Gabrielle shook her head. "There's no reason for me to go East. I don't have any other family, and . . . Mr. Kingsley—"

"Kirby."

She hesitated, then offered him a tremulous smile. "Thank you. Kirby. But, please, I don't want to go. I want to find out who killed my father."

"Oh, we'll find out, all right," he said. "And we'll let you know. But, meanwhile, you'll be safe. Jim would skin me alive if he were here and I let you stay on, knowing somebody's gunning for you."

Gabrielle's heart was racing. She couldn't leave

now. Not after they'd come this far. But she had no rational arguments to offer about why he should let her stay—except the truth. And she couldn't bring herself to put into words what she hardly dared let herself hope might come true if she were allowed to remain.

All she could do was look at him with her heart in her eyes and say, "Please. Please, don't make me go."

He studied her long and hard. Finally, he said, "It's Drew, isn't it?"

She knew he could read the answer on her face. She couldn't have hidden it if she'd tried.

He looked at her for another long minute without speaking. Then, finally, he sighed. "All right," he said. "You can stay—for *a while*."

"Oh, thank you," she breathed, relief rushing through her.

"Don't thank me yet," he warned. "I want you to keep looking like Gabe Lewis—or at least some approximation of him. And I don't want any of the drovers to know who you really are, not even my nephews. It's too easy for someone to slip."

"Thank you," she said. "I . . . I don't deserve it."

"You're Jim's daughter," he said simply. "You deserve it, all right."

And before she could reply, he turned and walked away.

Gabrielle stayed by the river. Wrapping her arms around herself, she huddled in their embrace, unsure and a little confused by the myriad feelings whirling inside her. She felt new, unburdened for the first time in months; she hadn't realized how heavy a toll it had taken on her to live a lie all day, every day.

She also felt humbled. She'd embarked on a quest to gun down a man who had turned out to be one of the best men she'd ever met. He might forgive her for being insane with grief, but she would never quite forgive herself for misjudging him so badly.

Mostly, she guessed, she felt frightened. Not of the

danger facing her—though she supposed she ought to be afraid of that—but of the future. She wanted to allow herself to envision a future with Drew, but she was afraid to hope, afraid to dream. Afraid that, after all her lies, he would never really trust her again. She didn't even dare for more, though her own heart cried out for it.

Staring blindly at the black water flowing past her, she stood waiting, wondering when, and even if, he would come to her.

Ha'Penny was asleep in his makeshift bed, and the dog lay next to him, a self-appointed sentinel. Drew sat on the back of the hoodlum wagon, watching them both with bemusement, a warmth creeping in to fill the empty hollows of his heart.

He wished a part of him wasn't leery of that warmth, that he knew how to accept without questioning these new, unfamiliar feelings.

If he went back to her tonight, he knew he would be taking that risk. He would be making a commitment as surely as if he'd spoken it before God and man. He'd never considered himself a gentleman, but neither had he ever played with female hearts for the sheer sport of it. All his past liaisons had been with experienced women, the simple rules of engagement known beforehand. He seldom returned more than once, thus avoiding even the slightest hint of personal involvement.

But Gabrielle . . . ah, Gabrielle was different. Even her name warmed him. Excited him. Made him ache with an intense wanting he'd never known. She somehow made him smile inside, made his heart beat with a yearning so strong he could barely breathe. He suspected bedding her was not the way to exorcise her from his system. He'd done that once, and it had only made him want her more. If he did it again, she'd become even more entwined in the threads of his being and, he feared, more essential to him.

Sighing, Drew jumped down from the wagon to get himself a cup of coffee, but as he walked toward the fire, he saw Kirby emerging from the dark shadows of the trees. Drew stood and watched his approach, bracing himself for the questions he knew were coming.

"Drew," Kirby acknowledged, coming to a stop beside him. "Gabrielle told me quite a story."

Drew nodded.

"She said you knew about it."

"Aye."

"Found yourself in quite a dilemma, didn't you?"

Hearing the note of amusement in Kirby's voice, Drew replied dryly, "Seems so. Ever since I stopped in that bloody saloon and overheard the men plotting the ambush."

Kirby grunted. "Can't say I'm totally sympathetic. I'd be dead if you hadn't."

"You think the same man who hired those gunmen killed Gabrielle's father?"

"I'm sure of it," Kirby said. "I'm just not sure why."

"So you knew her father?"

Kirby nodded. "We were friends once. Before we let a dangerous sonofabitch talk us into robbery—and murder."

Hesitating, Drew asked, "And Gabrielle? What will you do about her?"

Kirby eyed him thoughtfully. "She's staying on for a while. I don't think she'd be safe out there alone. Here, no one knows who she really is. I doubt anyone would connect our Gabe—or even our Gabrielle—with an actress named Maris Parker. At least, not anytime soon, they won't. But if someone's after her too, she won't really be safe until we discover who it is."

"I know," Drew said. "I'm guessing that the

gunman took a shot at her because he thought she might have seen him—not because of any connection with her father and you—and the old robbery."

"I agree," Kirby said.

"Any ideas about who hired the gunman?"

"I'd bet everything I have it's Cal Thornton. But we all changed our names, and I have no idea what he might be called today or even if I'd recognize him. I didn't know him long, and he's a quarter of a century older. I do remember his eyes, though. Light blue. And cold. Like ice." Kirby paused. "Gabrielle said she got a glimpse of the gunman. Said he was tall and lean and that he wears a hat with a silver band. Does that description fit any of the men you saw in the saloon?"

Drew tried to think back, tried to picture the three. But he'd been sitting with his back to them and hadn't really gotten a good look. They'd all seemed disgruntled cowhands out for an easy dollar. He shook his head. "I'm afraid not."

"Then we have to assume whoever is behind this has the resources to hire several killers."

"Inadequate, careless ones, though," Drew said. "They missed Gabrielle, and they never checked to make sure you were dead, back there in Indian Territory."

"I keep wondering about that," Kirby said. "Only thing I can figure is the gunman saw my horses gallop off and assumed that if I wasn't dead, I soon would be. Or something scared him off. I sure as hell would have been dead if you hadn't found me."

"So, what we need to know," Drew concluded, "is how long it will be before they find out exactly how wrong they were."

"And come looking and find Gabrielle as well," Kirby added.

Their eyes met, and Drew smiled. "Perhaps they'll find a trap instead."

"Exactly my thought," Kirby said. "If we can catch the sonofabitch, we can find out who hired him.

Except it could be dangerous for Gabrielle." Pausing, seeming a little uncomfortable, he asked, "Do you think you could persuade her to go back East? At least for a while?"

Drew uttered a brief laugh. "I think that would be like telling a tornado which direction to take."

Kirby grinned. "Yeah, she's got spunk, I'll give her that. Her father was my friend. I've missed him, but damn, his spirit lives on in her. Maybe that's why I took to Gabe Lewis, even when I didn't know who he . . . or *she* was."

Drew was silent. He was pleased that Kirby and Gabrielle had clearly made peace with each other. And it seemed that Kirby didn't blame him for his own lack of candor. Yet his friend's absolution didn't alleviate his sense of guilt over withholding possibly vital information.

"Dammit, Drew," Kirby said, interrupting Drew's musings. "I think the gal's waiting for you by the river. If it was me, I sure wouldn't be standing around jawing."

"Kirby . . ."

"If you're worrying about not telling me all this before, don't," the rancher said. "I held you to a secret, and Gabrielle did the same. I don't think less of you because you honored both. Besides, you seem to be my guardian angel, and I'd be a fool to risk going against Heaven."

"I'm one bloody odd guardian angel," Drew said bleakly. "It must be one of God's jokes."

"Joke or not, I'm grateful to you. Now go to Gabrielle. I think she's worried about you. And don't worry about the babe. Either Hank or I will be in camp, and we'll listen for him."

Drew nodded, some of the weight lifting from his soul. No more secrets. Yet a great deal of turmoil remained. He wanted Gabrielle. He wanted her more than he had any right to want a woman. But what did he have to give her in return?

Still, his legs moved him in the direction of the river and, as he approached, he saw her silhouette outlined against the black sky. Coming to a stop a few feet behind her, he spoke her name softly. "Gabrielle?"

She turned quickly, walked the few steps to him, and held out her hand. He took it, feeling the strength in it. She was such an appealing combination of vulnerability and toughness that his heart pounded from the sheer glory he felt being near her. Silently, they walked hand and hand far upstream, seeking privacy.

When the campfire was a mere dot of orange in the distance, he stopped. His arms went around her and he crushed her to him. Her arms circled his neck, holding tightly as if to keep him there forever.

Forever was a word he'd never used. *Forever* scared the hell out of him. And yet he melted under the pure, sweet savageness of her need, of his own. His heart throbbed, and he had to strain for breath.

"You were right," she whispered. "I should have gone to Kirby long ago."

But then he cut off any other words as his lips caught hers and they clung to each other, savoring a new intimacy rooted in budding trust as well as unrestrained passion. Her right hand entwined itself in his hair, and her mouth opened to his. Love was in her every caress, a tenderness he'd never felt, never known before she came into his life.

It deepened the lust in his body, this passion of the soul. He was astonished at the aching longing he had for her. He wanted to touch and feel every part of her. His hands moved up and down her back, causing her to tremble as his kiss deepened.

A soft purr came from her throat as his tongue ravished her mouth; then her tongue reached tentatively to spread flames of its own. Nothing mattered now to him but to feed the fires raging within. He could no longer control them—and he didn't try.

He moved his lips from her mouth to the nape of her neck, and again he felt her tremble. He was aware, in some fogged part of his mind, of her hands leaving his back and unbuttoning his shirt, and then his own hands were on her shirt, her trousers, his fingers unusually clumsy as they fought to release buttons that were suddenly much larger than the holes.

And then he felt her body, slim and lovely and soft. He took off his shirt and spread it on the ground, then carried her down with him to kneel on the fabric. He found her breast with his mouth, licking his way to the taut nipple, caressing, teasing, until he felt it grow hard, and her body shivered.

Her hands were on his waist, then his trousers, and he was suddenly free of the last vestiges of clothing. The clouds chose that moment to free the moon, as well, and he saw the wondrous expectation in her eyes, the elation.

His body echoed her obvious yearning, the frantic hunger of hers, as they came together. He felt the desire—God help him, the love—as their lips met again. The universe seemed to explode in that kiss. An elemental force, as potent as a storm-whipped ocean pounding the cliffs, locked them together, and his desperate prayer for sanity went unheeded. The current was too strong, the force too great. In a soundless minuet, they were flat on the ground, his body stretched out above her, his manhood touching the soft curve of her belly.

Her breathing was ragged, but her face told him everything he needed to know. "Drew," she whispered. "Andrew Cameron . . ." Any further words seemed caught in her throat.

Still, he knew what they were, but he didn't know how to answer. So he said instead, "Are you sure, lass?"

She nodded. "Very."

And again, he hesitated, then said, "I'll try to keep from getting you with child." He saw in her eyes the hurt he felt in the sudden stiffening of her body.

"I'll not trap you," she said in a broken whisper.

"I'm thinking of *you*, lass."

She didn't say anything more. Instead, she lifted a hand and her fingers touched his cheek. Her body trembled under his.

He felt his chest tighten as he surrendered to the raw yearning driving him. He entered her, slowly at first, then faster as the pulsing center of her gloved him. She gave a low, rasping cry of pleasure as his thrusts deepened, and their bodies joined in a magical dance, its rhythm quickening with every movement. He felt her arms tighten around him, felt the warm moisture inside her. Then he heard her small cry of rapture. He was barely able to control himself enough to withdraw and collapse upon her, quaking with his own surrender.

He rolled over, breathing heavily, his hand clasping hers. He'd wanted to stay within her. He'd wanted it so badly he'd almost betrayed both of them. But he would not get her with child. He would not bring a bastard into the world.

Gabrielle was quiet. Too quiet. Still, Drew swallowed the words he wanted to say, the promises he wished he could make. Because he hated promises nearly as much as he'd hated lies.

Gabrielle snuggled into Drew's arms, trying desperately to bridge the canyon she suddenly felt yawning between them. She'd seen the despair flicker in his eyes, and it had made her heart constrict painfully. Despite their stunning intimacy of moments ago, he seemed isolated again, detached, as if he'd hung out a red flag warning off anyone who might get too close.

But the warning was too late. She'd already lost her heart. And the arm around her was cold comfort when she felt the tension of Drew's body, as if he wanted to bolt.

Had he not forgiven her, after all?

Or was he really afraid she might try to trap him into a marriage he didn't want?

Had someone else tried to do that? Had there been women—a woman—he'd cared about in the past? One, perhaps, that he still cared about now?

Gabrielle thought there probably had been many women in Drew's bed over the years. As inexperienced as she was at lovemaking, she sensed his expertise. That knowledge hurt, but not nearly as much as thinking that there might have been one special woman.

Suddenly, she had to know.

"Drew?"

"Hmm?" he mumbled.

"Is there someone else? A woman?"

His arm tightened around her. "No, lass."

"Was there one?" Her voice sounded very small to her.

"No one. Until an urchin in the worst-looking hat I've ever seen fell into a river."

Emotion nearly choked her. It wasn't a girl's fondest dream of a compliment, but it was the closest he'd come to an endearment. And she would gladly take what she could get. She snuggled deeper into his arms, listening to the beat of his heart and feeling his chest rise and fall.

"I'm sorry I lied to you," she said. "And Kirby."

"Kirby?"

"He told me to call him that. He and my father were friends. Neighbors," she added shyly. She was still reeling a little from all the revelations of the day— discovering new pieces of her father's past, getting to know him better, and in the process, finding an old friend of his. She felt as if she'd unearthed a treasure. "They grew up together."

Drew didn't reply, but she went on, hoping to recapture the intimacy between them. "Papa *was* in a robbery with him," she admitted sadly, realizing she'd once hoped to learn it wasn't true. Now, at least, because of Kirby, she understood her father's reasons—and the pain he'd carried with him all the years of his life. She'd seen it alive in Kirby.

"I know," Drew said. "Kirby told me. It's the reason he's never married. He was always afraid his past would come back to haunt him."

"And he was right."

"Aye. It's been a high price to pay for one foolish mistake."

Wanting him to keep talking, but wanting to hear about him, not someone else, Gabrielle said quietly, "You never told me why you left Scotland."

His chest rumbled with a low, ironic sound. "Nearly half of Scotland has left for your western gold fields, and many more for your cities. You have a rich country, lass, and a fine one for a gambler."

"I once heard you and Kirby discuss ranching."

"Aye. I'm thinking on it. But it would take a bloody long time and a lot of money. 'Twould be no life for a lass, not for quite a while."

He'd made himself very clear. And whatever remnants of hope, of satisfaction, of rapture, Gabrielle had tried to cling to turned to ashes. The thought of losing him devastated her.

"Have you thought about where you'd want to go?" she said weakly.

"Colorado, I think," he said. "If I decide upon it. But I'm not sure I'd want roots. I wouldn't know what to do with them."

Another warning, even clearer. She bit down on her lower lip, swallowed the stone in her throat, and slowly moved away from him. Drawing the shirt around her, she sat hugging herself.

Drew reached to pull on his trousers, then rose with easy athletic grace. He held out his hand, and she took it, allowing him to lift her to her feet.

"Gabrielle . . ." he began, sounding uneasy.

She put a finger to his mouth. "No, don't say anything. You don't owe me anything. Far from it. I, on the other hand, owe you my life." She tried to stem the hot rush of tears, fumbling with the buttons of her shirt and combing her hair with her fingers.

She started almost blindly toward camp, but he grasped her and stopped her progress. "Blast it, Gabrielle."

She fought his hands. She wanted to get back to the wagon before the tears came. But he whirled her around until she faced him, and when she looked up at him through misted eyes, she saw agony etched on his face.

"Gabrielle," he said again. "Gabrielle . . ." And then his lips came down on hers with fierce possession.

Chapter Nineteen

Drew knew he should let Gabrielle go, but he couldn't. Not this way. Not with the tears she tried so desperately to hide glistening in her exquisite blue eyes.

"You don't owe me anything," she had said. But he did owe her. Because of her, he could feel again. True, he felt pain and loneliness as he hadn't since he was a child. But he also felt joy, joy as he had never experienced it. The sun was brighter than it had ever been, the grass greener, the sky bluer. He reveled in the world around him in a new way. And, too, he was tasting of the richer things life had to offer—friendship, loyalty. . . .

And love. He knew what he felt was love. His heart was bursting with it, even crying with it, as he saw the tears glistening in Gabrielle's eyes and knew he'd put them there. The tightness in his throat made it nearly impossible to breathe as he clasped her to him and, for the first time in his life, put his heart into a kiss.

He loved her. But he couldn't yet speak the words locked inside him. So he tried to tell her without words, tried to say *I love you* with the touch of his fingertips on her cheek, her hair. With a caress of his lips against her eyes, her throat . . . her lips. With his arms, he sheltered her body, trying desperately and with his entire being to tell her *I love you, Gabrielle, I love you.*

But then, unforeseen, an insidious thought snaked through his mind. *"I owe you my life."* Did she truly feel that she owed him something? Was that why she was here with him? Was that why she'd made love with him?

Drew's arms loosened, and his lips left Gabrielle's. He stepped back, taking her chin in his hand until she looked up at him. "You don't owe me anything," he said. "You never will."

The clouds chose that moment to dim the moon, and the telltale blue eyes that often revealed so much were obscured in shadow.

"Don't mistake gratitude for . . . for love," he continued, his voice harsher than he had intended.

"Is that what you believe I'm doing?" she said, her voice cracking slightly.

"I don't know," he said honestly. "I don't know much about . . . good women."

She touched his chest. His shirt was still unbuttoned, and her fingers lightly grazed his skin, sending tremors racing through him. His groin started aching again.

"I've been an actress—a performer—nearly all my life," she said. "Most people consider women who make the stage a career to be loose—fallen women— whether we are or not."

Drew winced, remembering that in his experience, actresses were usually fair game.

"You? A fallen woman?" he said, a finger going up to push back a wayward curl. "I don't think so."

Her smile penetrated the shadows, breaking

through the misery on her face, and he thought about how striking she must be onstage. Her smile alone would captivate a crowd. She hadn't smiled much recently, and he felt himself largely to blame.

"You're beautiful," he said, touching her cheek.

One of her hands went to her hair, to the short curls, in a self-conscious gesture.

"Don't regret cutting your hair?" he said suddenly.

"I don't," she said. "Not really. I love the freedom. I only miss it because it reminded me of my mother's hair. Mine was like hers."

"How long was it?" he asked quietly.

"Nearly to my waist," she said.

He tried to picture her with long ropes of dark hair, but that woman wouldn't be his Gabrielle. His Gabrielle. When had such possessiveness ever been a part of him?

Never. Yet, suddenly, the very thought of someone else touching her hair, or any part of her, was pure torment.

"Do you miss the stage?" he asked, even as he fought the shocking urge to carry her away to some remote hideaway and keep her there forever.

She shook her head. "I thought I would, but without Papa and my mother . . ."

"You miss them very much, don't you?" He remembered his own vague sorrow when his mother had died—not so much for what had been but for what he'd always hoped could be—and none at all at his father's passing. But then the earl of Kinloch had not really been his father.

She nodded. "I never spent a day without them until my mother died a few years ago. And then, at least, my father was still there."

Drew couldn't even imagine her life, her love for her parents, the safety she must have known, that safety suddenly gone with a gunshot.

He wished he could give her that safety again. But he had no security to give, no pledge. No future. Only an empty title that was pure mockery to him. So, he simply held her, her head resting against his heart, and wondered about the price of keeping her there. The price to him. The price to her.

Gabrielle finally eased away from Drew, leaning back to look up at him. Shadows shielded his eyes from her, but she sensed his inner turmoil—his reluctance to leave her warring with his fear of staying or of getting any closer than they already had.

"I have to get back to Ha'Penny," she whispered.

"Aye, and I to the cattle," he said. "Or Damien will ha' more to fret about."

"Do you really think anyone cares whether Damien frets?"

"Aye. I do," Drew said quietly. "He's trying bloody hard to live up to what he thinks Kirby wants. It's not always easy to stand tall in another man's shadow."

She heard the concern in his voice.

"Kirby cares for Damien, as he does for Terry," Drew said slowly. "And Damien cares for his uncle. The two simply don't know how to talk to each other."

It occurred to Gabrielle that Drew and Kirby had become friends because they were very much alike. Neither of them knew how to reveal their thoughts or feelings, and both feared any kind of intimacy. Yet each was capable of bone-deep loyalty and affection.

Still, Drew's understanding for someone whose blanket animosity was clear to all touched her. Again, she was astonished by his quiet insight and his compassion for the very people he tried so hard to keep at arm's length.

"You're smiling," Drew said, breaking into her reverie.

"At something Kirby said," Gabrielle replied.

"What?" he asked suspiciously.

"I'm not sure you'd want to hear it."

"Tell me."

"He said you try so hard to mind your own business—and you fail so miserably every time."

Drew scowled and muttered an oath.

She touched his face. "I like that in you. Your caring."

"I don't," he said stubbornly, like a small boy.

"Aye, but you do care, and everyone knows it. You're a fraud, Drew Cameron."

"Talk about frauds," he said with mock severity.

"I know," she said. "I'm a terrible one. But at least *I* admit it."

"Ah, Gabrielle. I wish I could reach up and hand you that moon and a fistful of stars, but I can't. My hand would hold only air. I could pluck a coin from behind your ear, but that's as far as my magic goes. I've never been good at anything but illusion, and it's impossible to live for long on that."

Not true, she wanted to cry out. He was good at everything he tried. Kirby himself had called him the best hand he had, and the rancher was a man who rarely paid compliments. And he would be good at trusting, too, if he decided to try—surely as good as he was at erecting fences between him and other people.

In an odd way, though, she loved him all the more that he was cautious. She'd heard declarations of love before that had been as meaningful, and as substantial, as a feather in the wind. When Drew Cameron finally admitted love, it would be forever. With all her heart, Gabrielle wanted to be the one to whom he made the declaration.

She took his hand. "We'd better get back," she said.

"Or Kirby will send out a posse," he agreed.

"Damien, at the very least."

"Most likely Damien," he said with a chuckle. "He's probably stewing by now."

Gabrielle nodded. She hurt for Drew, for his loneliness and lack of faith in his fellow man—and woman. But she was certain now that he loved her, and she thought he was coming closer to admitting it. A day? A month? Even a year?

She would wait however long it took.

The drive reached Caldwell two days later. Kirby stopped the herd three miles east of town and sent Drew and Gabrielle in for supplies.

He watched with a mixture of trepidation and amusement as Gabrielle donned her Gabe Lewis garb—a coat borrowed from one of the drovers—not as disreputable as her own had been but large enough to swallow her—and Hank's battered hat drooping over her eyes.

As he'd expected, all of the hands had protested, saying they deserved a drink or two—or three—and a night on the town. But Kirby knew he couldn't afford loose talk. He didn't want anyone to know he was still alive, and he didn't trust any of the hands not to let it slip. A few wrong words and a killer would know he had failed. He figured that only Drew and Gabrielle knew the stakes.

Hank volunteered to look after Ha'Penny, saying he'd raised a passel of younger brothers and sisters. After watching him with the baby, Gabrielle had finally agreed to leave the child in camp. Kirby wasn't sure whether she had more faith in Hank or in her dog; he was only grateful that he'd finally convinced her to accompany Drew, and he watched in relief as the two of them pulled out in the hoodlum wagon.

He never liked to send a drover into a town alone, but in this case, he had ulterior motives. He had watched the Scotsman and Gabrielle return from the river a couple of nights earlier, had seen traces of dried tears on Gabrielle's face and a hint of bleak despair on Drew's. He'd thought of Laura, how he'd lost his chance to love and be loved, and he was damn well determined that the same thing wouldn't happen to his friend and his old friend's daughter.

He caught himself thinking of Laura more and more lately. Maybe if exposure of his past wasn't so imminent—so likely—he might have tried to court her after all. Watching Gabrielle and Drew together, the way their gazes seldom strayed from each other, made him ache inside for what had never been and never could be.

He poured himself a cup of coffee from the pot Gabrielle had prepared before leaving.

Damien, who had just ridden in, joined him. "The men are angry," he said. "They want to go into town."

"I know," Kirby said wearily. "Tell them there will be a bonus at the end of the trail."

"They're not thinking about bonuses. They want a reason."

"You also want a reason, Damien, don't you?"

His nephew hesitated; then anger flickered in his eyes. "You confide in the Scotsman, don't you? I know you think he saved your life, but Terry and I are kin, after all."

"I don't *think* Cameron saved my life," Kirby said sharply. "I know it. And he damn well doesn't want anything that's yours, if that's what you're afraid of."

"No," Damien said stiffly. "It's just . . . It used to be the four of us, dammit. You and Pa and Terry and me. Now it's always you and Cameron."

Kirby heard the hurt in Damien's voice, and he wished he could ease it. But he and his brother had vowed years ago to say nothing about how they'd gotten the money to start the Circle K. Even Jon's late wife, Sarah Elizabeth, had never known about the bank robbery. And he couldn't confide in Damien without discussing it first with Jon.

More than that, although he loved Damien like a son, Kirby knew his nephew was still young and a little wild, and he knew all too well that liquor loosened tongues. He just plain didn't trust Damien with his life. Not yet.

But he did trust Drew Cameron. He might not know the details of the Scotsman's life, but he knew enough to recognize that, for a man so young, Drew Cameron had more life experience—and little of it good—than Damien ever would *want* to have. Drew knew how to keep secrets—his own and those entrusted to him by others.

But what was he going to do now, right this minute, about Damien?

In the end, he said only, "Scotty's been a good friend. A good hand."

"Better than Terry and me?"

"You're foreman, Damien, not Scotty."

"But you make all the decisions—like keeping Two-Bits on the drive."

Kirby sighed. He'd seen Damien's attempts to attract Gabrielle. The girl hadn't rebuffed him as much as she'd simply been totally unaware of anyone but the Scotsman. "You know anyone else who can cook?" he pointed out.

"No, but I still don't like it," Damien said. "A woman has no place on a trail drive. And why was she here to begin with? You sure it doesn't have anything to do with those ambushes?"

Kirby didn't like the calculating look in Damien's eyes, the suspicion fed by the boy's jealousy of Drew.

He wished he could say more, but he couldn't, not without putting a stick of dynamite in his volatile, if unwitting, nephew's hands. "Yes, I'm sure," he said simply. "Now, I'll check on the watches. You get some food and sleep."

Damien looked as if he wanted to protest, but he didn't. Kirby headed for the remuda. Once the drive was over, he would try to repair his relationship with his nephews. If, he qualified, he was alive and free to do so.

• • •

Caldwell, Kansas, sat stoically in the blistering heat, a jumble of rickety buildings rising from the prairie.

Gabrielle strained forward on her seat, after weeks on the trail eager for a glimpse of civilization. She wondered whether the town had a theater or a restaurant. Especially a restaurant. She'd never been so tired of anything as she was of beans.

Drew was handling the team of mules. He'd been extraordinarily quiet on the two-hour drive into Caldwell, even though she'd peppered him with questions about Edinburgh and London. He'd been to so many places she'd only read about, and she was hungry to learn more about them—and about him.

His answers, however, had mostly been monosyllabic. His golden eyes had remained fixed on the horizon, and she'd wondered whether he missed those fine cities, whether he missed his homeland.

She pushed back a curl that had fallen alongside her cheek; her hair was growing out, and she had to tuck it under her hat. She longed for a few pins. She really longed for a dress, a fine dress that would make Drew's eyes light up the way those of the men in her audiences had.

But she didn't have much money with her, and she planned to use what little she did have on clothes for Ha'Penny. He still had only the deerskin shift his mother had dressed him in.

As they reached the road that ran through the center of town, she searched the signs fronting the wooden buildings. There was one saloon after another: Cowboy's Rest, The Longhorn, The Maverick, Trail's End. Then she saw a gunsmith's, a blacksmith. Another gunsmith.

Drew stopped at a dry-goods store and turned to her. "You have a list?"

She nodded. She'd taken inventory and catalogued everything they would need to reach Abilene. She knew Kirby wanted to avoid towns from now on.

Drew climbed from the wagon seat and turned to offer her his hand. Then he stopped, his hand half-raised, a wry smile on his face. Gabrielle grinned back. In the past few days, they'd almost forgotten their roles as cowhand and louse.

She swaggered into the store behind Drew, effecting the strut she'd seen practiced by young boys playing at being men. A heavyset clerk met them inside, visibly judging their clothes and weighing their ability to pay. He frowned and seemed on the edge of turning his back when he noticed the wagon outside.

"Settlers?" he asked.

Drew shook his head. "We're with a cattle drive stopped a few miles east of town. We need supplies." He handed Gabrielle's list to the storekeeper as she looked around.

Two men standing at the counter muttered angrily. "Where'd you say you left them cattle, mister?" one asked.

"East," Drew replied calmly.

"My farm's that way," the other man said. "Last herd that went through trampled my crops. We're damned tired of you Texans riding roughshod over our land."

"You tell me where your farm is," Drew said politely, "and we'll be sure to stay clear of it. We don't want any trouble."

"Who's bossing the outfit?" asked the first farmer, his jaw set at a belligerent angle.

Drew hesitated fractionally, and Gabrielle held her breath. They had already discussed the question with Kirby when he'd given Drew the cash for their purchases, and they'd agreed on the best response. Still, she was certain Drew was finding it hard to lie.

"Damien Kingsley," came Drew's reply, uttered in perfectly normal tones.

Gabrielle breathed a little easier.

"Heard of them Kingsleys," the second farmer said. "Nothing good, either."

He was obviously spoiling for a fight, and Gabrielle watched the scene unfold with apprehension.

But Drew merely shrugged, saying, "He's no better or worse than most."

"You got cash money?" the storekeeper asked.

"Aye, I do."

"You ain't no Texan," the first farmer observed.

"Astute of you to notice," Drew said, straight-faced, and Gabrielle had to pretend to wipe her nose with her hand to hide a grin.

"What did you call me?" The man stepped forward, his face mottled with anger.

"I said you were observant," Drew replied seriously. "And now we would like to get our goods and be on our way."

The storekeeper looked at his other customers and shrugged. "Let me see your money first."

Drew reached into his shirt pocket and took out a roll of bills. "Will this be sufficient, do you think?"

The storekeeper nodded, took the list from his hand, and looked it over. "You'll have to get them oats at the feed store, next to the livery," he said as he started to search his shelves for the other supplies. The two farmers headed for the door without further comment.

Gabrielle gave an inward sigh of relief and found a counter stocked with bolts of cloth. She ran her hand down a bolt of dark blue silk, then gently fingered a reel of ribbon. She looked up to see Drew watching her with his amber eyes glowing. As he stood in a beam of light coming through the large glass window in the front of the store, his hair was sun-gilded, falling in copper strands over his forehead and down to touch the very top of his shirt collar. His clean-shaven face was dark from the sun, and as she looked at him, he peeled off his gloves, revealing strong, powerful hands that she knew could also be gentle.

Not now, she told herself, forcing her gaze away from him. But her body didn't listen to the admonition; it was reacting in that hungry way it always did every time she looked at him—her heart racing and her blood simmering.

She turned back to the ribbon, trying to keep from caressing it as a woman would. But she couldn't resist another quick glance at Drew. His lips had turned up in that devilish half-smile that always melted her heart. His eyes shifted to something beyond her, and she let her gaze follow his. There stood a manikin dressed in a pretty blue calico frock and a jaunty hat.

Her gaze flashed back to him, and she found his eyes measuring her, then the dress. She shook her head imperceptibly, but his grin widened. Dropping the reel of ribbon back onto the counter, she moved toward a table with bolts of strong, practical material.

"For Ha'Penny," she said in answer to Drew's raised eyebrow, and she pulled several bills out of her pocket and placed them on the counter.

Sighing as though in resignation, he stood quietly while the storekeeper cut the fabric she chose, wrapped the parcel, and handed it to her with her change.

Then he asked the man, "Is there a good restaurant in town?"

The man shook his head with disgust. "Just saloons and a few boardinghouses. Might git somethin' at the hotel, such as it is. Or you might try the Trail Dust Saloon down the street. They have good steaks."

Drew winced, and again Gabrielle had to hide a grin. He'd adopted a cowhand's code as his own: Thou shall not eat that which you are herding to market. The very suggestion of eating beef was nigh on to blasphemy.

Politely, Drew inquired, "Would I be likely to find any mutton available?"

The storekeeper's eyes widened. "You crazy, mister? Mention sheep around here and you can get dead real quick."

Gabrielle heard Drew's sigh and sympathized. "We'd best get back, anyways," she said.

Drew glanced her way as he paid the bill and lifted one of the heavy sacks. "You go on to the feed store and order the oats for the horses. I'll load these things and pick up you and the grain on the way out of town."

Gabrielle protested. "But you need help loading."

"No, I do not," Drew said. "You go. I'll be along directly." He lifted one of the large sacks, gave her a final glance, and ordered again, "Go."

Now, she figured, was no time to argue, not with the storekeeper watching. But she turned toward the door with decidedly mixed feelings. Drew might be gallant, but she resented his sudden imperiousness.

She hugged her package for Ha'Penny to her chest and walked out to the wagon, placing the parcel under the bench. Then she headed toward the feed store, passing several saloons along the way.

Heat radiated off the street, and she wished she could discard her jacket. It was too risky, though, for both for her *and* Kirby. The mental reminder put her nerves on edge as her gaze skimmed over the other loiterers outside the saloons.

She pulled Hank's hat down farther on her forehead and continued on her way. Each saloon she passed was much like the other. But as she tried to pass the entrance of the third one, a crowd of men blocked her way. Among them she recognized the two farmers from the dry goods store.

"Pretty small for a drover, ain't you?" one man asked.

"You think he's old enough to hold a beer?"

"Hell, no. But he's old enough to buy some for us, since his kind been spoiling our land and polluting our water."

"What 'bout it, boy?" another asked.

"I heard the other one say he had plenty of cash money."

More men were coming out of the saloon now, aroused by the commotion. Anxiety pricked at Gabrielle. And the muttering grew louder. She'd heard about the Kansas farmers' growing animosity toward the large herds of cattle being driven through the state. Several young drovers had even been hanged, it was rumored. Her eyes darted around, looking for a way out.

Then she saw him. A tall man on the edge of the crowd, listening intently. A tall man with a silver band around his hat.

Her hands clenched at her sides, but she dared not show any recognition. She wanted to look back toward the general store to see whether Drew was aware of what was happening, but she didn't want to draw attention to him either.

Someone jostled her. "You understand English, boy?" one of the farmers said. "Or are you a foreigner like that other one?"

Her gaze skipped over to the tall man again, memorizing his face. It was gaunt, the cheeks hollow, the eyes small and dark like those of a bird of prey.

"You dumb, too?" another man asked.

"Must be dumb to wear all them clothes in this heat," someone jeered.

Gabrielle tried to edge herself out of the knot of men. She didn't have to feign her growing fear. If they touched her, they would soon discover she wasn't what she seemed.

The tall man stepped closer, and the crowd parted for him as the seas had parted for Moses.

"You with the Kingsley herd?" the man asked.

She nodded.

"Heard you had some trouble. That Kingsley was killed."

There was no way he could have heard, Gabrielle knew. Not unless he was the one who had shot Kirby and now was making sure that his quarry was dead.

Her eyes went to the silver band again. She was

staring at the man who had killed her father and tried to kill her. Her head began to spin, and red spots appeared before her eyes, but she held on desperately to sanity and reason, knowing lives, including her own, depended upon it.

She wished she had her papa's Colt.

Her gaze took in the man's gun and the easy familiarity with which it rode on his thigh. None of the farmers would be a match for him, nor, she thought, would Drew. Not with the rifle still in the wagon. She hadn't seen a sheriff's office, either.

And the man was still awaiting an answer.

"Cowardly bushwhacker shot him, killed him dead," she finally said. "Nephew's running the drive now."

The man's eyes grew colder, and he stared at her face. For a moment, she wondered whether she'd gone too far. She put her hands in her pockets, and clenched her fingers into tight fists. Only that way could she keep herself from flailing out at him.

She glared at him, though, daring that much, wishing she could dare a great deal more.

The crowd of farmers had inched away from the man who was obviously a gunfighter and who made little pretense that he was anything else. She didn't want to back away from him. Everything in her protested at that. But if she didn't move, she knew Drew would eventually see them and come to her rescue. Actually, she was surprised he hadn't already appeared. He must be settling up with the shopkeeper.

Gabrielle forced herself to turn away from the man with the silver hat band. And she vowed she would say nothing to Drew about the encounter. Not now. Not for a few days.

Her legs seemed wooden as she moved on toward the feed store, unimpeded now by the men who had slunk away under the gunslinger's cold eyes. She felt the man's gaze follow her, burning a hole in her back.

She finally made it to the feed store. Hands shaking, she handed the clerk her list.

As had the other storekeeper, he asked, "Got cash money?"

She nodded. "My partner's loadin' supplies at the dry-goods store. He'll be here directly with the money."

Unlike the keeper of the dry-goods store, this man was rail thin and ready with an easy smile. "Kinda young for a drover, ain't you?"

Ordinarily, she might have played cocky Gabe Lewis to the hilt and acted unduly annoyed. But the clerk clearly meant no harm, and she had more important fish to fry. She ignored the comment and went after what she wanted to know. "Got any law in this town?"

"Nope. Last sheriff was gunned down by a drunken cowboy. You Texans ain't real popular right now."

"I'm finding that out," she said grimly. "Fact is, I just saw somebody on the street with a mean-lookin' gun and an attitude to match. Wore his Colt real low, like maybe he was a paid gun."

The clerk shrugged. "Cow towns are always full of gamblers, cowboys, and killers."

"This one had a silver band around his hat," she said.

"Ah. You must mean Killian. Has a real bad reputation. Been hangin' around town a few days. No one knows what he wants. You stay clear of him, y'hear? He's a bad 'un."

Her questions were answered. There was no law to go to. But she had a name: Killian. Once they returned to Texas, they could take the name Killian to a marshal, then let justice take its course. Meanwhile, she'd bought them some time; it gave her no small measure of satisfaction that Killian now believed Kirby dead.

Still, she felt sick inside. For she would have to lie to Drew again. She couldn't tell him about Killian. She'd seen his reckless courage over and over again.

Kirby had much the same sort of stubborn courage. But, as much as she admired them, she knew neither Kirby nor Drew was a match for a ruthless professional gunman. And she wasn't about to take even the slightest risk that they might decide to take on the gunslinger themselves.

Drew wouldn't appreciate her trying to protect him—especially if it meant lying to him. But she remembered her father's death, and she still felt guilty. She would not—would not—be responsible for another death.

You're an actress, she told herself. *Play a part. Play the most important role in your life.* She could do it. She *had* to do it. She straightened her spine, set her chin. Justice for her father would come in time. Silently, she begged his forgiveness, and she knew he would understand. But for now, nothing was more important than keeping Drew Cameron, her Scotsman, safe.

She watched as the clerk dragged three large bags of oats to the door for her. She grabbed the fourth, struggled out after him, and looked down the street. The gunman, Killian, had disappeared, probably into a saloon to celebrate yet another death. She shivered again in the hot noonday sun.

"You okay?" the clerk asked, his eyes on her coat. "You aren't sick, are you?" He stepped several feet back from her.

She was, but not from the kind of contagious illness he feared. She was spared an answer as she saw the Kingsley hoodlum wagon creaking down the dusty road. She waited, her body tense, hoping Killian didn't suddenly emerge from the saloon. She'd told Drew about the silver hat band, and that kind of decoration was an expensive rarity in these parts.

Drew stopped the wagon and leaped down. He took one look at her face and questioned her with his eyes, but he said nothing, instead going inside with the clerk to settle the bill. She tried to lift one of the sacks of oats into the wagon but failed. She tried again, compelled to do something, anything, to hurry their departure.

Then Drew came back, lifting the sack easily from her arms and setting it in the back of the wagon. The other three sacks followed, and she climbed up onto the bench.

He climbed up after her, took the reins, and snapped them. She didn't look at him, but just as she'd felt the gunman's eyes on hers, she now felt Drew's.

You're an actress, she told herself again.

But a huge lump formed in her throat, and she wanted to be sick as he turned the wagon and started east. The trip to Caldwell has been all too short. The return journey, she thought, would be all too long.

Chapter Twenty

✣

Drew leaned against a tree and listened to Gabrielle sing a poignant ballad from the Civil War.

He looked around at the rapt faces of the drovers. Kirby had persuaded her to entertain them, and she'd agreed willingly enough. Yet she'd seemed uneasy about putting aside her duties in favor of a more relaxed evening activity. Indeed, since Caldwell two days earlier, Drew had watched as she'd immersed herself in cooking and taking care of Ha'Penny and the rest of her brood, keeping frantically busy every minute of the day, as if each one might be her last. One thing she hadn't done was spend any time alone with him. Indeed, she'd avoided it like the plague.

Something was wrong. Something that worried her, and she was refusing to discuss it with him. More bloody secrets, driving another wedge between them.

He recalled her sitting, tense and silent, beside him as they'd ridden back from Caldwell. He'd been trying ever since to imagine what had happened to change the lighthearted sprite who had chattered all the way into town. She hadn't been out of his sight long, only the ten or fifteen minutes when she'd gone to the feed store.

During that time, he'd queried the storekeeper about any strangers who'd come to town recently, but to no avail. Apparently Caldwell always had strangers—drovers, gamblers, and such—passing through.

The real purpose, though, of his having sent Gabrielle to the feed store without him had been to give himself a few moments to make a special purchase. The package he'd bought still lay hidden in the back of the hoodlum wagon behind the sacks of oats. He wanted to give it to her. Bloody hell, he'd bought it for her. But something about her evasiveness—his suspicion she was lying or at least withholding something from him—kept him from giving it to her.

He'd tried. He'd asked questions, but he'd received vague, monosyllabic responses that reminded him of her lying days—days not so far in the past. Something had happened in Caldwell, and she wouldn't tell him a bloody thing about it.

The drovers were grinning as Gabrielle started singing "The Yellow Rose of Texas." Ha'Penny squirmed in Hank's grasp, and Honor nuzzled closer, keeping a careful eye on the child.

As she sang, Gabrielle looked anywhere but at Drew.

Blast it all, he had started to believe in her, and he'd thought she was returning that trust. Now he knew she wasn't. Trusting, he mused bitterly, was highly overrated.

The song came to an end.

"What about you, Scotty?" Hank yelled. "Don't you have a favorite?"

He shrugged and started to move away from the fire. It was time to get some sleep. He had the midnight watch.

"Drew?"

Gabrielle's voice stopped him, and he turned.

"I know some English songs," she said. "Would you like to hear one?"

"I'm a Scot," he said curtly. "I don't particularly care for the English." He saw surprise on the faces around the fire. He seldom snapped at anyone. Hell, he *never* snapped, having never cared about anything or anyone enough to bother.

He heard Damien ask Gabrielle, "Can you do 'Lorena'?"

She smiled at Kirby's nephew and nodded. It seemed an automatic smile, a performer's smile, but Drew still wanted to strike Damien. He strode off as he heard her strong contralto fill the quiet night.

Maybe he would go out on watch. As he approached the horses, the pinto came over to greet him, nuzzling his hand, then his face. Drew felt the weight of the animal's affection. Since his father had killed his first horse—a lesson, the old man had told him, not to ever get attached to an animal—he'd never kept a horse for very long. He'd never wanted that kind of pain again.

But needs were simmering inside him now, needs he'd always denied before. They were hammering at him, giving him no peace. For the first time in his life, he wanted to love, he wanted to need, he wanted to be needed. And he thought he'd found what he wanted.

Damn her.

He saddled the pinto, catching himself in the act of considering names for the bloody beast. Grudgingly, he allowed that perhaps it was all right to name the horse; he would need a mount after the drive, and he'd thought about asking Kirby if he could buy the pinto.

Walking the horse slowly until he was away from the herd, not wanting any quick movement to stir the cattle—the last thing they needed in Kansas was a stampede—he spurred his horse to an easy canter. A few more weeks and they would be in Abilene. And his grand adventure would end. He would have decisions to make, decisions about the rest of his life.

About whether he would continue to drift through the years, ever a wanderer, or try to make something worthwhile of his existence.

But whether he drifted or put down roots, remained a gambler or became a rancher, he couldn't, for the life of him, imagine any kind of future without Gabrielle.

Gabrielle watched Ha'Penny sleep, his long lashes lying on his cheeks, the little fingers of one hand clutched around a doll she had made him out of a coffee sack. The fingers of his other hand were buried in Honor's fur as the dog lay contentedly next to him. Gabrielle mused that the two of them—child and dog—seemed destined for each other, each making their own tragic journey to find the other.

She had thought that she and Drew were destined for each other, too, but now she wondered. She'd seen the coldness in his eyes over the past several days and worried that he would not understand yet another time why she'd lied to him—even if the lie was one of omission. He had his own private code of honor, one that beggared most, and she loved him for it, even as she violated that which he most valued.

Better his contempt than his death.

They were five days from Caldwell, but that was only a couple of days of hard riding if unencumbered by a herd of cattle. Was it safe yet to tell Drew and Kirby about Killian? She wasn't sure.

Sighing, she fussed for a moment over Ha'Penny, making sure he was not too warm, not too cold, then she climbed down from the wagon to stoke the fire and put on a fresh pot of coffee. Pepper had always tried to keep coffee available, and so did she.

The drovers not on duty were asleep in their bedrolls. The night sky was clear, the stars as bright as she'd ever seen them, the moon a brilliant crescent. In the distance, she saw the dark silhouettes of thousands of cattle. There was an odd serenity about the scene.

The loneliness inside her deepened, became agonizing, as she realized her days on the trail were coming to end. In such a short time, she'd grown close to the men with whom she was traveling, and she'd come to look forward to the physical demands, too, for they led to an intense satisfaction and even joy.

She'd never considered any career but performing. Now she found it difficult to think about returning to the stage, to the open leers as well as sincere appreciation, to the paint and the corsets and revealing dresses. She loved the freedom of her shirt and trousers; she enjoyed the easy company of men who appreciated her for what she was rather than how she looked.

She didn't want hundreds of men's appreciation. She only wanted one man's appreciation—and his trust and his love—for the rest of her life.

She swallowed tears, knowing she was losing the man she wanted. But she didn't dare tell him the secret she was harboring. Not yet. Not until they were farther north, much farther north. And by then, it might be too late.

She leaned against the wagon wheel, knowing sleep wouldn't come easily tonight.

Kirby couldn't sleep. Tonight it seemed that the ground was too hard, his bedroll too warm, and his thoughts too disturbed. So instead of frustrating himself any further, he sat up, looked around the campsite, and saw Gabrielle leaning against the hoodlum wagon. She was one of the things keeping him awake.

He studied his cook. She looked pale, her usual vitality absent, and her expression grim. She'd looked that way for five days, ever since Caldwell.

Kirby considered the possibility that she could be just plain tired; after all, keeping after the babe and the rest of her flock, in addition to her regular chores, would be exhausting for anybody. And, too, they'd been stopping earlier each day to keep the cattle rested and well-fed—weight was vital to buyers—which meant her cooking duties started earlier and lasted longer.

He might have been satisfied with that explanation for Gabrielle's dreary mood, except that she wasn't the only one looking so dreary.

In fact, the Scotsman was looking even worse. His composed, easygoing friend had suddenly developed a temper and a short fuse to go along with it. He avoided the other hands, and he was even more close-mouthed than usual.

Kirby figured it was about time he found out what the hell was going on, and he thought he'd more likely jerk it out of Gabrielle than the Scotsman.

Climbing out of his bedroll, he stood up and walked over to the fire, where he poured himself a cup of coffee. Taking a sip, he sauntered over and sidled up to his cook. She gave a quick swipe of her cheek with the back of her hand, then offered him a very brief, clearly uncomfortable smile.

"What's wrong between you and Scotty?" he asked, leaning back against the wagon.

She was silent for a moment. Then, letting out a resigned sort of sigh, she said, "There's something you should know. I—I couldn't tell you—or Drew—before. I'm not sure I should now. But he knows I . . ."

"That you're holding something back," Kirby finished for her.

She nodded.

"So, what is it?"

Hesitantly, she said, "I think I saw the man who shot my father. Back in Caldwell."

Kirby's heart missed a beat, then began to thud hard as he listened to her continue.

"He was asking about you, said he'd heard you'd been killed. No one could have known about that shooting except the man who did it."

Kirby scowled. "Why do you think it was the same man who gunned down your father?"

She waved an arm, as though seeing the man she described, standing there before her. "He had the same build—tall and lean—a lot like Drew's. And his manner, the way he walked, was familiar, too, and he wore a silver band around the crown of his hat."

Kirby's scowl deepened. "Where was Drew when you saw this sonofa—Uh, this man?"

"In the dry-goods store," she replied. "He sent me on to order the feed. Some angry farmers stopped me. Then this man—his name is Killian—came along, and the farmers sort of melted back." She drew a quick breath, her anxiety over the incident plain in her voice. "He asked me about you. I told him you were dead. I thought he'd head back to Texas, and when we returned you would at least have a name and—"

"Dammit!" Kirby exploded. "Girl, are you loco?" He watched her chin set stubbornly despite the uncertainty in her eyes.

"I was afraid you might go after him," she persisted. "You and Drew. The feed store clerk said Killian was a hired gun—a killer."

"*Dammit,*" Kirby cursed again. "Why didn't you tell us?"

Her chin lifted another notch, but her voice cracked as she replied. "He killed my father. I didn't want him to kill you and Drew, too. There was no law there. The last sheriff had been gunned down, and the people didn't like cattlemen. I was afraid that Drew—"

"I think," he interrupted her, "that Drew would surprise you. He's no fool, Gabrielle. And neither am I."

She lifted her gaze to stare at him, her eyes suddenly bleak, the fingers of her hands locked together at her waist. "I thought—"

"You thought Drew would walk down the street,

guns blazing?" He shook his head. "You've read too many dime novels."

He saw her lower lip tremble as her gaze fell away from his and her chin lowered. "I couldn't bear to lose anyone else," she whispered. "Not again. Not that way, and not if I could do something to keep it from happening."

"Ah, Gabrielle," he sighed. Some of Kirby's anger faded as he understood what her decision had cost her. Not only had she risked alienating Drew, she'd sacrificed her own hope for justice, the goal that had driven her from the life she had known into the hardship and perils of a cattle drive.

"I'll never forget that night," she said, her voice a thready whisper. "The blood, the look in Papa's eyes. I kept seeing Drew like that. . . ." She drew a sharp little breath, looked down for a moment, then back up at him with desperate, searching eyes. "But I just delayed things, didn't I?"

"Maybe," he said slowly. "But at least I now have a name. That's a start." He paused. "As for Drew, there's no reason to tell him yet. At the end of the drive, he'll go back to Colorado and be safely out of it."

Kirby thought about what he'd said for a few minutes and realized instantly that his solution was no good. A bullet had been meant for her, too. And if the would-be murderer discovered that she'd been on this drive, which he might well do once the drovers separated, the bastard would probably figure she knew way too much.

"Tell him," he said abruptly. "Tell Drew what you saw and why you didn't tell him."

She frowned. "But you said he would be safer if he didn't know."

"I was wrong," Kirby said. "We're both underestimating him. We're both taking away his choices. He might be physically safer, but we'd be cutting the man to pieces. We'd be taking away his heart, and

believe me, that's a much slower, more painful death."
He took her hand. "I'll always wish I'd had a daughter
like you, and Drew's a damnably lucky man."

Gabrielle looked at him with troubled eyes, still
unconvinced.

"Look here, girl. You chose to come on this drive.
You chose it out of love for your father, because your
heart guided you. What if somebody else, not you,
had heard your father's last words? Would you rather
he or she had never told you for fear you might do
something dangerous? Would you rather your choices
be taken away?"

He saw her waver. "I couldn't bear it if . . ."

"You can bear anything," he said. "You're a very
strong young woman. And Drew's a strong man. He's
also smart as hell. I don't think he's ever had much
reason to trust anyone. Don't take away the one
chance he might have. He loves you, you know. Don't
disappoint him."

"I already have," she said in a small voice.

"But I don't think it's too late."

"And if he's killed? How can I live with that?"

Kirby gave her a twisted smile. "I don't think your
Scotsman's as easy to kill as you think," he said. "And
neither am I."

She paused, looking at her hands, twisting at her
waist. "He'll go with you after Killian," she said.

"Probably," Kirby agreed.

Her gaze flashed up to his. "I'm going, too! I can
recognize him."

"Now, hold on just one minute," he objected.
"Neither Drew nor I are going to let you risk your life
like that."

"Are you going to take away my choices?" she
challenged.

Kirby glared at her for all of two seconds, then
found himself chuckling as his own words were turned
against him. "If I wasn't Drew's friend," he said, "I
might give him one hell of a race for you."

She smiled. "No, I don't think so. Every once in a while, I see a faraway gleam in your eye. A girl back in Texas, perhaps?"

The old ache returned. "I gave up on romantic notions long ago," Kirby said, embarrassed.

"Because of the bank hold-up?"

He nodded. "I never knew when it might come back to haunt me. I just knew it would. I didn't want anyone else hurt in the process."

"Is that why you keep Damien and Terry at a distance?"

Astonished at her observation, he stared at her. "Damn," he said softly.

Her eyes, full of compassion, glistened, and he knew that she understood.

"Go to him," he said. "Tonight. He comes off watch at midnight."

She nodded. "I'd better check on Ha'Penny."

"I imagine that dog is keeping good watch over him and the rest of Noah's Ark," Kirby observed. "And either Hank or Shorty or Terry will be in camp for the rest of the night. You know they'll listen for the babe."

She gave him a weak smile, then turned to climb inside the wagon. Kirby meandered over to the fire, feeling unaccountably pleased with himself. Maybe, he thought, it was time to do a bit of night duty himself. He knew just the man to relieve.

Drew unsaddled his horse. He'd been surprised to see Kirby riding out to him on watch, even more startled at the trail boss's order to return to camp. But he couldn't deny that he was tired. Sleep came hard if at all these days.

It was close to midnight. The sky was black but clear, and a million stars winked at him. He enjoyed such nights; Scotland had a few of them, but most were drenched in fog and mist. Not that he'd seen many nights in Scotland; most had been spent in smoke-filled clubs, not out under the sky.

A fire smoldered beneath the perpetual coffeepot, and Drew threw on a little extra wood, as they did at night, then went to the hoodlum wagon for a bedroll. He wondered whether Gabrielle would be asleep, wondered if he wanted her to be or not.

The night was quiet, disturbed only by the occasional restless movement of cattle and the quiet snoring of several hands, rolled up in blankets scattered around the campsite. He reached the wagon, looked inside for his belongings, and immediately became aware of the silent figure sitting beside Ha'Penny's makeshift bed, Honor at her feet. The dog raised his head, then lay it back down again, evidently feeling no threat to his tiny charge.

Despite the distance between Gabrielle and him, Drew felt a quickening of his pulse, the almost painful awareness that always stretched between them. As he gazed at her in silence, she slowly rose, stepped to the wagon flap, and held out a hand to him. He took it, then reached to lift her down.

She always felt so light in his arms. And right. As if she belonged there.

"Drew," she murmured. "I've been waiting for you."

His arm instinctively tightened around her waist, even as he warned himself against it. Blast it, he had spent the last few days trying to persuade himself of the folly of doing exactly what he was doing at that moment. But when she looked up at him, he had no will to let her go.

"Come with me for a while," she said. Her voice was little more than a whisper, but her fingers wrapped around his firmly to guide him away from the campfire and the sleeping drovers.

No stream or river broke the prairie here. The land stretched out in gently rolling hills and occasional ravines. Gabrielle led him to the other side of a hill, away from curious eyes, and by the time she halted, Drew's body was rigid with tension, sensing she was about to tell him something that he didn't want to hear.

As she turned to him, his hand seemed to propel her into his arms. He held her there, savoring the feel of her body next to his, his chin resting on her tousled hair. She smelled of soap and the slightest hint of flowers, and he wondered how she had managed that piece of magic. But then, she was a sorceress, full of mysteries and puzzles.

He resisted putting his lips to hers, knowing that if he did he would lose himself in her. He tried to maintain a coolness, a certain distance, but already his manhood was swelling against her. Angry that he had so little control, he took a step back.

"Gabrielle?"

She reached up to touch his cheek, then abruptly dropped her hand to her side. "I . . . I told Kirby tonight that I . . . that I saw the man who killed my father, back in Caldwell."

Drew sucked in a sharp breath, his body instantly going cold.

"The man said . . . he heard someone say I was with the Kingsley drive, and he asked me about Kirby, said he'd heard the trail boss was dead. There was only one way he could know."

Stunned, Drew stood there, unable to speak. Of all the things he'd imagined had gone wrong, of all the many excuses he'd invented for why she'd avoided talking to him, he'd never imagined anything like this.

"Why didn't you tell me?" he finally managed to ask.

"Why do you think?" she countered softly, brokenly. "With that huge heroic streak of yours, I was afraid you would try to face him down."

Swearing under his breath, Drew turned away, his mind whirling. Gabrielle had come a long way for justice for her father. And now she'd risked ever finding it to protect him. *Him*—Andrew Cameron. No one in his life had *ever* tried to protect him before. No one had ever given a bloody damn whether he lived or died.

Suddenly, all the barren places in his soul started to fill with a warmth so long denied him.

"Drew?" Her voice was tentative.

"You have precious little faith in me," he said roughly, turning back to her, hoping the mist in his eyes didn't show.

"Oh, I have faith," she whispered. "I have faith in your heart, in your courage. In your loyalty." Reaching out, she clasped his hand tightly. "I know you can do anything you put your mind to. And I know you're good with a rifle. But that man ... Drew, he wore his gun like it was part of him. And you're not a killer. You could *never* be a killer. And he is."

Drew knew he should be angry. Gabrielle had kept something from him that both he and Kirby had a right to know. But all he felt was a glowing, blinding joy.

Gabrielle had never wanted anything from him, never tried to take anything he wasn't willing to give. She had reached out and offered him her heart because she saw something in him no one else had bothered to find.

The lump in his throat threatened to choke him as he reached out and pulled Gabrielle to him. He clung to her, hearing her muffled sobs, offering her halting reassurances. "It's all right, lass," he said. "My brave, bonny lass. . . . It's all right, now."

Finally, he understood how much courage it had taken her to deceive him for his own sake. Just as it had taken courage to make every move she had made since her father's violent death. He'd been so sure about the black and white of truthfulness. He'd made his demons hers.

"I wanted to tell you," she sniffed. "I wanted to tell you so badly, but—"

"Hush, lass," he said, cradling her in his arms. "I said it's all right, and I meant it. And I thank you for caring. No one ever has before. But I want you to trust me, too. I'll not be running out and doing something foolish."

She lifted her face to his. "Do you promise?" she said in an almost childlike tone.

He had to smile. "Aye. But you must promise to do the same. Running off on a trail drive is not the most sensible thing I've ever heard of a lass doing."

"What about a Scots gambler running off on a trail drive?" she countered with another sniff.

He chuckled. "You have me there."

He looked down at her and felt he was looking at the face of an angel. Her eyes were swimming in tears but luminous in the light from a million stars. Love shone in her face as surely as the moon shone from above, and it shattered the last barrier to his heart as if it were no more than dust scattered by a warm summer breeze.

He loved and was loved.

He marveled over the miracle as his lips met hers.

Chapter Twenty-one

✦

Night had deepened into the wee hours before dawn, and Gabrielle sighed, snuggling deeper into Drew's arms.

Silently, she acknowledged that honesty had a great deal going for it. The frost of the past few days had melted at her confession, and she felt Drew had truly opened his heart for the first time and allowed her to slip inside. He hadn't said the words, had not uttered what she wanted to hear. And yet his kiss and his touch had offered, even promised, love in abundance. It was enough for now.

She found herself regretting that he'd been careful again not to spill his seed in her. She'd wanted it. But his will had been iron. "I'll not leave a bastard," he'd said in a strangled voice at the height of passion.

Recognizing the bitterness of his words, Gabrielle remembered the conversation they'd had not long ago. *"I'm a bastard in fact, if not in law."* She'd wanted to ask what he meant, wanted to know about his background, his family, but it had been no time for asking questions. Nor was it now. The pain in him ran deep and raw, and she would not, could not, salt the wounds. One day, in his own time, he would tell her, and perhaps then she could ease some of the pain she sensed.

She sighed with the warm, deep joy of lying next to him. She spent the past few hours wrapped in Drew's arms, humbly grateful to be there. It was so much more than she'd expected, dreamed of, hoped for. They had ventured to the brink of paradise time and time again, their lips meeting and melding and searching, their bodies clinging to each other. Even thinking about it, she ached to feel him within her once more.

How could one love so much, so deeply, so intensely? She didn't know, didn't want to question it; she simply wanted to feel every wonderful wondrous second. She did exactly that, then finally, reluctantly, opened her eyes. The sky had visibly lightened; the stars were fading fast, and the crescent moon had already fallen below the horizon. It was time to get back. Ha'Penny would wake soon and need to be fed, though she knew one fretful cry from the infant would bring every drover rushing to the wagon.

She stirred, rousing Drew who mumbled sleepily. He stretched, and his cheek brushed hers. His face was rough with stubble, but she loved the feel of it anyway, loved the intimacy of sharing the night with him. She didn't even want to think about how she looked; her hair a tangle of curls and her shirt completely rumpled.

But Drew grinned at her, reminding her of a boy who'd just played hooky from school to go fishing and had made his biggest catch ever. Her heart somersaulted at seeing him so obviously happy.

"I think we need to rise," he said lazily, his hand stroking her arm from shoulder to wrist.

"Probably," she agreed reluctantly.

He took her hand and raised it to his mouth, nuzzling it. "You taste delicious."

"It must be the peppers I put in the beans," she teased.

" 'Tis not peppers I taste," he disagreed with a smile, "though you have become a passable cook."

"Passable?"

"Fair, then?" he amended.

"I'll ban you from my bean pot," she threatened.

He groaned. "I vow I'll never eat another bean after this drive."

"I don't think I'll ever cook one, either," Gabrielle agreed heartily.

"Do you know how to make decent tea?"

For some reason, his question made her heart pound faster. Was he alluding to a future together? Or was she simply jumping to conclusions?"

"You don't like my coffee?" she ventured.

"Muddy brew from a tin pot is utterly uncivilized," he exclaimed.

"I thought you *liked* uncivilized. I thought you wanted an adventure. Now you tell me that you want *tea*!"

"I also like good brandy," he chuckled. "And a good cigar."

"What else?" she said, knowing she was fishing shamelessly for words of affection.

His fingers traced her cheek. "A game of chance. A sunrise." He sighed. "Ah, lass, I fear I'm a poor prize. I've little to show for my life but what's on my back and a name I've all but destroyed."

"I don't care about a name," she pointed out. "And I don't care about your lack of money. I have a little myself." She felt his hand tighten around hers.

"I won't be taking any money from a lass," he said.

"Oh, you won't?" Anger stirred in her. "You'll just take a roll in the hay, is that it? And here I thought— No." She fought her way out of his arms and rose to her feet. "No, maybe I didn't think. I believed you were different. But it seems you're just an arrogant ass."

She searched the ground for her trousers. She couldn't stomp back to camp in righteous indignation without her clothes.

"Looking for these?" Drew had stood and slipped on his own trousers, and he was dangling hers from his fingertips.

"Yes," she said primly as she reached out to grab them.

He moved, holding them out of her grasp. "An arrogant ass?" he asked ominously.

"An arrogant Scottish ass," she agreed.

"I didn't know you had such a temper, Of course, Gabe had one, but sweet Gabrielle? My, my, my."

"You inspire me," she shot back.

He chuckled. "What a termagant!"

"Better a termagant than the backside of a mule," she countered.

"I have a partiality for termagants," he admitted. "Might you have one for asses?"

His eyes were twinkling, and his voice had turned lazy and warm. She clenched her fists, trying to hold out against his irresistible charm. He used it to avoid certain subjects, to defuse and confuse, and for once she refused to succumb to it.

"I do not have any such partiality," she announced, reaching again for her trousers. It surprised her that he allowed her to snatch them.

"It wasn't a roll in the hay," he said quietly, all amusement gone. "I'll not have you believing that it was."

"Then why . . . ?"

"I'm not sure I can be what you deserve," he said.

"I want what you *are*," she replied fiercely.

"Ah, lass, you don't even know me."

Exasperated, she exclaimed, "You keep telling me that, and it isn't true. I *do* know you! I know all I need to know. I know your kindness, your gentleness, your loyalty. And I know that everyone looks up to you because of what you do so naturally, without thought."

He was silent for a moment. "I thought I was an ass."

"That, too," she agreed. "It sort of balances things out. One wouldn't want too much of a good thing."

His arms came around her, holding her tightly. Fiercely. "I don't think I could bear seeing disappointment in those blue eyes of yours."

She stopped the words with her fingertips pressed to his lips. "I love you, Drew Cameron. I don't think I could ever love anyone else the way I love you."

A choked sound came from his throat. "I—"

"No," she said. "Don't answer. Not now. But know that I love you and I want you. And I don't give up easily."

She fled then, her trousers in hand, her heart quaking at her own pronouncement. She knew she could have stayed and tried to drag a similar declaration out of him, but she didn't want it that way. She wanted him more than life itself. But as deep and strong as that emotion flowed within her, she had to know that he wanted her the same way, loved her with the same uncompromising strength. Next time, he would have to come to her.

"I'm going back to Texas with you," Drew said as he rode out with Kirby in the morning to scout the next ten miles.

"The hell you are," Kirby growled back. "If you go, Gabrielle will go. And I'll not have you both risking your necks for me."

"No, she won't," Drew said. "I'll send her to my brother-in-law's ranch near Denver."

Kirby looked incredulous. "You really think she'd stay there?"

"Not willingly," Drew replied, "But if anyone can

keep her in Denver, it's my sister Lisbeth and her husband Ben Masters."

"Hmph." Kirby scowled. "Dammit, Drew, you're no gunfighter."

"Neither are you," he replied.

"But it's my battle, not yours. Someone's after me for what *I* did."

"They're also after Gabrielle," Drew said quietly. "And that *is* my battle."

Kirby shot him a piercing glance. "Is it?"

"Aye," Drew said. "It most definitely is."

The older man studied him for a moment, then gave a short nod. "I'm glad to hear it. But why don't you just go East with her? Or even to Scotland? She'll be safe, then."

"Could you ever relax your guard," Drew asked, "knowing there was someone out there who wanted you—or someone you cared for—dead?"

He was gratified when Kirby stopped protesting.

"Apparently someone is prepared to go to any length to make sure you, and maybe Gabrielle, are dead. Killian probably didn't come cheap, and whoever it is must have spent a considerable amount of money for detectives to find Gabrielle's father and you. It seems to me the stakes are very high." Preparing himself for another argument, Drew said, "I think you should tell Damien. We might need him, and he's good with a gun."

As expected, Kirby shook his head. "I want to keep my family out of it."

"Jon could be the next target," Drew warned.

Kirby quickly turned toward him, and Drew saw the instant fear streak across his friend's face. "Damn . . ." The trail boss's voice was strained with tension. "Jon was outside the bank, holding the horses. He rode with us when we hightailed it out of town. Dammit, yes, Jon knows everything—and Cal Thornton knows that he knows."

"Then Damien should know," Drew said. "And

Terry. Whoever is behind this has already killed Gabrielle's father, tried to kill her, and has tried twice to kill you. It seems obvious that he isn't going to stop until everyone who had anything to do with the robbery is dead—and that includes Jon."

"Dear God," Kirby said. "They think I'm already dead. Killian could be on his way right now to . . ." His voice trailed off.

Drew was silent, only too aware of the implications.

"I'll have to resurrect myself sooner than I expected," Kirby said.

"We're only two weeks from Abilene," Drew said. "Damien can take the herd in."

Beside him, Kirby was riding with his gaze fixed straight ahead, his breathing heavy and disturbed. "There're a dozen ranchers depending on me," he said. "They're trusting me to get them the best price. Some of them might lose their ranches if I don't. I'm not sure Damien can handle it yet."

"Well, I bloody well can't," Drew admitted. "But I *can* go back to Texas."

"Killian has several days' head start."

"But he doesn't know we know about him."

"Drew, I can't ask you to go."

"Try to keep me from it," Drew said. "I'll leave at dawn tomorrow for Caldwell and telegraph Jon, warn him to be careful. You send Gabrielle to my brother-in-law in Denver. He's a former U.S. marshal, and he'll make sure she's safe. No one knows she's with us, so she won't be followed."

Kirby snorted. "Gabrielle will want to go with *you*."

"She won't know I'm gone until it's too late," Drew said, knowing she was going to hate his plan. He fully expected her to be as mad as a wet hen when she found out, but both he and Kirby had bloody few choices if they were to keep the people they loved safe.

And he most definitely intended to keep Gabrielle safe. He was still sifting through the miracle in his mind that someone loved him. *Really* loved him. And while he hadn't quite assimilated that astonishing fact enough to respond to it, he wasn't about to give up his chance of *ever* responding simply because he had failed to take a few reasonable precautions and, as a result, lost her. She could be as angry as she liked—as long as she continued to live.

Kirby growled something indecipherable, then spoke in half-embarrassed tones. "Are you sure you want to do this to her? Leave without so much as an explanation or goodbye."

"No," Drew said. "I'd rather be horsewhipped. And horsewhipping will probably be kinder than her reaction when I see her again. But I can't take a chance with her life."

Kirby looked dubious.

Drew gave him a dry smile. "You want to tie her up and keep her from following me? Once I'm gone long enough, she'll be easier to persuade to go Denver."

"All right," Kirby finally said, "I'll see that she gets on that train to Denver."

Drew nodded. "I'll write her a letter, explaining, and another to my brother-in-law. Explain to her how important it is that he receives it . . . *personally*. Perhaps that will help."

Kirby nodded. Then, gruffly, he said, "Drew, I don't know what to say. How do you thank—"

"You don't say anything," Drew cut him short.

Kirby looked at him, and for a moment their gazes held. Then the older man held out his hand across the space between their horses. Drew reached over and took it, clasping it firmly. And no more words were needed. None at all.

When Drew reached Caldwell, Killian was long gone. "And good riddance," the storekeeper said.

The man eyed Drew curiously when he'd asked

about the hired gun. He eyed him again when Drew inquired about sending a telegraph.

"I can do that for you," the man said. "Town ain't big enough for a full-time operator, so I fill in."

Drew passed him the message for Kirby's brother, warning Jon he might be in danger and advising him never to ride alone, particularly into town, and to be wary of strangers. Drew signed Kirby's name.

When he'd left camp, he'd taken two horses, the pinto and a bay known for its endurance. He'd stowed his bedroll and told Gabrielle that he would be scouting north for the next two days, that Kirby felt he was ready for the responsibility. He'd guided her behind the wagon, out of sight of curious eyes, and kissed her, long and deeply.

She had clung to him, as if sensing something, but she didn't ask questions. It was one of the things he liked best about her. She never pried, simply waited until he was ready to talk. The hell of it was, now that he *was* ready, he had something he had to do first.

He'd had to settle for saying to her, "Be careful while I'm gone, lass. I'll have a lot to say to you."

He'd wanted to tell her he loved her then and there. But that wouldn't be fair, not yet when his life was so uncertain. "Wait for me," he said instead, and saw the surprise in her eyes, then a soft joy.

"I'll always wait for you," she whispered.

"And trust me."

She nodded.

"Promise?"

"I promise."

He kissed her, praying as he'd never prayed in his life that it wouldn't be for the last time. Then, because he was dying inside, because he knew she really wouldn't understand, he whirled away and mounted the pinto, forcing himself to keep a normal pace until he was out of sight. And then he spurred the horse into a gallop.

Switching mounts periodically to keep them from

overtiring, he'd made Caldwell in one day. He didn't want to think, couldn't think, about Gabrielle. *"I don't like lies."* How many times had he told her that?

But he hadn't known any other way to keep her safe. He had to find Killian before the gunman killed anyone else. And he had to find the man alive; he was the only link to whoever had hired him.

Drew stayed in Caldwell long enough to buy a few supplies, then rode south. He had to make San Antonio before Killian got there.

Two days passed, and Drew did not return. Gabrielle missed him more than she would have thought possible. She found herself looking for the tall, lean figure who had become her whole world.

She had accepted his explanation about scouting because there had been no reason not to. He had been going out more and more with Kirby, and Damien had been taking more responsibility for the herd. But as night fell late on the second day of Drew's absence, she knew something was wrong. Really, she'd known it that morning when Kirby had ridden out alone and come back late. Why would both he and Drew be scouting?

Kirby had been avoiding her, too, now that she thought about it. She really hadn't paid much attention to his comings and goings from camp, being kept busy herself with her chores and taking care of Ha'penny. But earlier that evening, she'd seen Kirby lead Damien away from the campsite, and, now, as she watched them return, she noted that Damien's expression was stormy.

She waited until the younger Kingsley stalked off, then approached his uncle.

"Kirby?"

He turned toward her, his eyes wary in the firelight.

"Shouldn't Drew be back by now?"

A muscle flexed in his cheek. "He's gone, Gabrielle," he said tersely. "He left the drive."

Gabrielle gasped, feeling as if she'd been shot in the stomach. "I . . . don't understand."

"He said he had some business to take care of," Kirby told her. "He asked me to see you onto the train to Denver. Said he'll meet you there."

Shocked, her mind a whirlwind, Gabrielle didn't know what to think. She knew how she felt, though: hurt. Drew had asked her to trust him—made her *promise* to trust him—but he hadn't trusted her at all. He didn't want anyone lying to him, but he apparently had few scruples about withholding the truth himself.

The loner. Whatever had made her think she could change him? He was as unable and unwilling as he'd ever been to share his emotions, his thoughts, his plans. Maybe he always would be.

Her heart was breaking, crumbling into pieces. She turned away, not wanting Kirby to see the pain, the betrayal she felt, in her eyes.

"Gabrielle," he said, stopping her with his hand on her arm. "Drew loves you. He just wants to make sure you're safe."

"Without asking me? Without finding out what *I* think or need or want?" The words burst forth in a fury as anger solidified inside her. "That's not love!" she said. "That's not even the honesty he talks so much about."

She glared at the hand restraining her until Kirby withdrew it. "Where did he go?" she demanded.

Kirby cleared his throat. "He left a letter for you. And one for you to take to his brother-in-law, Ben Masters."

With deadly calm, she said, "And the two of you expect me to travel hundreds of miles to the home of strangers—while you go hunting a murderer?"

The alarm in Kirby's eyes told her that she'd hit the target. She wanted to hit *him*. Kick him. She wanted to toss the bean pot into the ashes. She wanted to take

Billy Bones and gallop away as hard and fast as she could. She wanted to murder the man in front of her—to say nothing of the one who'd left her—with her own two hands. If Killian didn't do it first. In all, Gabrielle had never been so angry in her entire life.

"Trust me. Promise?" She wanted to throw Drew's promises in his face. He'd known precisely what he was asking when he exacted that unfair promise from her.

"Trust me." Ha! She'd trust him, all right. She'd . . . she'd . . .

Suddenly, Gabrielle's inward fuming came to an abrupt halt. *Trust me.* It was the first thing, the *only* thing, that Drew had ever asked of her. Slowly, that realization filtered its way through her anger.

"He loves you," Kirby had just told her. Could he be right? Anger, fear, and hope all became jumbled in her mind, whirling around like colors in a kaleidoscope. Fear crowded its way to the forefront.

"He went alone?" she demanded.

Kirby's hands clenched at his sides. She watched various expressions flit across an usually impassive countenance, and she surmised that he was debating how to answer.

"Did he go after Killian *alone*?" she demanded again, her voice rising in stark terror.

Kirby shook his head in resignation. "No one knows Drew has a connection to me. Or to you. He's just another cowboy. And he's only going to my ranch to warn my brother. He's not out there looking for trouble."

Except trouble always seemed to find Drew Cameron, even when he tried to avoid it. She wanted to go after him. But it was impossible, and she knew it. She had Ha'Penny to think of. She couldn't drag a baby halfway across the country, alone, on horseback.

But how did one choose between loves?

You choose the one who needs you most, her heart answered.

She tried to remember what Drew had said about Denver, about his half-sister and brother-in-law. The man was a lawyer, had been a marshal once, and Drew had seemed certain that this man could protect her. It seemed to her that he might also protect a brother-in-law hell-bent on getting himself killed.

"All right. I'll go to Denver," she told Kirby. "But I want to go now, with Ha'Penny and Honor. And I want to know that Billy Bones and Samson will be taken care of."

Kirby heaved a huge sigh, and his expression cleared in evident relief. He gave her a lopsided smile. "Everything will be just fine, Gabrielle. I'll see to it."

"Who'll cook?" she asked.

He shrugged. "We'll manage."

"You'll probably have grit in the beans."

"Probably. Maybe even a horseshoe in the coffee."

Gabrielle felt tears well in her eyes. She would miss him. She would miss them all. They'd become her family. "I'll make loaves of bread before I leave."

He nodded. "I'll send someone with you north to the railhead. You can catch a spur to the Union Pacific." He took two letters from his pocket and gave them to her. "One is to you, the other to Drew's kin. I'll get someone to accompany you tomorrow. Oh, and one other thing. Wait here while I get it."

Walking over to the hoodlum wagon, he took out his own bedroll and pulled from it a parcel wrapped in brown paper. Then, tossing the bedroll back into the wagon, he came back to hand her the package.

"Drew asked me to give this to you."

Hesitantly, Gabrielle took the package, feeling it squish and the paper crackle in her hands. Looking up at Kirby, she asked, "Do you know what it is?"

He shook his head. "Haven't any idea." He started to turn away, then stopped, looking back at her as he spoke. "By the way, you've been the best damn louse I ever hired."

She gave him a smile. "And you've been the best trail boss I ever worked for."

"Make sure I'm the *only* trail boss you ever work for," he warned. Then, in softer tones, he added, "Take good care of our Scotsman."

"I will," she promised.

She watched Kirby walk away, then carried her letters and package into the marginal privacy of the hoodlum wagon, where Ha'Penny slept peacefully. Sitting cross-legged beside the baby's bed and laying the letters aside, she untied the strings around the parcel, unwrapped the paper, then sucked in a quick, sharp breath.

And instant later, she burst into tears.

There, folded neatly in her lap, its delicate lace collar pristine white, was the calico dress off the manikin in the Caldwell dry-goods store.

Chapter Twenty-two

***

Gabrielle peered out the dirty soot-smudged window of the train as it pulled into Denver. Ha'penny fretted in her arms for his dinner, and Honor lay at her feet, growling at any man who approached them. Those few whom an Indian baby didn't scare away, Honor's bared teeth did, the results being that Gabrielle had enjoyed a bench to herself the entire way.

She'd sent a telegram to Drew's brother-in-law from Ellsworth, which she and Hank had reached after three days of hard riding, taking turns carrying Ha'penny in a rigged sling. She'd been exhausted when they'd finally arrived at a rail spur of the Union Pacific.

Two days later—two days spent sleeping in snatches, sitting up, and trying to keep Honor and Ha'Penny from disturbing other passengers—she was arriving in Denver full of doubts. She knew nothing about Lisbeth and Ben Masters, had no idea whether they would accept an actress with an Indian child, and she froze inside at the prospect of invading the home of folks she didn't know. She had never asked favors of strangers.

And she had a very big favor to ask.

Would they even meet her at the station? Her telegram had been brief: "Friend arriving Monday train. Gabrielle Lewis. Please meet." And she'd signed Drew's name.

What would Drew's brother-in-law say when she told him she'd sent the telegram? When she asked him to go to Texas? And to take her with him?

As the train pulled into the station, she searched the platform. A number of men and women stood there, apparently waiting for new arrivals. Her stomach churned as she scanned their faces.

The train lurched to the stop, making her stomach turn over yet again. The conductor, who had been very kind when several other passengers had grumbled about Ha'Penny, stopped at her seat.

"Can I help you, miss?" he asked.

She nodded gratefully. She didn't have much luggage—barely anything, in fact. She wore her new calico dress, now sooty and rumpled from the train; her other belongings included a second dress she'd purchased in Ellsworth, her trail drive clothes, a few things for Ha'penny, and her father's Colt, all stuffed in a cheap travel bag.

She scanned the crowd again. Ben Masters, a former marshal, she reflected. Most of the lawmen she'd met were humorless and rigid. And Drew's half-sister, Lisbeth? Would she approve of an actress who'd just spent nearly three months in the company of over a dozen men? Yet Drew had asked her in his letter to come here, saying she could trust Ben and Lisbeth. Still, shivers of apprehension ran down her spine and her heart thundered, thinking about the enormous request she needed to make of these strangers.

She stood awkwardly, reluctant to descend from the train.

"I'll carry the boy and the bag, miss," the conductor said. "You just go on."

She looked at Ha'penny, who felt as if he'd grown several pounds during the journey, and gave the conductor a smile from under the hat she'd bought, which she hoped hid the shortness of her hair. "Thank you," she said.

He grinned. "A pleasure, miss. A real pleasure."

She had no more excuses. She stepped into the aisle and then made her way to the door and down the three steps to the platform, Honor crowding her legs. Taking Ha'penny and her bag back from the conductor, she gave him another smile, then searched the crowd one more time.

One couple, a tall man and a woman obviously with child, eyed her curiously before turning to look toward other passengers descending from the train. The woman appeared somewhat anxious.

Gabrielle moved a little closer, and she saw the woman's eyes. Hazel with flecks of gold. Drew's eyes.

The woman's gaze met hers, and when Gabrielle smiled tentatively, the woman moved forward, one hand drawing her male companion with her, the other outstretched.

"Gabrielle?" Her voice had a soft Scottish lilt to it, and Gabrielle dropped her bag, balanced Ha'penny, nodded her head, and offered her own hand.

The woman took it warmly. "I'm Lisbeth Masters, and this is my husband Ben." She inspected Gabrielle with frank, though not unpleasant, curiosity, then looked at Ha'penny. "A boy?" she asked, and when Gabrielle nodded, she added, "How wonderful. Our Sarah Ann's been hopping up and down, waiting for her new brother or sister, and now she has one to practice on." Her eyes went to the dog.

"And who is this?"

"Honor," Gabrielle said. "I hope you don't mind, but Honor considers himself the baby's protector, and I couldn't leave him behind."

"Of course, you couldn't," Lisbeth said, winking at her husband. "I can't wait till Honor meets Henry the Eighth. But how did you get him on the train?"

Gabrielle smiled. "Tears."

Lisbeth laughed. "Sometimes it's the only way."

"They wanted to stuff him in the baggage car," she said, "but he threatened to bite anyone who tried, so when pleas didn't work, I cried copiously."

"The ultimate weapon," Ben Masters grumbled.

"Only because men don't see reason," his wife rebuked. "Anyone can tell he's a very well-behaved dog."

"Maybe he can teach Henry something," Ben growled, but Gabrielle heard the fond amusement in his voice.

"And Annabelle, too," his wife inserted smoothly. "Annabelle," she explained to Gabrielle, "is Ben's cat."

"Henry is Lisbeth's dog." Ben added balefully.

Gabrielle looked from one to the other, felt the love flowing between them in their gentle teasing, and some of her apprehension evaporated. She'd heard no hiss of disapproval over an Indian baby or an unexpected dog, not to mention an uninvited guest. Only an open offer of friendship. Gabrielle felt a sense of kinship with these people already and wondered why Drew had said so little about his wonderful sister.

"Here, let me take the boy," Ben said. "And your bag. Cute little fellow," he added with a chuckle as Gabrielle gratefully handed Ha'Penny over. Then his gaze returned to study Gabrielle's face for a moment. "Welcome to Denver."

"Thank you," she replied, wondering how soon she could start explaining the circumstances of her trip. She glanced at Lisbeth Masters' swelling stomach, and her own stomach flip-flopped. Would Ben be willing to leave his wife in her condition?

Gabrielle realized her dismay must have been reflected in her expression, because Lisbeth warmly took her arm and guided her toward a buggy hitched to two lovely gray horses. "I'm sure you need a hot bath, and I want to hear all about Drew. Our ranch is a few miles out of Denver, and I hope you'll consider it your home."

Gabrielle felt as if a giant wave had picked her up and was sweeping her along, so powerful was the onslaught of warmth and welcome from these two people.

Ben Masters was tall, she noted, close to Drew's height, his build a bit heavier but without an ounce of fat on him. Where her Scotsman had always exuded pure devilish charm, hiding the deeper, more substantial qualities she'd found within, Ben radiated sureness and authority and strength. Likely qualities, she thought, for either a lawyer or a marshal.

He handed her up into the buggy, gave her Ha'penny, then assisted his wife with so much tenderness that Gabrielle's heart lurched. How could Drew be such a loner with these two people as kin?

Ben snapped the reins, and the horses stepped off smartly.

Gabrielle had played a theater in Denver with her father before they headed toward Texas, and her eyes stung as the carriage passed the hotel where they had stayed. She felt Lisbeth's hand press hers, and she realized the woman must have been watching her.

"I'm sorry," she said. "I—I must be more tired than I thought."

"Of course," Lisbeth said. "Travel is always exhausting. Perhaps you'd like me to hold the baby."

Gabrielle heard the hopeful note in Lisbeth's tone, realized the other woman was truly eager to hold Ha'penny. "That would be wonderful," Gabrielle replied, smiling as she handed Ha'penny to her. "Frankly, my arms feel permanently locked in holding position."

"Oh, he's adorable. What's his name?"

"Ha'penny," she said automatically, then flushed. "Temporarily."

"Interesting name," Ben Masters observed dryly.

Gabrielle sensed it was a question, but he was too well-mannered to ask outright. Well, they might as well know the worst. "I . . . well, I was called Two-Bits on the Kingsley cattle drive, and when we found the baby, orphaned and alone, he was so small that Drew started calling him Ha'penny."

"Sounds like Drew," Ben chuckled.

"You were on the cattle drive?" Lisbeth gasped, her voice full of astonishment but bearing no censure. "We knew Drew had joined one, but I've never heard of . . ." She trailed off.

Gabrielle twisted the folds of her dress in her hands. "It's a long story."

"Where's Drew?" Ben asked.

"On his way to Texas," she said.

"But the telegram—"

"I sent the telegram," Gabrielle admitted. "But I have a letter for you from him. And he probably didn't say anything about himself, but I think he needs your help."

Ben looked at her sharply.

Lisbeth's face paled.

And Ha'Penny, who had been so very stoic during the trip, chose that moment to start crying, cutting off any further conversation. The horses moved faster as Ben Masters snapped the reins again, and all further questions were postponed.

Gabrielle loved the ranch house that sprawled comfortably beside a wide, briskly flowing stream.

As Ben helped his wife, then her, from the buggy, he gestured toward the barn. "Drew helped us build that."

Just as he said the words, a small tornado burst from the barn door and hurtled herself into Ben's arms. She was followed by a massive dog who stopped short upon seeing Honor.

"We gotta a new f-foal," the little girl stammered in excitement.

Lisbeth leaned over and kissed the child's cheek. "That's wonderful. You'll have to show me later."

"I want to show you *now*."

"But we have a guest. Three guests," she corrected herself. "This is Miss Gabrielle Lewis, and she's a friend of your Uncle Drew's. And this, Miss Lewis, is our Sarah Ann."

The little girl performed a perfect curtsy, then dropped to her knees to greet Honor, who was regarding the much larger dog with a tentatively wagging tail. "He's beautiful!" Sarah Ann declared.

"His name is Honor," Gabrielle said. She stooped down and showed Sarah Ann the baby. "And this is Ha'penny."

"Ohh," Sarah Ann crooned. "He's even better than a pony. I'm going to have a baby."

"You are?" Gabrielle smiled. "You look a little small."

"I'm 'most five."

"Well, that's very big indeed," Gabrielle said, enchanted by the girl's red hair and sparkling green eyes.

"Yes, it is," Sarah Ann agreed seriously.

"I think Miss Lewis would like to freshen up after her journey," Lisbeth interrupted. "Why don't you stay with Pedro and take care of the foal, Sarah Ann?"

"But don't you want to see him?"

"Aye, I do," Lisbeth said.

Gabrielle thought of Drew, of the urgency of her mission. But a moment wouldn't hurt. "I do, too," she said.

Sarah Ann grabbed Gabrielle's hand and pulled her toward the barn, followed by Ben Masters and his wife. A beaming Mexican met them at the door.

"Señor, Señora, Glory has dropped a colt. *Muy bueno.*"

The four of them went to a stall and peered in. A lovely black mare was nuzzling a dark gray colt, which took a few steps, faltered, then righted itself.

"He's beautiful," Gabrielle sighed. She'd never seen a newborn colt before; it was all legs and sweetness.

"He *is* beautiful, isn't he, Mama?" the little girl said.

"Indeed, he is," Lisbeth agreed. "Would you like to name him?"

The little girl nodded. "I'll have to consider it."

"You do that," Ben said, his voice warm and amused. "And we'll take Miss Lewis to the house while you consider."

Sarah Ann, already engrossed in her appointed task, nodded.

Urgency began clawing at Gabrielle again as they walked to the house, Ben carrying Ha'Penny and Honor following closely behind. The large woolly dog that looked more pony than canine loped after them, his tongue lolling out the side of his mouth.

"That's Henry the Eighth," Lisbeth explained. "He loves everyone, particularly women."

Gabrielle couldn't help but smile. She'd never met a more delightful family, not even among her most eccentric theater cronies. Once inside the house, she noted that the furnishings seemed selected for comfort and informality.

A woman dressed in a colorful blouse and skirt protected by an apron hurried out of the kitchen to meet them, a huge smile on her face. "Señora, you saw the foal?"

Ben balanced Ha'penny in his arms. "We did, and we even have another wee one for you to feed." He turned to Gabrielle. "This is Serena. She's Pedro's wife, and she looks after us all. Serena, this is Drew's friend, Señorita Lewis."

"Señorita," the woman acknowledged. "How is Señor Drew?"

"My question exactly," Lisbeth said. "Gabrielle, you said Drew might need our help. Is he in some kind of trouble?" Concern laced her gentle Scots voice.

"It's a very long story," Gabrielle said, "and my name is Parker. It's . . . well, it's a long story."

Ha'Penny was squirming again, whimpering. Serena reached out and took the baby. "I'll feed him, and start supper."

"And something cool to drink for the señorita," Ben added, turning to Gabrielle with concern. "Would you like a bath first, or some rest?"

She shook her head. "There's no time."

"Then please sit," he said, "and tell us about Drew."

"You have to go, Ben," Lisbeth said. "You know Drew. He's like a dog with a bone. He won't let go."

"But the baby," Ben protested.

"It's still two or three months away," Lisbeth said. "And Pedro and Serena are here. Gabrielle and Ha'penny can stay with us, as well."

'No," Gabrielle said. "I have to go, too."

Both Lisbeth and her husband stared at her. They'd been listening intently for over an hour, distress visibly mounting in Lisbeth as Gabrielle explained that Drew might be on his way to confront a killer, or killers.

Ben had listened in silence, occasionally punctuating Gabrielle's tale with a pointed question. His eyes had gone ice cold and an almost feral expression had appeared on his face when she'd mentioned Killian's name. "I know him," he'd said tersely. And Gabrielle saw fear invade Lisbeth's eyes at his comment.

"Drew's gotten himself into one hell of a mess this time," Ben said.

Gabrielle stiffened at what she perceived as a slight aimed at Drew. "He saved my life. He saved the life of one of the drovers during a stampede, risking his own. He saved Kirby Kingsley's life. He's very brave and very competent. It's just that . . ." Without warning, emotion overcame her, and her lower lip trembled. "It's just that he's not a gunfighter."

Lisbeth's eyes glowed. "You love him, don't you?"

Gabrielle could only nod.

Ben scowled. "Dammit! I should have known the man couldn't stay out of trouble. Couldn't do it in Scotland, either. I was a damn fool to suggest he head south."

Lisbeth studied Gabrielle for a moment. "I don't think so," she said with a smile. "I think he finally found what he's been looking for." She turned to Ben. "You can find some marshals to help you, can't you?"

He nodded, asking Gabrielle, "And you say Kingsley doesn't know who's behind these shootings?"

When Gabrielle hesitated, Ben pounced on it immediately. "Gabrielle, this is no time to withhold information."

She shook her head. "I'm not. Kirby doesn't actually know. He's got an idea, but ... well, it's something he'll have to tell you himself. Even then, he has no evidence. It's just a guess. The only one who really knows is Killian."

Ben nodded. "I've heard of Kingsley. Why in the hell would anyone be after him?"

Gabrielle swallowed hard. It wasn't her place to tell Ben—a former U.S. marshal, no less—about Kirby's past sins. So far, she'd said only that her father and Kirby had been friends years ago, that their ranches had been stolen, and that both had been attacked recently. Anything else that Ben learned would have come from Kirby himself. Still, she wasn't about to lie. Oh, no. She was through with lies forever.

Ben was waiting.

"As I said, you'll have to ask Kirby," she said.

Ben gave her a narrow-eyed look, but he didn't press the point. Instead, he asked, "How long since Drew left for Texas?"

"Five days," she said. "He and Kirby are afraid Killian might go after Kirby's brother Jon."

"So it might be too late," Ben finished grimly.

Gabrielle shook her head. She wouldn't let herself believe that. "I don't think Drew will really go after Killian until Kirby joins him. He only wants to make sure Jon Kingsley is protected."

"And you?" Lisbeth inserted gently.

"And Ha'penny," Gabrielle said. "He's very fond of Ha'penny."

"I'm sure he is," Lisbeth said with a small laugh. "He's very good with children. Sarah Ann adores him, but he's always been like quicksilver, never staying anyplace long." She cast a knowing glance at her husband.

Ben raised one eyebrow and grinned. "She likes to think she tamed me, but it's more the other way around. She used to go galloping across the countryside, flying over six-foot fences, wrecking carriages, and creating general havoc."

Gabrielle suddenly felt very alone, witnessing their obvious love for one another. Would Drew ever be able to love her like that?

"I want to go," she said again. "Please, don't make me stay behind."

Ben scowled. "You aren't going to start crying if I say no, are you?"

"Well . . . I might. Will it help?"

"Hmph," he grunted noncommittally. "What about the child? You aren't planning on asking to take him, too, are you?"

"He's my responsibility, and I can't simply leave him."

Ben rolled his eyes heavenward.

"Of course, you can," Lisbeth interjected. "He'd be fine here. But we won't talk about it anymore until after supper. Gabrielle needs to wash and get some rest. Serena will take care of the baby. I'll show you to your room," she told Gabrielle. "It's the same one Drew used."

Gabrielle didn't want to waste time. She wanted to head south immediately. But she had to persuade Ben to take her with him, and he wasn't ready to agree. Having met Drew's brother-in-law, she already had faith in him. Instinct told her he was a very competent man as well as a compassionate one. He'd said he would go to Texas; that was the first and biggest hurdle. Now she would have to play by his rules—though she still planned to nudge them a bit.

She followed Lisbeth into a very pleasant room dominated by a large double bed and already graced with a basin of warm water along with towels and soap.

"I'll have Pedro bring in water for your bath," Lisbeth said, hovering at the door. Gabrielle sensed she wanted to ask questions but her good manners prevented it. She was curious, too, and had a hundred questions for Drew's sister.

"I miss Drew," Lisbeth said. "I didn't even know he was my brother until we reached America seven months ago. He'd told Ben back in Scotland, before we left, but he waited until we arrived here to break the news to me. Now he's as dear to me as if we'd been raised together. I had hoped he would stay with us longer, but I think family . . . well, perhaps it made him uncomfortable."

It was clear to Gabrielle that Lisbeth was trying to tell her something and didn't quite know how.

"Drew says so little about his past," Gabrielle said. "I know he believes his father despised him—"

Lisbeth made a sound of disgust. "Enough to bankrupt his estate so that he would leave Drew nothing but an empty title."

Gabrielle stared at her. "A title?"

"Yes. Earl of Kinloch," Lisbeth said—then shut her mouth abruptly at Gabrielle's shocked look. "Oh, dear."

"He's an *earl*?" Gabrielle heard her voice and knew it sounded strangled.

Hurriedly, Lisbeth explained, "Drew hates the title. It doesn't mean anything to him."

But Gabrielle was still grappling with the astonishing revelation and the fact that Drew hadn't deemed it important enough to tell her himself. *I don't like lies.* Well, all right, he'd never *actually* lied to her about who he was, but surely a lie of omission was still a lie. He called himself a gambler, a wanderer, a horseman who rode in steeplechases. He'd even, she recalled, labeled himself a "poor prize." She thought, in all that, he might have mentioned in passing that he also happened to be an earl.

She didn't know whether to be angry or hurt or both. He'd made her promise to trust him when he'd trusted her not at all. Not even enough to tell her basic truths about himself.

"I think I could use some rest after all," she said to Lisbeth, trying to conceal her despair.

Lisbeth gazed at her sympathetically, then made another sound of disgust. "Men!" she exclaimed, then started out the door. She stopped and turned back to Gabrielle. "If he told you anything about his family at all, then he's already told you far more than he's ever told anyone else," she said softly. "And he must love you a great deal to have sent you here."

"I'm not sure he can love anyone," Gabrielle said.

"Of course, he can," Lisbeth said. "It'll take time, though. Time and faith. Drew's been alone all his life." Then she slipped quietly out of the room, closing the door behind her.

Gabrielle knew she would never learn exactly what Lisbeth had said to Ben, but after supper he announced that she could go to Texas with him. Actually, Gabrielle thought, the decision must have been made earlier in the couple's bedroom, for Ben put up only token resistance.

"I wish I could go, too," Lisbeth said as Ben saddled two horses the next morning. "But Serena and I will take good care of Ha'Penny, and I'm sure Sarah Ann will practice sisterhood on him. And we'll look out for Honor, too."

She smiled down at the great lummox of a dog continually trailing Honor, who responded with an occasional wag of his tail as he continued to guard his small charge.

Gabrielle had donned her shirt and trousers, knowing she would be more comfortable and, therefore, that they would make better time. Much to her relief, neither Ben nor Lisbeth had disapproved.

Gabrielle held out her hand to the woman who'd become an instant friend. "I can't thank you enough."

"You can by being patient with Drew," Lisbeth said. "Don't be angry with him for not telling you about his title. He truly does hate it. He told me it's only been a constant reminder of the man he called father and a mother unfit for the name."

Gabrielle nodded. God knew nothing could ever stem the love she felt for her Scotsman. But hurt ran deep, so deep it threatened to undermine any hope she might have for a future with him. Despite his last words to her, he'd continually insisted he was a wanderer with no ties. And now she knew how much he'd kept from her, how much of himself he'd kept private and inviolate. And exactly how far from being a cowhand he truly was.

After a last tearful goodbye with Ha'Penny, who gurgled happily in Lisbeth's arms, she swung up into the saddle of one of the Masters' fine horses. She felt a small surge of pride when Ben eyed her, then gave a nod of approval.

He leaned down from his saddle to give his wife a kiss that was just long and lingering enough to remain decent for public viewing.

"Take care of yourself," she heard Lisbeth whisper.

"I will, love," he replied. "And I'll bring that rogue brother of yours home."

Gabrielle prayed that he was right.

Chapter Twenty-three

Drew missed Gabrielle with every fiber of his being. During the long hours of hard riding, with little else to occupy his thoughts, he often wondered how someone could crawl so completely into his heart in so short a time.

His journey seemed endless and achingly lonely. He rode throughout the daylight hours, switching horses to relieve them. Killian, he guessed, would travel at his ease, thinking his job was nearly done. While it had taken the herd two-and-a-half months to reach central Kansas, it took him only fifteen days to return to the Circle K.

He arrived, bone weary and in worse need of a bath and shave than he could ever remember, to discover that Jon had received his telegram and, although deeply puzzled, had taken his advice to heart. When Drew handed him the letter that Kirby had sent, Jon read it quickly and sank into a chair, shocked.

"Dear God," he said.

Drew didn't know how much Kirby had told Jon, so he waited in silence.

Jon smothered a groan. "I always knew it would catch up with us someday," he said finally. He looked up at Drew. "Thanks for being there with Kirby. And for coming back."

Drew shrugged and moved on to more important matters. "How many men do you have here?"

"Right now, we're shorthanded. Most of our hands went with Kirby. There's fifteen men here, barely enough to look after the ranch, horses, and cattle."

"Add another," Drew said. "Kirby sent me to stay with you. I don't think you should ride off the ranch until he returns. If you need anything from town, either I or one of the other hands can fetch it."

Jon stared at him. "Why are you doing this?"

"Your brother is my friend. And I have a bone of my own to pick with Killian. So, don't worry, I don't want anything from you. Once this is over, I'm going to Colorado." Drew replaced the hat he'd taken off to come inside. "I'll put my things in the bunkhouse."

"No," Jon said. "Stay in the house. I'd welcome the company."

Drew didn't argue. Thoughts of a real bed and a bath were akin to thoughts of heaven.

Still, over the following days, Drew came to wonder how—or why—he'd ever spent so much of his life indoors. He'd ridden horses, yes, but he'd whiled away so many afternoons and evenings in clubs and saloons and taverns—wherever he could find a card game—arising late the following day. Now that he knew the glory of a sunrise and the wonder of a sunset and the deep pleasure of a clear, moonlit sky, he couldn't imagine returning to his previous habits. Moreover, he'd gone months without a drink, something he once couldn't have imagined, and he felt better than he'd ever felt before.

What made the most difference, though, was that

he now knew that he had something to go to, rather than run from. He had Gabrielle.

He helped out around the ranch, often working with the horses, staying close to the house and Jon Kingsley. Jon liked to talk, asking intelligent questions and giving thoughtful replies. He was, Drew decided, a gentle, considerate man, and he understood why Kirby had felt the need to protect him.

After two weeks had passed, one of the hands brought in a newspaper. The headline was emblazoned, "Kirby Kingsley Herd Reaches Abilene." The paper reported that Kingsley had received record prices for the beef.

"That should give someone a nightmare," Drew said, passing the paper to Jon.

"I'm not so sure he should have advertised the fact he's still alive," Jon worried. "He wouldn't have, if it weren't for me."

"No one could have kept it secret forever," Drew said. "Not with all our drovers getting drunk in Abilene."

Jon chuckled. "You're flat right about that. And Kirby knows the country. No one will find him now he's aware someone is after him."

"I wish we knew for certain who was behind this."

"*I* know," Jon said quietly.

Drew started. "What?"

Jon's face flushed. "Well, actually, I think I know. But I've always been good at faces."

"So ..." Drew prompted, feeling his impatience rising. "Who?"

Jon plucked the paper from Drew's hands, turned a page, then returned it to him, pointing at a brief article. "Philip Thorpe to Run for Governor. Prominent Austin Businessman Declares Candidacy."

"Bloody hell!" Drew exclaimed. "A candidate for governor?"

"I saw a poster with a sketch of Thorpe several weeks ago when I was in San Antonio," Jon said.

"The name didn't mean anything, but something about the face caught me. I just didn't figure it out until you told me about Kirby and Jim Davis—the man you call James Parker. This man Thorpe—he's Cal Thornton. I'm almost sure."

Drew let his breath whistle out through clenched teeth. "He must have thought himself safe," he said. "James Parker was dead, and Killian's reputation almost guaranteed your brother's demise."

"And maybe he thought I was too young at the time to remember much," Jon mused. "Or that Kirby's death would ensure my silence. Of course, he also might have had second thoughts."

"Governor," Drew said again. He didn't know much about American politics, but he'd learned enough to know that candidates for public office traveled extensively, held rallies, did whatever they could to spread their news and bonhomie, working hard for every vote. "It seems unlikely that Thorpe—or Thornton—would want to leave any loose ends," he murmured.

"He's very wealthy," Jon observed. "According to the newspaper account, he practically owns Austin."

"Gabrielle said she couldn't get the law to act against Kirby, a powerful cattle rancher, when she thought him guilty of her father's murder. It will be even more difficult to go after this man."

Jon nodded. "Especially since we no longer have the Texas Rangers. The National Police is little more than protectors of the Republican carpetbaggers. Thornton probably already has them in his pocket."

A powerful man had ordered the killings of the father of the woman he loved and a man who was his friend, on the remote chance that they might someday recognize him and somehow expose his past, despite the risk to themselves. No matter how angry he felt, he knew he was helpless to do anything that would leave Jon Kingsley unprotected. He had to wait for Kirby. Together they could do . . . what?

He didn't know. But he bloody well was going to think of something.

Gabrielle was actually becoming comfortable in the saddle. Or maybe she was too tired to care. She knew only one thing for certain: She wasn't going to complain.

She and Ben had become friends during the trip, though he was a reticent man. She'd chattered about her adventures both in the theater and on the cattle drive, drawing a few chuckles as she told him about Pepper's sourdough starter and the pebbly beans. She tried to extract information about Drew, but Ben's mouth always seemed to slam shut when she did. Drew's business, apparently, was his own. Yet she could tell that Ben liked his brother-in-law, even admired him.

Once, when she'd worried aloud about Drew's safety, he'd stared her straight in the eye and said, "Don't ever underestimate Drew Cameron. He's a survivor."

At last, the Kingsley ranch came into view. Gabrielle ached to dig her heels into her mount's side and race ahead, but fear held her back. What if Drew was furious that she hadn't stayed in Denver? What if he didn't want her here? And what was she going to say to him? The news that he was an earl still rankled, filling her with foreboding.

What would she say to an earl who wanted to be foot-loose and fancy-free, who demanded her secrets but withheld his own?

She wanted to punch him in the stomach. Right after she made sure he was safe. Right after she kissed him.

Further evidence she was no lady.

As she and Ben approached the ranch, they heard a single gunshot. Ben was instantly alert, his rifle out of the scabbard and tucked under his arm. But they saw no one, nor were there more shots forthcoming. They stopped near the corral in time to see Drew come out of a barn with a rifle in his hand. When he saw them, he immediately dropped the rifle to his side and waved an arm at a man perched in the open door of the barn loft. She then realized that the gunshot must have been an alarm, established to warn of approaching riders.

She had no time to realize anything else, nor did she have eyes for anything but the tall, lean figure who squinted at her against the sun as he strode over to them.

"Gabrielle! What in the bloody hell are you doing here?" Drew exploded.

"Now, that's no way to greet a lady who's ridden all this way to see you," Ben growled.

Only then did Drew shift his gaze to her companion, and his eyes narrowed. "So, *you* tell me, Ben, why did you bring her?"

"Because, like you, she doesn't take no for an answer," Ben replied comfortably as he dismounted. "Your manners have certainly deteriorated since you left Denver. It's the last time I'll suggest you go to Texas."

While the two men were glaring at each other, Gabrielle slipped down from her horse, feeling a little sick inside. She'd dreamed of being grabbed up and hugged and told how much she was missed, followed by declarations of love.

Ha!

She held her spine stiff as a rod and did some glaring of her own. "You're a bloody fraud," she told Drew.

Both men turned and stared at her. "Earl of Kinloch, indeed," she said, fury coloring her voice. "I'm almost regretting trying to save your sorry hide."

She grabbed the reins of her horse and started toward the barn, aware of the sudden silence behind her. She got inside the barn before her shoulders drooped and the magnitude of her despair socked her in the stomach. He didn't love her. He'd never loved her. She'd merely been a plaything to a titled rogue. But this time she wouldn't cry. She would die before she cried for him again.

Yet she found herself burying her face in the mane of her horse. She would leave for Denver tomorrow. Then she would find a home of her own where she and Ha'penny—and Honor and Billy and Sammy—could build a future together. *Without* the maddening Scotsman.

A sob escaped her throat. And she got madder.

Then a hand touched her shoulder, and she whirled around, ready to flail out. Instead, Drew caught her in his arms, and somehow her arms ended up wound around him.

She looked up at his ravaged face. She'd never seen so much longing in a man's eyes.

She didn't want to be moved. Didn't want to be mollified. She didn't want to reach out and touch his face.

But she did, with her heart thundering like a cattle stampede. And her anger turned into another kind of ache that lodged in her throat and made it difficult to breathe.

"Gabrielle," he said raggedly. "I've missed you so."

"You glared at me like I was the pox," she said, unable to keep the pain from her voice.

A groan came from deep inside his chest. "I wanted you to go to Denver so you wouldn't be in danger."

Emotions were roiling through her so fast that she didn't know which way to turn. She couldn't think when she was this close to him. Her mind ceased functioning when he looked at her with so much tenderness. Her anger was rapidly cooling. Nothing else was, though. The air between them had turned decidedly steamy.

Torrid.

Blistering.

And then his mouth descended on hers, and she didn't care about anger or sanity or truth or lies or anything else. She cared only about the man in her arms.

Drew had never been so glad to see anyone in his life. He didn't even mind the sparks of anger in Gabrielle's eyes. He loved everything about her, particularly that independent and indomitable spirit that thumbed its nose at all things safe and comfortable and conventional.

Contrarily, though, the very qualities that attracted him to Gabrielle worried him bloody near to distraction. He didn't want to change her, but he *did* want her safe. He wanted her here with him, but he didn't want her exposed to any violence that might ensue.

But such thoughts fled his mind the moment their lips met. The kiss was like spontaneous combustion, their responses to each other frantic and desperate and needing. Somewhere in the back of his mind he'd registered her hurt but furious reference to his damnable title. Despite her fevered passion he knew her well enough to realize that her wounded anger was probably gunpowder to the explosion happening between them. It would have to be dampened, her feelings salved. But later.

Right now, he buried his hands in her hair, so soft and sweet, as his lips tried to tell her how much he cared. He should have told her in words, rather than leaving as he had, but he hadn't known how. Not then. Not even now. So he just held on for dear life, binding her to him with his arms, with his lips, with his body.

Then he heard the clearing of a throat, a not-completely-polite interruption. Gabrielle stiffened, and he fought the sudden urge to kill his brother-in-law. He reluctantly straightened and glared at Ben, who was grinning at him.

"This young lady is under my protection," Ben said smoothly, "I would like to know your intentions."

"My intentions?" Drew said dangerously. "Maybe to make my sister a widow."

"Now is that any way to greet a brother-in-law who's come to lend a helping hand?"

"I don't need a helping hand." Drew turned his glare on Gabrielle, who looked up at him defiantly.

"Well, then, I'll just take care of my horse," Ben said. "And Gabrielle's," he said pointedly. "They've earned a rest."

"Did you have to bring her?" Drew demanded.

Ben shrugged. "She was coming one way or another. I thought you would prefer she had an escort." He shook his head in mock sadness. "Such ingratitude!"

Drew hesitated a moment. He was bloody unused to friendship, to generosity. When he'd sent Gabrielle to Ben and Lisbeth, he had never meant for him to travel to Texas on his behalf. And his brother-in-law's trail-weary appearance, unshaven, dusty, had come as a shock. So he responded with the irritable challenge that characterized their relationship.

"Shouldn't you be home with Lisbeth?" he grumbled. "What about the baby?"

"Not due for several more months, and Serena is with her," Ben said. "She insisted I come. She was worried about you."

"So now she'll worry about you, too," Drew countered.

"She knows I can take care of myself."

Now Drew really wanted to throw a punch. "And I can't?"

"As Gabrielle said, you're not a gunman." Ben was suddenly serious, all amusement gone. "Drew, I have experience that you don't. And contacts with other law officers."

Drew couldn't deny that. Still, the interference rankled.

Ben held out his hand. The banter was over. "It's good to see you again, Drew."

Drew swallowed his pride and took Ben's hand. "I *do* thank you for coming."

It was a solemn moment, but neither man could countenance deep emotion for very long. Amusement soon crept back into Ben's voice.

"From what Gabrielle said, you've turned into a real-live hero. Again."

Drew winced, even as his heart lurched crazily. Gabrielle wasn't entirely angry with him, though he'd given her reason enough to be.

Ben chuckled at his discomfort. Then the smile disappeared. "You going to tell me what's going on?"

"Kirby and I have a plan," Drew said.

"I can imagine," Ben replied, a gleam in his eyes. "Let's take care of the horses and talk about it."

Drew glanced at Gabrielle. She looked exhausted and stunned and not a little frustrated at being left out of the men's conversation. Devil take it, but she was beautiful. Stubborn and beautiful and reckless and wonderful.

"I won't go away," she said quietly to him.

"I know," he said gently. "I know."

They waited for Kirby. One week. Ten days. There was no telegram, but then Drew expected none. Kirby would come his own way, in his own time. He wanted to leave no clues for Killian until they were ready.

Ben spent some time in San Antonio, using the telegraph, querying law enforcement friends about Philip Thorpe. He learned that the man had come to Texas five years earlier at the end of the war, one of the many Northern businessmen descending upon the state to plunder the Confederacy. Though Drew knew that Ben had fought for the North, his brother-in-law expressed only contempt for the carpetbaggers, especially, he said, after making friends with a Rebel renegade who had saved his life. He had fought as fiercely for the man he called Diablo as he'd once fought for the Union.

Drew received his brother-in-law's help with mixed feelings. Though he had often been reckless, he'd never considered himself a fool. He'd known the risks he and Kirby were willing to make. Still, Ben's arrival had narrowed the odds considerably. A former U.S. marshal and now a lawyer, Ben Masters was formidable indeed.

But Drew had never asked for help in his life, had taken pride in his ability to handle himself in almost any situation. But it wasn't his life that was at risk. It was Kirby's and Gabrielle's and Jon's. He'd become embroiled in these people's lives, was no longer responsible only for himself, and he was edgy, nervous, and distinctly uncomfortable having to depend on others and having others depend on him.

It also made him sullen, irritable, and impossible to get along with. As much as he loved having Gabrielle near, he withdrew into himself. He was grateful that she seemed to sense that he was like dynamite on a short fuse, ready to explode at any moment. She gave him his distance, but he often caught her looking sad, which made him feel even worse. Maybe it was just her loneliness for Ha'penny, he told himself. Hell, he was missing the little bairn, too.

Drew frankly didn't understand what was happening to him, didn't begin to comprehend the new needs that were tugging his emotions every which way. And until he *did* understand it, he concluded, he had no right to speak—or even to trust—his heart.

So he waited. Gabrielle waited. They all waited.

Gabrielle sensed how impatient Ben was growing, how much he must want to return to Lisbeth. And she saw how irritable Drew was becoming. She had never seen an irritable Scotsman before; she didn't think she wanted to again.

She tried to persuade herself that it was the waiting and not her that made him so moody. After all, his eyes still lit when she came into a room, and they followed her every move. She decided he simply wasn't willing to admit the strength of his feelings yet, and she didn't want to push him. Ben had taken her aside one afternoon and told her that he had been much like Drew himself, afraid to believe in love, afraid *to* love. It took time, he warned her, to overcome a lifetime of distrust.

Kirby and Damien arrived two weeks after Gabrielle and Ben. Terry and the other hands would follow in the next week or so with Billy Bones, Samson, and the string of cow ponies.

Finally, the men and Gabrielle sat down to refine their plans for drawing out Killian's employer. Ben had discovered a great deal about Philip Thorpe. He was very rich, and he owned a huge amount of land around Austin. He had also helped pay for a new school. But dark rumors about his past business practices abounded. Some claimed he was a war profiteer, other claimed that he had sold weapons to anyone with cash, including rifles to warring Indians. Witnesses to these activities always seemed to disappear, however, and open gossip had subsided since his arrival in Texas.

"Keeping his nose clean," Ben said.

Puzzled, Gabrielle asked, "But why would he run for governor and risk exposing himself?"

Ben's lips thinned with cynicism. "Contracts," he said. "Railroad contracts, road contracts, building contracts. All available with bribes, substantial bribes. And power for power's sake draws many men to politics. He probably thought he'd long since outrun his past. Something—or someone—must have jolted him out of his complacency."

Kirby took a sip of brandy. "We know James Parker wasn't the cause," he said. "And until now I didn't even suspect Thorpe was Thornton. That leaves Sam Wright."

Ben leaned forward. "Tell me everything you know about Sam Wright."

Kirby shrugged. "He followed Cal Thornton around like a puppy. Didn't have much in the way of brains. Easily influenced. Drank a lot."

"What did he look like?"

"Back then, he was tall and skinny, regular features, black hair." Kirby narrowed his eyes, remembering. "He had a small finger missing. Something happened when he was a kid."

Ben nodded. "I'll wire a friend in Austin, see whether anyone with a missing finger has turned up dead."

"You think . . ."

"This Sam Wright doesn't sound bright enough to make it on his own. He probably never left Texas," Ben said. "Maybe he tried to blackmail Thorpe."

Gabrielle could almost see Ben's mind click, adding and discarding possibilities. But it was Drew who presented the next possible conclusion.

"And," Drew said, "Thorpe suddenly realized that all of you who had been involved with him in the robbery were possible dangers."

"But how did he find us?" Kirby asked.

"You never left Texas," Ben replied. "Detectives could have tracked you down easily enough. Gabrielle's father may have been an accident. Thorpe might have seen him on stage." He shrugged. "Or maybe James Parker wrote to you, Kirby, after seeing your sketch in the San Antonio paper. The article came out several days before he was killed, didn't it? Might your father have done that, Gabrielle?" Ben queried, turning to her.

Gabrielle was stunned at the thought. Running through her father's last words in her mind once more, she thought, yes, perhaps that *was* what her father had tried to tell her. Perhaps he hadn't been *accusing* Kirby but rather he'd wanted her to *warn* him.

"I—I don't know," she stammered honestly. "The only letter he left was addressed to me, but he did say Kirby's name and the words *danger* and *be careful*. I suppose he could have been trying to tell me to warn Kirby about Thorpe."

Ben turned back to Kirby. "It's also possible that if Thorpe had detectives on you Kingsleys, they might well have intercepted mail. A bribe here and there can work wonders."

Still stunned by the possibility that she could have so misinterpreted her father's dying words, Gabrielle looked up to see Drew watching her. His gaze held a world of understanding. He knew, his eyes told her, how guilty she'd felt for her role in convincing her father to return to Texas. *Don't let this make you feel even more guilty*, he seemed to be saying to her. Then, amid the comfort and tenderness she saw in his amber gaze, another message came through: *We'll find your father's killer. His death won't go unavenged.*

A shiver raced up her spine. She appreciated his commitment and his desire to help her. But if the price of vengeance—or justice—was his life, she wasn't willing to pay it.

"We can't prove any of this, of course," Ben was saying.

"But we know it's gotta be true," Damien put in. He was sitting next to his father and had been listening silently. All his former bluster was gone, Gabrielle noted. He'd even been cordial to Drew.

"We have to be able to prove it," Kirby said to his nephew.

Apprehension snaked down Gabrielle's back at Kirby's calm comment. She'd guessed that was the intent, but somehow it seemed more dangerous put into words. She didn't want to see any of these men in peril.

"When?" she asked quietly.

All the men turned toward her.

It was Drew who finally answered. "The sooner the

better. Even if Killian took his time coming back, he'll have heard the news you're alive. I'll bet anything he's hanging around San Antonio, waiting for news of Kirby's return."

Kirby drew on the cigar he was smoking. "If we get Killian alive, we can get Thorpe. And Killian wants me."

"I hope you're not saying what I think you're saying," Jon said.

"I'm going to San Antonio tomorrow to transact some business. I'll stay a few days. There's no other way," Kirby said. "Either I make myself a target, or none of us will be safe."

"I'll be there," Ben said. "And Drew. Neither Thorpe nor Killian knows us."

"I want to go with you," Damien said.

"I need you to stay with your father," Kirby said. "He's probably a target himself. And," he added, "I need someone I can trust to take care of the ranch." Kirby gave his nephew a smile of approval.

Damien sat up straighter, and Gabrielle thought that he had grown up a great deal on the drive.

Gabrielle turned her attention toward Kirby, mentioned the possibility that had been worrying her. "It's possible that the law will find out about the bank robbery, isn't it?"

Kirby's lips thinned. "That damned secret has caused too much heartache already. If it comes out, well, I'm ready. God knows, I've lived with it all my life. No need to involve Jon, though. He was only holding the horses; he didn't know what was happening."

"Well, maybe it won't be necessary," Ben said. His gaze rested on Kirby for a moment, as if considering the ethics of a former marshal and present lawyer ignoring a crime, even if it was twenty-five years ago.

Kirby shrugged. "I don't care anymore. I would just as soon it all came out."

Damien jumped to his feet. "Dammit, you shouldn't have to pay *forever*."

"A man died," Kirby said. "That fact's haunted me all my life. I'll go to San Antonio tomorrow, stay in town until Killian shows."

Gabrielle hated the helpless feeling in the pit of her stomach. She knew Kirby was doing this as much for her as for himself. The others would assist him for the very same reasons. And all of them would be in peril. But Ben and Kirby and Drew had made up their minds. And all she could do was pray.

The three of them—Ben, Kirby, and Drew—reached San Antonio the next day. They took separate rooms in the town's most popular hotel, then separated. Kirby stayed in his room, and Drew and Ben sought out saloons—and the information that always circulated there.

Killian was already in town, had been for several days.

Drew and Ben conferred. Neither was known to Killian, and thus had some freedom of movement that Kirby didn't. Ben decided to track Killian down and follow him. Drew would sit in the lobby of the hotel, watching for the killer.

The afternoon passed slowly for Drew. He hadn't realized how difficult it was to try to look relaxed while scrutinizing every visitor, searching for a tall lean man with a silver hat band. Then Ben appeared, and Drew followed him up to Kirby's room.

"He's been asking about Kirby, saying he's looking for a job," Ben said when they were all inside the rancher's room. He turned all his attention to Kirby. "He knows you're here. He'll probably wait until he thinks you're asleep. We'll arrange a surprise for him."

The three of them placed a bedroll under the blankets on Kirby's bed, making it appear as if someone were sleeping there. Then Ben turned to Drew. "Go downstairs and wait for him to come back in after he's gone to supper."

Drew raised an eyebrow in question.

"When he enters the lobby door, you head for the stairs, act drunk and bump against Kirby's door on the way to your room. Then go on to the room."

Drew looked at him suspiciously, wondering whether Ben was merely trying to get him out of the way.

"We need to know he's on the way," Ben pointed out. "There's no other way."

Drew had to surrender. What Ben had said made sense. But he planned to be close by and ready in the event that anything went wrong. He headed downstairs to the lobby, found a chair, and pulled his hat down over his eyes, listening for footfalls.

Kirby sat with Ben on the floor of the room, guns in their hands.

It was the waiting, Kirby thought. It was the waiting that tore at a man's gut, that made him think, made him remember what had brought him to this point. And Kirby knew he didn't deserve the help he was getting.

The hours went by slowly in total silence. Then came a bump at the door, followed a minute later by something rasping in the lock. Ben was standing now, as was Kirby. The door opened, light filtered in from a lamp in the hallway, and feathers from the bedding flew as the sound of a gunshot filled the room.

Ben slammed the door, trapping the killer inside.

"Don't move," he said. "There's two guns pointed right at your head."

But Killian did move, swiftly swinging his gun to point unerringly at Kirby. Before he could move, Kirby heard another loud blast—and saw Killian crumple to the floor.

Ben swore, bending down over the man. "Who sent you?" he asked.

Killian moaned.

"Dammit, who?"

But the moan ended in a sigh, and the body went limp.

They wouldn't learn anything from Killian.

Chapter Twenty-four

———✦———

"I'm going to go to the law and tell them exactly what happened twenty-five years ago," Kirby said. "I won't have any other lives on my conscience."

Drew had returned to the ranch with Kirby and Ben after Ben pacified the San Antonio law. Since Ben was a former marshal and was able to prove that Killian was in a room that wasn't his own the local sheriff was willing to accept that the killing was justified. Drew had not been involved, his name not even mentioned.

"It'll be your word against Thorpe's about who killed that clerk, Kirby," Ben said. "You won't be able to prove a thing. And if you ruin Thorpe's chances for the governorship, he'll come after you for sure, and probably Gabrielle and Jon as well."

Kirby swore.

"Drew has another idea to bring Thorpe out into the open," Ben told him. "He may be wary now, because Killian's dead. But if we dangle a large enough prize in front of his eyes, he might just bite, particularly if he thinks you might talk and ruin his hopes for the governorship. He can't know that you already realize who he is, but he has to know you might well figure it out."

Leaning casually against the wing chair in which Gabrielle was sitting, Drew listened, satisfied to let Ben explain his plan to Kirby.

"If," Ben finished, "Thorpe is as voracious as we think he is, he'll jump at the opportunity to sell some land to a wealthy Scotsman. The English are buying land all over the West right now, investing in huge cattle spreads, so he wouldn't suspect anything. And, given the right encouragement, he might well try to keep the money *and* the land if he thinks he can get away with it. That's the key. We have to make the opportunity so inviting he can't resist."

Kirby scowled. "And if he doesn't take the bait?"

"Drew pulls out, says he changed his mind, and we try something else."

Silence descended on the room.

"Drew would be more believable as a rich real-estate speculator if he had a wife," Gabrielle pointed out.

Drew's gaze flashed downward to her, an instant protest springing to his lips. "No," he said, hearing the edge of panic in his own voice. "He may know what you look like."

"Not when I get through with myself," she said, turning in her chair to look up at him. "A blond wig will do wonders. Any good dressmaker will have them available."

Drew's hands were suddenly cold, and he became even more aware of it when Gabrielle reached up and took one of his hands in her warm one.

"I can't live the rest of my life worrying about someone behind every tree," she said quietly. "It's my battle as much as Kirby's."

Drew looked to Ben for support. "Ben, please, tell her that this is a dreadful idea."

Ben shook his head. "Can't. She's right. A husband and wife would be better."

Drew's hand clenched around Gabrielle's. "No," he said again.

Gabrielle twisted around further so that she could look at him directly. "Drew, you're going to risk your life. I have the right to do the same. And I will. For my father, if for no other reason."

Drew knew her too well. If he didn't let her go with him, she would find some way of doing it on her own, just as she had braved the cattle drive alone. At least with him and Ben, she would have some protection.

"You two won't be alone," Ben pointed out. "I have a few friends who will help. Men I can trust."

The assurance didn't calm the fear in Drew's heart. But he knew of no argument that would change Gabrielle's mind, and if he didn't take her with him, she might well do something on her own. He couldn't risk that. So he glared at Ben. "If anything happens to her . . ."

Ben looked at him, then around the room. "I think Philip Thorpe has finally met his match."

The Austin hotel room was one of the finest Gabrielle had ever occupied. She and her parents had never had much money and usually had stayed in clean but economical boardinghouses.

Ben had insisted on the Grand because it offered suites, the kind a wealthy Scot might require. A suite, with adjoining rooms, also allowed for better protection. Ben engaged one suite for Andrew Cameron, Lord Kinloch, and his wife, Catherine. He engaged a second adjoining suite for a rich Colorado mine owner named Dan Forsyth.

Gabrielle looked around the suite with awe and not a little apprehension. As an earl, she realized that Drew must be used to lavish lodgings like this. But the luxury itself made her feel out of place.

Two sharp-eyed strangers joined Ben, or Dan Forsyth, next door. One of them, a man named Kane O'Brien, deftly unlocked the door separating the suites without a key. Gabrielle soon discovered he'd once been an outlaw named Diablo—the man she'd heard mentioned several times before. She wasn't entirely sure how he'd come to be here, but it was plain that Ben trusted him implicitly, and he certainly looked deadly enough. Their other accomplice, a man named Jud Merrill, was a former law officer who, she gathered, owed Ben a favor. She wondered who had been dispatched to the Circle K to guard Kirby and Jon. Ben's resources seemed limitless, his commitment to this venture complete.

She and Drew went shopping. She purchased two very fine dresses, Drew two expensive suits. They had pooled their funds to do so, and Kirby, who'd made a great deal on the cattle drive, was providing the cash to "buy" the land.

The next step was locating a blond wig, and when she mentioned her requirements in the men's hearing, Kane O'Brien appeared with one later that day. She didn't ask questions, but she admitted to herself that the man had a good eye. The wig fit over her short hair perfectly and, with a hat, she would look quite elegant.

She worked with Drew for several hours on learning a Scottish accent, and her years as an actress served her well. His own accent deepened, and all traces of the western lingo he'd picked up on the trail disappeared.

Once they felt ready, Drew wrote a formal note to Philip Thorpe, saying that he, the Earl of Kinloch, was in America to buy a considerable parcel of land, that he was hopeful of a rapid transaction, and that he'd been informed that Philip Thorpe was just the man to help him. He added that he wanted all dealings confidential at this time. Would Mr. Thorpe be amenable to an immediate meeting in his hotel suite?

A hotel messenger was dispatched with the note.

And then they waited. Ben and Kane O'Brien joined them in their parlor and reviewed details. Neither Drew nor Gabrielle was ever to be left alone. O'Brien and Merrill would follow them wherever they went, and Drew was to make sure the two never lost them. Ben would stay at the hotel until it appeared Thorpe might make his move.

Gabrielle noticed that Drew and O'Brien immediately took a liking to each other, leading Ben to comment wryly that they deserved each other. Rogues, both of them, he said. Merrill was more like Ben—quiet, reserved, watchful.

They reviewed the scheme again. If Thorpe checked, he would discover there really was an Earl of Kinloch in America, and one with a less than savory reputation. Drew had winced slightly at the characterization but then shrugged it off.

Gabrielle had watched his face as he'd made the gesture. So much of him was still a mystery, yet it was plain to her that Lisbeth had been correct—he clearly hated his title. Seeing that, the last vestiges of injury she'd felt at not being told about it evaporated.

She wanted to go to him, touch him, comfort and love him. She wanted to lie in his arms. But she was beginning to think they would never be alone again. Ben in particular had been staying close, and she wasn't sure that it was altogether for their physical safety. He seemed to have taken on the role of big brother—big *protective* brother—to her, and as much as she appreciated his efforts in this intricate venture, she wished he would allow her some privacy with Drew.

"You sure you feel comfortable with that gun?" he asked her.

She nodded. She'd produced her father's Colt, causing shocked male stares. Then she'd had to prove to them all that she knew how to use it. She hadn't missed the look of pride in Drew's gaze when she'd passed the test.

Still, Ben seemed to feel concerned. "You shoot close up," he said. "That's if you have to shoot at all."

Sighing inwardly, she didn't argue.

A knock at the door prompted Ben and his friends to conceal themselves in the bedroom. Drew opened the door and accepted a formal-looking envelope from a messenger boy.

"I was told to wait for a reply," the boy said.

Drew opened the envelope and quickly read its contents. "Tell Mr. Thorpe that tomorrow at ten is quite acceptable."

The boy nodded and disappeared down the corridor. Drew closed the door and called an all-clear toward the bedroom. The three men emerged.

"Thorpe took the bait, gentlemen," Drew announced.

Philip Thorpe's face was florid, his body well padded, his tailoring and grooming otherwise impeccable. He obviously ate well, drank well, and lived well. He also had cold eyes even when his face was wreathed in smiles.

Gabrielle hid her revulsion as she watched him, standing in the parlor of their hotel suite, extend a hand to Drew.

"My lord," he fawned.

Gabrielle glanced sideways at Drew and sensed that, as he shook Thorpe's hand, he was inwardly contemptuous. Yet he handled himself with the amiable condescension she would have expected anyone of his class to display. He would do well as an actor, she thought fleetingly.

"And this is Lady Kinloch," Drew said, his hand touching the small of her back in a possessive gesture.

"It's a great pleasure, Lady Kinloch," Thorpe said.

She did not offer her hand, merely raised what she hoped was an aristocratic eyebrow.

Thorpe turned back to Drew. "I understand you're looking for land."

"Aye," Drew said with a deep exaggerated brogue. "But I donna want it known. I ha' come into some money recently, but I also owe a few debts, if ye ken my meaning. I know of an Englishman who has made a great success of a ranch out here, in your wilderness. I, too, wish to purchase a ranch and find someone to run it—all verra quietly. My friend said I could triple my investment verra quickly."

"The land deed has to be filed," Thorpe said carefully.

"Aye, I thought it would," Drew said. "My wife's maiden name should do." He shrugged. "Before long I should ha' found the funds to pay my debts, and all will be well."

"Why did you come to me?" Thorpe asked cautiously.

"I am told ye own a lot of property here," Drew said. "And that ye might be selling some of it to raise money to run for . . . what do ye call it?"

"Governor," Thorpe said expansively.

"Aye. And I've been assured ye are a shrewd businessman wi' an eye toward opportunity. 'Tis nothing I see illegal aboot this transaction. I just want to stress the need for . . . discretion."

"How much money do you have?" Thorpe asked.

Gabrielle could almost see him licking his lips like a cat with cream on its whiskers.

"Nearly two hundred thousand of your American dollars," Drew said.

Philip Thorpe blinked. "In cash?"

"Aye. I donna believe in banks," Drew said.

A strangled noise came from Thorpe's throat. "Surely you don't carry it with you?"

Drew shrugged. "I keep a pistol in my carriage," he said complacently. "I would ha' the money available."

Gabrielle could almost see Thorpe's brain working.

He would have already verified by telegraph that an Earl of Kinloch was indeed in the United States.

"I *do* have some land you might like," Thorpe said tentatively. "If you would like to see a map . . ."

Drew nodded.

The man unrolled a map on the desk. "It's three miles out of Austin. Property used to be a cotton plantation. Owner died during the war, and I bought it from the widow. Land's just been sitting there, waiting for the right buyer. Real pretty place. Rolling hills. Good stream for water. Of course, I have had other inquiries. In fact, just yesterday . . ." His voice trailed off.

Drew turned to Gabrielle.

She shuddered delicately. "Wha' aboot Indians?"

"They're long gone from this area, Lady Kinloch," Thorpe assured her. "And you wouldn't find a prettier piece of land in Scotland."

"I want t' go back to Scotland," she said plaintively to her "husband."

Drew's voice grew firm. "Ye know that is not possible. The law—" He stopped suddenly, as if belatedly remembering Thorpe's presence. "How soon can we be aboot closing the transaction, Mr. Thorpe, if the property pleases us?"

Thorpe's eyes were greedy now. Very, very greedy, Gabrielle noted with satisfaction.

"Surely you have a friend, an acquaintance, a lawyer who would like to advise you?" Thorpe probed.

"Do I look like a man who requires someone else's opinion?" Drew said disdainfully. "A . . . provincial's opinion, at that?" He turned to his "wife." " 'Twill only be a few months, my dear. Things will be sorted out."

"The disgrace, the shame," Gabrielle said, wilting against Drew's shoulder. "My family canna hold their heads up again because ye—"

"Mr. Thorpe is not interested in all that, my dear,

not interested at all. When we show a profit, show them all what we've accomplished . . ."

Gabrielle sighed loudly.

"You will like the property, Lady Kinloch," Philip Thorpe said hastily. "And there's a lovely little house."

"Little?" she said in a horrified tone.

"I think we'd best be seeing the property," Drew interjected. "As soon as possible."

Thorpe nodded. "I can meet you out there tomorrow," he said. "I'll give you directions. If you think you're interested, I can bring the papers with me. There *is* another buyer coming to see it."

Drew's eyebrows rose in mock alarm. "I'll bring the money with me. We can be after signing the papers there, if all is satisfactory."

Thorpe sat at the desk and sketched them a map. Then he looked up at them. "Noon tomorrow?"

"Aye," Drew said with satisfaction.

"It's a pleasure doing business with you, Lord Kinloch."

"Indeed," Drew said with more than a hint of condescension.

Resentment flared briefly in Thorpe's eyes but was quickly replaced with an expression of geniality. "If you settle in Texas, I would welcome your vote for me as governor," he said.

"Ah, yes," Drew said noncommittally. "Elections," he said with a sneer. "You Yanks do have strange customs."

Thorpe's face reddened. But he managed a "Good day," before taking his leave.

Gabrielle stood beside Drew, holding her breath, until the sound of footsteps in the hall had disappeared. Then they looked at each other—and burst into laughter.

●   ●   ●

"If two hundred thousand dollars doesn't appeal to his avarice, nothing will," Jud Merrill said as he stared at Thorpe's map.

"He'd been trying to be respectable," Kane O'Brien argued. "He'll be a fool to risk everything now."

"Ah, but a greedy man can't resist a sure thing," Ben said. "Kinloch has no friends. He has cash. And the law's apparently looking for him. What better mark?"

Drew glanced at him. "Have you always been this devious?"

"Yes," Kane said. "I'll tell you about it someday."

Drew looked at his brother-in-law. "Does my sister know this side of you?"

Gabrielle smiled at the bantering between the two men. Though they often resembled a pair of bulldogs challenging each other, she sensed the affection that underlay their competition.

"Ask her yourself," Ben quipped.

"I believe I shall," Drew shot back.

The men returned their attention to Thorpe's map—Ben, O'Brien, and Merrill comparing it with their knowledge of Austin and its environs.

"He won't risk a shooting on his own property," O'Brien ventured.

"I agree," Ben said. "It will be on a public road someplace. An ordinary robbery of two careless foreigners nobody cares about."

"Here," Merrill said, pointing to a spot on the map. "This road forks off the main one toward Thorpe's property. I know it. There's hills on both sides. It's an ideal spot for an ambush."

Kane agreed.

"And Thorpe believes you have only a single pistol," Ben said, smiling a little as he added, "If we're lucky, he even thinks it's probably some ancient family relic, taken off the walls of your family castle."

"It's a big risk for Thorpe to take alone," Merrill cautioned.

"But I don't think he'll chance hiring anyone this close to home. And with Killian gone, he'd have to find another gunslinger, and he hasn't got time for that. Unless, of course, he's got one stashed away we don't know about."

"A lot of ifs," Kane said.

"Yes," Drew agreed. "But, gentlemen, if I might point out, this plan is all we've got."

The men looked at Drew, and Gabrielle could see that although they didn't like it, they all knew that he was right. They'd done all the planning they could do. Nature—human nature—would now have to take its course.

Drew had chosen the rented buggy carefully. Enclosed on three sides, the vehicle seemed ambush proof. A fringe at the front would further hinder any clear view—or shot. A shooter would have to come out into the open and face them head on. And yet it was exactly the kind of fancy buggy Lord and Lady Kinloch would select.

He drove it to an alley behind the hotel, where Kane O'Brien joined him and Gabrielle, who was sitting tensely beside him. O'Brien crouched in the back with two rifles and a handgun. Drew also had a handgun tucked in his boot, and Gabrielle's Colt was under the front seat.

Ben had ridden ahead to the first possible ambush site. Merrill had stationed himself at Philip Thorpe's home just after midnight and planned to follow the man when he ventured out. They had plotted every move carefully, precisely timing when the buggy would reach each point on the map. That way, in the event Merrill lost Thorpe, he could catch up with them readily enough.

Drew was beginning to understand why Ben had been such a good marshal. He left nothing to chance, which, Drew realized with some amusement would also have made him a good criminal.

As they rode out of town, Gabrielle was quiet, her eyes intent on every rock, every hill they passed. So much depended on Thorpe doing what they wanted him to do, risking everything he'd built for one large prize. Would he be content with selling a large piece of land at a good price, or would he want everything? Would he risk seeing the sale fall through? Would he wait and inspect the bundle of money they carried, real bills on top, plain paper on the bottom? If he did, Drew would suddenly change his mind about the property, or Gabrielle would faint, whichever seemed more effective at the time.

He felt Gabrielle's hand sneak over to rest on his thigh, and he flashed her what he hoped was a re-assuring grin. As her hand remained in place, he had to shove aside the arousal it produced in him. This was no time to get distracted. Yet it was difficult. They'd had no private time together since being reunited. Ben had stayed in their suite as protection, and they could not very well have retired to the one bed in his presence. He himself had ended up sleeping on a sofa in the parlor, with Ben spreading a bedroll on the floor.

Seeking a distraction from the distraction, Drew began to whistle a few tunes as he drove the carriage. When he came to the end of the song, O'Brien's muffled voice came from behind him.

"Don't stop."

"How did you get to know Ben?" Drew asked him.

"It's a long, miserable story," O'Brien said. "I hated the sonofabitch for years."

Drew chuckled. "I can appreciate the sentiment. I felt somewhat the same way for a while. He tends to grow on one, though."

"Does he?" O'Brien growled from his position behind the seat. "I haven't noticed."

"Then why are you here?" Gabrielle asked, keeping her eyes forward.

"Damned if I know," O'Brien said. "He wired and said he was in need of my particular criminal talents. It was a request I couldn't refuse. Masters being something less than righteous and noble I just had to see."

Despite the cynical words, Drew detected a note of admiration in the man's voice. "Besides," O'Brien added reluctantly, "like Merrill, I guess I owe him."

Drew was going to owe him, too. He wondered how many other markers his brother-in-law had accumulated over the years.

They were coming to the turnoff in the road, and Drew directed the horses left. The first possible ambush site was a mile ahead. He felt himself tense, not for himself but for Gabrielle.

Silence fell among them, the only audible sound being the clip-clopping of the horses' hooves and the rattling of the wheels. Drew sensed O'Brien moving behind him, knew he was readying his rifle.

Gabrielle's fingers bit into his thigh, and he gave her a quick smile and started whistling a new tune. Her fingers dug deeper.

He saw the hill ahead, the incline rising to the right. He looked for a telltale glint of sunlight on metal but saw nothing. Nor did he see any sign of Ben.

The buggy continued toward the next possible hill, a half-mile away.

His hands tightened around the reins. Bloody hell, but he hated this waiting, hated using Gabrielle as bait. Shifting the reins to one hand, he reached to take her hand, and held it. He turned to gaze at her for a moment, finding her returning his gaze. Her eyes were incredibly blue, full of emotion. She was so brave, so gallant.

Was he insane bringing her along? Had he a choice?

He wanted to pour out his heart to her. He wanted to do it now, in case something would happen to him.

He would make bloody sure nothing would happen to her.

But the words lodged in his throat. Now was not the time. When this was over . . .

He tried, though, to tell her with his eyes, with the hand he rested on her lap.

And she knew. Joy flooded her eyes, making his heart pound and his hands tremble.

Promises were made during the silence. Lasting promises.

A voice from the back broke the moment. "Keep your eyes open," Kane O'Brien said dryly as if sensing their distraction with each other.

The warning was enough. Drew knew he shouldn't endanger someone else, and he bloody well didn't want to endanger himself, either—not this time. Not when the future stretched out in front of him, bright and full of promise.

They passed the gully without incident. The road was completely empty. Where in the hell was Ben?

The next turn in the road would reveal the site both Ben and O'Brien thought the likeliest for an ambush. Gabrielle stiffened at his side, and pride rushed through him. God, he loved her.

The road swung left, hills rising on both sides, and he saw several small logs lying in the road, as if they had spilled from a wagon. A steely calm came over him, as his right hand went for his hidden gun.

He slowed the horses. Thorpe was no fool. He'd known that his quarry would have to get out of the buggy to move the logs. Drew realized he would be out in the open, alone, and Gabrielle would be an easier target, too, without him beside her. She might even get down with him. Where in the bloody hell were Ben and Merrill?

But Drew knew what needed to be done. Thorpe would have to fire at them to be charged with attempted robbery and murder. He wondered how good a shot the man was and whether he had, after all, obtained help. If he had, Drew was sure Ben or Merrill would have discovered that fact by now.

If they were still alive.

Why in the bloody hell had he allowed Gabrielle to convince him to bring her with him?

As if turning to talk to her, he informed O'Brien, "There are logs lying in the road. I'll have to move them."

"No," Gabrielle said, her voice frightened.

"It's the only way, Gabrielle," he said. "We have to trust Ben."

A snort came from the back.

"Do you have any better ideas, O'Brien?" Drew challenged.

" 'Fraid not," the man said as Drew brought the buggy to a stop. "Unless you just sit there, too aristocratic to move a few pieces of wood. Our friend might get impatient."

Drew was actually considering the idea when O'Brien offered another thought.

"Or," O'Brien said slowly, "you might consider that the man will want the sun at his back, not in his eyes. That would mean he's positioned somewhere to your right. Move the horses as close as you can to the logs, then get down. Keep the horses and carriage to the right of you. Kick the first log out of the way and move the horses to the next one."

Drew took a deep breath. It could work. "You and Ben must have been formidable, working together."

"Hell, we were on different sides," O'Brien said.

"Drew?"

He turned, and Gabrielle leaned over and kissed him, her lips sweet and loving against his.

"Be careful," she whispered.

"You stay back in the seat, out of sight," he ordered as he handed her the reins, aware that O'Brien's hands were nearby in case of trouble. "O'Brien, get her on the floor if firing starts."

He stepped down, careful to keep the horses

between him and the hill, kicking aside first one log, then another, trying to look as nonchalant and careless as possible while planning and timing every step. Only for a fraction of a second was he clear of the buggy.

And in that instant he heard a shot ring out and felt the impact of a bullet hit his shoulder. He heard Gabrielle scream as he stumbled, stunned.

The horses reared. He was aware of movement to calm them down, but they jolted a few feet ahead, leaving him exposed.

Where in the hell was Ben?

He heard another shot. Dirt splattered an inch away from him. Then a whirl of skirts descended from the carriage, even as O'Brien apparently fought to keep the horses steady.

"No," he yelled. "No."

But she kept coming, and then he saw the rifle in her hands. She threw it to him and he rolled over, facing toward the origin of the shot.

He thought he saw a glint of a rifle stock just as another shot hit where he had been seconds ago. He aimed and fired, though he had little hope of hitting anything.

Just then he heard other shots, and the carriage backed up, the team finally under control by O'Brien.

Drew managed to get to his knees, then his feet, pushing Gabrielle toward the carriage as another shot rang out, then a volley echoed through the air.

The horses reared again. Ignoring the pain that was now raging through him, he grabbed the edge of the carriage and managed to shove Gabrielle up into the backseat as O'Brien fought the frantic horses.

"Go," he told O'Brien. "Get the hell out of here," he added, slapping the rear of one of the horses to make sure his order was obeyed, and the carriage took off, leaving him alone.

He fell to the ground again, clutching the rifle. His eyes searched the hill and then he saw something move. He aimed again, but another shot rang out from a different direction and then a third. The movement in the rocks stilled for a moment, then something started to fall, rolling over and over.

He watched until the object reached the bottom and he saw two horsemen approach it. Then he relaxed his hold on the rifle, and rolled over on his back, fighting against the pain.

He had to know that Gabrielle was all right.

Part of him—only a part—heard approaching horses. His eyes closed for a second. He was so tired. But he forced them back open and saw Ben lean over him.

"It's over," he said. "That was the damnedest shot I've ever seen."

"I couldn't have . . ." Drew started.

"No, you couldn't have but somehow you did," Ben said. "At least you crippled him enough that he missed me when I came in his gunsights. My bullet killed him, but he was already wounded. You never told me you could shoot like that. Sorry to be so damned late. He'd circled. We thought he was headed to a place farther ahead. We heard the shots and raced here. There wasn't any time to be subtle so we came straight in. If you hadn't hit him . . ."

But he didn't continue because the carriage was back. Drew vaguely heard the horses, but he didn't miss the flurry of skirts nor the kisses cooling his face.

She was all right. He closed his eyes for a moment of thanks.

"Don't you dare!" Gabrielle's voice was insistent, demanding, and he felt something wet on his face, something other than the soft feel of her lips. "Darn you," she said. "Look at me."

He did. The fancy hat sat askew on her head, its plumage bent and dusty. Her blond wig was half turned around, apparently upset when he'd pushed her into the carriage. He had to grin at the picture. She looked almost, not quite, but almost as disreputable as the old Gabe.

She shook her head as she stared at him, then finally grinned back, seeing herself through his eyes. Her fingers touched his cheek. "I love you," she said softly, "and that darn silly smile of yours."

Then her eyes turned serious as they stared at his new suit, much of it turning a bright red. "Drew," she whispered.

"Not very bad," he whispered, not really understanding why his voice was so weak.

"Damn," Kane O'Brien, who was now crowding Ben, said. "No time for that now," he chided them both. "We've got to stop that bleeding."

Drew moved and couldn't quite stifle a small groan. Gabrielle gripped his hand as if it were a lifeline.

Ben stirred beside him. "Lisbeth will have my hide for this," he growled, apparently oblivious to anything but that fact. He started unbuttoning Drew's blood-soaked frockcoat and shirt. "Too many damned clothes," he muttered, getting frustrated and finally ripping the shirt open. He frowned as he saw the scars from Drew's earlier wounds, and his frown deepened as he looked at the fresh one. "Move your arm," he commanded.

Drew did as Ben asked, the pain going deeper. But his arm moved properly, as did his hand.

"Just a flesh wound," he said, shrugging casually, and Drew knew he was doing it for Gabrielle's sake. Her eyes were full of panic.

He decided to play his own part. "Is Thorpe really dead?" he inquired.

"Completely," Ben said wryly. "And two ex-lawmen are on hand who will testify that they saw him attack the carriage of a naïve Scottish earl who was taking his lady for a buggy ride."

Drew grimaced. "Is it necessary to put it like that?"

Ben grinned. "I sort of like it."

"Who the hell cares how it's put?" O'Brien inserted.

"Let's get that wound bandaged and get Cameron to a doctor. I have a wife to get home to."

"So do I," Ben said. "And she'll probably never forgive me for letting her precious brother get shot." He glared at Drew, then took off his own jacket and started to unbutton his shirt.

"Don't even think about it," Drew said. "I don't need your shirt and I don't need your doctoring."

"What in the hell . . ."

"I have a louse to do it," Drew said, struggling to lighten Gabrielle's still stricken face.

"A louse?" O'Brien questioned, puzzled.

"Me," Gabrielle said, her eyes brightening with understanding. She released Drew's hands and pulled up her skirts to display her petticoat. She calmly tore it into strips, pressed a piece of cloth to the wound and competently tied it firmly. Her hands were extraordinarily gentle, tender, and her eyes were wide with love and compassion and pride.

Pride. He felt ten feet tall lying in the dirt.

O'Brien watched in amazement. "A louse," he said, shaking his head.

Drew managed a shaky grin. "A bloody good one."

She smiled slightly, even while her eyes worried over him. "He needs a doctor," she said. "The bullet didn't come out."

Two of the three men helped him into the carriage as Merrill held the carriage horses steady. Gabrielle climbed into the backseat and cradled his head in her lap as the carriage headed back to Austin. Her hands felt good. So did her lap. But the pain was growing. So was the weakness.

And the drowsiness. He could barely keep his eyes open, could barely move, and then he felt nothing.

He woke to the smell of flowers, to the touch of a warm hand, to a pure voice softly singing his Scottish lullaby.

And pain.

His eyes fluttered open, and he looked up into the bluest eyes he'd seen and a smile that could make angels sing. "At last," she whispered.

He tried to move, but he was weak and swathed in bandages. Then he remembered: the drive back to Austin, the doctor, chloroform. The bullet had to be dug out. How long had he been here?

He looked around. The room was full. Ben. O'Brien. Merrill. Kirby. Even Damien. At his first movement, they grouped around him as he surveyed worried faces, then relieved smiles. All these people. People who cared.

Gabrielle's hand crept into his. Her eyes were suspiciously wet.

"Didn't think you were ever going to wake up," Ben said, his mouth spreading into a grin.

"I thought you were heading ... home to your wife," Drew said. His gaze cut to O'Brien. "And you."

Both men shrugged self-consciously and shifted their feet.

"Lisbeth would have horsewhipped me," Ben said wryly, "if I left without knowing you were ... in one piece. Besides, I wanted to see for myself. I don't have that many brothers-in-law to dismiss one so easily."

"Well, I *am* in one piece," Drew said grumpily, moving slightly and wincing painfully as he did. "I think." He sighed. "So you can go."

"Such gratitude," Ben said.

Drew glared at him. "You were supposed to *be* there."

"*You* weren't supposed to get in the line of fire," Ben retorted, his eyes sparking with competitive fire.

"Truce," O'Brien said. "I *do* have to get home." He stepped up to Drew, held out his hand. "Anytime you need anything ..." Then he turned and left.

Kirby was next, pushing forward. He stood there

for a moment silently, his face filled with emotion. "I can never thank you properly. . . . I . . ."

Drew's gaze cut to Gabrielle, to her hand lying in his, then to the men standing around. "You gave me more than I ever thought to have, Kirby." He stopped talking as his emotions overwhelmed him. Kirby had taught him friendship. Loyalty. Commitment. He'd never known how incomplete a man he'd been until now. His pride in earning respect and affection from men like these grew with each moment. He would never be alone again. Never.

And he had Gabrielle. As his gaze fixed on hers, he was aware, but only barely, of the men filing out, leaving them alone.

His hand squeezed hers. "I love you," he said, finally able to say the words that had eluded him all his life. He had something to offer now. Not land or money. But a soul that was whole, a heart that had opened, a future that was limitless because he had friends. Because he could feel. He could care.

Because he could love.

Gabrielle's face dissolved, and tears shimmered in her eyes.

"Is the prospect that bad?" he whispered, suddenly afraid.

"Oh no," she said in a ragged whisper. "I just thought . . . I was afraid . . . you would never say it." She leaned down, her lips touching his in a caress so full of love and tenderness it felt like an angel's kiss. Maybe it was.

He believed in angels now. In magic. In miracles. In love.

Drew heaved a contented sigh. Lying prostate on a bed, his shoulder burning and every movement pure agony, he'd never felt better in his life.

When Gabrielle lifted her lips from his, he pulled her down next to him with his good arm. "I think," he said slowly, "that it's time I had a wife to come home to." He hesitated, his voice cracking a little. "If she can love a wandering Scotsman without much more than his name to offer her."

Her smile was brilliant. It lit up his entire world.

"Ah," she said, "but we have a great deal. Including a son."

"And a fine horse named Billy Bones," he said.

"Sir William," she corrected. "I've renamed him. And we have our first head of cattle. Samson will make a fine father for a herd."

"And a dog," he added, still counting blessings he'd never thought to have.

"Aye," she said. "All that and more."

"Much, much more," he agreed as he leaned forward and their lips met in a long, lingering kiss.

About the Author

Patricia Potter has become one of the most highly praised writers of historical romance since her impressive debut in 1988, when she won the Maggie Award and a Reviewer's Choice Award from *Romantic Times* for her first novel. She received the *Romantic Times* Career Achievement Award for Storyteller of the Year for 1992 and more recently a Career Achievement award in Western Romance. She has worked as a newspaper reporter in Atlanta and was president of the Georgia Romance Writers Association. She is now on the board of the River City Romance Writers.

Ben Masters had to travel across the ocean to Scotland to find his true love. Discover this poignant romance in
THE MARSHAL AND THE HEIRESS

Kane O'Brien had agreed to a desperate bargain, then found himself having to choose between betraying his country—or the woman he'd come to love.
Thrill to this adventure-filled romance in
DIABLO

Titles are available wherever Bantam Books are sold.
Or turn to the back of the book for an order coupon.

Look for Patricia Potter's short story
in the anthology
WHEN YOU WISH . . .
on sale Fall 1997

Turn the page for an early look at this
enchanting collection of original stories.

The moon rode high against the soft blackness of the night sky. The great stones of the circle threw their shadows across the sleeping plain. The girl waited in the grove of trees. He had said he would come when the moon reached its zenith.

She shivered despite the warmth of the June night, drawing her woolen cloak about her. The massive pillars of Stonehenge held a menacing magic, even for one accustomed to the rites that took place within the sinister enclosure. The thought of venturing into the vast black space within the circle terrified her as it terrified all but the priests. It was forbidden ground.

Her ears were stretched for the sound of footsteps, although she knew that she would hear nothing as his sandaled feet slid over the moss of the grove. She stepped closer to the trunk of a poplar tree, then jumped back as she touched its encrustation of sacred mistletoe.

"Move into the moonlight."

Even though she'd been waiting for it, the soft command sent a thrill of fear shivering in her belly, curling her toes. She looked over her shoulder and saw him, shrouded in white, his hood pulled low over his head, only his eyes, pale blue in the darkness, gave life to the form.

The girl stepped out of the grove onto the moonlit plain. She felt him behind her. The priest who held the power of the Druid's Egg. She stopped, turned to face him. "Will you help me?"

"Are you certain you know what you're asking for?" His voice rasped, hoarse as if he'd been shouting for hours. The pale blue eyes burned in their deep sockets.

She nodded. "I am certain." With a sudden movement, she shook off her hood. Her hair cascaded down her back, a silver river in the moonlight. "Will the magic work?"

A smile flashed across his eyes and he reached out to touch her hair. "It has the power of desires and dreams."

"To make them come true?" Her voice was anxious, puzzled.

He said nothing, but drew from beneath his cloak a thick-bladed knife. "Are you ready?"

The girl swallowed, nodded her head. She turned her back to the priest. She felt him take her hair at the nape of her neck. She felt the knife sawing through the thick mass, silvered by the moon. She felt it part beneath the blade. And then she stood shorn, the night air cold on her bare neck. "Now you will give it to me?"

He was winding the hank of hair around his hand and didn't answer as he reveled in the richness of the payment. The hair of a maiden had many useful properties but it was a potent sacrifice that few young virgins were voluntarily prepared to make. He opened a leather pouch at his waist and carefully deposited the shining mass inside, before taking out an object of green glass. It lay on his flat palm.

She looked closely at it. A green glass bottle with a chased silver top. Vertical bands of chased silver flowed down the bottle from the stopper, like liquid mercury. There was something inside it. She could see the shape in the neck behind the glowing glass. Would it work? It had to work. Only the magic of a man who held the power of the Druid's Egg could enable her to make the right decision.

She reached out and touched it tentatively with her fingertip. "The spell is within?"

"You will read it within."

"What must I do? Must I open it in a certain way? Read it in a certain way?"

"You will read it as it is meant to be read." The smile was there again as he took her hand and placed the bottle on her palm. "As it is meant to be read for you," he added.

Her fingers closed over the bottle. She frowned, wondering what he could mean. A spell was a spell, surely. It could only be read one way.

When she looked up, the priest had gone.

The Druid's Egg was hatched by several serpents laboring together. When hatched it was held in the air by their hissing. The man who had given her the spell had caught the egg as it danced on the serpents' venom. He had caught it and escaped the poison himself. Such a man . . . such a priest . . . had the power to do anything.

Holding the bottle tightly in her fist, the girl turned her back on the stone pillars. She tried to walk but soon was running across the plain toward the village nestled in a fold of land beside the river that flowed to the sea. She had never seen the sea, only heard tales of a vast blueness that disappeared into the sky. But the river flowing between sloping banks was her friend.

She sat down on the bank outside the village and with trembling fingers opened the bottle. A scrap of leather, carefully rolled, lay inside. She drew it out, unfurled it, held it up to the bright moonlight.

Runes were scratched into the leather at the top, and at the sight of the magic symbols her heart leaped. She hadn't sold her hair for nothing. Here was the incantation she had bought. She squinted at the strange marks and wondered what she was to do with them. Only when she turned the leather over did she see the writing in legible strokes inked onto the leather.

"To thine own wish be true. Do not follow the moth to the star."

The girl stared in disbelieving dismay. What did it mean? It told her nothing. There was nothing magic about those words. She looked again at the runes and knew in her bones that they would add nothing to the message. They were decoration for a simple truth. She thrust the scrap of leather back into the bottle and corked it.

Be true to her own wish. Was it telling her she must face the consequences of her desires? If she wished for the stars, she would burn like the moth at the candle.

Slowly, she stood up. She held her hand over the swift flowing water and opened it. The little bottle dropped, was caught by the current and whisked away toward the distant sea. As distant as the stars.

The choice was still hers to make. The road still branched before her. She had sold her hair for the druid's power and she was left, as always, with only her own.

And don't miss Patricia Potter's
next thrilling historical romance
STARCATCHER
available Winter 1997

Turn the page for a sneak peek.

Highlands of Scotland
1648

She was eight years old and destined to be his bride.

Patrick Sutherland saw the small, slight figure huddled at the corner of one of the parapets of Abernie Castle as he walked there for the last time in what would probably be years.

Tomorrow, he would join his clansmen and go to war in Ireland. He would leave the Gunns—the family with whom he'd been fostered—and his best friend with whom he'd been trained in the ways of war.

And though he knew he would miss Abernie, and Gavin, excitement and anticipation coursed through him. He was sixteen, at last considered a man ready to do a man's service. He would return in ten years to claim his bride, according to the betrothal agreement signed this day by Marsali's father and his own.

Patrick had not objected to his match with the Lady Marsali. Since his birth he'd been taught that the interests of his clan came before any personal consideration. Marriage was almost always a matter of convenience: an alliance for protection, money or bloodlines. He'd always understood that, and Marsali, who was like a little sister to him, was an endearing little sprite with a happy disposition, quick mind and sweet face. He'd always liked the minx, who followed him around like a puppy. Even at eight, she had a winning way about her.

But now she looked heartbroken and he wondered whether the formal betrothal ceremony had frightened her more than any of them realized.

He looked up at the sky. It seemed extraordinarily bright. The moon was a huge luminous globe. Stars, some so bright he felt he could reach out and grab them, crowded the sky.

His eyes went back to Marsali. She had not noticed him as she hugged one of the small creatures she usually had with her. She had made pets of a pair of ferrets as well as an orphaned baby rabbit she'd found on a walk.

"Marsali," he said softly. "Shouldn't you be abed?"

She whirled around. She was dressed only in a nightrail that emphasized her small, lithe body. The bright moon revealed trails of tears down her face.

One ferret crouched protectively on her shoulder while another stilled at her feet. They both looked ready to tear him to pieces if he made the slightest threatening move.

"Are you so unhappy then," he asked gently, "at today's ceremony? I promise not to beat you," he added with a quick grin that had always brought a smile to her lips.

Her eyes widened. "Oh no, Lord Patrick."

"Then why the tears?" he asked, tucking a finger under her chin and forcing her to look up to him.

She bit her lip. Long dark hair, unbound by a cap, fell over her cheek. "I will . . . miss you."

Real sorrow edged her words, and he felt humbled. He was sixteen, a man, and he'd paid little attention to his best friend's sister, even when she trailed him as her ferrets trailed her every step.

He took a long look at her face. Even at eight, she showed signs of being a true beauty. Her eyes were a dark blue, and they glistened with tears and moonlight. Her face was delicately molded, and her wide mouth smiled frequently with true delight for the world around her.

Something gentle and tender moved within him as she stared at him with total adoration. No one had looked at him that way. No one, in fact, had ever regarded him with fondness. His mother had died at his birth, and his stepmother had considered him a hindrance to his half-brother's inheritance. His father, a rough and prideful man, cared only for a warrior to carry on tradition, and Patrick had been raised as such.

"I'll be back before you have a chance to sprout," he said.

"Promise you won't get killed," she demanded forcefully, her dark blue eyes boring into his. There was no meekness in her words now, only a command.

"Aye," he said. "I swear it." And he could, in all honor. He felt invincible. Even at sixteen, he could defeat much older, much heavier men in combat. He was quick with movements, adept at the sword. He would vanquish his enemies and live forever.

She watched him steadily, too steadily for a child. It was as if she were willing his words to be true, making them true by the force of her desire.

The ferret moved down her arm and she caught it in her right hand, the left rubbing the animal's head.

"Antony and Cleopatra will miss you, too," she said. "They will pray for you, as will I."

"And now," he said solemnly, "I know I have nothing to fear."

Her eyes appeared to dance for a moment, appreciative of his response. But then they grew solemn again.

He bowed slightly. "You must hurry back to bed, but first a favor to carry with me."

Her mouth widened into a smile. "I have nothing."

"You have a ribbon," he said, looking at the ribbon that graced her neck of her nightrail.

Her eyes lighting at being treated like a true lady, she beamed at him and her small hands untied the ribbon, snaking it through the small holes of the cloth. She shyly handed to him.

"I thank you, my lady," he said.

"Do I get one, too?" she asked.

He looked down at his clothing. He wore only the kilt of his clan. His dagger and sporan were in his room. "A star, Marsali?" he said, wondering at his own whimsy since he was not a whimsical man. He turned and looked up at the sky. "Can I pluck one for you?"

"But then there will be an empty space where there should be brightness," she replied. "Tell me which one, and I will look at it every night and remember it's mine, and that you're my star-catcher."

He stared at her for a moment. She seemed much older than her eight years.

Patrick searched the skies carefully for exactly the right star, one she could always find. It stood at the heel of a formation of stars, one that never changed. His tutor had pointed it out to him long ago as a pattern by which one could determine direction.

He stooped down, balancing himself on his balls of his feet as he explained its pattern carefully.

She listened intently. "I'll look for it every night," she promised.

"And so will I," he said, knowing that he would not. But the lie was worth the joy that leaped into her eyes.

His wife to be. It was difficult to imagine this child in that role, nor himself as a husband. But that was years away. In the meantime, he felt like an older brother.

"Ye'd best be off to bed before Jeanie finds you gone," he warned.

She leaned over and swiftly kissed him on the cheek before turning away, small feet flying as she disappeared down a set of steep stairs.

He was left with the scent of roses, a piece of silk ribbon, the feel of silken hair against his cheek, and a lingering sense of the first sweetness he'd ever known.

The Highlands
1660

It was a splendid day for a wedding. Everyone said so.

The sun fairly sparkled, its rays dappling the rich green fields and nearby loch. The cold wind of several days earlier had eased into a gentle breeze.

A good omen for a future filled with happiness, Marsali's father had insisted. A fine day. A splendid alliance.

That he—and others—said it with straight, sincere faces impressed the bride. The level of self-delusion among her clan had risen to a new high, she thought wryly as she allowed Jeanie to brush her waist-length hair, then braid it with fresh flowers.

"Edward Sinclair is a bonny man," Jeanie said hopefully.

"Aye," Marsali agreed. She could not quarrel with that assessment of the man her father now intended as her husband, but she could not believe that no one else saw the cold depths of his eyes, the ruthlessness in a smile that, to her, was no smile at all.

Four more hours. She had four more hours of freedom. Four more hours to dream of a young man who had offered to catch her a star.

What had happened to him? What was he thinking this day? Was he even alive? She'd heard no news for such a long time. No one knew whether he was alive or dead.

So many years had passed since the evening he'd shown such kindness to child. She had never forgotten it, nor his visit six years later when she was reaching womanhood. The look in his eyes had changed from kindness to something else altogether, something that made her tingle inside with delight and anticipation. She treasured both.

It seemed she had waited for him all her life, that she had prepared herself all these years just for him, for the day she would become his bride. But he had gone to war to fight against Cromwell, then been outlawed. Their wedding had been postponed first one year, then another. In all that time, only two messages reached her, both stilted and formal and saying only that he was alive.

And now she would become someone else's bride. Her heart was breaking, but she had no choice. If she did not go through with the marriage, her fifteen-year-old sister would replace her at the altar.

A splendid day for a wedding, they all continued to insist. Her brother. Her father. Even Jeanie, who was her best friend as well as her maid.

Then why did her heart feel like a stone? Why did she feel it was a better day for a funeral?

One of her ferrets, Tristan, climbed on her lap.

Tristan and Isolde had replaced Cleopatra and Antony whom she was sure had ascended to ferret heaven. She wasn't sure why she had named them after legendary—and tragic—lovers. Perhaps another omen.

A tear trickled down her face and dropped on the elongated, furry animal.

"Ah now, lass," Jeanie said. "It is so bad for ye?"

Marsali bit her lip. She didn't want to force her unhappiness on anyone else. There was nothing to be done. No one had heard from Patrick for two years now, and in any event her father would never permit that marriage—not since he'd declared a blood feud against Patrick's family and the betrothal had been cried off by both families. The two families were far more likely to kill each other than feast together, though many of both families had blood ties.

It was a wretched situation for everyone, one created by Marsali's aunt, Margaret, who had married Patrick's father the same day Marsali was betrothed to his son. There had been much rejoicing then by both clans.

But more than a year ago, Patrick's father accused her aunt of adultery and publicly branded her a whore. He had sought a divorce through Parliament, but the only two witnesses had disappeared and the divorce was denied for lack of proof. Margaret vanished a week later. Murdered, Marsali's father claimed. Murdered by the man he once called friend. Murdered by Patrick's father, the Marquis of Brinaire.

Marsali didn't know the truth of it. No one did. All she knew was that her aunt had been her father's only sister, and he felt that his honor, and the honor of his clan, had been impugned.

The accusations had escalated. Her father had filed charges of murder against Brinaire, but again there had been no proof, and they were dismissed. Marsali had watched her father rage, his hatred grow until he lost reason, until he decided to use his daughters as pawns in his quest for revenge. She'd realized then she would never have Patrick as a husband, even if he still lived.